KU-431-845

PENGUIN BOOKS

MAIGRET MEETS A MILORD

Georges Simenon was born at Liège in Belgium in 1903. At sixteen he began work as a journalist on the *Gazette de Liège*. He has published over 212 novels in his own name, many of which belong to the Inspector Maigret series, and his work has been published in thirty-two countries. He has had a great influence upon French cinema, and more than forty of his novels have been filmed.

Simenon's novels are largely psychological. He describes hidden fears, tensions and alliances beneath the surface of life's ordinary routine which suddenly explode into violence and crime. André Gide wrote to him: 'You are living on a false reputation – just like Baudelaire or Chopin. But nothing is more difficult than making the public go back on a too hasty first impression. You are still the slave of your first successes and the reader's idleness would like to put a stop to your triumphs there . . . You are much more important than is commonly supposed'; and François Mauriac wrote, 'I am afraid I may not have the courage to descend right to the depths of this nightmare which Simenon describes with such unendurable art.'

Simenon has travelled a great deal and once lived on a cutter, making long journeys of exploration round the coasts of Northern Europe. A book of reminiscences, *Letter to My Mother*, was published in England in 1976. He is married and lives near Lausanne in Switzerland.

GEORGES SIMENON

MAIGRET MEETS
A MILORD

PENGUIN BOOKS

Penguin Books Ltd, Harmondsworth, Middlesex, England
Penguin Books, 40 West 23rd Street, New York, New York 10010, U.S.A.
Penguin Books Australia Ltd, Ringwood, Victoria, Australia
Penguin Books Canada Ltd, 2801 John Street, Markham, Ontario, Canada L3R 1B4
Penguin Books (N.Z.) Ltd, 182–190 Wairau Road, Auckland 10, New Zealand

Fifth Business first published in Canada by The Macmillan Company
of Canada Limited 1970
First published in the United States of America by The Viking Press 1970
Published in Penguin Books 1977
Copyright © Robertson Davies, 1970

The Manticore first published in the United States of America
by The Viking Press 1972
Published in Canada by The Macmillan Company of Canada Limited 1972
Published in Penguin Books 1976
Copyright © Robertson Davies, 1972

World of Wonders first published in Canada by The Macmillan Company
of Canada Limited 1975
First published in the United States of America by The Viking Press 1976
Published in Penguin Books 1977
Copyright © Robertson Davies, 1975

Published in one volume in King Penguin as *The Deptford Trilogy* 1983
Copyright © Robertson Davies, 1983
All rights reserved

Made and printed in Great Britain
by Richard Clay (The Chaucer Press) Ltd,
Bungay, Suffolk

Contents

MAIGRET MEETS
A MILORD

TRANSLATED BY
ROBERT BALDICK

CHAPTER I

Lock 14

NOTHING could be deduced from the most minute reconstruction of the facts, except that the find by the two carters from Dizy was so to speak impossible.

That Sunday – it was the 4th of April – the rain had started pouring down at three o'clock in the afternoon.

At that time, in the port above Lock 14, which marked the junction between the Marne and the canal, there were two motor-barges going downstream, one boat unloading, and a dredger.

Shortly before seven o'clock, when dusk was beginning to fall, a tanker, the *Éco III*, had arrived and entered the lock.

The lock-keeper had been in a bad temper, because some relations of his had called. He had shaken his head at a horse-barge which had arrived a minute later, moving at the slow pace of its two nags.

Not long after he had gone back into his house, the carter, a man he knew, had come in.

'Can I go through? The skipper wants to get to Juvigny by tomorrow night.'

'You can go through if you like. But you'll have to work the gates yourself.'

The rain was falling more and more heavily. From his window, the lock-keeper saw the stocky figure of the carter trudging from one gate to the other, urging his horses forward, and fastening the mooring-ropes to the bollards.

The barge rose little by little above the walls. It was not the skipper who was holding the wheel, but his wife, a fat Brussels woman with peroxided hair and a shrill voice.

At twenty past seven the *Providence* was moored in front of the Café de la Marine, behind the *Éco III*. The horses were taken on board. The carter and the skipper made for the café, where there were some other seamen and two pilots from Dizy.

At eight o'clock, when darkness had fallen completely, a tug arrived at the gates with the four boats it had in tow.

This added to the company in the Café de la Marine. There were six tables occupied, with people calling from one table to another. The men coming in left puddles of water behind them and shook the mud off their boots.

In the next room, which was lit by an oil-lamp, the women were doing their shopping.

The air was heavy. There was talk of an accident which had occurred at Lock 8 and the delay which might be suffered by boats going upstream.

At nine o'clock the wife of the *Providence*'s skipper came to fetch her husband and the carter, who went off after farewells all round.

At ten o'clock the lights were out on board most of the boats. The lock-keeper accompanied his relations as far as the main road to Épernay, which crossed the canal two miles from the lock.

He saw nothing unusual. As he was passing the Café de la Marine on his way back, he looked inside and was hailed by a pilot.

'Come and have a drop! You're soaking wet . . .'

He had a rum, still standing. Two carters got to their feet, sluggish with red wine, their eyes shining, and made for the stable adjoining the café, where they slept on the straw, next to their horses.

They were not exactly drunk. But they had had enough wine to send them into a heavy sleep.

There were five horses in the stable, which was lit only by a storm-lantern with the wick turned down low.

At four o'clock one of the carters roused his companion and the two of them started attending to their horses. They heard the horses on the *Providence* being brought off the barge and harnessed.

At the same time the proprietor of the café was getting up and lighting the lamp in his bedroom, on the first floor. He too heard the *Providence* moving off.

At half past four the diesel engine of the tanker started spluttering, but it did not leave until a quarter of an hour later, after the skipper had drunk a hot toddy in the café, which had just opened.

He had scarcely gone out and his boat had not yet reached the bridge before the two carters made their find.

One of them was pulling his horses towards the tow-path. The other was rummaging in the hay for his whip when his hand came into contact with something cold.

Startled by the touch of what felt like a human face, he went to get his lantern, and cast its light over the corpse which was going to send Dizy into a turmoil and upset the whole life of the canal.

*

Chief-Inspector Maigret of the Flying Squad was recapitulating these facts and putting them in their context.

It was the Monday evening. In the morning the Épernay magistrates had made their statutory visit to the scene of the crime, and after the Records Office men and the police doctors had done their work, the corpse had been taken to the mortuary.

It was still raining, a fine, cold, steady rain which had gone on falling all night and throughout the day.

Silhouettes were moving about on the gates of the lock, in which a boat was rising imperceptibly.

During the hour that he had been there, the Chief-Inspector had thought of nothing but of how to familiarize himself with a world which he had suddenly discovered and about which, on his arrival, he had only vague, mistaken ideas.

The lock-keeper had told him:

'There was hardly anything in the canal reach: two motor-barges going downstream, one motor-barge going upstream which made the lock in the afternoon, a dredger, and two Panamas. Then the kettle arrived with her four boats . . . .'

And Maigret had learnt that a kettle is a tug, and that a Panama is a boat which has neither an engine nor any horses on board but hires a carter with his horses for a given distance, an operation known as 'getting a snatch'.

Arriving at Dizy, he had seen nothing but a narrow canal, three miles from Épernay, and a small village near a stone bridge.

He had had to splash through the mud along the tow-path as far as the lock, which itself was two miles from Dizy.

And there he had found the lock-keeper's grey stone house with its signboard reading: 'Lock Office.'

And he had gone into the Café de la Marine, which was the only other building in the place.

On the left, a shabby bar-room, with brown oilcloth on the tables, and walls painted half brown, half dirty yellow.

But there was a characteristic scent in the air which was enough to distinguish the place from an ordinary country café. It smelt of stables and harness, tar and groceries, petrol and diesel oil.

The door on the right was fitted with a little bell and there were some transparent advertisements stuck on the glass panes.

The room behind was packed with goods for sale: oil-skins, clogs, linen garments, sacks of potatoes, barrels of cooking oil and crates of sugar, peas and beans, all mixed up with vegetables and crockery.

There was not a customer to be seen. In the stable the only horse left was the one the proprietor harnessed to go to market, a big grey animal as friendly as a dog, which was not tied up and occasionally ambled about the yard, among the hens.

Everything was streaming with rain. That was the dominant note. And the people passing by were dark, shining figures, bent forward.

12

A hundred yards away, a little Decauville train travelled backwards and forwards across a building yard, and its driver, at the back of the miniature engine, had fixed up an umbrella under which he was standing shivering, with his shoulders hunched up.

A barge moved away from the bank and punted along as far as the lock, from which another barge was emerging.

How had the woman got there, and why had she come? That was the question which the Épernay police, the officials from the Public Prosecutor's department, the doctors, and the technicians from the Records Office had asked themselves in amazement and which Maigret was turning over and over in his great head.

She had been strangled, that was one thing which was certain. Death had occurred on the Sunday evening, probably about half past ten.

And the corpse had been found in the stable shortly after four o'clock in the morning.

There was no road in the vicinity of the lock. Nothing could bring anybody there who was not concerned with navigation. The tow-path was too narrow for a motor-car. And that particular night, anybody walking along it would have had to wade up to his knees through mud and water.

But the woman obviously belonged to a class more accustomed to travelling in limousines and sleeping-cars than on foot.

She was wearing nothing but a cream-coloured silk dress and a pair of white buckskin shoes which were more suitable for the beach than for the town.

The dress was crumpled but they had not found a single mud-stain on it. Only the toe of the left shoe was still wet when the body was discovered.

'Between thirty-eight and forty,' the doctor had said after examining the woman.

Her ear-clips were two genuine pearls, worth about fifteen thousand francs. Her gold and platinum bracelet, shaped in an ultra-modern style, was ornate rather than expensive, but bore the signature of a jeweller in the Place Vendôme.

The hair was brown and waved, cut very short at the nape of the neck and at the temples.

As for the face, which had been disfigured by strangulation, it had obviously been remarkably pretty.

From all appearances a gay society woman.

Her finger-nails, which were manicured and polished, were dirty.

No handbag had been found near her. The police of Épernay, Rheims, and Paris had been provided with a photograph of the corpse and had been trying in vain all day to establish its identity.

And the rain went on falling relentlessly on an ugly landscape. To the left and right, the horizon was barred by chalky hills streaked with black and white, where the vines, at this time of the year, looked like wooden crosses in a war cemetery.

The lock-keeper, whose only mark of identity was a cap trimmed with silver braid, circled miserably round his lock, in which the water started bubbling every time he opened the sluices.

And every sailor, while a boat was rising or falling, had to listen as he told the story.

Sometimes the two men, once the necessary papers had been signed, strode into the Café de la Marine and had a glass of rum or a mug of white wine.

The lock-keeper never failed to jerk his chin towards Maigret who, prowling aimlessly around, must have given the impression that he was nonplussed.

It was a fact. The case was quite exceptional. There was not even a single witness to question.

For the officials from the Public Prosecutor's department, after questioning the lock-keeper and coming to an understanding with the local Government engineer, had decided to allow all the boats to continue on their way.

The two carters had been the last to leave, about midday, each convoying a 'Panama'.

As there was a lock every three or four miles, and as these locks were linked by telephone, it was possible to know at at any given moment where any given boat was to be found and bar its way.

What was more, a police inspector from Épernay had questioned everybody, and Maigret had at his disposal the record of these interrogations from which nothing could be deduced, except that reality was improbable.

All the people who had been at the Café de la Marine the day before were known either to the proprietor or the lock-keeper, and more often than not to both.

The carters slept at least once a week in the same stable, and always in the same condition bordering on intoxication.

'You see, we have a drink at every lock. . . . Nearly every lock-keeper sells wine. . . .'

The tanker which had arrived on Sunday afternoon and left on Monday morning was carrying petrol and belonged to a big company in Le Havre.

As for the *Providence*, whose skipper was also her owner, she went through twenty times a year, with her two horses and her old carter. And the same was true of the others.

Maigret was in a grumpy mood. A hundred times he went into the stable, then into the café or the shop.

He was seen walking as far as the stone bridge and giving the impression of counting his steps or looking for something in the mud.

With a scowl on his face, and dripping with water, he watched a dozen boats go through the lock.

People wondered what his theory was, but in fact he had none. He was not even trying to find a clue properly speaking, but rather to steep himself in the atmosphere, to familiarize himself with this canal life which was so different from all that he knew.

He had made sure that he could borrow a bicycle if he wanted to catch up with one or other of the boats.

The lock-keeper had lent him the *Official Handbook to Inland Navigation*, in which obscure places like Dizy took on an unexpected importance for topographical reasons, or on account of a junction, a crossing, or the presence of a port, a crane, even an office.

He tried to follow in imagination barges and carters:

'*Ay: Port. Lock 13.*'

'*Mareuil-sur-Ay: Boat-building yard. Port.*'

'*Lock 12. . . .*'

Then '*Bisseuil. Tours-sur-Marne, Condé, Aigny. . . .*'

At the far end of the canal, beyond the Langres plateau, which the boats mounted lock by lock and went down on the opposite slope, the Saône, Chalon, Mâcon, Lyons. . . .

'What was that woman doing here?'

In a stable, with her pearl ear-clips, her stylish bracelet, her white buckskin shoes.

She must have arrived alive, since the crime had been committed after ten o'clock at night.

But how? But why? And nobody had heard a thing. She had not screamed. The two carters had not woken up.

If it had not been for the whip which had been mislaid, the corpse would probably have been found only a fortnight or a month later, accidentally, by someone poking about in the hay.

And other carters would have come and snored beside that woman's body.

In spite of the cold rain, there was still something heavy and implacable about the atmosphere. And the rhythm of life was slow.

Feet in boots or clogs trailed across the walls of the lock or along the tow-path. Dripping horses waited for the end of the locking to move off again, straining forward in a repeated effort and thrusting back with their hindlegs.

And dusk was about to fall, just like the day before. Already the barges going upstream were not continuing on their way but mooring for the night, while the bargees were sluggishly making their way in groups towards the café.

Maigret went to have a look at the bedroom which had just been prepared for him next to the proprietor's. He stayed there for ten minutes or so, changed his shoes, and cleaned his pipe.

Just as he was going downstairs a yacht steered by a seaman in oilskins moved gently along beside the bank, went astern, and came smoothly to a stop between a couple of bitts.

The seaman carried out all these manoeuvres by himself. Two men came out of the cabin a little later, glanced wearily around them, and finally made for the Café de la Marine.

They too were wearing oilskins. But when they took them off they were seen to be dressed in open-necked flannel shirts and white trousers.

The bargees looked at the new-comers without causing them the slightest embarrassment. On the contrary, this sort of surroundings seemed to be familiar to them.

One of them was a tall, heavily-built man with greying hair, a brick-coloured complexion, and prominent sea-green eyes with a gaze which slid over people and things as if it did not see them.

He leant back on his straw-bottomed chair, pulled a second chair towards him for his feet, and snapped his fingers to call the proprietor.

His companion, who must have been about twenty-five, was talking English to him with a nonchalance which savoured of snobbery.

It was he who asked without any trace of an accent:

'Have you any still champagne?'

'Yes.'

'Bring us a bottle.'

They were smoking Turkish cigarettes with cardboard tips.

17

The bargees' conversation, which had been interrupted for a moment, gradually started up again.

Shortly after the proprietor had brought the wine, the seaman came in, dressed in white trousers too, with a sailor's blue-striped jersey.

'Over here, Vladimir. . . .'

The bigger of the two men yawned, displaying a massive boredom. He drained his glass with a grimace which was only half-satisfied.

'Another bottle!' he whispered to the younger man.

And the other repeated in a louder voice, as if he was accustomed to transmitting orders in that way:

'Another bottle! . . . The same again!'

Maigret came out of his corner, where he had been sitting in front of a bottle of beer.

'Excuse me, gentlemen. . . . May I ask you a question?'

The older man pointed to his companion with a gesture which signified:

'Ask him!'

He showed neither surprise nor interest. The seaman poured himself a drink and cut off the end of a cigar.

'You've come here by way of the Marne?'

'Yes, of course.'

'Were you moored a long way from here last night?'

The big fellow turned his head and said in English:

'Tell him that's no business of his.'

Maigret pretended not to have understood, and without saying anything more, took the photograph of the corpse out of his wallet and placed it on the brown oilcloth on the table.

The bargees, sitting at the tables or standing in front of the bar, were following the scene with their eyes.

The yachtsman scarcely moved his head to look at the photograph. Then he examined Maigret and sighed:

'Police?'

He had a pronounced English accent and a tired voice.

'Yes. A murder was committed here last night. So far it hasn't been possible to identify the victim.'

'Where is she?' asked the other man, standing up and pointing to the photograph.

'In the mortuary at Épernay. Do you know her?'

The Englishman's face was inscrutable. But Maigret noticed that his huge, apoplectic neck had turned purple.

He picked up his white cap, put it on his bald head, and turning to his companion, muttered in English:

'More complications!'

Then, unconcerned by the interest being shown by the bargees, he puffed at his cigarette and stated:

'*C'est mon femme.*'

The pattering of the rain on the window-panes and even the creaking of the lock machinery could be heard much more clearly. The silence lasted a few seconds, completely unbroken, as if life had been suspended.

'You pay, Willy. . . .'

The Englishman threw his oilskins over his shoulders, without putting his arms in the sleeves, and growled at Maigret:

'Come on board. . . .'

The seaman he had called Vladimir finished off the bottle of champagne and then went out as he had come in, accompanied by Willy.

The first thing the Chief-Inspector saw when he arrived on board was a woman in a dressing-gown, her feet bare, her hair tousled, dozing on a red-velvet couch.

The Englishman touched her shoulder and with the same calm as before, in a tone of voice devoid of courtesy, said:

'Go outside.'

Then he waited, his eyes wandering over the folding table on which there was a bottle of whisky and half a dozen dirty glasses, as well as an ash-tray overflowing with cigarette ends.

He ended up by automatically pouring himself a drink

and pushed the bottle towards Maigret with a gesture which signified:

'If you want some . . .'

A barge went by on a level with the portholes and the carter fifty yards farther on stopped his horses, whose bells could be heard tinkling.

CHAPTER 2

The Southern Cross

MAIGRET was almost as tall and bulky as the Englishman. At the Quai des Orfèvres his sang-froid was a byword. Yet this time he was irritated by the other man's calm.

And that calm seemed to be the order of the day on board. From the seaman Vladimir to the woman who had just been roused from her sleep everyone had the same unconcerned or apathetic look. They were like people who had been dragged out of bed the morning after a tremendous binge.

One detail among a hundred. While she was getting up and looking for a packet of cigarettes, the woman caught sight of the photograph which the Englishman had placed on the table and which had got wet in the course of the brief journey from the Café de la Marine to the yacht.

'Mary?' she asked, with scarcely a start of surprise.

'Yes, it's Mary.'

And that was all. She went out through a door which opened forward and which presumably led to the bathroom.

Willy came on deck and went down in front of the hatchway. The saloon was tiny. The partitions of polished mahogany were extremely thin, and anyone forward could probably hear everything, for the owner looked that way first and then at the young man, saying with a certain impatience:

'Hurry up! Come in!'

And to Maigret he said curtly:

'Sir Walter Lampson, retired colonel of the Indian Army.'

He accompanied his own introduction with a stiff little bow and a wave towards the bench.

'And this gentleman?' asked the Chief-Inspector, turning to Willy.

'A friend of mine ... Willy Marco. ...'

'Spanish?'

The colonel shrugged his shoulders. Maigret looked hard at the young man's obviously Jewish features.

'Greek on my father's side ... Hungarian on my mother's. ...'

'I shall have to ask you a certain number of questions, Sir Walter. ...'

Willy had perched nonchalantly on the back of a chair and was swaying to and fro while smoking a cigarette.

'I'm listening.'

But just as Maigret was going to begin, the yachtsman said in halting French:

'Who did it? Do you know?'

'We have no idea as yet. That is why you can help me considerably in my inquiries by clearing up certain points.'

'Rope?' the Englishman asked, touching his throat.

'No. The murderer used just his hands. When did you last see Mrs Lampson?'

'Willy ...'

Willy was undeniably the general factotum, expected to do everything from ordering drinks to answering questions put to the colonel.

'At Meaux on Thursday evening,' he said.

'And you didn't inform the police that she had disappeared?'

'What for? She did as she pleased.'

'She often went off like that?'

'Sometimes.'

The rain was pattering on the deck above them. Dusk was giving place to night and Willy Marco turned on the electric light.

'Are the batteries charged?' the colonel asked him in English. 'It won't be like the other day, will it?'

Maigret was making an effort to give a definite direction to his interrogation. But he was constantly being distracted by new impressions.

22

In spite of himself he was looking at everything and thinking about everything at the same time, so that his head was full of a seething mass of shapeless ideas.

He was not so much outraged as embarrassed by this man who, in the Café de la Marine, had glanced at the photograph and stated without a tremor:

'*C'est mon femme.*'

He recalled the woman in the dressing-gown asking:

'Mary?'

And now Willy was swaying to and fro all the time, a cigarette between his lips, while the colonel was worrying about batteries!

In the neutral atmosphere of his office, the Chief-Inspector would probably have conducted an orderly interrogation. Here he began by taking his coat off without being asked, and picked up the photograph, which was as sinister as any other photograph of a corpse.

'You live in France?'

'France and England.... Sometimes Italy.... Always with my boat, the *Southern Cross*....'

'Where have you come from?'

'Paris,' replied Willy, to whom the colonel had motioned to speak. 'We stayed there a fortnight, after spending a month in London.'

'You were living on board?'

'No. The boat was at Auteuil. We put up at the Hôtel Raspail, in Montparnasse....'

'The colonel, his wife, the lady I saw just now, and yourself?'

'Yes. The lady is the widow of a Chilean politician, Madame Negretti.'

Sir Walter gave an impatient sigh and spoke again in English:

'Hurry up, or he'll still be here tomorrow morning....'

Maigret did not bat an eyelid. But from then on he put his questions with a hint of brutality:

'Madame Negretti isn't a relation of yours, is she?' he asked Willy.

'No.'

'So she isn't connected in any way with you and the colonel. . . . Would you mind telling me how the cabins are arranged?'

'Forward there's the crew space where Vladimir sleeps. He was once a cadet in the Russian navy. He served in Wrangel's fleet. . . .'

'There are no other seamen? No servants?'

'Vladimir does everything. . . .'

'And then?'

'Between the crew space and this saloon, there's the galley on the right and the bathroom on the left.'

'And aft?'

'The engine.'

'So there were four of you in this cabin?'

'There are four bunks. . . . First of all the two benches you can see, which turn into divans . . . and then . . .'

Willy went over to one of the partitions and opened a sort of long drawer, revealing a complete bed.

'There's one on each side. . . . You see?'

Maigret was indeed beginning to see things a little more clearly and realized that it would not be very long before he had uncovered the secrets of this strange company.

The colonel's eyes were glazed and moist like those of a drunkard. He seemed to have lost interest in the conversation.

'What happened at Meaux? And first of all, when did you get there?'

'Wednesday evening. . . . Meaux is one day's journey from Paris. . . . We had brought along a couple of girls from Montparnasse. . . .'

'Go on.'

'It was a fine night. . . . We brought out the gramophone and danced on deck. . . . About four o'clock in the morning

24

I took our friends to the local hotel and they presumably caught a train back to Paris the next day.'

'Where was the *Southern Cross* moored?'

'Near the lock.'

'Did anything special happen on Thursday?'

'We got up very late, after being continually woken up by a crane loading stones into a barge next to us. . . . The colonel and I had an apéritif in town. . . . In the afternoon. . . wait a minute . . . the colonel had a nap . . . . I played chess with Gloria . . . Gloria is Madame Negretti. . . .'

'On deck?'

'I think Mary went out for a walk.'

'And she never came back?'

'Oh, yes! She had dinner on board. . . . The colonel suggested spending the evening in a dance-hall and Mary refused to come with us. . . . When we got back, about three in the morning, she wasn't here. . . .'

'You didn't make any inquiries?'

Sir Walter started drumming his fingers on the polished table.

'The colonel has already told you that his wife was free to come and go as she pleased. . . . We waited for her until Saturday and then we moved on. . . . She was familiar with the route we were taking and she knew where she could join us. . . .'

'You're on your way to the Mediterranean?'

'To the island of Porquerolles, opposite Hyères, where we spend the greater part of the year. . . . The colonel has bought an old fort there, the Petit Langoustier. . . .'

'Did everybody stay on board all day Friday?'

Willy hesitated, then replied rather hurriedly:

'I went to Paris. . . .'

'What for?'

He laughed, an unpleasant laugh which gave a peculiar twist to his mouth.

'I've already mentioned our two friends from Montparnasse . . . I wanted to see them again . . . one of them at least. . . .'

'Can you give me their names?'

'Their Christian names . . . . Suzy and Lia. . . . They're at the Coupole every night. . . . They live at the hotel on the corner of the rue de la Grande Chaumière. . . .'

'Professionals?'

'Sweet little things. . . .'

The door opened. Madame Negretti, who had put on a green silk dress, appeared in the doorway.

'May I come in?'

The colonel replied with a shrug of the shoulders. He must have been on his third whisky and he was drinking them with very little water.

'Willy . . . . ask about the formalities.'

Maigret did not need a translation to understand. This odd, casual way of asking him questions was beginning to get on his nerves.

'Naturally you will have to identify the body first of all. . . . After the post-mortem you will probably be able to obtain the burial permit. You choose the cemetery and . . .'

'Can we go straight away? Is there a garage where I can hire a motor?'

'At Épernay.'

'Willy . . . telephone for a motor . . . straight away. . . .'

'There's a telephone at the Café de la Marine,' said Maigret while the young man was grumpily putting on his oilskins.

'Where's Vladimir?'

'I heard him come back just now.'

'Tell him we're having dinner at Épernay. . . .'

Madame Negretti, who was a plump woman with shining black hair and pale flesh, had sat down in a corner, under the barometer, and was following the scene, her chin in her hand, with an absent-minded or deeply thoughtful expression.

'Are you coming with us?' Sir Walter asked her.

'I don't know. . . . Is it still raining?'

Maigret's nerves were on edge and the colonel's last question was not calculated to calm him down.

'How many days do you think we shall need for everything?'

He retorted fiercely:

'Including the funeral, I suppose?'

'Yes. . . . Three days?'

'If the police doctors issue the burial permit and if the examining magistrate doesn't oppose it, you could get it all over, materially speaking, within twenty-four hours. . . .'

Did the other man grasp the bitter irony of these words?

Maigret, for his part, felt the need to look at the photograph: a broken, dirty, crumpled body, a face which had once been pretty and powdered, with scented rouge on the lips and the cheeks, and whose grimace could not be looked at now without a shiver going down one's spine.

'Have a drink?'

'No, thanks.'

'Well, then . . .'

Sir Walter Lampson stood up to signify that he considered the conversation at an end, and called out:

'Vladimir! . . . a suit!'

'I shall probably have other questions to ask you,' said the Chief-Inspector. 'Perhaps I may have to search the yacht. . . .'

'Tomorrow . . . Épernay first, eh? . . . How long will it take by motor?'

'You're leaving me by myself?' Madame Negretti asked anxiously.

'With Vladimir. . . . You can come along if you like. . . .'

'I'm not dressed.'

Willy burst in and took off his dripping oilskins.

'The motor will be here in ten minutes. . . .'

'Then if you don't mind, Chief-Inspector . . .'

The colonel showed him the door.

'We have to dress . . .'

Maigret would have liked to punch somebody in the face as he left, he was so exasperated. He heard the hatchway shut behind him.

From outside, nothing could be seen but the light of eight portholes and the white lantern hooked on to the mast. Less than ten yards away the squat stern of a barge stood out in silhouette, and on the left, on the bank, a big pile of coal.

Perhaps it was an illusion. But Maigret had the impression that the rain was falling faster, that the sky was lower and darker than he had ever seen it.

He made for the Café de la Marine where the voices suddenly fell silent on his arrival. All the bargees were there, in a circle round the cast-iron stove. The lock-keeper was leaning on the bar, close to the daughter of the house, a tall, red-headed girl in clogs.

On the oilcloth on the tables there were bottles of wine, tumblers, puddles.

'Well, is it really his missus?' the proprietor asked at last, taking his courage in both hands.

'Yes. Give me a beer. No . . . something hot . . . toddy. . . .'

The bargees gradually started talking again. The girl brought the hot glass, brushing against Maigret's shoulder with her apron.

And the Chief-Inspector imagined the three people getting dressed in the narrow cabin, with Vladimir there as well.

He imagined a good many other things, but idly and not without a certain repugnance.

He knew the lock at Meaux, which was all the more important in that, like the one at Dizy, it formed a junction between the Marne and the canal, where there was a port in the shape of a half-moon, always crowded with barges packed tightly together.

There, in the midst of the barges, the *Southern Cross*

all lit up, with the two women from Montparnasse, fat Gloria Negretti, Mrs Lampson, Willy, and the colonel dancing on the deck to music from the gramophone, and drinking . . .

In a corner of the Café de la Marine, two men in blue overalls were eating sausages, which they were cutting with their pocket-knives as they went along, at the same time as their bread, and drinking red wine.

And somebody was describing an accident which had happened in the morning at the 'vault', in other words at the place where the canal, in order to cross the highest part of the Langres plateau, went underground for a distance of five miles.

A bargee had had his foot caught in the tow-rope; he had shouted without being able to make the carter hear him and, when the horses moved off after a rest, he had been thrown into the water.

There was no light in the tunnel. The barge carried only one lantern which cast only a faint gleam over the water. The bargee's brother—the boat was called *The Two Brothers* – had jumped into the canal.

Only one of them had been fished out, when he was already dead. They were still looking for the other. . . .

'They only had two annual instalments left to pay on their boat. But it seems that according to the contract their wives won't have to pay them. . . .'

A taxi-driver wearing a leather cap came in and looked round.

'Who ordered a motor here?'

'I did,' said Maigret.

'I've had to leave it at the bridge . . . I don't fancy diving into the canal. . . .'

'Are you eating here?' the proprietor asked the Chief-Inspector.

'I don't know.'

He went out with the taxi-driver. The white-painted *Southern Cross* made a milky patch in the rain and two boys

29

from a near-by barge, oblivious of the downpour, were gazing at her in admiration.

'Joseph!' shouted a woman's voice. 'Bring your brother back . . . you're in for a hiding!'

'*Southern Cross,*' the taxi-driver read on the bows. 'They're English, are they?'

Maigret crossed the bridge and knocked. Willy, who was ready, very smart in a dark suit, opened the door, revealing the colonel, red-faced and in his shirt-sleeves, having his tie done by Gloria Negretti.

The cabin smelt of eau-de-Cologne and brilliantine.

'Has the motor arrived?' asked Willy. 'Is it here?'

'It's at the bridge, two miles away.'

Maigret stayed outside. He heard the colonel and the young man talking together in English. Finally Willy came out and said:

'He doesn't want to wade through the mud. Vladimir's going to lower the dinghy . . . we'll join you over there. . . .'

'Hmm!' muttered the taxi-driver, who had heard what he said.

Ten minutes later, he and Maigret were walking up and down on the stone bridge, beside the motor whose sidelights were burning. Nearly half an hour went by before they heard the throb of a little two-stroke engine.

Finally Willy's voice called out:

'Is it here? . . . Chief-Inspector!'

'Here, yes.'

The motor-boat described a circle and hove to. Vladimir helped the colonel on to the bank and agreed on a time for the return journey.

In the motor Sir Walter did not say a word. Despite his corpulence he was remarkably smart. Ruddy-faced, well groomed, and phlegmatic, he was very much the English gentleman as depicted in nineteenth-century prints.

Willy Marco smoked one cigarette after another.

'What a rattle-trap!' he sighed as the motor jolted over a gully.

Maigret noticed that he was wearing a platinum signet-ring with a big yellow diamond.

When they arrived in the town with its streets glistening with rain, the driver raised his window and asked:

'What's the address you want?'

'The mortuary!' replied the Chief-Inspector.

*

It did not take long. The colonel scarcely opened his lips. There was only one attendant in the building, where three bodies were stretched out on the slabs.

All the doors were already locked. The locks could be heard squeaking. A light had to be switched on.

It was Maigret who lifted the sheet.

'Yes.'

Willy was more upset, more impatient to get away.

'You recognize her too?'

'It's her all right. . . . As she is now . . . .'

He did not finish what he was saying. He was visibly turning pale. His lips were going dry. If the Chief-Inspector had not taken him outside he would probably have been sick.

'You don't know who did it?' said the colonel.

Perhaps it might have been possible to distinguish a scarcely perceptible tremor in his voice. But then that was probably the effect of all the whisky he had drunk.

All the same, Maigret made a mental note of that tiny weakening.

They found themselves outside on a pavement dimly lit by a street-lamp, opposite the motor whose driver had not left the wheel.

'You'll have dinner with us?' said Sir Walter, without even turning towards Maigret.

'No, thank you. I want to see to a few matters while I'm here.'

The colonel did not press him.

'Come along, Willy.'

31

Maigret remained for a moment in the doorway of the mortuary while the young man, after conferring with Sir Walter, bent forward to speak to the driver.

It was a question of finding out which was the best restaurant in the town. People went by, as well as clanking, brightly lit trams.

A few miles away lay the canal and, all the way along it, near the locks, sleeping barges which would move off at four o'clock in the morning, in a smell of stables and hot coffee.

CHAPTER 3

Mary's Necklace

WHEN Maigret had gone to bed, in a room whose characteristic smell caused him a certain queasiness, he spent some time comparing two pictures.

At Épernay first of all, seen through the brightly lit windows of the Bécasse, the best restaurant in the town, the colonel and Willy having dinner, surrounded by high-class waiters.

It was less than half an hour after the visit to the mortuary. Sir Walter Lampson was holding himself a little stiffly and the impassivity of his brick-red face, surmounted by a few silver hairs, was amazing.

Beside his elegance, or rather his breeding, Willy's, casual though it was, rang false.

Maigret had dined in another restaurant, and had telephoned first to the Prefecture and then to the Meaux police.

Then, all alone in the rainy night, he had walked along the long ribbon of the road. He had caught sight of the lighted portholes of the *Southern Cross* opposite the Café de la Marine.

And he had been inquisitive enough to go on board, under the pretext of a pipe he had left behind.

It was there that he had registered the second picture: In the mahogany cabin, still in his striped seaman's jersey and with a cigarette between his lips, Vladimir was sitting opposite Madame Negretti, whose oily hair was once again hanging down over her cheeks.

They were playing cards, a Central European game called Sixty-six.

There was a brief moment of amazement. But not even a start of surprise. Breaths were caught for a second. After that Vladimir had got up to look for the pipe. Gloria Negretti had asked with a lisp:

'Aren't they back yet? ... It really is Mary?'

The Chief-Inspector had felt like getting on his bicycle and following the canal so as to catch up with the barges which had spent the night between Sunday and Monday at Dizy. The sight of the soaking tow-path and the black sky had discouraged him.

When there was a knock on his door he realized, even before opening his eyes, that the grey light of dawn was filtering through the window into his room.

He had had a disturbed sleep, full of the stamping of horses, vague shouts, footsteps on the stairs, clinking glasses down below, and finally whiffs of coffee and hot rum which had come up to him.

'What is it?'

'Lucas. Can I come in?'

And Inspector Lucas, who nearly always worked with Maigret, pushed open the door and shook the moist hand which his chief held out to him through an opening in the sheets.

'Have you got something already? You're not too tired, old man?'

'Not really. Straight away after getting your phone call I went to the hotel in question, on the corner of the rue de la Grande Chaumière. The girls weren't there. I got their names in any case ... *Suzanne Verdier, known as Suzy, born at Honfleur in 1906 ... Lia Lauwenstein, born in the Grand Duchy of Luxemburg in 1903. . . .* The first arrived in Paris four years ago as a housemaid, then worked for some time as a model. . . . The Lauwenstein girl has lived mostly on the Riviera. Neither of them, I checked on that, is on the Vice Squad's lists ... but they might just as well be.'

'Look, old man, would you mind passing me my pipe and ordering some coffee?'

Water could be heard splashing in the lock and a diesel engine running slowly. Maigret got out of bed and went

34

across to a pitiful dressing-table where he poured some cold water into the bowl.

'Carry on. . . .'

'I went to the Coupole as you told me to. . . . They weren't there, but all the waiters know them. They sent me to the Dingo, then to the Cigogne. . . . Finally, in a little American bar whose name I've forgotten, in the rue Vavin, I found them by themselves, and not a bit stand-offish. . . . Lia isn't at all bad . . . she's got a style of her own. . . . Suzy is a sweet, harmless little blonde who would have made a good wife and mother if she'd stayed in her home-town . . . she's got freckles all over her face and . . .'

'You can't see a towel anywhere can you?' Maigret broke in, his face streaming with water and his eyes shut. 'Incidentally, is it still raining?'

'It wasn't raining when I arrived but it's going to start again any minute. At six o'clock this morning there was a fog that froze the air in your lungs. . . . Well, I offered the young ladies a drink. . . . They promptly asked for sand-wiches, which didn't surprise me to begin with . . . but after a while I noticed the string of pearls the Lauwenstein girl had got round her neck . . . . I bit on them by way of a joke. . . . They are absolutely genuine . . . not an American millionairess's necklace, but worth a hundred thousand all the same. . . . Well, when girls of that sort prefer chocolate and sandwiches to cocktails . . . .'

Maigret, who was smoking his first pipe of the day, went to open the door for the girl who had brought some coffee. Then he glanced out of the window at the yacht, where there was no sign of life as yet. A barge was passing the *Southern Cross*. The sailor at the wheel was looking at his neighbour with grudging admiration.

'Right . . . go on. . . .'

'I took them somewhere else, to a quiet café. . . . There I suddenly showed them my badge, then pointed to the necklace and said on the off-chance:

'"Those are Mary Lampson's pearls, aren't they?"'

35

'The two of them probably didn't know that she was dead. In any case, if they did know, they played their parts perfectly.

'It took them a few minutes before they opened up. It was Suzy in the end who told the other girl:

'"You'd better tell him the truth, seeing that he knows so much already."

'And it was quite a story.... Do you want a hand, chief?'

Maigret was in fact trying in vain to catch hold of the braces which were hanging down his thighs.

'The most important point first: they both swore that it was Mary Lampson herself who gave them the pearls last Friday in Paris, where she came to see them. ... You probably understand better than I do, because I know nothing about the case except what you told me over the phone. ...

'I asked if Willy Marco was with Mrs Lampson. They say not, and maintain that they haven't seen Willy since Thursday, when they left him at Meaux ...'

'Hold on a minute!' said Maigret, knotting his tie in front of a greyish mirror which deformed his reflection. 'On Wednesday evening the *Southern Cross* arrives at Meaux. ... Our two young things are on board. ... They have a gay time that night with the colonel, Willy, Mary Lampson, and the Negretti woman. ...

'Late at night Suzy and Lia are taken to a hotel and they leave by train on Thursday morning. ... Were they given any money?'

'Five hundred francs, they say.'

'They met the colonel in Paris?'

'A few days earlier. ...'

'And what happened on board the yacht?'

Lucas gave a peculiar smile.

'Some not very pretty fun and games. ... It seems that the Englishman lives for nothing but whisky and women ... Madame Negretti is his mistress. ...'

36

'Did his wife know?'

'Oh, yes! She herself was Willy's mistress. . . . Not that that prevented them from taking Suzies and Lias along with them. . . . You cotton on? . . . And on top of that, Vladimir danced with all the women. . . . At dawn there was a quarrel because Lia Lauwenstein complained that five hundred francs was just a tip. . . . The colonel didn't even answer them, leaving that to Willy. . . . Everybody was drunk. . . . The Negretti woman was asleep on the roof and Vladimir had to carry her into the cabin. . . .'

Standing at the window, Maigret let his gaze wander along the dark line of the canal and on the left he could see the little Decauville train still carting earth and rubble around.

The sky was grey, with, lower down, scraps of black clouds, but it was not raining.

'Go on. . . .'

'That's about all. . . . On Friday Mary Lampson is supposed to have gone to Paris where she met our two young ladies and gave them her necklace. . . .'

'Well, well! Just a little token gift!'

'Oh, no! She gave it to them to sell it and give her half the price they got for it. . . . She told them that her husband never let her have any ready money. . . .'

The wallpaper of the room had a pattern of little yellow flowers. The enamel jug added a pale note to the scene.

Maigret saw the lock-keeper hurrying along with a bargee and his carter to drink a glass of rum at the bar.

'That's all I got out of them,' concluded Lucas. 'I left them at two in the morning, telling Inspector Dufour to keep a discreet eye on them. Then I went to the Prefecture to go through the files, in accordance with your instructions. I found a card on Willy Marco, who was expelled from Monaco four years ago after a rather obscure gambling affair, and held at Nice the following year on a complaint by an American woman who had been relieved of a few jewels. But the complaint was withdrawn, I don't know why, and Marco allowed to go free. You think it was he who . . .?'

'I don't think anything. And I swear that I mean that. Don't forget that the murder was committed on Sunday after ten o'clock at night, when the *Southern Cross* was moored at La Ferté-sous-Jouarre. . . .'

'What do you think of the colonel?'

Maigret shrugged his shoulders and pointed to Vladimir, who had climbed out of the forward hatchway and was coming towards the Café de la Marine, dressed in white trousers, canvas shoes, and a sweater, with an American beret over one ear.

'Somebody wants Monsieur Maigret on the telephone,' the red-headed girl shouted from behind the door.

'Come downstairs with me, old man. . . .'

The telephone was in the corridor, next to a coat stand.

'Hullo . . . is that Meaux? What's that you said? . . . Yes, the *Providence*. . . . She spent all day Thursday taking on cargo at Meaux? . . . Left on Friday at three in the morning. . . . No others? . . . The *Éco III*. . . . She's a tanker, isn't she? . . . Friday night at Meaux . . . left Saturday morning. . . . Thank you, Chief-Inspector. . . . Yes, ask questions as you think fit . . . I'm still at the same address!'

Lucas had listened to this conversation without understanding it. Before Maigret had time to open his mouth to explain, a police cyclist appeared at the door.

'An urgent message from Police Headquarters!'

The policeman had mudstains up to his belt.

'Go and dry yourself and drink my health in a hot toddy. . . .'

Maigret took the inspector out on to the tow-path, opened the envelope, and read in an undertone:

'*Summary of the first analyses made in connexion with the Dizy case: many traces of resin found in the victim's hair as well as chestnut-coloured horse-hairs. . . . The stomach, at the time death occurred, contained some red wine and some preserved beef of the type sold under the name of corned beef.*'

'Eight horses out of ten have got chestnut hair!' sighed Maigret.

*

Vladimir, in the shop, was asking about the nearest place where he could do his shopping and there were three people advising him, including the police cyclist from Épernay, who finally went off with the seaman in the direction of the stone bridge.

Maigret, followed by Lucas, made for the stable where, the previous evening, the proprietor's grey horse had been joined by a broken-kneed mare that there was talk of killing.

'She can't have picked up the resin here,' remarked the Chief-Inspector.

He followed the path from the canal to the stable twice over, going round the buildings.

'Do you sell resin?' he asked, catching sight of the proprietor pushing a wheelbarrow full of potatoes.

'Well, it isn't really resin. . . . We call it Norwegian tar. . . . They use it on the wooden barges above the water-line. . . . Farther down they make do with coal-tar, which is twenty times cheaper. . . .'

'Have you got any in stock?'

'There's always a couple of dozen cans in the shop . . . but we don't sell any in this weather. . . . The bargees wait for the sun before doing up their boats. . . .'

'Is the *Éco III* made of wood?'

'No, iron like most motor-barges.'

'And the *Providence*?'

'Wood . . . Have you found anything?'

Maigret did not reply.

'You know what they're saying?' continued the man, who had put down his wheelbarrow.

'Who are *they*?'

'The canal folk, the bargees, the pilots, the lock-keepers. A motor-car would have a job to go along the tow-path . . . but what about a motor-bike? And a motor-bike can go a long way, without leaving much more trace than a push-bike. . . .'

The door of the cabin of the *Southern Cross* opened. But nobody could be seen yet.

For a moment one point in the sky turned a yellowish colour, as if the sun were at last going to break through. Maigret and Lucas paced silently up and down beside the canal.

Before five minutes had gone by the wind was bending the reeds and a minute later the rain was pouring down.

Maigret held out his hand in a mechanical gesture. In a gesture no less mechanical, Lucas took a packet of grey tobacco out of his pocket and handed it to his companion.

They stopped for a moment in front of the lock, which was empty and being made ready, for an invisible tug had hooted three times in the distance, which meant that she was towing three boats.

'Where do you think the *Providence* is now?' Maigret asked the lock-keeper.

'Wait a minute . . . Mareuil . . . Condé . . . near Aigny there are a dozen barges in a row and they'll slow her up. . . . The lock at Vraux has only got two of its sluices working. . . . I'd say she's at Saint-Martin. . . .'

'Is that far from here?'

'Just twenty miles.'

'And the *Éco III*?'

'She ought to be at La Chaussée . . . but a fellow going downstream told me last night that she'd broken her propeller at Lock 12 . . . so that you'll find her at Tours-sur-Marne, ten miles from here. . . . They've only themselves to blame. . . . The regulations forbid them to carry a load of two hundred and eighty tons, and they all insist on doing it. . . .'

*

It was ten o'clock in the morning. When Maigret got on the bicycle he had hired, he caught sight of the colonel sitting in a rocking-chair on the deck of the yacht and opening the Paris newspapers which the postman had just delivered.

'Nothing special!' he said to Lucas. 'Stay around here . . . don't let them too much out of your sight. . . .'

The rain thinned out. The road was straight. At the third lock the sun appeared, still a little pale, making the raindrops glisten on the reeds.

From time to time Maigret had to get off his bicycle to pass a barge's horses which, harnessed together, took up the whole width of the tow-path, moving one leg after another, in an effort which threw every muscle into relief.

Two horses were being led by a little girl between eight and ten, wearing a red dress and carrying her doll at arm's length.

The villages, for the most part, were at a fair distance from the canal. The result was that that regular ribbon of still water seemed to stretch away in absolute solitude.

A field here and there, with men bent over the dark earth. But nearly always woods. And reeds five or six foot high added still further to the impression of calm.

A barge was taking on a load of chalk near a quarry, in a cloud of dust which was whitening her hull and the men working on her.

In the lock at Saint-Martin there was a boat sure enough, but it was not the *Providence*.

'They must be having dinner in the reach above Châlons,' said the lock-keeper's wife, who was coming and going from one lock to the other, followed by two children clinging to her skirts.

Maigret had a stubborn nature. He was surprised, about eleven o'clock, to find himself in a spring-like setting, an atmosphere vibrating with sunshine and warmth.

In front of him, the canal stretched away in a straight line for five miles, lined on both sides by fir-woods.

Right at the end, one could just make out the

light-coloured walls of a lock whose gates were oozing trickles of water.

Half-way along, a barge was stationary, a little askew. Her two horses had been unharnessed and each with its head buried in a bag, were eating oats and stretching themselves.

The first impression was gay or at least restful. There was not a house in sight. And the gleams of light on the calm water were broad and slow.

A little more pedalling, and at the stern of the barge the Chief-Inspector could see a table laid underneath the awning protecting the tiller. The oilcloth was a blue-and-white check. A fair-haired woman was putting down a steaming dish in the middle.

He got off his bicycle after reading the name *Providence* on the round, shining hull.

One of the horses looked hard at him, moved its ears, and gave a peculiar moan before beginning to eat again.

*

Between the barge and the bank there was only a thin, narrow plank which bent under Maigret's weight. Two men were eating, following him with their eyes, while the woman came to meet him.

'What do you want?' she asked, buttoning her half-open blouse over a buxom bosom.

Her accent was almost as musical as that of the south of France. She was not in the least uneasy. She waited. She seemed to be protecting the two men with her joyous corpulence.

'Some information,' said the Chief-Inspector. 'You probably know that a murder has been committed at Dizy. . . .'

'The people on the *Castor et Pollux*, which passed us this morning, told us about it. . . . Is it true? . . . It's almost impossible, isn't it? . . . How could anybody have done it? . . . And on the canal, where everybody's so quiet!'

Her cheeks were blotchy. The two men went on eating,

without taking their eyes off Maigret. The latter automatically glanced at the dish which was full of a dark-coloured meat with a smell which puzzled him.

'A kid I bought this morning at Aigny Lock. . . . You wanted to ask us for some information? . . . But we'd gone before they found the corpse. . . . Incidentally, have they found out who the poor lady was?'

One of the two men was short and dark, with a drooping moustache and something gentle and docile about him.

He was the husband. He had simply given the intruder a casual nod, leaving his wife to do the talking.

The other man was probably about sixty. His hair, extremely thick and badly cut, was white. An inch or two of beard covered his chin and the greater part of his cheeks, so that, what with his thick eyebrows, he looked as hairy as an animal.

In contrast his eyes were bright and expressionless.

'It's your carter that I'd like to ask a few questions. . . .'

The woman laughed.

'Jean? . . . I'd better warn you that he doesn't talk much. . . . He's our bear! . . . Just look at him eating. . . . But he's the best carter you could find. . . .'

The old man's fork had stopped moving. He was looking at Maigret with curiously limpid eyes.

Certain village idiots have that sort of look in their eyes, and also certain animals used to gentle treatment when they are suddenly treated roughly.

A dazed expression. But something else too, something indescribable, a sort of withdrawing into one's shell.

'What time did you get up to see to your horses?'

'Usual time. . . .'

He had shoulders of a breadth which was all the more astonishing in that he had very short legs.

'Jean gets up every morning at half past two,' the woman broke in. 'Just look at our horses . . . they're groomed like race-horses every day . . . and at night you'll never get him to have a drink before he's rubbed the horses down. . . .'

'Do you sleep in the stable?'

Jean looked as though he did not understand. Once again it was the woman who pointed to a taller construction in the middle of the boat.

'That's the stable,' she said. 'He always sleeps there. We've got our cabin aft. Do you want to see it?'

The deck was spotlessly clean, the brasses more highly polished than on the *Southern Cross*. And when the woman opened a pair of doors in deal, with a stained-glass skylight over them, Maigret saw a touching little saloon.

There was the same fake antique furniture in oak as in the most traditional of lower-middle-class homes. The table was covered with a cloth embroidered with silks of different colours and held vases, framed photographs, and a flower-stand overflowing with green plants.

There were more embroidered cloths on a sideboard. The arm-chairs were protected by net covers.

'If Jean had wanted, we'd have fixed up a bed for him near us ... but he says he can't sleep anywhere except in the stable ... even though we're always afraid of him getting kicked one day. ... It's all right him saying the horses know him. ... When they're asleep ....'

She had started eating, the typical housewife cooking for others who picks the worst food for herself without even thinking about it.

Jean had stood up and kept looking, now at his horses, now at the Chief-Inspector, while the skipper was rolling a cigarette.

'And you didn't see anything or hear anything?' Maigret asked, gazing hard at the carter.

The man turned towards the skipper's wife who answered him with her mouth full:

'You can be sure that if he'd seen anything he'd have said so.'

'The *Marie*'s arriving!' her husband announced anxiously.

For a few moments the air had been filled with the throbbing of an engine. Now the silhouette of a barge could be seen behind the *Providence*.

Jean looked at the woman, who looked hesitantly at Maigret.

'Look,' she said in the end. 'If you've got to talk to Jean, would you mind doing it on the move? . . . In spite of her engine, the *Marie* goes slower than we do. . . . If she gets in front of us before the lock, she'll block our way for three days. . . .'

Jean had not waited for these last sentences. He had removed the bags of oats from the heads of his horses, which he was leading a hundred yards in front of the barge.

The skipper picked up a tin trumpet and blew a shaky blast on it.

'Are you staying on board? . . . We'll tell you all we know, you understand. . . . Everybody knows us on the canals, from Liège to Lyons. . . .'

'I'll join you at the lock,' said Maigret, who had left his bicycle on the bank.

The gangway was removed. A figure had just appeared on the lock gates and the sluices were being opened. The horses moved off to an accompaniment of bells, waving the red pompons they wore on their heads.

Jean walked along beside them, slow, indifferent.

And the motor-barge, two hundred yards behind, slowed down on seeing that she had arrived too late.

Maigret followed, holding the handlebar of his bicycle with one hand. He could see the woman hurriedly finishing her meal, and her husband, a tiny, thin, inconsistent figure, practically lying over a tiller which was too heavy for him.

CHAPTER 4

The Lover

'I've had my lunch!' announced Maigret, coming into
the Café de la Marine where Lucas was sitting by a
window.

'At Aigny?' asked the proprietor. 'It's my brother-in-
law who keeps the inn there. . . .'

'Bring us some beer.'

It was like a wager. The Chief-Inspector, toiling away on
his bicycle, had scarcely come within sight of Dizy before
the weather had clouded over. And now raindrops were
slashing the last ray of sunshine.

The *Southern Cross* was still in her place. There was
nobody to be seen on deck. And there was no sound coming
from the lock, so that for the first time Maigret had the
impression of being in the country on hearing the hens
clucking in the yard.

'Nothing new?' he asked the inspector.

'The seaman came back with his shopping. The woman
appeared for a moment, wearing a blue dressing-gown. The
colonel and Willy came in here for an apéritif. They gave
me a suspicious look, I think. . . .'

Maigret took the tobacco his companion offered him and
filled his pipe while he waited for the proprietor who had
served them to disappear into his shop.

'I've got no news either,' he growled. 'Of the two boats
which could have brought Mary Lampson, one has broken
down ten miles from here and the other is creeping along
the canal at two miles an hour. . . .

'The first is made of iron . . . so it's impossible for the
corpse to have picked up any resin on it. . . .

'The second is a wooden boat. The bargee's name is
Canelle. . . . A nice motherly body who insisted on making

46

me drink a glass of horrible rum, and a tiny husband running round her like a spaniel.

'The only person you could possibly suspect is their carter. . . . Either he's playing dumb, and in that case he's an amazingly good actor, or else he's a stupid brute. . . . He's been with them for eight years. . . . If the husband's a spaniel this fellow Jean's a bulldog. . . .

'He gets up at half past two in the morning, sees to his horses, gulps down a bowl of coffee, and starts walking along beside the animals. . . .

'Like that he pulls the barge along twenty or twenty-five miles a day, at the same steady pace, with a glass of white wine at every lock. . . .

'In the evening he rubs the horses down, has supper without saying a word, and drops on to his bale of straw, usually fully dressed. . .

'I've seen his papers: an old military pay-book in which you can scarcely turn the pages, they're so filthy. His name is Jean Liberge, and he was born at Lille in 1869.

'That's all . . . or rather, no . . . you'd have to assume that Mary Lampson was taken on board on Thursday evening, at Meaux. . . . Well, she was alive then . . . and she was still alive when she arrived here on Sunday evening. . . .

'It's physically impossible to hide a human being two days against her will in the stable on that boat . . .

'So that all three of them would have to be guilty. . . .'

And Maigret's grimace showed that he did not believe this.

'As for the idea that the victim went on board of her own free will. . . . You know what you're going to do, old man? Ask Sir Walter for his wife's maiden name . . . get on the phone and find out all you can about her. . . .'

There were still some rays of sunshine in two or three places in the sky, but the rain was falling more and more heavily. Lucas had scarcely left the Café de la Marine, making for the yacht, before Willy Marco came down the gangway, a loose-limbed, nonchalant figure in town clothes, with a vacant look in his eyes.

It was definitely a common feature of the entire company of the *Southern Cross* to look all the time like people who have not had enough sleep or who are suffering from a hang-over.

The two men passed each other on the tow-path. Willy appeared to hesitate when he saw the inspector go on board, then, lighting another cigarette from the one he had just finished smoking, he made straight for the café.

It was Maigret he was looking for, without attempting to disguise the fact.

He did not take off his soft hat, which he touched casually with one finger, murmuring:

'Good morning, Chief-Inspector. . . . Slept well? . . . I'd like to have a word with you. . . .'

'Fire away. . . .'

'Not here, if you don't mind. . . . We couldn't go up to your room, for instance, could we?'

He had lost nothing of his nonchalance. His little eyes were sparkling with what was almost an expression of mischievous pleasure.

'Cigarette?'

'No, thank you.'

'I was forgetting you were a pipe-smoker. . . .'

Maigret decided to take him up to his room, which had not yet been cleaned. Straight away, after a glance at the yacht, Willy sat down on the edge of the bed and began:

'Naturally you've already checked on my record. . . .'

He looked round for an ash-tray, failed to find one, and dropped his ash on the floor.

'Not so good, is it? . . . Not that I've ever tried to pass myself off as a little saint. . . . And the colonel tells me three times a day that I'm a skunk. . . .'

What was extraordinary was the frank expression on his

48

face. Maigret even admitted to himself that after making an unpleasant impression on him at first, the man now struck him as quite tolerable.

A peculiar mixture. Craftiness, cunning. But at the same time a spark of decency which redeemed the rest, and a hint of roguishness too, which was disarming.

'Mind you, I was educated at Eton, like the Prince of Wales. . . . If we were the same age, we'd probably be the best of friends . . . only my father is a fig-merchant at Smyrna . . . and I can't bear that sort of thing! . . . I got into one or two scrapes. . . . The mother of one of my friends at Eton helped me for a while. . ,. You don't mind if I don't tell you her name, do you? . . . . A charming woman . . . but her husband became a Cabinet minister and she was afraid of compromising him. . . .

'After that . . . You must have heard about Monaco and then the business at Nice. . . . The truth isn't really as ugly as that . . . let me give you a piece of advice: never believe anything you're told by a middle-aged American woman who spends her time having fun on the Riviera and whose husband arrives without warning from Chicago. . . . Stolen jewels aren't always stolen . . . but let's forget about that. . . .

'Now about the necklace. . . . Either you know already or you haven't found out yet. . . . I'd have liked to talk to you about it last night, but in view of the circumstances it probably wouldn't have been decent. . . .

'The colonel is a gentleman after all. . . . Admittedly he's a bit too fond of his whisky . . . but that isn't surprising. . . . He ought to have ended up as a general and he was one of the coming men in Delhi when on account of a woman – she was the daughter of an important Indian personage – he was put on the retired list. . . .

'You've seen him yourself . . . . a splendid man, with tremendous appetites. . . . Out there, he had thirty boys, orderlies, secretaries, and heaven knows how many motors and horses at his disposal . . . and then, all of a sudden, nothing: something like a hundred thousand francs a year . . . .

'Did I tell you that he'd already been married twice before meeting Mary? . . . His first wife died in India. . . . The second time he divorced, taking all the blame on himself, after finding his wife with a boy. . . . A real gentleman! . . .'

And Willy, leaning back on the bed, swung one leg slowly to and fro, while Maigret, his pipe between his teeth, stood motionless with his back to the wall.

'And there you are. . . . Nowadays he spends his time as best he can. . . . At Porquerolles he lives in his old fort, the Petit Langoustier. . . . When he's saved enough money he goes to Paris or London. . . . But just think that in India he used to give a dinner every week to thirty or forty guests. . . .'

'Was it about the colonel that you wanted to speak to me?' murmured Maigret.

Willy did not bat an eyelid.

'The fact is, I was trying to put you in the picture . . . seeing that you've never lived in India or in London, and never had thirty boys and heaven knows how many pretty girls at your disposal. . . . I'm not trying to annoy you . . .

'To cut a long story short, I met him two years ago. . . . You didn't know Mary when she was alive. . . . A charming woman but with a bird-brain. . . . A bit hysterical too. . . . If people weren't fussing over her all the time she'd throw a fit or start a scene. . . .

'Do you know how old the colonel is? . . . Sixty-eight. . . . She made him tired, you understand? . . . Admittedly she let him play around – because he still likes his little bit of fun – but she was a bit of a nuisance. . . . She fell for me . . . I was quite fond of her. . . .'

'I suppose that Madame Negretti is Sir Walter's mistress?'

'Yes,' admitted the young man, pulling a face. 'It's hard to explain to you. . . . He can't live or drink on his own. . . . He needs people around him. . . . We met her one day when

we'd put in at Bandol. . . . The next morning she didn't
go. . . . For him, that's enough! . . . She'll stay as long as
she likes. . . .

'With me, it's a different matter . . . I'm one of the few
men who can hold whisky as well as the colonel . . . except
perhaps Vladimir, whom you've seen, and who puts us in
our bunks nine times out of ten. . . .

'I don't know if you really understand my position. . . .
Admittedly I don't have to worry about money . . . even
though we sometimes stay a fortnight in a port waiting for
a cheque from London to be able to buy some petrol!

'Why, the necklace I was talking about just now has been
to the pawnshop a score of times. . . . Still, we don't often
run out of whisky. . . . It isn't a life of luxury . . . but we
sleep as long as we like . . . we come and go. . . . For my
part, I prefer this to my father's figs. . . .

'In the beginning, the colonel had given his wife a few
jewels. . . . She would ask him for some money now and
then . . . for her clothes, you know, and to have a little
ready cash. . . .

'Whatever you think, I swear it was a real shock for me
yesterday to see that it was Mary in that awful photo. . . .
For the colonel too, for that matter! . . . But he'd rather be
torn to pieces than show it. . . . That's how he is! A real
Englishman!

'When we left Paris last week – it's Tuesday today, isn't
it? – the exchequer was very low. . . . The colonel wired to
London to ask for an advance on his pension. . . . We were
waiting for it at Épernay. . . . The money-order may have
arrived by now. . . .

'The trouble was, I'd left a few debts in Paris. . . . Two
or three times already, I'd ask Mary why she didn't sell her
necklace. . . . She could have told her husband that she'd
lost it, or that it had been stolen. . . .

'On Thursday night there was the little party you know
about. . . . You mustn't get any wrong ideas about it. . . .
As soon as Lampson sees some pretty girls, he's got to

invite them on board ... then, a couple of hours later, once he's tight, he gives me the job of getting rid of them as cheaply as possible.

'On Thursday, Mary was up much earlier than usual, and when we got out of our bunks she was already outside. ...

'After lunch we stayed alone together for a little while, she and I. ... She was very affectionate, in a strange rather sad sort of way. ...

'At one point she put her necklace in my hand and said: "'You'll be able to sell it. ...'"

'I don't care if you don't believe me .... I was a bit embarrassed, a bit upset. ... If you'd known her, you'd understand. ... Just as she could be unpleasant sometimes, at other times she could be very touching. ...

'You wouldn't understand. ... She was forty years old. ... She did her best to keep her end up ... but she must have felt that she was finished. ...

'Somebody came in ... I put the necklace in my pocket. ... In the evening the colonel took us to the dance-hall and Mary stayed behind. ...

'When we got back, she wasn't there. ... Lampson didn't worry, because it wasn't the first time she'd gone off like that. ...

'And not on the spree, either. ... Once, for instance, during the Porquerolles festival, there was a regular orgy at the Petit Langoustier that went on for nearly a week. ...

'The first day or two, Mary was the liveliest of us all. ... The third day she disappeared ... and do you know where we found her? In an inn at Grien, where she was spending her time mothering two filthy little kids. ...

'The business of the necklace worried me. ... On Friday I went to Paris. ... I nearly sold it. ... Then I told myself that if there were any complications, I might get into trouble. ...

'I thought of the two girls who'd been with us the day before. ... You can do what you like with those kids. ...

Besides, I'd already met Lia at Nice and I knew I could count on her.

'I left the necklace with her . . . just in case, I told her, if anyone asked her, to say that Mary had given it to her herself to sell. . . .

'It's as simple as that. . . . Stupid, really . . . I'd have done better to keep quiet. . . . The fact remains that unless I happen on some intelligent coppers, it's the sort of thing to land me in the Assize Court. . . .

'I realized that yesterday when I heard that Mary had been strangled. . . .

'I'm not asking what you think . . . indeed, to be perfectly frank, I quite expect to be arrested. . . .

'That would be a mistake, that's all . . . but if you want me to help you, I'm ready to give you a hand. . . . There are several things which may strike you as peculiar and which are really very simple. . . .'

He was practically lying on the bed and still smoking, his eyes fixed on the ceiling.

Maigret went and planted himself in front of the window to hide his perplexity.

'Does the colonel know about your coming to see me?' he asked, swinging round suddenly.

'No more than he knows about the business of the necklace . . . and . . . I'm in no position to make conditions, I realize that . . . but I'd rather he went on knowing nothing about it. . . .'

'Madame Negretti?'

'A dead weight! A pretty woman incapable of anything but lying on a divan, smoking cigarettes, and drinking liqueurs. . . . She started the day she arrived on board, and she's never stopped. . . . Oh, I beg your pardon! She plays cards too . . . indeed, I think it's her only passion. . . .'

The screech of rusty iron announced that the lock gates were being opened. . . . . Two donkeys went past the house and stopped a little farther on, while an empty barge went gliding along on its course as if it wanted to climb the bank.

Vladimir, bent double, was baling out the rain-water collecting in the dinghy.

A motor-car crossed the stone bridge, tried to drive on to the tow-path, braked, carried out a few clumsy manœuvres, and finally came to a complete stop.

A man in black got out. Willy, who had stood up, glanced out of the window and said:

'The undertaker.'

'When does the colonel expect to move on?'

'Straight after the funeral.'

'And that will take place here?'

'Why not? He's already got one wife buried near Delhi, and another married to a New-Yorker who'll end up under American soil. . . .'

Maigret glanced at him in spite of himself, to see if he was joking. But Willy Marco looked perfectly serious, except for that ambiguous little gleam in his eyes.

'Let's hope the money-order has arrived! . . . Otherwise the funeral will have to wait. . . .'

The man in black hesitated in front of the yacht, spoke to Vladimir who answered him without interrupting his work, and finally went on board, where he disappeared into the cabin.

Maigret had seen nothing more of Lucas.

'Off you go!' he said.

Willy hesitated. An anxious expression passed fleetingly over his features.

'Are you going to speak to him about the necklace?'

'I don't know. . . .'

It was finished already. Carefree once more, Willy connected the fold in his soft hat, gave a wave of the hand, and went downstairs.

When Maigret went down in his turn, there were two bargees at the bar, each with a mug of beer.

'Your friend's on the phone,' the proprietor told him. 'He asked for Moulins.'

A tug hooted in the distance. Maigret automatically counted the hoots and muttered under his breath:

'Five.'

That was canal life. Five barges arriving. The lock-keeper, wearing clogs, came out of his house and made for his sluices.

Lucas came back from the telephone with his face red.

'Whew! . . . That was a job!'

'What is it?'

'The colonel told me that his wife's maiden name was Marie Dupin. . . . For the marriage ceremony she produced a birth-certificate in that name, issued at Moulins. . . . I've just phoned there, saying it was a priority call. . . .'

'Well?'

'There's only one Marie Dupin registered at Moulins. She's forty-two, has three children, and is married to a certain Piedbœuf who's a baker in the rue Haute. . . . The Town Clerk who answered me saw her only yesterday behind her counter and it seems she weighs all of thirteen stone. . . .'

Maigret said nothing. Like a gentleman of leisure with nothing to do, he went over to the lock without bothering about his companion, and watched the whole operation. But every now and then he thrust his thumb furiously into the bowl of his pipe.

A little later Vladimir came up to the lock-keeper, and after touching his white cap, asked where he could fill up with drinking-water.

CHAPTER 5

The Y.C.F. Badge

MAIGRET had gone to bed early, while Lucas, to whom he had given his instructions, had set off for Meaux, Paris, and Moulins.

When he had left the bar-room there were three people drinking there, a couple of bargees and the wife of one of them, who had come to join her husband and was knitting in a corner.

It was gloomy and close. Outside, a barge had moored less than six feet from the *Southern Cross*, whose portholes were all lit up.

All of a sudden the Chief-Inspector was roused from a dream so vague that he could remember nothing about it as he opened his eyes. Somebody was hammering on his door while a frantic voice was shouting.

'Chief-Inspector! . . . Chief-Inspector! . . . Quick! . . . My father . . .'

Still in his pyjamas, he ran to open the door and the next moment the innkeeper's daughter hurled herself upon him in an unexpected frenzy, literally throwing herself into his arms.

'There! . . . Hurry. . . . No, stay . . . I don't dare to stay here alone . . . I don't want to . . . I'm frightened. . . .'

He had never paid much attention to her. He had regarded her as a solid, well-built girl without any nerves.

And here she was, her face ravaged, her body heaving, clinging to him with embarrassing fervour. Trying to free himself, he went over to the window and threw it open.

It must have been six o'clock in the morning. Day was just breaking, as cold as a winter dawn.

A hundred yards from the *Southern Cross*, in the direction

of the stone bridge and the Épernay road, four or five men were trying to get hold of something floating in the water, with the aid of a heavy boat-hook, while a bargee had untied his punt and was beginning to row.

Maigret was dressed in crumpled pyjamas. He threw his overcoat over his shoulders and looked for his shoes, which he put straight on his bare feet.

'You know! . . . It's *him*. . . . They've . . .'

With an abrupt movement he freed himself from the strange girl's embrace, went downstairs, and arrived outside just as a woman carrying a baby was approaching the group.

He had not been present when Mary Lampson's body had been discovered. But this new find was perhaps even more sinister, for with another crime an almost supernatural anguish hung over this stretch of the canal.

The men kept calling out to each other. The proprietor of the Café de la Marine, who had been the first to see a human body floating in the water, was directing their efforts.

Twice the boat-hook had touched the corpse. But the hook had slipped. The body had gone a few inches under the water before coming to the surface again.

Maigret had already recognized Willy's dark suit. He could not see the face because the head, being heavier, was submerged.

The bargee in the punt suddenly bumped into it, grabbed the dead man by the chest, and hauled him out of the water with one hand. But then he had to be dragged over the side of the boat.

The man had no feelings. He lifted the legs one after the other, threw his mooring-rope ashore, and wiped his streaming forehead with the back of his hand.

For a brief moment Maigret caught sight of Vladimir's sleepy head emerging from the hatchway on the yacht. The Russian rubbed his eyes. Then he disappeared.

'Don't touch anything.'

A bargee behind him protested, muttering that his

brother-in-law, in Alsace, had been brought back to life after spending nearly three hours in the water.

The café proprietor for his part, pointed to the corpse's throat. There, clearly visible, were two black finger-marks, like those on Mary Lampson's neck.

This tragedy was the more disturbing of the two. Willy's eyes were wide open, even bigger than usual. His right hand was clutching a fistful of reeds.

Maigret had the impression of an unusual presence behind him, and turned round to find the colonel standing there, likewise in pyjamas, with a silk dressing-gown over them and blue kid slippers on his feet.

His silver hair was tousled, his face a little puffy. And it was odd to see him there, dressed like that, among the bargees in their clogs and rough clothes, in the damp, muddy dawn.

He was the tallest and broadest of them all. He gave off a vague smell of eau-de-Cologne.

'It's Willy!' he said in a hoarse voice.

Then he said a few words in English, too fast for Maigret to understand, bent down, and touched the young man's face.

The girl who had woken the Chief-Inspector was leaning against the door of the café, sobbing. The lock-keeper came running up.

'Telephone the police at Épernay. . . . A doctor. . . .'

The Negretti woman herself appeared barefoot and dis-hevelled, but did not dare to leave the deck of the yacht, and called to the colonel:

'Walter! . . . Walter!'

In the background there were people nobody had seen arrive: the driver of the little train, some navvies, and a peasant whose cow went on following the tow-path by herself.

'Carry him into the café . . . touching him as little as possible.'

There could be no doubt that he was dead. The smart

suit, which was now nothing but a rag, trailed on the ground while they were lifting the body.

The colonel followed slowly and his dressing-gown, his blue slippers, and his brick-coloured head on which a few long hairs were stirring in the wind made him look at once ridiculous and hieratical.

The girl started sobbing louder than ever when the corpse passed near her, and ran to shut herself up in the kitchen. The proprietor was yelling into the telephone:

'No, Mademoiselle! ... The police! ... Hurry! ... It's a murder ... Don't cut me off ... Hullo? ... Hullo?'

Maigret stopped most of the onlookers from coming in. But the bargees who had found the corpse and helped to fish it out were all in the café where the tables were still littered with glasses and empty bottles from the day before. The stove was rumbling. There was a broom in the middle of the floor.

Through one of the windows the Chief-Inspector caught sight of the silhouette of Vladimir, who had found time to put on his American sailor cap. The bargees were talking to him, but he was not replying.

The colonel was still gazing at the corpse stretched out on the reddish flagstones and it would have been hard to say whether he was moved or bored or frightened.

'When did you last see him?' asked Maigret, going up to him.

Sir Walter sighed and gave the impression of looking around for the man to whom he usually gave the job of replying for him.

'It's horrible,' he said at last.

'He didn't sleep on board?'

With a wave of the hand the Englishman drew his attention to the bargees who were listening to them. It was like a reminder of the proprieties. It meant:

'Do you think it necessary and proper for these people ...'

Maigret got them to leave.

'It was ten o'clock last night. . . . There was no whisky left on board . . . Vladimir hadn't found any at Dizy. . . . I decided to go to Épernay . . .'

'Willy went with you?'

'Not for long . . . Just past the bridge he left me. . . .'

'Why?'

'We had a few words . . .'

And while the colonel was saying this, his eyes fixed on the dead man's pale, ravaged, twisted face, his features softened.

Perhaps it was the fact that he had not slept long enough and that his flesh was puffy which made him look moved. In any case Maigret would have sworn that there were tears behind his thick eyelids.

'You quarrelled?'

The colonel shrugged his shoulders, as if resigning himself to this vulgar, commonplace expression.

'You were blaming him for something?'

'No! I wanted to know . . . I kept on saying: "Willy, you're a skunk. . . . But you've got to tell me . . ."'

He fell silent, thoroughly upset, and looked around him to avoid being hypnotized by the dead man.

'You were accusing him of murdering your wife?'

He shrugged his shoulders again and sighed:

'He went off by himself. . . . That happened sometimes. . . . The next day we would drink our first whisky together and forget all about it. . . .'

'You walked all the way to Épernay?'

'Yes.'

'You had a few drinks?'

The colonel gave him a pitying glance.

'I played the tables too, at the club. . . . They had told me at the Bécasse that there was a club. . . . I came back in a taxi. . . .'

'What time was that?'

He indicated with a wave of the hand that he had no idea.

'Willy wasn't in his bunk?'

'No ... Vladimir told me while he was undressing me....'

A motor-cycle with a side-car drew up outside the door. A police-sergeant got off, followed by a doctor. The door opened and shut.

'I'm from Police Headquarters,' said Maigret, introducing himself to his colleague from Épernay. 'Will you keep people away and phone the Public Prosecutor's department....'

The doctor needed only a brief examination to declare:

'He was dead at the time of immersion.... Look at these marks.....'

Maigret had seen them. He knew. He glanced automatically at the colonel's right hand, which was powerful, with square-cut nails and prominent veins.

*

It would take at least an hour to get the local magistrate and his officials together and bring them to the scene of the crime. Some police cyclists arrived and formed a cordon round the Café de la Marine and the *Southern Cross*.

'May I get dressed?' asked the colonel.

And in spite of his dressing-gown, his slippers, and his bare ankles, he was amazingly dignified as he walked through the crowd of onlookers. He had scarcely gone into the cabin before he put his head out and called:

'Vladimir!'

All the hatchways on the yacht were closed.

Maigret started questioning the lock-keeper, whom a motor-barge was summoning to his gates.

'I suppose there isn't any current in a canal. So that a body is bound to stay where it is thrown in....'

'That's true of the long reaches, of eight or ten miles.... But this reach isn't even five miles long.... If a boat comes down through Lock 13, above mine, I can feel the water arriving a few minutes later ... and if I lock through a boat going downstream, I take hundreds of gallons of water from the canal which create a temporary current. . . .'

'What time do you start work?'

'In theory, at sunrise. . . . In fact, much earlier. . . . The stable-barges, which move slowly, leave about three in the morning and generally lock through themselves without us hearing them. . . . We don't say anything, because we know them. . . .'

'So that this morning . . .'

'The *Frédéric*, which spent the night there, must have left about half past three and locked through at Ay at five o'clock. . . .'

Maigret went back the way he had come. A few groups had formed in front of the Café de la Marine and on the tow-path. As the Chief-Inspector passed them, making for the stone bridge, an old pilot with a grog-blossomed nose came up to him.

'Do you want me to show you where the young man was thrown into the water?'

And he gave a proud glance at his friends who hung back.

He was right. Fifty yards from the stone bridge, the reeds were lying flat over a distance of several yards. Not only had somebody walked on them, but a heavy object had been dragged along the ground, for there was a wide trail of flattened reeds.

'See that? . . . I live a quarter of a mile from here, in one of the first houses in Dizy. . . . When I came along this morning, to see if there were any boats going down the Marne that needed me, I was struck by that straight away. . . . Especially as I found this thingummy-bob on the towpath. . . .'

The man was tiresome, with his knowing looks and the glances he kept darting at his companions who were following at a distance.

But the object he took out of his pocket was of the greatest interest. It was a delicately wrought enamel badge which, together with a kedge anchor, bore the initials: Y.C.F.

'Yachting Club de France,' explained the pilot. 'They all wear that in their buttonhole. . . .'

Maigret turned to look at the yacht, which was about a mile away, and, under the words *Southern Cross* made out the same letters: Y.C.F.

Without paying any further attention to his companion, who had handed the badge over to him, he walked slowly as far as the bridge. On the right stretched the Épernay road, absolutely straight, with motor-cars roaring along it. On the left the path bent sharply into the village of Dizy. On the far side of the bridge, on the canal, there were a few barges under repair, in front of the General Navigation Company's yards.

Maigret retraced his steps, feeling a little on edge, because the local magistrate was going to arrive and for an hour or two there would be the usual fuss and bother, questions, comings and goings, ridiculous theories.

When he reached the yacht he found its hatchways still closed. A uniformed policeman was pacing up and down, telling onlookers to keep moving, but unable to prevent a couple of journalists from Épernay from taking photographs.

The weather was neither good nor bad. The sky was a luminous grey, as uniform as a ceiling of frosted glass.

Maigret went up the gangway and knocked on the door.

'Who's there?' asked the colonel's voice.

He went in. He had no desire to waste time talking. He saw the Negretti woman as dishevelled as ever, drying her eyes and snivelling, with her hair hanging down over her cheeks and the back of her neck.

Sir Walter, sitting on the bench, was holding his feet out to Vladimir who was putting a pair of brown shoes on them.

There must have been some water boiling somewhere on a stove, for he could hear a jet of steam.

The colonel's bunk and Gloria's had not been made yet.

And there were playing-cards lying about on the table, as well as a map of the inland waterways of France.

The same vague, spicy smell still hung in the air, recalling at one and the same time bar, boudoir, and bed. A white yachting cap was hanging on the coat-stand, next to an ivory-handled riding-crop.

'Did Willy belong to the Yachting Club de France?' asked Maigret, in a voice which he tried to keep casual.

The colonel's shrug of the shoulders indicated that the question was absurd. As indeed it was, for the Y.C.F. was one of the most exclusive of clubs.

'I do,' said Sir Walter. 'And to the Royal Yacht Club.'

'Would you mind showing me the jacket you were wearing last night?'

'Vladimir . . .'

He had his shoes on. He stood up and bent down to look inside a little cupboard which had been fitted out as a cocktail cabinet. There was no bottle of whisky to be seen in it, but there were some other spirits, between which he hesitated.

Finally he took out a bottle of brandy and murmured casually:

'Will you have some?'

'No, thank you.'

He filled a silver goblet from a rack over the table and looked around for a syphon, frowning like a man whose habits have been disturbed and who cannot get used to it.

Vladimir came back from the bathroom with a black tweed suit and a gesture from his master ordered him to hand it over to Maigret.

'The Y.C.F. badge used to be in the buttonhole of this jacket?'

'Yes . . . Haven't they finished yet? . . . Is Willy still on the floor over there?'

He had emptied his glass, in a series of sips, and was hesitating as to whether to have another.

64

He glanced out of the port-hole, saw some legs, and gave a muffled groan.

'Will you listen to me for a moment, Colonel?'

He nodded. Maigret took the enamel badge out of his pocket.

'This badge was found this morning at the place where Willy was dragged through the reeds before being pushed into the canal.'

The Negretti woman gave a half-cry, threw herself on to the red velvet bench, and, her head in her hands, started sobbing convulsively.

Vladimir, for his part, did not move. He was waiting for the jacket to be handed back to him so that he could hang it up again in its place.

The colonel gave a peculiar laugh and said four or five times:

'Yes . . . Yes . . .'

At the same time he poured himself another brandy.

'In England the police have a different method of asking questions. . . . They have to remind you that anything you say may be used in evidence against you . . . only once, of course. . . . Haven't you got to write all this down? I shan't go on repeating myself . . .

'We had a few words, Willy and I . . . I kept asking. . . . Never mind . . .

'He isn't a skunk like all the others. . . . There are some likeable skunks . . .

'I said a few harsh things and he grabbed my jacket here. . . .'

He pointed to the lapels, darting an impatient glance at the feet in clogs or heavy shoes which could still be seen through the port-holes.

'That's all . . . I don't know. . . . Perhaps the badge fell on the ground. . . . It was on the far side of the bridge . . .'

'But the badge was found on this side . . .'

Vladimir did not even seem to be listening. He picked

up things that were lying around, disappeared forward, and came sauntering back.

In a strong Russian accent he asked Gloria, who had stopped crying but was lying stretched out, motionless, her head between her hands:

'Do you want anything?'

Footsteps rang out on the gangway. There was a knock on the door and the sergeant's voice said:

'Are you there, Chief-Inspector? ... It's the Public Prosecutor's department ...'

'I'm coming!'

The sergeant did not move, invisible behind the mahogany door with the brass handles.

'One more question, Colonel. ... When is the funeral?'

'At three o'clock.'

'Today?'

'Yes ... I've got no other reason to stay here.'

When he had drunk his third three-star brandy, his eyes took on that vague expression which Maigret had already seen in them.

And, calm, indifferent, the perfect English gentleman, he asked as the Chief-Inspector was getting up to go:

'Am I under arrest?'

The Negretti woman jerked her head up, deathly pale.

CHAPTER 6

The American Cap

THE end of the conversation between the magistrate and the colonel was almost solemn, and Maigret, who stayed in the background, was not the only one to notice this. The Chief-Inspector's eyes met those of the Public Prosecutor's deputy and read the same feeling in them.

The examining magistrate and his officials had installed themselves in the bar-room of the Café de la Marine. One of the doors opened into the kitchen, where the clatter of saucepans could be heard. The other door, which had a pane of glass covered with transparent advertisements for noodles and rock soap, afforded a glimpse of the bags and crates in the shop.

A policeman's peaked cap passed to and fro outside the window, and farther off a crowd of onlookers was massed, silent but stubborn.

A mug which still contained a little liquid had been left near a pool of wine on one of the tables.

The clerk of the court, a sour expression on his face, was sitting on a bench, writing.

As for the corpse, once the necessary particulars had been taken, it had been deposited in the corner farthest from the stove and temporarily covered with a brown oilcloth taken from a table whose uneven planks were now exposed to view.

The smell was as persistent as ever: spices, stable, tar, wine.

And the magistrate, who had the reputation of being one of the most unpleasant in Épernay – a certain Clair-fontaine de Lagny who prided himself on his noble parti-cules – stood with his back to the fire, polishing his pince-nez.

Right at the start he had said in English:

'I suppose you would rather speak your own language. . . .'

He himself spoke it fluently, with perhaps a touch of affectation, that twisting of the lips common to those who try in vain to acquire the correct accent.

Sir Walter had nodded, had slowly answered all the questions, keeping an eye on the clerk of the court as he wrote and waiting every now and then for the latter to catch up with him.

He had repeated, without adding anything, what he had told Maigret in the course of their two conversations.

For the occasion he had put on a navy-blue suit of almost military cut. In his hand he held a cap with a big gilt crest bearing the arms of the Yatching Club de France.

It was all very simple. One man was asking questions. Another who bowed almost imperceptibly every time before answering.

The fact remained that Maigret was filled with admiration, at the same time feeling a certain humiliation at the memory of his own intrusions on board the *Southern Cross*.

He did not know enough English to grasp the finer shades of meaning. But at least he understood the final exchanges.

'I must ask you, Sir Walter,' said the magistrate, 'to hold yourself at my disposal until these two cases have been cleared up. I also find myself obliged for the moment to refuse permission for the burial of Lady Lampson. . . .'

A nod of the head.

'Have I your permission to leave Dizy with my boat?'

And the colonel waved his hand towards the onlookers gathered outside, the scene around them, the very sky.

'My home is at Porquerolles. . . . It takes me a week just to reach the Saône. . . .'

It was the magistrate's turn to nod his head.

They did not shake hands, but they came close to doing so. The colonel glanced around him, appeared not to see the doctor who looked bored, nor Maigret who turned his head away, and bowed to the Public Prosecutor's deputy.

The next moment he was crossing the narrow space separating the Café de la Marine from the *Southern Cross*.

He did not even go into the cabin. Vladimir was on the deck. He gave him some orders and installed himself at the wheel.

And, to the amazement of the bargees, the seaman in the striped jersey went down into the engine-room, started the engine, and standing on the deck, jerked the mooring-ropes from their bitts with a precise gesture.

A few moments later, a little group of gesticulating figures made off towards the main road, where the motor-cars were waiting: it was the magistrate and his party.

Maigret was left alone on the bank. He had at last been able to fill his pipe, and he thrust his hands into his pockets with a plebeian gesture which was more plebeian than usual, at the same time muttering:

'As you were!'

For now he had to start all over again.

The magistrate's inquiry had yielded only a few points of detail whose importance it was impossible to judge as yet.

First of all, apart from the marks of strangulation, Willy Marco's body had bruises on the torso and the wrists. According to the doctor, the idea of an ambush had to be rejected in favour of the theory of a fight with an adversary of exceptional strength.

Then Sir Walter had declared that he had met his wife at Nice where, although divorced from an Italian called Ceccaldi, she was still using his name.

The colonel had been vague. His deliberately ambiguous remarks suggested that at that time Marie Dupin, *alias* Ceccaldi, was in a state bordering on poverty and lived on the generosity of a few friends, without actually descending to prostitution.

He had married during a visit to London and it was

69

then that she had had a birth certificate in the name of Marie Dupin sent from France.

'She was an absolutely charming woman . . .'

Maigret recalled the colonel's fleshy, solemn, brick-coloured face while he was saying these words, without any affectation and with a simplicity which the magistrate had seemed to appreciate.

He had to step back to make way for the stretcher which was taking away Willy's body.

And suddenly, shrugging his shoulders, he went into the café, dropped on to a bench, and said:

'A beer!'

*

It was the girl who served him, her eyes still red, her nose shining. He looked at her with interest and, before he could ask her any questions, she looked round to make sure that nobody could hear her and murmured:

'Did he suffer much?'

She had a plain face, thick ankles, plump red arms. She was none the less the only person to worry about the elegant Willy who, the day before, had perhaps given her a playful pinch – if that!

This reminded Maigret of the conversation he had had with the young man, half stretched out on the unmade bed upstairs, and smoking one cigarette after another.

The girl was called somewhere else. A bargee said to her:

'Seems you're proper upset, Emma. . . .'

And she tried to smile, giving Maigret a conspiratorial glance.

Traffic on the canal had stopped since the morning. There were seven boats, including three motor-barges, opposite the Café de la Marine. The women came across to do their shopping and every time the shop-bell tinkled.

'You can have your lunch whenever you like,' the proprietor told Maigret.

'In a few minutes.'

And from the doorway he looked at the place where only that morning the *Southern Cross* had been moored.

In the evening two fit, healthy men had come off the yacht. They had set off in the direction of the stone bridge. If the colonel was to be believed, they had parted after a quarrel and Sir Walter had continued on his way along the straight, deserted road, two or three miles long, which led to the first houses in Épernay.

Nobody had seen Willy alive again. When the colonel had come back, in a taxi, he had not noticed anything unusual.

No witnesses. Nobody had heard anything. The Dizy butcher, who lived about a quarter of a mile from the bridge said that his dog had barked, but as he had not worried about this, he could not say what time it had been.

The tow-path, with its puddles and pools, had been trodden by too many men and horses for any useful tracks to be found on it.

The previous Thursday, Mary Lampson, likewise fit and healthy, and in an apparently normal state of mind, had left the *Southern Cross*, where she was alone.

Beforehand – according to Willy – she had handed her lover a pearl necklace, the only valuable she possessed.

And all traces of her had been lost. Nowhere had she been seen again alive. Two days had gone by without so much as a glimpse of her.

On the Sunday evening she was strangled, hidden under the straw in a stable at Dizy, sixty miles from her point of departure, and two carters spent the night snoring beside her corpse.

And that was all. On the magistrate's orders, the two bodies were going to be placed in a refrigerator at the mortuary.

The *Southern Cross* had just left on its way to the south, to Porquerolles, to the Petit Langoustier which had seen so many orgies.

Head down, Maigret walked around the buildings of

71

the Café de la Marine. He pushed away a furious goose which came at him with its beak open in a hoarse cry of anger.

There was no lock on the stable door, just an ordinary wooden latch. And the gun-dog prowling round the yard, its paunch over-filled, rushed to meet every visitor, circling round them in joy.

Opening the door, the Chief-Inspector found himself face to face with the proprietor's grey horse, which was as unattached as it had been on other days and which took the opportunity to go for a canter outside.

The broken-kneed mare was still lying sad-eyed in her stall.

Maigret pushed the straw with his foot, as if he hoped to find something which had escaped his notice on his first examination of the place.

Two or three times he muttered crossly to himself:

'As you were!'

He had almost made up his mind to go back to Meaux, even to Paris, and retrace step by step the route taken by the *Southern Cross*.

All sorts of odds and ends were lying around: old reins, pieces of harness, a candle-end, a broken pipe . . .

From a distance he saw something white sticking out of a pile of hay and he went over to it without much hope. The next moment he was holding an American sailor's cap like Vladimir's.

The material was covered with mud and dung, and twisted as if it had been pulled in all directions.

But it was in vain that Maigret hunted around for another clue. Some clean straw had been thrown over the place where the body had been found, to make it less sinister.

'*Am I under arrest?*'

He could not have explained why that question of the colonel's should have come back to him while he was making for the stable door. At the same time he pictured Sir Walter to himself, at once aristocratic and besotted,

with his big moist eyes, his latent drunkenness, his astonishing calm.

He remembered his brief dialogue with the snobbish
magistrate in that bar-room full of tables covered with brown
oilcloth which the magic of a few intonations, a few atti-
tudes, had transformed for a moment into a drawing-room.

And he twisted the cap about in his hands suspiciously,
a sly look in his eyes.

'Go cautiously!' Monsieur de Clairfontaine de Lagny
had told him, giving him a perfunctory handshake.

The goose, in a ferocious mood, was following the horse
around and screaming abuse at it, while it hung its big head
and sniffed at the rubbish littering the yard.

On either side of the door there was a corner-stone, and
the Chief-Inspector sat down on one of them, without
letting go of the cap, or of his cold pipe.

In front of him there was nothing but a huge pile of
manure, then a hedge with gaps in it here and there, and
beyond that, fields where nothing was growing yet and the
hill streaked with black and white on which a cloud with
a jet-black centre seemed to be pressing with all its weight.

From one edge came an oblique ray of sunshine which
put sparks of light on the manure.

'*A charming woman,*' the colonel had said of Mary
Lampson.

'*A real gentleman,*' Willy had said of the colonel.

Only Vladimir had said nothing, simply coming and
going, buying food and petrol, filling the water tanks with
drinking-water, baling out the dinghy, and helping his
master to dress.

Some Flemings went by along the road, talking loudly.
Suddenly Maigret bent forward. The yard was paved with
uneven stones. And six feet away, between two of them,
something had just been caught by the sun and was gleaming brightly.

It was a gold cuff-link crossed by two threads of platinum.
Maigret had seen a pair of similar cuff-links at Willy's

wrists the day before, when the young man had been lying on his bed, blowing the smoke from his cigarettes at the ceiling and talking nonchalantly.

From then on he paid no further attention to the horse or the goose or anything else around him. A little later he was turning the handle of the telephone.

'Épernay. . . . Yes, the mortuary. . . . This is a police call . . .'

One of the Flemings, who was coming out of the café, stopped to look at him in astonishment, he was so excited.

'Hullo! . . . Chief-Inspector Maigret here, from Police Headquarters. . . . A body has just been brought along to you . . . No, I'm not talking about the motor accident. . . . The drowned man from Dizy. . . . Yes. . . . Go to the office straight away and have a look at his personal effects. . . . You ought to find a cuff-link there. . . . Tell me what it's like . . . I'll wait, yes. . . .'

Three minutes later he hung up, satisfied, still holding the cap and the cuff-link in one hand.

'Your lunch is ready. . . .'

He did not bother to answer the red-headed girl, for all that she had said that to him as sweetly as possible. He went out, feeling that he might be holding the key to the mystery, but at the same time terrified of dropping it.

'The cap in the stable. . . . The cuff-link in the yard. . . . And the Y.C.F. badge near the stone bridge. . . .'

It was in that direction that he started walking, striding out. Theories took shape in his mind, only to collapse.

Before he had covered a mile he looked in front of him in amazement.

The *Southern Cross*, which had left a good hour before in tremendous haste, was moored to the right of the bridge, in the reeds. There was no sign of anybody.

But when the Chief-Inspector was only a hundred yards away, on the opposite bank, a motor-car coming from Épernay drew up near the yacht and Vladimir, still in his

seaman's jersey, who was sitting beside the driver, jumped
out and ran towards the boat.

Before he reached it the hatchway opened and the colonel
came out on deck, holding his hand out to somebody inside.

Maigret made no attempt to conceal himself. He could
not tell whether the colonel had seen him or not.

The scene was brief. The Chief-Inspector could not hear
what was being said. But the characters' movements gave
him a fairly clear idea of what was happening.

It was the Negretti woman that Sir Walter was helping
out of the cabin. For the first time Maigret saw her wearing
outdoor clothes. Even from a distance he could see that
she was in a rage.

Vladimir had picked up a couple of suitcases which were
waiting and was carrying them to the taxi.

The captain held his hand out to the woman to help her
down the gangway, but she refused to take it and rushed
forward so abruptly that she nearly fell head-first into the
reeds.

And she walked on without waiting for him. He followed her impassively a few paces behind. She threw herself
into the taxi with the same fury, put her head out of the
window for a moment, and shouted something which must
have been an insult or a threat.

Yet Sir Walter bowed courteously as the taxi moved off,
then watched it disappear, and came back towards his boat
with Vladimir.

Maigret had not stirred. He had a very definite impression
that a change was taking place in the Englishman. He did
not smile. He was still as calm as ever. But, to take one
example, just as he got to the wheel-house, still talking, he
touched Vladimir's shoulder with a friendly, even affectionate gesture.

And the manoeuvre was superb. There were only the two
men left on board. The Russian pulled in the gangway and
with a single movement jerked the ring-bolts of the
mooring-ropes free.

The bow of the *Southern Cross* was embedded in the reeds. A barge was coming up astern and sounded its hooter.

Lampson turned round. He must almost certainly have seen Maigret, but he gave no sign of it. With one hand he put the engine into gear. With the other he gave the brass wheel a couple of turns and the yacht glided astern, just far enough to free itself, avoided the stem of the barge, stopped in time and moved off again, leaving behind a trail of bubbling foam.

She had not gone a hundred yards before she gave three hoots to warn the lock at Ay of her arrival.

*

'Keep going . . . Straight ahead. . . . Catch up with that taxi if you can . . .'

Maigret had stopped a baker's van which was going towards Épernay. The Negretti woman's taxi could be seen about a mile away, but it was moving fairly slowly, for the surface of the road was greasy and slippery.

As soon as the Chief-Inspector had revealed his identity, the delivery-man had looked at him with amused curiosity.

'You know, it wouldn't take me five minutes to catch up with them. . . .'

'Not too fast. . . .'

And it was Maigret's turn to smile at seeing his companion hunching himself over the wheel like a detective in pursuit of a criminal in an American film.

There were no dangerous manoeuvres to carry out, no difficulties to overcome. In one of the first streets in the town the taxi stopped for a few moments, presumably to allow the woman to confer with the driver, then moved off again, drawing up three minutes later in front of a fairly luxurious hotel.

Maigret got out of his van a hundred yards away and thanked the baker, who refused to accept a tip but, determined to see a bit more, went and parked close to the hotel.

A porter carried in the two suitcases. Gloria Negretti hurried across the pavement.

Ten minutes later the Chief-Inspector asked to see the manager.

'The lady who has just arrived?'

'Room 9. . . . I guessed there was something fishy . . . I've never seen anybody so worked up. . . . She jabbered away incredibly fast, using a lot of foreign words . . . I gathered that she didn't want to be disturbed and that she wanted a packet of cigarettes and some Kümmel taken up to her room. . . . There won't be any scandal, I hope?'

'None whatever,' Maigret assured him. 'I just want to ask her a few questions. . . .'

He could not help smiling as he approached the door marked with a figure 9. For there was an absolute din coming from the room. The young woman's high heels were clattering up and down the floor.

She was walking around in all directions. He could hear her shutting a window, moving a suitcase around, turning on a tap, throwing herself on the bed, getting up, and finally hurling a shoe to the other end of the room.

Maigret knocked on the door.

'Come in!'

The voice was shaking with anger and impatience. The Negretti woman had not been there ten minutes and yet she had had time to change her clothes, rumple her hair, and altogether resume, in a more rejected form, the appearance she had on board the *Southern Cross*.

When she recognized the Chief-Inspector, there was a glint of anger in her brown eyes.

'What do you want? . . . What have you come here for? . . . This is my room . . . I've paid for it and . . .'

She went on in a foreign language, presumably Spanish, and opened a bottle of eau-de-Cologne, pouring the greater part of the contents over her hands before moistening her burning forehead with it.

'May I ask you a question?'

77

'I told them I didn't want to see anybody. . . . Get out! . . . Do you hear?'

She was walking in her stockinged feet, and presumably her silk stockings had no garters, for they started to slip down her legs, already revealing a very pale, fleshy knee.

'You'd do better to keep your questions for those who can answer them. . . . But you don't dare to, do you? . . . Because he's a colonel. . . Because he's *Sir* Walter. . . . A fine *sir* he is . . . Why, if I told you only half of what I know. . . . Look at this. . . .'

She rummaged feverishly in her handbag and took out five crumpled thousand-franc notes.

'That's what he's just given me! . . . And I've lived with him for two years, I've . . .'

She threw the notes on to the carpet, then, changing her mind, picked them up and put them back in her handbag.

'Of course he promised to send me a cheque. . . . But I know what his promises are worth. . . . A cheque? . . . He won't even have enough money to get as far as Porquerolles. . . . Not that that will stop him getting drunk on whisky every day . . .'

She was not crying and yet there were tears in her voice. There was something very special about the hysteria of this woman whom Maigret had always seen steeped in blissful lethargy, in a hot-house atmosphere.

'His precious Vladimir's the same. . . . He had the nerve to say "Good-bye, Madame" while he was trying to kiss my hand. . . .They've got a gift for that sort of thing. . . . But when the colonel wasn't there, Vladimir used to . . .

'That's none of your business. . . . Why do you go on standing there? . . . What are you waiting for? Are you hoping I'm going to tell you something? Not a thing! All the same, you've got to admit I'd be in my rights if I did. . . .'

She kept on moving around, taking things out of her suitcase and putting them down somewhere, only to pick them up again and place them somewhere else.

'Leaving me at Épernay. . . . In this filthy rainy hole. . . .
I begged him to take me at least to Nice, where I have
friends. . . . It was for his sake that I left them . . .

'It's true that I ought to be glad that he hasn't killed
me. . . .

'I'm not saying anything, mind you. . . . You can clear
out . . . I loathe the police! . . . As much as the English. . . .
If you're capable of doing it, go and arrest him. . . .

'But you wouldn't dare! . . . I know only too well how
these things are arranged. . . .

'Poor Mary! . . . People can say what they like about
her. Of course she had a bad temper, of course she'd have
done anything for that Willy I've never been able to
stand. . . .

'But to die like that . . .

'Have they gone? . . . Then who are you going to arrest
in the end? . . . Me, perhaps? Why not? . . .

'Well, listen. . . . I'm going to tell you something after
all. . . . Just one little thing. . . . You can do what you like
with it. . . . This morning, when he was dressing up for
the magistrate – because he's always got to impress people
– Walter told Vladimir, in Russian, because he thinks I
don't understand that language . . .'

She was talking so fast that she was beginning to run
out of breath, getting tongue-tied and using Spanish words
again.

'He told him to try to find out where the *Providence*
was. . . . You understand. . . . It's a barge that was near
us at Meaux. . . .

'They want to catch up with it and they're afraid of
me. . . .

'I pretended I hadn't heard . . .

'But I know perfectly well you wouldn't dare . . .'

She looked at her open suitcases, at the room which in a
few minutes she had managed to turn upside down and fill
with her pungent scent. . . .

'Have you got a cigarette at least? . . . What sort of

79

‘

hotel is this? . . . I ordered a packet of cigarettes and some Kümmel . . .'

'Did you see the colonel talking to anybody from the *Providence* at Meaux?'

'I didn't see anything. . . . I wasn't taking any notice. . . . I just heard what he said this morning. . . . Why should they bother about a barge, otherwise? . . . Does anybody know how Walter's first wife died, out in India? . . . And if the other one got a divorce, she probably had her reasons. . . .'

A waiter knocked on the door, bringing cigarettes and liqueur. The Negretti woman took the packet and flung it out into the corridor, shouting:

'I said *Abdullahs*!'

'But Madame . . .'

She clasped her hands together in a gesture which suggested that an attack of hysterics was not far off. and groaned:

'Oh! . . . These people! . . . These . . .'

She turned towards Maigret who was looking at her with interest and snarled at him:

'Why are you still waiting here? . . . I'm not saying any more! I don't know anything! I haven't said anything! . . . You understand? . . . I don't want to be bothered with this business. . . . It's bad enough that I've wasted two years of my life. . . .'

The waiter, as he left the room, gave a meaning look at the Chief-Inspector. And when the young woman, her nerves frayed out, threw herself on to her bed, Maigret went out too.

In the street the baker was still waiting.

'What? You haven't arrested her?' he asked, looking disappointed. 'I thought . . .'

Maigret had to walk as far as the station to find a taxi to drive him back to the stone bridge.

CHAPTER 7

The Pedal

WHEN the Chief-Inspector passed the *Southern Cross,* whose
wash went on stirring the reeds long after she had gone
by, the colonel was still at the wheel and Vladimir was
standing forward, coiling a rope.

Maigret waited for the yacht at Aigny Lock. The
manœuvre was carried out without a hitch, and once the
boat had been moored the Russian went ashore to produce
her papers and give the lock-keeper a tip.

'This cap *is* yours, isn't it?' the Chief-Inspector asked,
going up to him.

Vladimir examined the cap, which was now just a dirty
rag, then his questioner.

'Thank you,' he said at last, taking the cap.

'Just a moment! Can you tell me when you lost it?'

The colonel was following the scene without betraying
the slightest emotion.

'It fell into the water last night,' explained Vladimir,
'when I was leaning over the stern, using a boat-hook to
clear away some weeds that were fouling the propeller. . . .
There was a barge behind us. . . . The woman was kneeling in the dinghy, rinsing her washing. . . . She fished
the cap out of the water and I left it on the deck to dry
out. . . .'

'In other words, it was on the deck last night?'

'Yes. . . . This morning I didn't notice it had gone.'

'Was it already dirty yesterday?'

'No. When the woman fished it out, she dipped it in
the soap-suds she was using. . . .'

The yacht was rising jerkily and already the lock-keeper
was holding the wheel of the upstream gate with both
hands.

'If I remember rightly, it was the *Phénix* behind you, wasn't it?'

'I think so. . . . I haven't seen her again today. . . .'

Maigret gave a wave of the hand and went back to his bicycle while the colonel, as impassive as ever, started up the engine and nodded his head as he passed the lock-keeper.

The Chief-Inspector stood for a while, thoughtfully watching him move away, and disturbed by the amazing simplicity with which things happened on board the *Southern Cross*.

The yacht continued on its way without troubling about him. At the very most the colonel, from his position at the wheel, put a question to the Russian, who answered with a single phrase.

'Is the *Phénix* far ahead?' asked Maigret.

'She may be in the Juvigny reach, three miles from here. . . . She doesn't move as fast as that thing. . . .'

Maigret arrived there a few moments before the *Southern Cross*, and Vladimir must have seen him, from a distance, questioning the skipper's wife.

The details were correct. The day before, while she was rinsing her washing, which could be seen, puffed out by the wind, on a wire stretched above the barge, she had fished the seaman's cap out of the water. A little later the man had given her boy two francs.

It was four o'clock in the afternoon. The Chief-Inspector got back on his bicycle, his head heavy with vague theories. There was some gravel on the tow-path and the tyres crunched over it, sending little pebbles flying on both sides of the wheels.

At Lock 9 Maigret had a good start on the Englishman.

'Can you tell me where the *Providence* is now?'

'Not far from Vitry-le-François. They're going at a good speed, because they've some fine horses, and above all a carter who isn't afraid of work. . . .'

'Do they seem to be hurrying?'

'No more and no less than usual. On the canal, you know, folk are always in a hurry.... You never know what's ahead of you.... You can lose hours at a single lock just as you can spend ten minutes ... and the faster you go, the more you earn....'

'You didn't hear anything unusual last night?'

'No.... Why?... Was there something?'

Maigret went off without answering, and after that stopped at every lock, at every boat.

He had had no difficulty in summing up Gloria Negretti. While refusing to say anything whatever against the colonel she had in fact come out with everything she knew.

For she was incapable of keeping anything back. Incapable of lying too. Or if not, she would have invented something infinitely more complicated.

So she really had heard Sir Walter ask Vladimir to find out where the *Providence* was.

Now the Chief-Inspector too was interested in this barge which had arrived on the Sunday evening, not long before Mary Lampson's death, coming from Meaux, and which, being a wooden boat, was coated with resin.

Why did the colonel want to catch up with her? What connexion was there between the *Southern Cross* and the heavy boat moving at the slow pace of her two horses?

Bowling along through the monotonous canal scenery and bearing down more and more wearily on the pedals, Maigret went on sketching out theories, but they led him only to fragmentary or unacceptable conclusions.

Yet didn't the Negretti woman's angry accusation throw some light on the matter of the three clues?

A score of times Maigret had tried to reconstruct the movements of the various characters in the drama, in the course of that night about which nothing was known, except that Willy Marco was dead.

Every time he had been conscious of a gap; he had had the impression that there was a character missing, who was neither the colonel, nor the dead man, nor Vladimir ...

And now the *Southern Cross* was going after somebody on board the *Providence*.

Somebody who had obviously been involved in the recent events. Wasn't it reasonable to assume that that somebody had taken part in the second drama, namely the murder of Willy, as well as the first?

It is possible to cover a considerable distance in a short time at night, on a bicycle for example, keeping to a towpath.

'Did you hear anything last night? ... Did you notice anything unusual on board the *Providence* when she went past?'

It was thankless, disappointing work, especially in the thin drizzle which was falling from the low-lying clouds.

'No, nothing ...'

The gap was widening between Maigret and the *Southern Cross*, which was losing at least twenty minutes at every lock. The Chief-Inspector got back on his bicycle more wearily every time, and stubbornly picked up one of the threads of his reasoning in the solitude of a reach.

He had already covered twenty-five miles when the lock-keeper at Sarry answered his question.

'My dog barked ... I think something must have gone past along the road. ... A rabbit perhaps. ... I went back to sleep straight away. ...'

'Do you know where the *Providence* spent the night?'

The man did a sum in his head.

'Wait a minute. Wouldn't be surprised if she'd got as far as Pogny. ... The skipper wanted to be at Vitry-le-François tonight. ...'

Another two locks. And no luck. Maigret had to follow the lock-keepers on to their gates, for the farther he went, the heavier he found the traffic. At Vésigneul three boats were waiting their turn. At Pogny there were five.

'Noise? No,' growled the keeper at this last lock. 'But I'd like to know who had the nerve to use my bike. ...'

The Chief-Inspector mopped his brow at this hint of

a clue. He was breathless and parched. He had just covered thirty miles without drinking so much as a glass of beer.

'Where is your bicycle?'

'Open the sluices yourself, will you, François,' the lock-keeper called out to a carter.

And he led Maigret towards his house. In the kitchen, which opened on to the tow-path, some bargees were drinking white wine which a woman was pouring out for them without letting go of her baby.

'You aren't going to report me, I hope? We aren't allowed to sell wine. . . . But everybody does it. . . . It's really just to do people a service. . . . Here we are . . .'

He pointed to a wooden shed built against a wall. There was no door.

'This is the bike. . . . It's my wife's. . . . Just imagine, the nearest grocer's shop is two miles from here. . . . I keep telling her to bring the bike inside for the night, but she says it dirties the house. . . . Mind you, the chap who used it is a queer sort of cuss. . . . I might never have noticed anything. . . .

'As it happens, the day before yesterday my nephew, who's a mechanic at Rheims, came here for the day. . . . The chain was broken. . . . He mended it and while he was at it he cleaned the bike thoroughly and oiled it. . . .

'Yesterday nobody used it. . . . Oh, and the back wheel had been fitted with a new tyre too. . . .

'Well, this morning the bike was perfectly clean, although it rained all night. . . . You've seen the mud on the tow-path. . . .

'But the left pedal is out of truth and the tyre looks as if it had done at least fifty miles. . . .

'Can you make anything of it? . . . The bike has travelled, that's certain. . . . And the chap who brought it back took the trouble to clean it. . . .'

'What are the boats which spent the night near here?'

'Wait a minute. . . . The *Madeleine* must have gone to La

Chaussée, where the skipper's brother-in-law keeps a pub
– The *Miséricorde* spent the night below my lock. . . .'

'Has she come from Dizy?'

'No. She's come downstream from the Saône. . . . There's
only the *Providence*. . . . She locked through yesterday at
seven in the evening. . . . She went on to Omey, a mile
from here, where there's a good port. . . .'

'Have you got another bicycle?'

'No. . . . But I can still use this one. . . .'

'I'm afraid not. I want you to lock it up somewhere . . .'
Hire another if necessary. . . . I'm counting on you.'

The bargees were coming out of the kitchen and one of
them called out to the lock-keeper:

'Is that how you entertain your friends, Désiné?'

'Just a minute. . . . I'm talking to this gentleman. . .

'Where do you think I can catch up with the *Providence*?'

'Well, she's still going at a good speed. . . . I'd be surprised if you caught up with her before Vitry. . . .'

Maigret was going to set off. He came back, took a
spanner out of his tool-bag, and removed the two pedals
from the lock-keeper's bicycle.

When he left, the pedals, which he had stuffed into his
pockets, made two lumps in his jacket.

*

The lock-keeper at Dizy had told him jokingly:

'When it's fine everywhere else, there are at least two
places where you can be sure to see it raining: here and
Vitry-le-François. . . .'

Maigret was approaching this town and it started raining
again: a thin, lazy, steady drizzle.

The appearance of the canal was changing. There were
factories along the banks and for a long time the Chief-
Inspector threaded his way through a swarm of working-
girls coming out of one of them.

Almost everywhere there were boats unloading and
others waiting half-empty.

86

And there were some little suburban houses again with rabbit hutches made out of old crates, and pathetic gardens.

Every mile there was a cement factory or a quarry or a lime-kiln. And the rain was mixing the white powder in the air with the mud on the tow-path. The cement shrouded everything: the tiled roofs, the apple-trees, and the grass.

Maigret was beginning to adopt that movement from right to left and left to right which is the mark of the tired cyclist. He was thinking without thinking. He kept lining up ideas which it was not yet possible to bring together in a solid bundle.

When he finally caught sight of the lock at Vitry-le-François, darkness was falling, speckled with the white lights of about sixty boats in Indian file.

Some were overtaking others, or broaching to. And when a barge approached in the opposite direction, shouts, oaths, and messages filled the air.

'Hey, there! ... *The Simoun!* ... We saw your sister-in-law at Chalon-sur-Saône, and she asked us to tell you that she'll see you on the Burgundy canal. ... The christening can wait. ... Pierre sends his regards. ...'

On the lock gates there were about a dozen figures bustling around.

And over everything, a bluish, rainy mist, in which the silhouettes of motionless horses could be made out, and men going from one boat to another.

While Maigret was reading the names on the sterns of the barges, a voice called out to him:

'Good evening, Monsieur!'

It took him a few seconds to recognize the skipper of the *Éco III.*

'Repairs finished already?'

'It was nothing! ... My boy's a fool. ... The mechanic who came from Rheims took only five minutes over it.'

'You haven't seen the *Providence*, have you?'

'She's ahead of us. ... But we'll go through before her

for all that. . . . This jam means that we'll be locking through all night and maybe tomorrow night too. . . . Just imagine, there are at least sixty boats here and they're still coming. . . . Generally speaking, motor-barges have precedence over horse-barges. . . . This time, the engineer has decided to lock us through alternately, one horse-barge and then one motor-barge. . . .'

And the man, a likeable fellow with an open face, pointed into the distance.

'Look! . . . Just opposite the crane. . . . I can recognize her white tiller. . . .'

Passing the barges, Maigret could see, through the hatchways, people eating in the yellow light of oil-lamps.

Maigret found the skipper of the *Providence* on the quayside, deep in discussion with some other bargees.

'Of course the motor-barges shouldn't have precedence over us! . . . Take the *Marie*, for instance. . . . We gain a mile over her in a five-mile reach, but with this system she'll lock through ahead of us. . . . Why, it's the Chief-Inspector!'

And the little man held out his hand, as he would to a friend.

'Are you here with us again? . . . The missus is on board. . . . She'll be pleased to see you again, because she says that, as coppers go, you're a good sort. . . .'

In the darkness the red tips of cigarettes could be seen glowing, and the lamps so close to one another that it was a mystery how the boats could still move about.

Maigret found the plump woman from Brussels straining her soup. She wiped her hand on her apron before holding it out to him.

'You haven't found the murderer yet?'

'I'm afraid not. . . . I've come to ask you for some more information. . . .'

'Sit down. . . . Will you have a drop of something?'

'No, thank you.'

'You can't mean that! . . . Come, now! In this sort of

weather, it can't hurt anybody. . . . At least you haven't come from Dizy, on a bike, have you?'

'Yes, I have.'

'But that's over forty miles!'

'Is your carter here?'

'He must be at the lock, arguing. . . They want to cheat us of our turn, and this isn't the moment to give in, because we've already lost enough time. . . .'

'Has he got a bicycle?'

'Who? Jean? . . . No!'

She laughed, and then explained, going back to her work:

'I can't see him riding a bike, with his little legs. . . . My husband's got one. . . . But he hasn't used it for at least a year, and I think the tyres are punctured. . . .'

'You spent last night at Omey?'

'That's right. We always try to moor at a place where I can do my shopping. . . . Because if you're unlucky enough to stop during the day, there are always some other boats that will pass you. . . .'

'What time did you arrive?'

'About this time. We pay more attention to the sun than the time, you know. . . Another little drop? . . . It's some gin we bring back from Belgium on every trip. . . .'

'Did you go to the grocers?'

'Yes, while the men were having their apéritifs. . . . It must have been just after eight that we turned in. . . .'

'Jean was in the stable?'

'Where else would he have been? . . . He's only happy when he's with his horses. . . .'

'You didn't hear any noise during the night?'

'Not a thing. . . . At three o'clock, as usual, Jean came along to make the coffee. . . . He always does that. . . . Then we moved off. . . .'

'You didn't notice anything out of the ordinary?'

'What do you mean? . . . You don't suspect old Jean, I hope? . . . You know, he looks a bit odd when you don't know him. . . . But he's been with us now for eight years. . . . And, well, if he left us, the *Providence* would never be the same again. . . .'

'Does your husband sleep with you?'

She laughed again. And as Maigret was close to her, she gave him a dig in the ribs.

'Get along with you! Do we look as old as all that?'

'Can I have a look at the stable?'

'If you like. . . . Take the lantern that's on the deck. . . . The horses have been left outside because we still hope to lock through tonight. . . . And once we've got to Vitry, we're all right. . . . Most of the boats take the Marne canal to the Rhine. . . . It's quieter towards Saône. . . . Except for that five-mile tunnel that always frightens me. . . .'

Maigret went by himself towards the middle of the barge where the stable was to be found. Picking up the storm-lantern which served as a navigation-light, he stole into Jean's domain, with its warm smell of dung and leather.

But it was in vain that he floundered about in it for a quarter of an hour, hearing all the time the conversation continuing on the quay-side between the skipper of the *Providence* and the bargees.

When he arrived a little later at the lock, where, to make up for lost time, everybody was working at once in a din of rusty machinery and bubbling water, he caught sight of the carter on one of the gates, his whip round his neck like a collar, working a sluice.

As at Dizy, he was dressed in an old corduroy velvet suit and a faded felt hat which had long ago lost its ribbon.

A barge left the lock, propelled along by a boat-hook, for there was no other way of moving among the crowded boats.

The voices calling from one barge to another were hoarse and bad-tempered, and the faces, which were sometimes lit up by a match, deeply marked by fatigue.

All these people had been on the move since three or four in the morning, and dreamed of nothing but their soup and then the bunks on to which they would finally drop.

But every one of them wanted to make the crowded lock first, so as to be able to start the following day's journey under the most favourable conditions.

The lock-keeper bustled to and fro, grabbing people's papers as he passed, running into his office where he signed and stamped them, and thrusting the tips he was given into his pocket.

'Excuse me . . .'

Maigret had touched the carter's arm. The man turned round slowly and looked at him with his eyes almost hidden behind his thick bushy brows.

'Have you got any other boots than those you are wearing?'

Jean did not seem to understand at first. His face wrinkled up more than ever. He stared at his feet in bewilderment.

Finally he shook his head, took his pipe out of his mouth, and simply murmured:

'Any others?'

'Those are the only boots you've got?'

A slow nod of the head.

'Can you ride a bike?'

Some people drew near, intrigued by this conversation.

'Come along here,' said Maigret. 'I want a word with you. . . .'

The carter followed him in the direction of the *Providence*, which was moored about two hundred yards away. As he passed his horses, which were standing in the rain with their heads down and their backs gleaming, he stroked the neck of the one nearer to him.

'Come on board. . . .'

The skipper, a thin, tiny figure, was pushing at a boat-hook stuck in the canal bed and levering his boat against the bank to allow a barge going downstream to pass.

He saw the two men going into the stable, but he had no time to pay any attention.

'Did you sleep here last night?'

A grunt which meant yes.

'All night? You didn't borrow a bike from the lock-keeper at Pogny?'

The carter had the unhappy look of a simpleton who is being teased or of a dog which has always been kindly treated and which is suddenly beaten for no reason.

He pushed his hat back and rubbed his head, which was covered with white hair as hard as bristles.

'Take your boots off.'

The man did not move, but glanced at the bank where the horses' legs could be seen. One of them neighed as if it had realized that the carter was in difficulties.

'Your boots. . . . Quick!'

And suiting the action to the word, Maigret made Jean sit down on a plank running along one of the walls of the stable.

Only then did the old man become submissive, and, looking reproachfully at his tormentor, he set about taking off one of his boots.

He was not wearing socks, but strips of cloth greased with tallow were wound round his feet and ankles, so that they seemed inseparable from his skin.

The lantern shed only a dim light. The skipper, who had finished his manoeuvre, came and squatted on the deck to see what was happening in the stable.

While Jean, scowling angrily, was lifting up his other leg, Maigret used some straw to clean the sole of the boot he was holding.

Then he took the left pedal out of his pocket and fitted it against the boot.

The bewildered old man gazing at his feet was a strange sight. His trousers, which must have been made for a man even shorter than himself, or which had been cut down, reached only half-way down his legs.

And the strips of greasy cloth were a dark grey, pitted with dirt and bits of straw.

Standing close to the lamp, Maigret compared the pedal, some of the treads of which were broken, with the scarcely visible marks on the leather.

'You took the lock-keeper's bicycle at Pogny last night!' he said slowly and accusingly, without taking his eyes off the two objects. 'How far did you go?'

'Hey, there! The *Providence*! Move up! The *Étourneau* has given up her turn and she's spending the night in the reach. . . .'

Jean turned towards the people moving about outside, then towards the Chief-Inspector.

'You can go and make your lock,' said Maigret. 'Here! Put your boots on. . . .'

The skipper was already wielding his boat-hook. His wife came running up.

'Jean! . . . The horses! . . . If we miss our turn. . . .'

The carter slipped his legs into his boots, hoisted himself up on deck, and called out in a curious voice:

'Ho! Gee up!'

And the horses snorted and moved off, while he jumped ashore and slowly followed behind them, his whip still round his neck.

'Ho! Gee up!'

While her husband pushed with the boat-hook, the woman bore with her whole weight on the wheel so as to avoid the barge coming in the opposite direction, whose rounded stem and haloed lantern at the stern were scarcely visible.

The lock-keeper's impatient voice shouted:

'What's the matter, the *Providence*? Are you going to take all night?'

She glided silently forward over the dark water. But she bumped into the stone wall three times before slipping into the lock, occupying its entire breadth.

CHAPTER 8

Ward 10

USUALLY the four sluices of a lock are opened only one after another, little by little, to avoid the wash which might break the boat's mooring-ropes.

But sixty barges were waiting. The bargees whose turn was approaching were helping to work the machinery, leaving the lock-keeper nothing to do but stamp their papers.

Maigret was on the quayside, holding his bicycle with one hand, and watching the shadows moving about in the darkness. The two horses had stopped of their own accord fifty yards from the upstream gates. Jean was turning one of the wheels.

The water poured in with a torrential din. It could be seen, all white, in the narrow gaps left by the *Providence*.

Suddenly, just as the flood was reaching its height, there was a muffled cry, followed by a thud on the bow of the barge and a confused hubbub.

The Chief-Inspector guessed rather than saw what happened. The carter was no longer in his place on the gate. And the others were running along the walls. Everybody was shouting at once.

There were only two lamps to light up the scene: one in the middle of the lift-bridge before the lock, the other on the barge which was continuing to rise fast.

'Shut the sluices!'

'Open the gates!'

Somebody passed with a huge boat-hook which hit Maigret in the face.

Some bargees came running up. And the lock-keeper came out of his office, panic-stricken at the idea of his responsibility for the accident.

'What is it?'

'The old man ...'

On either side of the barge, between the boat and the wall, there was not more than a foot of water. And this water, coming from the sluices, was surging and foaming into the narrow space.

There were some clumsy blunders. For instance somebody opened one of the sluices in the downstream gate, and this gate could be heard straining at its hinges while the lock-keeper rushed to repair the damage.

It was only later that the Chief-Inspector learnt that the whole reach could have been flooded and fifty barges damaged.

'Can you see him?'

'There's something dark down there.'

The barge was still rising, but more slowly. Three sluices out of four had been closed. But every few moments the boat thudded against the side of the lock, possibly crushing the carter.

'What depth?'

'At least three foot under the boat.'

It was horrifying. In the feeble glow of the stable-lantern, the skipper's wife could be seen running in all directions with a lifebelt in her hand.

She wailed plaintively:

'I don't think he can swim!'

And Maigret heard a solemn voice near him say:

'All the better! He won't have suffered so much. . . .'

*

All this lasted a quarter of an hour. Three times people thought they saw a body coming to the surface. But it was in vain that boat-hooks were plunged into the water at the places indicated.

The *Providence* slowly emerged from the lock and an old carter muttered:

'I'll bet you anything you like he's caught under the tiller. I've seen that happen at Verdun. . . .'

He was wrong. The barge had scarcely come to a stop fifty yards farther on before some men who were poking at the downstream gate with a pole called for help.

A dinghy had to be brought up. They could feel something under the water, about three feet deep. And just as somebody was getting ready to dive in, while his wife, with tears in her eyes, tried to hold him back, a body suddenly rose to the surface.

It was hauled out of the water. A dozen hands at once grasped the corduroy jacket, which was torn, for it had caught on one of the bolts on the gate.

The rest was like a nightmare. The telephone could be heard ringing in the lock-keeper's house. A boy had gone off on a bicycle to fetch a doctor.

But it was useless. The old carter's body had scarcely been laid on the bank, motionless and apparently lifeless, before a bargee took off his jacket, knelt down beside the drowned man's huge chest, and began rhythmical traction on the tongue.

Somebody had brought the lantern. The body looked shorter and stockier than ever, the dripping mud-stained face was livid.

'He's moving! . . . I tell you he's moving!'

There was no jostling in the crowd. The silence was such that the slightest word sounded as loud as in a cathedral. And all the time a jet of water could be heard gushing from a sluice which had not been properly closed.

'Well?' asked the lock-keeper coming back.

'He's alive . . . but only just.'

'We ought to have a mirror. . . .'

The skipper of the *Providence* ran to fetch one he had on board. The man who was practising artificial respiration was dripping with sweat and another took his place, pressing harder on the drowned man.

By the time the doctor came, arriving in a motor by a

side-road, everybody could see old Jean's chest slowly rising and falling.

His jacket had been removed. The open shirt revealed a chest as hairy as any animal's. Under the right breast there was a long scar and Maigret caught a glimpse of something which looked like a tattoo-mark on the shoulder.

'Next boat!' shouted the lock-keeper cupping his hands round his mouth. 'After all, you can't do anything to help. . . .'

And one bargee moved regretfully away, calling his wife who was talking to some other women some way off.

'You haven't stopped the engine, I hope?'

The doctor asked the onlookers to move away, frowning as soon as he felt the chest.

'He's alive, isn't he?' the first life-saver asked proudly.

'I'm from Police Headquarters,' Maigret broke in. 'Is it serious?'

'Most of his ribs are broken. . . . Admittedly he's alive. . . . But I'd be surprised if he lived for long. . . . Was he trapped between a couple of boats?'

'Probably between a boat and the lock.'

'Feel here . . .'

And the doctor made the Chief-Inspector feel the left arm, which was broken in two places.

'Is there a stretcher?'

The injured man gave a faint sigh.

'I'd better give him an injection in any case. . . . But have a stretcher brought here as quickly as possible. . . . The hospital is a quarter of a mile away. . . .'

There was a stretcher in the lock-keeper's house, in accordance with regulations, but it was in the attic, where, through the skylight, the flame of a candle could be seen moving about.

The skipper's wife was sobbing at some distance from Maigret, whom she was looking at reproachfully.

Ten men lifted the carter, who gave a fresh groan. Then a lantern moved away in the direction of the main road, shedding a halo around a compact group of men, while a motor-barge, showing its green and red navigation lights, sounded its hooter three times and went to moor in the middle of the town, so as to be the first to leave the next day.

*

Ward 10. It was purely by chance that Maigret saw the number. There were only two patients there, one of whom was wailing like a baby.

The Chief-Inspector spent most of the time pacing up and down the white-paved corridor, with nurses running by and passing on orders in an undertone.

In Ward 8, opposite, which was full of women, questions were being asked about the new patient and forecasts made.

'If they've put him in Ward 10! . . .'

The doctor was a plump man wearing horn-rimmed spectacles. He went past two or three times, in his white coat, without saying anything to Maigret.

It was nearly eleven o'clock when he finally came up to him.

'Do you want to see him?'

It was a baffling sight. The Chief-Inspector could hardly recognize old Jean, who had at last been shaved so that two cuts he had suffered on the cheek and the forehead could be treated.

There he was, all clean, in a white bed, in the neutral light of a lamp with a frosted-glass chimney.

The doctor drew back the sheet.

'Look at that carcass! . . . He's built like a bear. . . . I don't think I've ever seen a body like that. . . . How did he get smashed up?'

'He fell off the lock-gate while the sluices were open. . . .'

'I see. . . . He must have been crushed between the wall and the barge. . . . The chest is literally bashed in. . . . The ribs have given way. . . .'

'The rest?'

'We'll have to examine him tomorrow, my colleagues

98

and I, if he's still alive.... It's a ticklish job... The slightest slip might kill him...'

'Has he recovered consciousness?'

'I just don't know. That's perhaps the most baffling thing about it.... Just now, when I was probing his injuries, I had a distinct impression that his eyes were half-open and that he was watching me.... But as soon as I looked at him he dropped his eyelids.... He hasn't been delirious.... At the very most he gives a groan now and then...'

'What about his arm?'

'That's nothing serious. The double fracture has already been reduced.... But you can't mend a chest like a humerus.... Where does he come from?'

'I don't know.'

'I asked you that because he's got some queer tattoo-marks.... I've seen those of the African Battalions, but these are different.... I'll show them to you tomorrow when we take the plaster off for the examination....'

The porter came up to say that some people were insisting on seeing the injured man. Maigret himself went into the lodge, where he found the couple from the *Providence* who had dressed in their Sunday best.

'We can see him, can't we, Chief-Inspector?... It's your fault, you know.... You upset him with your questions.... Is he any better?'

'He's a little better.... The doctors will make their diagnosis tomorrow....'

'Let me see him!... Even if it's only from a distance.... He was so much part of the boat...'

She did not say *of the family* but *of the boat*, and perhaps that was even more touching.

Her husband stood shyly behind her, ill at ease in a blue serge suit, his scraggy neck enclosed by a celluloid collar.

'I advise you not to make any noise....'

The two of them looked at him from the corridor, from where nothing could be seen but a vague shape under the sheet, a little ivory in place of the face, a few white hairs.

A dozen times the skipper's wife was on the point of rushing forward.

'Look here ... If we paid something, would he be treated better?'

She did not dare to open her handbag, but fidgeted nervously with it.

'There are hospitals, aren't there, where if you pay... At least the other patients haven't got anything catching, I hope?'

'Are you staying at Vitry?'

'Why, of course we aren't going to leave without him! ... It doesn't matter about the load. ... What time can we come tomorrow morning?'

'Ten o'clock,' said the doctor who had been listening impatiently.

'There isn't something we could bring him, is there? ... A bottle of champagne? Some Spanish grapes?'

'We'll give him everything he needs. ...'

And the doctor pushed them gently towards the porter's lodge. When she got there, the good woman furtively took a ten-franc note out of her bag and pressed it on the porter, who looked at her in astonishment.

*

Maigret went to bed at midnight, after wiring to Dizy to forward any messages which might arrive for him there.

At the last moment he had learnt that the *Southern Cross*, after overtaking most of the barges, had arrived at Vitry-le-François and had moored at the end of the line of waiting boats.

The Chief-Inspector had taken a room at the Hôtel de la Marne, in the town, a fairly long way from the canal, and here he found nothing of the atmosphere in which he had lived for the last few days.

The guests who were playing cards were commercial travellers.

One of them, who arrived after the others, announced:

'It seems there's been a man drowned in the lock. ...'

'Come and make up a foursome.... Lamperrière is losing like nobody's business.... Is the fellow dead?'

'I don't know.'

That was all. The manager's wife was dozing behind the cash-desk. The waiter scattered some sawdust on the floor and stoked up the stove for the night.

There was a bathroom, just one, in which the bath had lost part of its enamel. For all that, Maigret took a bath at eight o'clock the next morning, and sent the waiter to buy him a new shirt and a collar.

But as time went by he began to lose patience. He was in a hurry to see the canal again. When he heard a siren he asked:

'Is that for the lock?'

'For the lift-bridge.... There are three of them in the town....'

It was a grey, windy day. He could not remember how to get to the hospital and had to ask his way several times, for every street brought him back without fail to the market place.

The porter recognized him and came to meet him, exclaiming:

'You'd never have believed it, would you?'

'What?... Is he alive?... Is he dead?'

'You mean you don't know? The director has just phoned to your hotel...'

'Tell me quick...'

'Well, he's gone..... Done a flit.... The doctor swears that it's impossible, that he couldn't have gone a hundred yards in the state he was in.... All the same, he's vanished....'

Maigret heard some voices in the garden, behind the building, and rushed in that direction.

He found an old man whom he had not seen before and who was the director of the hospital. He was speaking sternly to the doctor whom Maigret had seen the previous day and to a red-haired nurse.

'I swear that's the truth!' the doctor was saying. 'You know as well as I do what it's like. . . . When I say ten broken ribs it's probably an underestimate. . . . Not to mention the drowning and the shock. . . .'

'How did he get out?' asked Maigret.

They showed him the window, which was about five feet above the ground. In the earth could be seen the marks of two bare feet, as well as a long trail which suggested that the carter had fallen headlong straight away.

'There you are! . . . The nurse, Mademoiselle Berthe, spent the night in the duty-room as usual. . . . She didn't hear anything. . . . About three o'clock she had to attend to a patient in Ward 8, and she glanced into Ward 10. . . . The lamps were out. . . . Everything was quiet. . . . She can't say whether the man was still in bed. . . .'

'What about the other two patients?'

'One of them has to have an emergency operation. . . . We're waiting for the surgeon. . . . The other didn't wake up at all during the night. . . .'

Maigret's eyes followed the tracks, which led to a flower bed where a little rose-bush had been trampled on.

'Is the gate always left open?'

'This isn't a prison!' retorted the director. 'And how can we foresee that a patient is going to jump out of the window? . . . Only the main door of the building was locked, as usual. . . .'

Outside, there was no point in looking for tracks, for there was a paved road. In between a couple of houses could be seen the double line of trees along the canal.

'The fact is,' added the doctor, 'I was practically sure that we should find him dead this morning. . . . And seeing that there was nothing to be done. . . . That's why I put him in Ward 10. . . .'

He was somewhat truculent, for he was still smarting from the reproaches the director had levelled at him.

Maigret walked round and round the garden for a while

like a circus horse, and suddenly, touching the brim of his bowler hat by way of farewell, he set off for the lock.

The *Southern Cross* was just entering it. Vladimir, with the skill of a real seaman, tossed the loop of a rope over a bitt and brought the boat to a dead stop.

As for the colonel, dressed in long oilskins and his white cap, he was standing impassively at the little wheel.

'The gates!' shouted the lock-keeper.

There were only about twenty boats left to lock through.

'Is it her turn?' asked Maigret, pointing to the yacht.

'It is and it isn't. . . . If you regard her as a *motor-vessel* she has precedence over a *horse-boat*. . . . But as a *pleasure-craft*. . . . Still, we get so few of them we aren't very strict about the regulations. . . . And as they tipped the bargees. . . .'

It was the latter who were working the sluices.

'Where's the *Providence*?'

'She was blocking the way. . . . This morning she went and moored on the bend, a hundred yards farther on, just before the second bridge. . . . Have you any news of the old man? . . . I'll probably have to pay dearly for that business. . . . But I'd like to see you manage any other way. . . . Strictly speaking, I ought to do the locking through myself. . . . But if I did, there'd be a hundred boats waiting every day. . . . . Four gates! . . . Sixteen sluices! . . . and have you any idea how much I'm paid? . . .'

He had to move away for a moment, because Vladimir was holding out his papers and a tip.

Maigret took the opportunity to walk off along the canal. At the bend he caught sight of the *Providence*, which by now he could have recognized among a hundred barges.

A little smoke was coming out of the chimney; there was nobody on deck; all the hatches were closed.

He nearly went up the after-gangway, leading to the bargees' quarters.

Then he changed his mind and climbed the wide gangway which was used to take the horses on board.

One of the hatches covering the stable had been removed.

The head of one of the horses was poking out, sniffing the wind.

Looking inside, Maigret made out a dark figure stretched out on the straw behind the animal's legs. And, close to it, the skipper's wife was squatting with a bowl of coffee in her hand.

In a curiously gentle, motherly voice, she was murmuring:

'Come along, Jean. . . . Drink it while it's hot! . . . It'll do you good, you old silly. . . . Do you want me to lift up your head?'

But the man lying beside her did not move but gazed at the sky.

Against that sky was silhouetted Maigret's head, which he must have seen.

And the Chief-Inspector had the impression that across the face, which was criss-crossed with sticking-plaster, there passed a happy, ironic, even truculent smile.

The old carter tried to lift his hand to push away the cup the woman was holding to his lips. But it fell limply by his side, wrinkled, horny, and speckled with little blue spots which must have been the vestiges of old tattoo-marks.

CHAPTER 9

The Doctor

'You see? He's dragged himself home like a wounded dog. . . .'

Had the woman any idea of the injured man's condition? In any case she was not panicking. She was as calm as if she were nursing a child down with influenza.

'Coffee can't do him any harm, can it? . . . But he won't drink any. . . . It must have been four in the morning when my husband and I were woken up by a tremendous noise on board. . . . I took the revolver . . . I told him to follow me with the lantern. . . .

'Believe it or not, Jean was there, looking pretty much as he is now. . . . He must have fallen from the deck. . . . That's about a six-foot drop. . . .

'To begin with, we couldn't see very clearly . . . I thought for a moment he was dead. . . .

'My husband wanted to call some of our neighbours to help lift him on to a bed. . . . But Jean understood . . . he started squeezing my hand . . . squeezing it so hard! . . . It was as if he was hanging on to it like grim death. . . .

'And I could see him sniffing. . . .

'I understood. . . . Because in the eight years he's been with us, you know . . . He can't talk . . . but I think he can hear what I'm saying. . . . Am I right, Jean? . . . Are you in pain?'

It was difficult to know whether the injured man's eyes were shining with intelligence or fever.

The woman brushed away a piece of straw which was touching his ear.

'Me, you know, my life's my little household, my brasses, my bits and pieces of furniture . . . I do believe

that if somebody gave me a palace, I'd be downright unhappy. . . .

'For Jean, it's his stable . . . and his horses. . . . How can
I explain? . . . There are naturally days when we don't move
because we're unloading. . . . Jean has got nothing to do
. . . he could go to the pub. . . .

'But no! He lies down here. . . . He leaves an opening
for a ray of sunlight to come in. . . .'

And Maigret imagined himself where the carter was,
seeing the partition coated with resin on his right, with the
whip hanging on a twisted nail, the tin cup hooked on to
another, a patch of sky between the boards above, and on
the right the horses' muscular croppers.

The whole scene gave off an animal warmth, a sensation
of full-blooded life which took one by the throat like the
harsh wine of certain hill-sides.

'He can be left here, can't he?'

She beckoned to the Chief-Inspector to follow her outside. The lock was working at the same rhythm as the day
before. And all around were the streets of the town, with
their bustling life which had nothing to do with the canal.

'He's going to die after all, isn't he? . . . What has he
done? . . . You can tell me, you know . . . but you must
admit that I couldn't say anything. . . . In the first place,
I don't know anything. . . . Once, and only once, my husband found Jean with his chest bare. . . . He saw the tattoo-
marks . . . not like those some sailors wear. . . . We guessed
what you would have guessed. . . .

'I think I felt fonder than ever of him after that. . . . I
told myself that he probably wasn't what he seemed to be,
that he was hiding . . .

'I wouldn't have questioned him for all the money in
the world. . . . You don't think he killed the woman, do
you . . . or if he did, well, I'm sure she deserved it. . . .

'Jean . . . Jean is . . .'

She searched for a word which would express what she
meant, but failed to find one.

'Ah, there's my man getting up. . . . I packed him off to bed, because he's never been very strong in the chest. . . . Do you think if I made a really strong soup . . .?'

'The doctors will be coming. In the meantime it would be better. . . .'

'Have they got to come? . . . They're going to make him suffer, spoil his last moments which . . .'

'It's absolutely essential . . .'

'He's so happy here with us. . . . Can I leave you for a minute? . . . You won't bother him, will you? . . .'

Maigret gave a reassuring nod, went back into the stable, and took out of his pocket a metal box containing a little pad soaked in oily ink.

It was still impossible to tell whether the carter was conscious. His eyelids were half-open. Between them there filtered a serene, neutral gaze.

But when the Chief-Inspector picked up the injured man's right hand and pressed his fingers on to the pad, one after another, he had the impression that for a split-second at the most the shadow of a smile touched his lips again.

He took the finger-prints on a sheet of paper, looked at the dying man for a moment, as if he were hoping for something, threw a last glance at the partitions and at the croppers of the two horses which were showing signs of impatience, and went out.

Beside the helm, the skipper and his wife were having their breakfast of bread and coffee and looking in his direction. Less than five yards from the *Providence*, the *Southern Cross* was moored, with nobody on deck.

The day before, Maigret had left his bicycle at the lock, where he found it waiting for him. Ten minutes later he was at the police station, sending a motor-cyclist to Épernay with instructions to transmit the finger-prints to Paris by the Belin telephotograph.

When he came back on board the *Providence*, he was accompanied by two doctors from the hospital with whom he was soon involved in an argument.

The doctors wanted to take their patient back to hospital. The skipper's wife, thoroughly alarmed, threw beseeching glances at Maigret.

'Can you cure him?'

'No. The chest has been smashed in. One rib has entered the right lung. . . .'

'How long has he got to live?'

'Anybody else would be dead already . . . He might last another hour, another five . . .'

'In that case, leave him here.'

The old man had not moved, had not stirred a muscle. As Maigret passed the skipper's wife, she touched his hand shyly, in a gesture of gratitude.

The doctors looked disgruntled as they crossed the gangway.

'Allowing him to die in a stable!' grumbled one of them.

'Oh, what does it matter? . . . After all, he was allowed to live in it . . .'

All the same, the Chief-Inspector stationed a policeman close to the barge and the yacht, with instructions to inform him if anything happened.

From the lock he telephoned to the Café de la Marine at Dizy, and was told that Inspector Lucas had just been in and that he had hired a taxi at Épernay to drive him to Vitry-le-François.

There followed a long, empty hour. The skipper of the *Providence* took advantage of this respite to tar the dinghy he had in tow. Vladimir polished the brasses on the *Southern Cross*.

As for the woman, she was seen constantly crossing the deck, going from the kitchen to the stable. Once she was carrying a pillow of dazzling whiteness, another time a bowl of steaming liquid, presumably the soup she had insisted on making.

About eleven o'clock Lucas arrived at the Hôtel de la Marne, where Maigret was waiting for him.

'How are you, old man?'

'All right. But you look tired, Chief...'

'Did your inquiries produce any results?'

'Not much. At Meaux nothing, except that the yacht created a minor scandal. The bargees couldn't sleep on account of the music and singing, and threatened to break everything up...'

'Was the *Providence* there?'

'She took on a load less than twenty yards from the *Southern Cross*... But nobody noticed anything special...'

'And in Paris?'

'I saw the two girls again.... They admitted that it wasn't Mary Lampson who had given them the necklace, but Willy Marco.... I got confirmation of that at the hotel, where the staff recognized her photo and hadn't seen Mrs Lampson ... I'm not sure, but I think that Lia Lauwenstein knew Willy more intimately than she likes to admit, and that she had already helped him at Nice....'

'And at Moulins?'

'Not a thing! I went to see the baker's wife, who is indeed the only Marie Dupin in the place.... A nice, respectable body who can't understand what's going on and keeps complaining that this business will damage her reputation.... The copy of the birth certificate was made eight years ago.... Now there's been a new Town Clerk for the last three years and his predecessor died last year.... They've hunted through the archives without finding anything concerning that document....'

After a pause Lucas asked:

'How about you?'

'I don't know yet.... Nothing ... or everything ... I shall know any time now.... What are people saying at Dizy?'

'That if the *Southern Cross* hadn't been a yacht, she wouldn't have been allowed to leave, and that Mrs Lampson wasn't the colonel's first wife....'

Maigret said no more, but led his companion through the streets of the little town as far as the post office.

'Get me the Police Records Office in Paris. . . .'

The telephotograph of the carter's finger-prints ought to have reached the Prefecture nearly two hours before. After that it was a matter of luck. The card corresponding to the finger-prints could be found straight away, among eighty thousand others, just as the search could last for hours.

'Take an earphone, old man . . . Hullo . . . Who's that speaking? . . . Is it you, Benoît? . . . Maigret here . . . Did you get my message? . . . What's that you say? . . . It was you who looked for the file? . . . Wait a minute . . .'

He left the call-box and went over to the counter.

'I may need the line for a long time. Make sure that I'm not cut off on any account. . . .'

When he picked up the receiver again, his eyes were brighter.

'Sit down Benoît, because I want you to read me the whole file . . . Lucas is here beside me and he'll take notes. . . . Fire away. . . .'

He could picture Benoît as clearly as if he had been in front of him, for he knew the rooms, up in the attics of the Palais de Justice, where steel cabinets contain the cards of all the criminals of France and a good many foreign law-breakers too.

'First of all his name . . . .'

'Jean Évariste Darchambaux, born at Boulogne, now aged fifty-five . . .'

Maigret automatically tried to recall a case of that name, but already Benoît's unemotional voice, pronouncing each syllable distinctly, was droning on, with Lucas writing everything down.

'Doctor of Medicine . . . Married at twenty-five to a certain Céline Mornet of Étampes . . . Settled at Toulouse, where he had done his medical training. . . . A fairly hectic life. . . . Can you hear me, Chief-Inspector?'

'Yes, very well indeed. Go on. . . .'

'I got the whole file out, because the record-card says hardly anything. . . . The couple were soon up to their necks in debt. .... Two years after his marriage, at twenty-seven, Darchambaux was accused of having poisoned his aunt, Julia Darchambaux, who had come to live with the couple at Toulouse and disapproved of her nephew's way of life. .... The aunt was a wealthy woman. .... The Darchambaux were the sole heirs. ...

'The police investigation lasted eight months, because no positive proof could be found. .... The murderer maintained – and he was backed up by a number of experts – that the medicine prescribed for the old woman was not a poison in itself and that it was simply a case of a bold, unorthodox treatment. ...

'There was considerable argument on the subject. .... You don't want me to read the reports, do you? ...

'The trial was a stormy one and the court had to be cleared several times. .... Most people thought that Darchambaux would be acquitted, especially after the testimony of his wife, who came and swore that her husband was innocent and that if he was sent to a penal settlement she would go and join him. ...'

'What did he get?'

'Fifteen years' hard labour ... Wait a minute. .... That's all there is in our files. .... But I've sent a dispatch-rider to the Ministry of the Interior. .... He's just got back ...'

They could hear him talking to somebody standing behind him, and then turning over some papers.

'Here we are ... There isn't very much. .... The governor of Saint-Laurent-du-Maroni wanted Darchambaux to work in one of the hospitals in the penal settlement. .... He refused. .... His record out there was good. .... A docile convict. .... Only one attempt at escape, with fifteen fellow-convicts who had incited him to join them. ...

'Five years later a new governor attempted what he called a rehabilitation of Darchambaux, but noted straight away in his report that there was nothing in the convict who was brought before him which recalled the former intellectual, nor even the well-educated man. ...

'Right. . . . Does this interest you? . . .

'He was given a job as a medical orderly, but asked of his own accord to be sent back to the chain-gang. . . .

'He was gentle, stubborn, silent. One of his medical colleagues, interested by his case, examined him from the mental point of view and was unable to come to a definite conclusion.

'He noted, underlining these words in red ink, that there was a sort of progressive extinction of the intellectual faculties, matched by a hypertrophy of the physical faculties.

'Darchambaux committed two thefts. On both occasions it was food that he stole, the second time from a fellow-member of the chain-gang who wounded him in the chest with a sharpened flint. . . .

'Visiting journalists advised him in vain to ask for a pardon.

'When his fifteen years were over, he stayed out there under supervision, and took a job as a groom at a saw-mill where he looked after the horses.

'At forty-five he was finished with the law. All trace of him was lost . . .'

'Is that the lot?'

'I can send you the file . . . I've only given you a summary of the contents. . . .'

'There's nothing about his wife, is there? . . . You did say that she was born at Étampes, didn't you? . . . Thank you, Benoît. . . . No need to send me the papers. . . . What you've told me is enough.'

When he came out of the call-box, followed by Lucas, he was dripping with sweat.

'Ring up the Town Hall at Étampes. They'll tell you if Céline Mornet is dead. . . . At least if she's died under that name. . . . Ring up Moulins too and ask if Marie Dupin has any relatives at Étampes. . . .'

He crossed the town without seeing anything, his hands in his pockets, and had to wait for five minutes beside the canal, because the lift-bridge was up and a heavily loaded barge was moving along at a snail's pace, dragging its flat belly along the canal bed, from which the mud was rising to the surface together with bubbles of air.

In front of the *Providence* he went up to the policeman he had posted on the tow-path.

'You can go now . . .'

He noticed the colonel pacing the deck of his yacht.

The bargee's wife came running up, much more agitated than she had been that morning, with shining furrows on her cheeks.

'It's awful, Chief-Inspector . . .'

Maigret went pale, and asked, grim-faced:

'Is he dead?'

'No . . . Don't say that. . . . Just now I was alone with him . . . Because I ought to tell you that, while he was fond of my husband too, he had a preference for me. . . .

'I'm much younger than he is. . . . Well, in spite of that, he used to consider me rather as a mother . . .

'We used to go for weeks without talking . . . Only . . . Just to give you an idea . . . Usually my husband forgets the date of my name-day . . . St Hortense's Day. . . . Well, for the last eight years, Jean has never once forgotten to give me some flowers. . . . Sometimes, when we were in the depths of the country, I wondered where he got them. . . . And that day he used to put cockades on the horses' blinkers. . . .

'Well . . . I was sitting beside him just now . . . these are probably his last hours. . . . My husband would like to take the horses out, because they aren't used to being shut in such a long time . . . .

'I won't let him, because I'm sure that Jean wants them to stay with him too . . .

'I took his big hand . . .'

She started crying, but not sobbing. She went on talking, with tears running down her blotchy cheeks.

'I don't know how it happened . . . I haven't any

children. . . . We had even decided to adopt one when we reached the age required by law . . .

'I told him that it was nothing, that he'd get better; that we'd try to get a load for Alsace, where the countryside is so pretty in summer . . .

'I felt his fingers squeeze mine . . . I couldn't tell him that he was hurting me . . .

'It was then that he tried to speak . . .

'Can you understand that? . . . A man like him, who only yesterday was as strong as his horses. . . . He opened his mouth and made such a tremendous effort that his veins stood out on his forehead and went all purple . . .

'And I heard a hoarse noise, like an animal cry . . .

'I begged him to keep calm. . . . But he went on trying. . . . He sat up on the straw, heaven knows how . . . and he kept on opening his mouth . . .

'Some blood came out of it and trickled down his chin. . . .

'I should have liked to call my husband. . . . But Jean was still holding me . . . he frightens me . . .

'You can't imagine what it was like . . . I tried to understand . . . I asked him if he wanted something to drink. . . . No . . . Had I to go and fetch somebody? . . .

'He was so desperate at not being able to say a word. . . . I ought to have guessed . . . I tried hard enough . . .

'What do you think it could have been that he wanted to ask me? . . . Because now he's got something torn in his throat . . . I don't know . . .

'He had a haemorrhage. Finally he gritted his teeth and lay down again, right on his broken arm. . . . It must be hurting him and yet anybody would think he couldn't feel a thing. . . .

'He just lies there gazing straight in front of him . . .

'I'd give a lot to know what he'd like before . . . before it's too late. . . .'

Maigret walked noiselessly over to the stable and looked through the open hatchway.

It was as fascinating and pathetic as the death-agony of an animal with which one has no means of communicating.

The carter's body was doubled up. He had torn away part of the surgical appliance which the doctor had fitted round his torso that night.

And, at long intervals, the whistling sound of his breathing could be heard.

One of the horses had caught a foot in its tether but was standing motionless, as if it had realized that something solemn was happening.

Maigret too hesitated. He called to mind the dead woman hidden under the straw in the stable at Dizy, and then Willy's body, floating in the canal with people in the cold morning air trying to catch it with a boat-hook.

His hand, in his pocket, felt the Y.C.F. badge and the cuff-link.

And he recalled the colonel bowing to the examining magistrate and asking in a steady voice for permission to continue his journey.

In the mortuary at Épernay, in an icy room lined with metal lockers like the vaults of a bank, two bodies were waiting, each in a numbered box.

And in Paris, two women with crudely applied make-up on their faces were probably dragging their fear with them from one bar to another.

Lucas came into sight.

'Well?' Maigret called out from a distance.

'Céline Mornet has given no sign of life at Étampes since the day she applied for the papers required for her marriage to Darchambaux.'

The Inspector looked inquisitively at Maigret.

'What's the matter?'

'Ssh!'

But Lucas glanced around him in vain: he could see nothing to justify the slightest emotion.

Then Maigret took him to the stable hatchway and showed him the figure stretched out in the straw.

The skipper's wife wondered what they were going to do. From a passing motor-boat a voice called out gaily:

'Hullo! . . . Broken down?'

She started crying again, without knowing why. Her husband came back on board with a bucket of tar in one hand and a brush in the other, and announced from the stern:

'There's something burning on the stove. . . .'

She hurried automatically to the kitchen. And Maigret said to Lucas, almost regretfully:

'Let's go down . . .'

One of the horses neighed softly. The carter did not move.

The Chief-Inspector had taken the photograph of the dead woman out of his wallet, but he did not look at it.

CHAPTER 10

The Two Husbands

'LISTEN, Darchambaux. . . .'

Maigret had said that standing up, scrutinizing the carter's face. Without even realizing what he was doing, he had taken his pipe out of his pocket, but he did not think of filling it.

Perhaps the reaction was not what he had hoped for? The fact remains that he sat down on the stable bench, bent forward, his chin in his hands, and went on in a different tone of voice:

'Listen. . . . Don't get excited . . . I know that you can't talk . . .'

An unexpected shadow passing over the straw made him raise his head, and he saw the colonel standing on the deck of the barge, at the edge of the open hatchway.

The Englishman did not move, but went on following the scene from above, his feet higher up than the heads of the three men in the stable.

Lucas kept to one side, as far as the cramped conditions allowed. Maigret, feeling a little more nervous, continued:

'You aren't going to be taken away from here. . . You understand, Darchambaux? . . . In a few minutes I shall be going . . . Madame Hortense will take my place. . . .'

It was pathetic, though it would have been hard to say exactly why. Maigret, in spite of himself, was talking almost as gently as the skipper's wife.

'First of all, I want you to answer a few questions by blinking your eyes. . . . Several people are in danger of being accused and arrested at any moment. . . . You don't want that to happen, do you? . . . In that case I need you to confirm the facts. . . .'

And, while he was talking, the Chief-Inspector did not

take his eyes off the man, or stop wondering which he had in front of him at that moment, the sometime doctor, the stubborn convict, the besotted carter, or the infuriated murderer of Mary Lampson.

The body was brutish, the features coarse. But wasn't there a new expression in the eyes, an expression from which all irony had gone?

An expression of infinite sadness.

Twice Jean tried to speak. Twice they heard a noise which resembled the groaning of an animal and beads of pink saliva appeared on the dying man's lips.

All the time Maigret could see the shadow of the colonel's legs.

'When you were transported as a young man, you were convinced that your wife would keep her promise and follow you out there. It was she whom you killed at Dizy!'

Not a movement. Nothing. The face took on a greyish hue.

'She didn't come and . . . you lost heart. . . . You . . . you tried to forget everything, even your own personality. . . .'

Maigret was talking faster, as if he were losing patience. He was in a hurry to have done with it all. Above all he was afraid of seeing Jean die in the course of this horrifying interrogation.

'You came across her again by accident, when you had become a different man. . . . That was at Meaux, wasn't it? . . .'

He had to wait quite a while before the carter obediently blinked his eyes in confirmation.

The shadow of the legs moved. The barge rocked for a moment as a motor-boat went by.

'*She* had remained the same. . . . Pretty . . . and smart . . . and gay. . . . They were dancing on the deck of the yacht. . . . You didn't think of killing her straight away . . . otherwise there was no need to take her to Dizy first. . . .'

Could the dying man still hear what he was saying?

Lying in the position he was in, he must have seen the colonel just above him. But his eyes expressed nothing. Or at least, nothing intelligible.

'She had sworn to follow you everywhere. . . . You had been in a penal settlement. . . . You were living in a stable . . . and the idea suddenly occurred to you of taking her back, just as she was, with her jewels, her make-up, her white dress, and making her share your straw. . . . Wasn't that how it was, Darchambaux?'

The eyes did not blink. But the chest rose and fell. There was another groan. Lucas, who could scarcely stand it shifted in his corner.

'That's it! I'm sure it is!' exclaimed Maigret, speaking more and more quickly, as if he were growing giddy. 'Faced with his former wife, Jean the carter, who had almost forgotten Dr Darchambaux, was visited by memories of the past . . . and a strange vengeance began to take shape in his mind. . . . A vengeance? . . . Not exactly . . . an obscure desire to bring down to his level the woman who had promised to be his for life. . . .

'And Mary Lampson lived for three days hidden in this stable, almost of her own free will. . . .

'For she was afraid . . . afraid of the ghost whom she felt to be capable of anything, who ordered her to follow him. . . .

'All the more afraid in that she was conscious of the cowardice she had shown. . . .

'She came of her own accord . . . and you, Jean, you brought her corned beef, and coarse red wine. . . . You joined her, for two nights in succession, after the endless journeys along the Marne . . .

'At Dizy. . . .'

Once again the dying man stirred. But he had no strength in him. He fell back, weak and nerveless.

'She must have revolted. . . . She could not stand that sort of life any longer. . . . You strangled her in a moment of anger, rather than allow her to leave you a second time. . . . You carried the corpse into the stable. . . . Is that right?'

He had to repeat the question five times and at last the eyelids moved.

'Yes,' they said wearily.

There was a slight noise on deck. The colonel was holding back the skipper's wife who wanted to come nearer. She obeyed, impressed by his grave expression.

'The tow-path . . . Your life again along the canal. . . . But you were worried . . . You were afraid . . . For you are afraid of dying, Jean. . . . Afraid of being imprisoned again . . . afraid of transportation. . . . Above all, horribly afraid of leaving your horses, your stable, your straw, your little nook which has become your world. . . . So one night you took the lock-keeper's bicycle . . . I had questioned you. . . . You guessed at my suspicions . . .

'You came to prowl around Dizy with the idea of doing something, anything, to divert them. . . .

'Is that right?'

Jean was now so completely still that he might have been dead. His face no longer showed anything but boredom. All the same, his eyelids dropped once again.

'When you arrived, the *Southern Cross* was in darkness. You imagined that everybody was asleep. On the deck a sailor's cap was drying out. . . . You picked it up. . . . . You went to the stable to hide it under the straw. . . . That was a way of changing the course of the investigation and diverting it towards the people on the yacht.

'You couldn't know that Willy Marco, who was outside by himself, and who had seen you take the cap, was following you step by step. . . He waited for you outside the stable, where he lost one of his cuff-links . . . .

'Intrigued, he followed you on your way back to the stone bridge, where you had left your bicycle . . .

'Did he call out to you . . . Or did you hear a noise behind you? . . .

'There was a struggle. . . . You killed him with your

terrible fingers, which had already strangled Mary Lampson,
You dragged his body to the canal . . .

'Then you must have walked away with your head
down. . . . On the tow-path you saw something shining, the
Y.C.F. badge. . . . And, on the spur of the moment, knowing that the badge belonged to somebody, having seen it
perhaps in the colonel's buttonhole, you dropped it where
the struggle had taken place. . . . Answer me, Darchambaux.
That *was* how things happened, wasn't it?'

'Have you broken down, the *Providence*?' called another
bargee, whose boat passed so close that his head could be
seen gliding past, level with the hatchway.

And – a strange disturbing sight – Jean's eyes filled with
tears. He blinked his eyes rapidly, as if to admit everything
and have done with it. He heard the skipper's wife reply
from the stern, where she was waiting:

'It's Jean who's been injured . . .'

Then Maigret, standing up, went on:

'Last night, when I examined your boots, you realized
that I was bound to discover the truth. . . . You tried to
kill yourself by jumping into the lock. . . .'

But the carter was so weak and was breathing with such
difficulty that the Chief-Inspector did not even wait for a
reply. He motioned to Lucas and looked round him for the
last time.

A ray of sunshine was slanting into the stable and lighting
up the carter's left ear and a hoof of one of the horses.

Just as the two men were going out, unable to think of
anything else to say, Jean tried again to speak, making a
violent effort, without regard to the pain he was suffering.
He pulled himself up into a sitting position, his eyes glaring
wildly.

Maigret did not give his attention straight away to the
colonel. He beckoned the woman, who was looking at him
from a distance.

'Well? . . . How is he?' she asked.

'Stay with him . . .'

'Can I? . . . You won't come again and . . .'

She did not dare to finish what she was saying. She had frozen into immobility on hearing the vague appeals of Jean, who seemed to be afraid of dying all alone.

Then all of a sudden she ran towards the stable.

*

Vladimir, sitting on the capstan of the yacht, with a cigarette between his lips and his white cap cocked over one ear, was splicing a rope.

A policeman was waiting on the quayside and Maigret asked him from the barge:

'What is it?'

'The answer has come from Moulins . . .'

He held out a note which said simply:

The baker's wife Marie Dupin states that she used to have a distant cousin at Étampes called Céline Mornet.

Then Maigret looked the colonel up and down. He was wearing his white cap with the big crest. His eyes were only just turning sea-green, which probably meant that he had drunk comparatively little whisky.

'You were suspicious about the *Providence*, were you?' the Chief-Inspector asked him point-blank.

It was so obvious. Wouldn't Maigret too have suspected the barge if his suspicions had not fallen for a moment on the yacht's company?

'Why didn't you say anything to me?'

The answer was worthy of the conversation between Sir Walter and the examining magistrate at Dizy.

'I wanted to settle the matter myself . . .'

And that was enough to express the colonel's contempt for the police.

'My wife?' he asked almost immediately.

'As you said yourself, as Willy Marco said, she was a charming woman . . .'

Maigret was not being sarcastic. Besides, he was paying more attention to the noises coming from the stable than to this conversation.

He could hear the soft murmur of a single voice, that of the skipper's wife, who sounded as if she were comforting a sick child.

'When she married Darchambaux she already had a hankering after luxury ... And it was probably for her sake that the poor doctor he was helped his aunt to die. ... I'm not saying that she abetted him. ... I'm saying that he did it for her sake ... and she was so well aware of this that she swore in the Assize Court that she would go and join him. ...

'A charming woman ... Which isn't the same thing as a heroine ...

'Her love of life proved stronger ... You must understand that, colonel. ...'

There was sunshine, wind, and threatening clouds all at once. It could start raining at any moment. The light was doubtful.

'It's so rare for men to come back from transportation ... She was pretty ... All the pleasures of life were within her reach. ... The only obstacle was her name ... So, on the Côte d'Azur, where she had met an admirer who was ready to marry her, she hit on the idea of writing to Moulins for a copy of the birth certificate of a little cousin of hers whom she remembered ...

'It's easy! So easy that there's talk at the moment of taking the finger-prints of new-born children and putting them on the registers of births ...

'She divorced her husband ... She became your wife. ...

'A charming woman ... No harm in her, I'm sure of that. ... But she liked life, didn't she? ... She liked youth, love, luxury ...

'But at the same time, every now and then, she suffered a pang of remorse which sent her out on some inexplicable escapade ...

'You know, I'm convinced that she followed Jean not so much because of his threats as from a longing to win his forgiveness. . . .

'The first day, hidden in the stable on this boat, among all the strong smells, she must have felt a vague satisfaction at the idea that she was atoning for her treachery. . . .

'The same satisfaction she felt in the Assize Court, when she cried out to the jury that she would follow her husband to Guiana.

'Charming creatures, whose first impulse is always good, even theatrical. . . . They are full of good intentions. . . .

'The trouble is that life, with its acts of cowardice, its compromises, its insistent needs, is stronger . . .'

Maigret had spoken rather heatedly, listening all the time to the sounds in the stable while his eyes followed the movements of the boats entering or leaving the lock.

The colonel stood in front of him with his head bowed. When he raised it again, it was to look at Maigret with obvious liking, and perhaps even with suppressed emotion.

'Will you come and have a drink?' he said, pointing to his yacht.

Lucas stood a little way off.

'You'll let me know, won't you?' the Chief-Inspector said to him.

There was no need for explanations between them. The inspector had understood and prowled silently round the stable.

The *Southern Cross* was as shipshape as if nothing had happened. There was not a single speck of dust on the mahogany walls of the cabin.

In the centre of the table there was a bottle of whisky, a siphon, and some glasses.

'Stay outside, Vladimir.'

Maigret was conscious of a novel impression. This time he had not come here in an attempt to discover some particle of truth. He was less clumsy, less abrupt.

And the colonel treated him as he had treated Monsieur de Clairfontaine de Lagny.

'He's going to die, isn't he?'

'Yes, any minute now. . . . He's known that since yesterday. . . .'

The soda-water spurted from the siphon. Sir Walter said solemnly:

'Your health!'

And Maigret drank, just as thirstily as his host.

'Why did he leave the hospital?'

The rhythm of the answers was slow. Before replying, the Chief-Inspector looked around him, noting the smallest details of the cabin.

'Because . . .'

He searched for his words, while his companion was already filling the glasses again.

'. . . a man without any ties . . . a man who has cut all links with his past, with his former personality . . . He has to have something to hang on to! . . . And that something is his stable . . . the smell . . . the horses . . . the scalding-hot coffee gulped down at three in the morning before walking all day. . . . His lair, if you like . . . his own nook. . . . Full of his animal warmth. . . .'

And Maigret looked the colonel in the eyes. He saw him turn his head away. He added, picking up his glass:

'There are all sorts of lairs. . . . There are some which smell of whisky, eau-de-Cologne, women . . . With a gramophone playing and . . . .'

He stopped talking to have a drink. When he raised his head again, his companion had had time to empty a third glass.

And Sir Walter was looking at him with his big, bleary eyes, and holding out the bottle.

'No, thank you,' protested Maigret.

'Yes . . . I need . . .'

Wasn't there a certain affection in his gaze?

'My wife . . . Willy . . .'

At that moment a startling thought crossed the Chief-Inspector's mind. Wasn't Sir Walter just as lonely, just as helpless as Jean, who was dying in his stable?

And then the carter had his horses beside him, and his skipper's motherly wife.

'Have another . . . I insist. . . . You're a gentleman . . .'

He was almost begging Maigret to accept. He was holding out his bottle with a rather shame-faced expression. Vladimir could be heard walking up and down the deck.

Maigret held out his glass. But there was a knock on the door. Lucas called out.

'Chief-Inspector!'

And with the door only half-open he added:

'It's all over! . . .'

The colonel did not move. He watched the two men walk away with a morose expression on his face. When Maigret turned round he saw him empty at one gulp the glass he had just filled, and heard him shout:

'Vladimir!'

Near the *Providence* a few people had collected, for sobbing could be heard from the bank.

It was Hortense Canelle, the skipper's wife, who was kneeling beside Jean and still talking to him, even though he had been dead for several minutes.

Her husband, on the deck, was watching for Maigret to arrive. He hurried over to him, a thin agitated figure, and murmured despairingly:

'What shall I do? . . . He's dead . . . My wife . . .'

A sight Maigret would never forget: in the stable, seen from above, and encumbered by the two horses, a body almost curled up into a ball, with half the head buried in the straw. And the woman's fair hair catching the sunlight while she groaned softly, murmuring every now and then:

'My little Jean . . .'

As if Jean had been a child and not that old man, hard as granite, with a gorilla's body, who had baffled the doctors.

CHAPTER 11

Overtaking

NOBODY noticed except Maigret. Two hours after Jean's death, while the body was being carried on a stretcher to a waiting ambulance, the colonel, with bloodshot eyes, but a dignified bearing, had asked:

'Do you think they'll give me the burial permit?'

'Tomorrow, yes. . . .'

Five minutes later, Vladimir, with his usual precise movements, was casting off the mooring-ropes.

Two boats were waiting outside the lock at Vitry-le-François, on their way towards Dizy.

The first was already being punted into position when the yacht brushed past her, went round her curved bow, and entered the open lock.

There were cries of protest. The bargee shouted to the lock-keeper that it was his turn, that he would make an official complaint, and a great deal besides.

But the colonel, in his white cap and officer's uniform, did not even turn round.

He stood at the brass wheel, impassive, looking straight ahead.

When the lock-gates were closed, Vladimir went ashore, presented his papers, gave the traditional tip.

'Well, I'll be damned! Those yachts can get away with anything!' grumbled a carter. 'With ten francs at every lock . . .'

The canal-reach below Vitry-le-François was crowded. It scarcely seemed possible for the yacht even to punt its way between the boats waiting their turn.

And yet the gates were hardly open before the water started bubbling round the propeller. With a casual movement the colonel moved the gear-lever forward and let in the throttle.

And at one go the *Southern Cross* reached her full speed, passed close to the heavy barges, in the midst of shouts of protest, but did not touch a single one.

Two minutes later she disappeared round the bend and Maigret said to Lucas, who had accompanied him:

'They are both dead-drunk!'

Nobody had guessed. The colonel was dignified and correct, with the huge gold crest in the centre of his cap.

Vladimir, in a striped jersey, with his forage cap on the top of his head, had not made a single false move.

But if Sir Walter's apoplectic neck was purple, his face was sickly pale, his eyes underlined with heavy pouches, his lips colourless.

As for the Russian, the slightest shock would have thrown him off his balance, for he was asleep on his feet.

On board the *Providence* everything was closed and silent. The two horses, a hundred yards from the barge, were tied to a tree.

And the skipper and his wife had gone off into the town to order mourning clothes.

MAIGRET
AND THE HUNDRED
GIBBETS

TRANSLATED BY
TONY WHITE

CHAPTER I

Inspector Maigret Commits a Crime

No one noticed what was going on. No one suspected that a drama was being played out in the waiting-room of the small railway station where only six depressed-looking passengers were waiting, amid the smell of coffee, beer, and lemonade.

It was five o'clock in the afternoon and night was falling. The lamps had been lit, but through the windows the German and Dutch Customs and railway officials could still be seen pacing up and down in the murk of the platform.

Neuschanz railway station is located in the extreme north of Holland, on the German frontier.

It is not an important station; Neuschanz is barely a village. No main lines pass through it. There are trains only in the mornings and evenings for the German workmen who, attracted by the high wages, work in the Dutch factories.

The same ritual is repeated each time. The German train stops at one end of the platform. The Dutch train waits at the other end.

The officials wearing orange caps and those in greenish or Prussian blue uniform meet, and together while away the hour's wait for Customs formalities.

Since there are only about twenty passengers on each trip, and they are regulars who call the Customs officers by their Christian names, the formalities are soon completed.

The passengers then go and sit in the buffet which is typical of all frontier buffets. The prices are marked in both *cents* and *Pfennigs*. A showcase contains Dutch chocolate and German cigarettes. Both gin and *schnapps* can be had.

It was close that evening. A woman was dozing at the cash-desk. A jet of steam was coming from the percolator. The kitchen door was open and you could hear a radio whistling as a child was fiddling with it.

It all seemed ordinary, yet there were a few odd details which were enough to make the atmosphere heavy with a vague sense of mystery and adventure.

The uniforms of the two countries, for instance; and the contrast between the advertisements for German winter sports and for the Utrecht Trade Fair.

And a figure in one corner: a man of about thirty, with threadbare clothes and a pallid, ill-shaven face, wearing a soft hat of some kind of grey, who looked as if he might have wandered all round Europe.

He had arrived on the train from Holland. He had shown a ticket for Bremen, and the ticket collector had explained to him in German that he had picked the most roundabout route, with no fast trains.

The man had indicated that he did not understand. He had ordered some coffee, in French, and everyone had stared at him inquisitively.

His eyes were feverish and very deep-set. He smoked with his cigarette stuck to his lower lip, a mere detail, but enough to indicate either exhaustion or contempt.

At his feet was a small fibre suitcase, the kind sold in all cheap stores. It was new.

After he'd got what he'd ordered, he fished out of his pocket a handful of loose change which included French and Belgian coins and tiny Dutch silver pieces.

The waitress had to pick out the necessary coins herself.

Less notice was taken of a passenger sitting at the next table, a tall, heavy, broad-shouldered man. He was wearing a thick black overcoat with a velvet collar, and the knot of his tie was held up by a celluloid device.

The first man seemed tense and never stopped watching the officials through the glass door, as if he were afraid of missing his train.

The second, puffing away at his pipe, studied him calmly and steadily.

The nervous passenger left his seat for a couple of minutes to go to the W.C. Then the other, without even stooping, drew the small suitcase towards him with a simple movement of his foot, and pushed an identical one into its place.

Half an hour later, the train left. The two men settled themselves in the same third-class compartment, but did not speak to each other.

At Leer, the train emptied, but continued on its way for the benefit of these two passengers.

It was ten o'clock when the train pulled in beneath the massive glass roof at Bremen, where everyone's face looked grey in the arc-lights.

*

The first passenger could not have known a word of German, because he lost his way several times, went into the first-class restaurant and, only after several comings and goings, landed up in the third-class buffet, but did not sit down at a table.

He pointed to some small rolls filled with a piece of sausage, indicated that he wished to take them away, and again paid by holding out a handful of change.

For more than half an hour he wandered through the broad streets by the station, with his small suitcase, as if he were looking for something.

The man with the velvet collar, who was following him patiently, at last understood what was on when he saw his companion plunge into a poorer district which stretched away to his left.

All he was looking for was a cheap hotel. The young man was beginning to feel tired; he looked suspiciously at a few of them before choosing a low-class establishment over the door of which was a large white frosted-glass ball.

He was still holding his suitcase in one hand and his sausage-rolls wrapped in grease-proof paper in the other.

The street was full of people. The fog was beginning to thicken, blurring the lights in the shop windows.

The man in the heavy overcoat had some difficulty getting the room next to the previous visitor.

It was a poor room, like poor rooms all over the world, with perhaps only this difference, that poverty is nowhere so depressing as in northern Germany.

But there was a communicating-door between the two rooms, and the door had a keyhole.

So the man was able to watch the suitcase being opened. All it contained was old newspapers.

The traveller went so white that it was a painful sight, and he turned the case over and over in his shaking hands, scattering the newspapers about the room.

The rolls were on the table, still in their wrapping, but the young man, who had eaten nothing since four in the afternoon, did not even glance at them.

He dashed out towards the station, losing his way and asking it a dozen times, and repeating in an accent which distorted the word so much that he was barely understood:

'*Bahnhof?* . . .'

He was in such a state that, to make himself better understood, he imitated the noise of a train!

He got to the station. He wandered about the vast departure hall, noticed a pile of luggage, and crept up to it like a thief to make sure that his case was not there.

He gave a start every time somebody passed with a suitcase of the same make.

His companion kept following him, never once letting him out of his sight.

It was midnight before they returned, one behind the other, to the hotel.

The keyhole was not big enough to show the young man slumped in his chair with his head between his hands. When he got up, he snapped his fingers in an angry yet resigned gesture.

That was the end. He took a revolver from his pocket, opened his mouth wide, and pressed the trigger.

*

A moment later, there were ten people in the room. Inspector Maigret, who had not taken off his overcoat with the velvet collar, tried to stop them going in. The words *Polizei* and *Mörder*, which means murderer, were to be heard repeatedly.

The young man was even more pathetic dead than alive. There were holes in the soles of his shoes, and his trouser-leg, which had rucked up when he fell, revealed an extraordinary red sock and a hairy, white shin.

A policeman arrived, rapped out a few orders, and everyone collected on the landing, except Maigret, who showed his Police Headquarters Inspector's badge. The policeman spoke no French, Maigret only a few stumbling words of German.

Ten minutes later, a car pulled up opposite the hotel, and some officials in civilian clothes burst in.

On the landing, the word *Franzose* had now been replaced by the word *Polizei*, and the Inspector had become an object of curiosity. But a few orders soon put a stop to the excitement, and the noise came to an end as abruptly as if someone had turned off a switch.

The visitors went back to their rooms. In the street, a silent group kept a respectful distance.

Inspector Maigret still had his pipe between his teeth, but it had gone out. His fleshy face, looking as if it had been modelled from thick clay by means of a vigorous thumb, wore a look that suggested either fear or failure.

'I must ask your permission to carry out my inquiry at the same time as yours,' he said. 'One thing is certain: this man committed suicide. He's a Frenchman.'

'Were you following him?'

'It would take too long to explain. I should like your

technical staff to take as detailed photographs as possible from all angles.'

Instead of silence, there was now excitement in the room; only two or three people were now moving about.

One of them, young and pink-faced, with a shaven head, was wearing a morning-coat and striped trousers and, from time to time, wiped the lenses of his gold-rimmed spectacles. His official title was something like *Doctor of Pathology*.

The other, equally pink, but less formally dressed, was making a thorough search, and trying hard to speak French.

They found nothing, except a passport in the name of Louis Jeunet, mechanic, born in Aubervilliers.

The revolver bore the mark of the Herstal (Belgium) arms factory.

Back at Police Headquarters, on the Quai des Orfèvres, no one suspected, that evening, that Maigret, silent, as if crushed by events, was helping his German colleagues, standing aside to make room for the photographers and police doctors, and waiting with a stubborn frown, his pipe still out, for the pathetic loot which was handed him at about three in the morning: the dead man's clothes, his passport, and a dozen photographs which the flashlights had succeeded in making strangely delusory.

He was not far, in fact he was very near believing that he had just killed a man.

Yet he did not know this man. He knew nothing about him. There was no proof that he had any accounts to settle with the law.

*

It had started the previous evening in Brussels in a most unexpected way. Maigret was there on a job. He had been conferring with the Belgian C.I.D. about some Italian refugees who had been expelled from France and whose activities were causing anxiety.

It was a job which was more like a pleasure trip. His

talks had been shorter than he had expected. The inspector had a few hours to himself.

Out of sheer curiosity, he had gone into a little café on the Montagne aux Herbes Potagères. It was ten in the morning. The café was practically deserted. But while the cheerful, friendly proprietor was chatting away to him, Maigret noticed another customer sitting at the far end of the room, in the semi-darkness, curiously employed.

The man was scruffy. He was a 'professional un-employed', the sort that exists in every capital, on the look-out for an opportunity.

He was pulling thousand-franc notes out of his pocket, counting them, wrapping them in brown paper, tying them up into a parcel, and writing an address on it.

There were at least thirty notes! Thirty thousand Belgian francs! Maigret had frowned and, when the stranger had paid for his coffee and gone out, had followed him to the nearest post office.

There, he had been able to read, over his shoulder, the address which was written in a by no means uneducated hand:

> *Monsieur Louis Jeunet*
> *18, rue de la Roquette*
> *Paris*

But what struck him most was the description: *Printed Matter*.

Thirty thousand francs travelling as printed matter, like ordinary advertising hand-outs! The package was not even registered. The postal clerk weighed it, and said:

'Seventy centimes . . .'

The sender paid and went out. Maigret had noted down the name and address. He had followed his man and, for a moment, he had been amused by the chance of making the Belgian police a present. He could have gone along later to the head of the Brussels C.I.D. and said in an off-hand way:

'By the way, while I was having a glass of Gueuse-Lambic,

137

I ran across a crook. All you'll have to do is pick him up at such-and-such a place . . .'

Maigret was in high spirits. The town was bathed in a soft autumn sun which filled it with currents of warm air.

At eleven o'clock, the stranger bought an imitation leather, or rather imitation fibre suitcase, for thirty-two francs from a shop in the rue Neuve. Maigret, just for fun, bought a similar one, without trying to work out where it might lead him.

At half past eleven, the man entered a hotel in an alleyway, the name of which the Inspector was unable to read. He left it shortly afterwards and took the train to Amsterdam from the Gare du Nord.

This time the Inspector hesitated. Possibly the feeling that he had already seen that face somewhere influenced his decision.

'I dare say it's some trivial affair. But supposing it were something important?'

There was nothing urgent to take him back to Paris. At the Dutch frontier, he was struck by the fact that the man, with a deftness which suggested that he was used to this sort of trick, hoisted his suitcase on to the roof of the carriage before arriving at the Customs.

'We'll soon see when he stops somewhere. . . .'

But he didn't stop at Amsterdam. He merely bought a third-class ticket for Bremen. Then they crossed the flat Dutch countryside, its canals full of sailing-boats which seemed to be scudding along through the middle of the fields.

Neuschanz . . . Bremen . . .

Maigret had played his hunch and swapped over the suitcases. For hours, he had tried unsuccessfully to place the fellow in one of the categories known to the police.

'Too nervous to be a genuine international crook. Or could he be the sort of underling who gets his bosses arrested? A conspirator? An Anarchist? But he only speaks French, and there are hardly any conspirators in France, or

138

even any active anarchists! Or a small-time crook operating on his own?'

But would a crook be living in such poverty after sending off thirty thousand francs in an ordinary brown-paper package?

The man did not drink spirits. All he did, at stations where there was a long wait, was swallow down some coffee and sometimes a roll or a *brioche*.

He did not know the line, because he kept asking for information, and worrying if he were going in the right direction, worrying unduly, in fact.

He was not strong. Yet his hands bore the marks of manual labour. His nails were black but too long, which indicated that he had not worked for some time.

His complexion suggested anaemia, maybe poverty.

Maigret had gradually forgotten the trick he was going to play on the Belgian police by bringing them a criminal bound hand and foot, as a joke.

The problem fascinated him. He kept finding excuses for himself:

'Amsterdam isn't so far from Paris. . . .'

Or:

'Bah, I can get back in thirteen hours from Bremen, by express. . . .'

*

The man was dead. He had nothing suspicious on his person, and there was nothing to indicate what he was up to except an ordinary revolver of the most common make in Europe.

He seemed to have killed himself simply because someone had stolen his suitcase. If not, why had he bought those rolls at the station buffet and not eaten them?

And why that day's journey from Brussels where he could have blown his brains out just as easily as in a German hotel?

There remained his suitcase, which might provide the

key to the enigma. That was why, when the body had been taken away, wrapped naked in a sheet and lifted into an official van, and after it had been examined, photographed, and studied from the soles of its feet to the crown of its head, the Inspector shut himself up in his room.

His face was drawn. Though he filled his pipe, as he always did, with little prods of his thumb, it was purely and simply to try and convince himself that he was calm.

The agonized face of the dead man preyed on his mind. He could see him again and again snapping his fingers and then straight away opening his mouth wide and firing a shot into it.

This sense of distress, almost of remorse, was so strong that he hesitated before touching the fibre suitcase.

Yet this suitcase must contain something to justify what he had done. Would he find in it evidence that the man, for whom he had been weak enough to feel sorry, was a crook or a dangerous criminal, perhaps even a murderer?

The keys were still hanging from a string tied to the handle, just as when they left the shop in the rue Neuve. Maigret lifted the lid and took out first a dark grey suit, not so worn as that of the dead man.

Under the suit were two shirts, dirty and frayed at the collars and cuffs, and rolled up into a ball.

Then a collar, with narrow pink stripes, which had been worn for at least a fortnight, because it was quite black where it had rubbed its owner's neck. Black and theadbare.

That was the lot. The bottom of the suitcase had a green paper lining, and the two straps with new buckles and tabs had not been used.

Maigret shook the clothes and went through the pockets. They were empty.

An uncertainty which he couldn't explain seized him by the throat. He went on trying to find something, because he wanted to, because he had to.

Hadn't a man killed himself because this suitcase had

been stolen from him? Yet all it contained was an old suit and some dirty linen.

No papers. Nothing that even resembled a document. Not even a trace of anything which bore on the dead man's past.

The room was freshly papered with cheap wallpaper, in a loud, garish flower-pattern. By contrast, the furniture was worn, wobbly, and falling to bits, and on the table there was a piece of cretonne so dirty it would have been revolting to touch.

The street was deserted. The shops had put up their shutters. But at the traffic junction, a hundred yards away, cars never stopped flowing past with a reassuring hum.

Maigret looked at the communicating-door, though he no longer dared to stoop down to the keyhole. He remembered that the experts, thinking ahead, had drawn the outline of the body on the floor of the next room.

He went in on tiptoe, so as not to waken the other visitors, but perhaps also because the mystery was weighing him down; he was still holding the crumpled suit from the suitcase.

The outline on the floor was contorted yet mathematically exact.

When he tried to fit the jacket, trousers, and waistcoat to it, his eyes lit up, and he bit the stem of his pipe without realizing.

The clothes were at least three sizes too big! They were not the dead man's!

What this tramp was so carefully preserving in his suitcase, and to which he attached such value that he killed himself because he'd lost it, was a suit belonging to somebody else!

CHAPTER 2

Monsieur Van Damme

THE Bremen papers merely carried an announcement of a few lines that a Frenchman named Louis Jeunet, a mechanic, had committed suicide in one of the town's hotels, and that his motive seemed to be poverty.

But by the time these lines appeared the next morning, the information was no longer accurate. In fact, when examining the passport, Maigret had been struck by a curious detail.

On the sixth page, for the description, where there are columns headed: *age, height, hair, forehead, eyebrows,* etc. . . . the word *forehead* came before the word *hair* instead of after it.

Now, six months earlier, the Paris C.I.D. had discovered, in Saint-Ouen, a complete factory for forged passports, army pay-books, foreign identity cards, and other official papers. A certain number of these documents had been seized, but the forgers had themselves admitted that hundreds of these forgeries from their printing-presses had been in circulation for some years and that, as they kept no books, they were unable to supply a list of their customers.

The passport proved that Louis Jeunet was one of these customers and that, consequently, his name was not Louis Jeunet.

As a result, the only more or less solid basis for an inquiry vanished. The man who had killed himself that night was no more nor less than a person unknown!

*

The authorities had given the Inspector the necessary permission, so at nine o'clock he arrived at the mortuary where the public were allowed in, once the doors were opened.

He tried unsuccessfully to find a dark corner from where he could watch, though in fact he didn't expect very much. The mortuary was a modern one, like the greater part of the city and all its public buildings.

It was more sinister even than the old mortuary in the Quai d'Horloge in Paris. More sinister for the very reason that its lines and perspective were clean, and that its uniformly white walls reflected a harsh light, and that it had cold storage units, gleaming as if in some power-station.

It suggested a model factory, a factory where the raw material was the human body.

The so-called Louis Jeunet was there, less mutilated than might have been expected, because the specialists had to some extent reconstructed his face.

There was also a young woman, and a drowned man who had been fished up in the harbour.

The attendant, glowing with health, and laced into a spotless uniform, looked more like a museum attendant.

Contrary to expectations, about thirty people filed through within an hour. When a woman asked to see a body which was not on view in the hall, electric bells rang and numbers were rapped out over the telephone.

In a section on the first floor, one of the drawers of a huge cupboard that filled an entire wall slid on to a goods-lift and, a few seconds later, a steel box appeared on the ground floor, just as books arrive in the reading-rooms of some libraries.

It was the body which had been requested! The woman leant over it, sobbed, and was led away to an office at the far end of the hall where a young clerk took down her statement.

Few people paid any attention to Louis Jeunet. However, about ten o'clock, a smartly-dressed man got out of a private car, came into the hall, looked round for the suicide and examined him closely.

Maigret was only a few steps away. He went up closer

and, looking the man over, had the impression that he was not dealing with a German.

What was more, as soon as the man saw the Inspector move, he gave a start, looked embarrassed and must have had the same impression about Maigret as the latter had had about him.

'Are you French?' he got in first.

'Yes. Are you, too?'

'In actual fact, I'm Belgian. But I've been living in Bremen for some years.'

'And do you know a man named Jeunet?'

'No! I ... I read in the paper this morning that a Frenchman had committed suicide in Bremen. I lived in Paris for a long while. I was curious and came to have a look. ...'

Maigret was imperturbably calm, as he always was on such occasions. In fact, he looked so obstinate and unsubtle as to seem almost bovine.

'Are you from the police?'

'Yes. Police Headquarters.'

'And you came here on purpose? What am I talking about? You couldn't have, because the suicide only took place last night. Do you know some other Frenchmen in Bremen? No? If not, perhaps I can be of some help to you? May I offer an *apéritif*?'

Shortly afterwards, Maigret followed him out and got into the car which his companion was driving himself.

Words poured from the latter's mouth. He was, in fact, the typical hearty, energetic business-man. He seemed to know everyone, hailed passers-by, pointed out buildings, and explained things:

'That's the Norddeutscher Lloyd. Have you heard about the new liner they've launched? They're clients of mine.'

He pointed out a building nearly all of whose windows bore different names.

'On the fourth floor, to the left, you can see my office. ...'

On the windows, in enamel letters, were the words: *Joseph Van Damme, Import and Export Agent.*

'Would you believe it, I sometimes go a month without having a chance to speak French? My staff and even my secretary are German. Essential – for business reasons.'

No one could have read a thought from Maigret's face. Subtlety seemed his least likely characteristic. He nodded approval. He admired what he was asked to admire, including the car. Van Damme was boasting about its patent suspension.

He accompanied him into a large *brasserie*, packed with business-men talking noisily, to the accompaniment of a tireless Viennese orchestra and the clink of beer-mugs.

'You can't imagine how many millions the customers here are worth!' Van Damme enthused. 'Listen! Do you understand German? The man next to us is selling a cargo of wool which is at this very moment *en route* from Australia to Europe. He owns thirty or forty ships. I could show you others. What will you drink? I can recommend the Pilsener. . . .

'By the way . . .'

Maigret didn't even smile at the change of subject.

'By the way, what do you make of this suicide? Was he a down-and-out, as the papers here claim?'

'It's possible. . . .'

'Are you making inquiries about him?'

'No. That's up to the German police. So, as the suicide is established . . .'

'Of course. Mind you, it only occurred to me because he was a Frenchman. So few come to the North!'

He got up to shake hands with a man who was leaving and came back hurriedly.

'You must excuse me! The director of a big insurance company. He's worth a few hundred million . . . But, look here, Inspector, it's almost midday. You will come and lunch with me, won't you? I shall have to invite you to a restaurant because I'm a bachelor. It won't be like eating in

Paris. However, I'd try and see that you didn't lunch too badly. That's settled, then, is it?'

He called the waiter over and paid. As he took his wallet from his pocket, he made a gesture which Maigret had often noticed among business-men of his kind round the Bourse, an inimitable gesture, a way of leaning backwards, sticking out the chest, drawing in the chin, and opening with casual satisfaction that sacred object, a leather case stuffed with notes.

'Let's go!'

*

It was five o'clock before he let the Inspector go, after taking him to his office where there were three clerks and a typist.

He also promised Maigret that if he did not leave Bremen that day, they would spend the evening together at a well-known cabaret.

The Inspector was once again back in the crowd, alone with his thoughts which were far from ordered. They could hardly even be described as thoughts.

In his mind, he was comparing two figures, two men, and trying to establish a link between them.

Because there *was* one! Van Damme had not gone out of his way to visit the mortuary and peer at the corpse of someone he didn't know. Nor was it merely the pleasure of speaking French that had impelled him to invite Maigret to lunch.

Besides, he had only really become natural when the Inspector appeared uninterested in the affair – or even stupid!

He had been worried that morning. His smile lacked spontaneity.

But when the Inspector had left him, he had changed and had once again become the little business-man who comes and goes, gets worked up, talks, enthuses, rubs shoulders with the big financiers, drives his car, telephones, raps out orders to his typist, gives expensive dinners, and is proud and happy to be what he is.

On the other side of the coin was a homeless, sickly-looking man in old clothes and with holes in his shoes, who had bought some sausage-rolls, never suspecting that he would not eat them.

Van Damme must have found some other companion for his evening *apéritif*, in the same atmosphere of Viennese music and beer.

At six o'clock, a metal drawer would slide noiselessly along, close on the naked body of the so-called Jeunet, and the lift would take it up to the cold storage unit where it would occupy a numbered compartment till the next day.

Maigret set off towards the Polizei Proesidium. Some policemen, stripped to the waist in spite of the time of year, were doing P.T. in a yard surrounded by bright red walls.

In the laboratory, a dreamy-eyed young man was waiting for him by a table where all the dead man's possessions were laid out and decorated with labels.

He spoke correct, academic French, and took a pride in finding the right word.

He began with the greyish suit which Jeunet was wearing when he committed suicide, explaining that the lining had been unpicked and all the seams examined, but that nothing had been found.

'The suit comes from the Belle Jardinière in Paris. The cloth is fifty per cent cotton. It is therefore a cheap garment. Grease-spots have been removed, including mineral grease which seems to indicate that the man had worked or had often been in a factory, workshop, or garage. His underclothing was unmarked. The shoes were bought in Rheims. The same goes for the suit: popular quality, mass-produced. The socks are cotton, the sort sold from stalls at four or five francs a pair. They are in holes, but have never been darned.

'All these clothes were put in a strong paper bag, shaken, and the dust collected and analysed.

'In this way, we obtained confirmation of the origin of the grease-spots. In fact, the cloth was impregnated with a fine metallic dust found only on the person of fitters, metal workers, and, in general, people who work in mechanical workshops.

'There is no such evidence in the case of the clothing which I shall call *Clothing B* and which has not been worn for several years, at least six.

'Another difference: in the pockets of *Clothing A*, we found some particles of French government tobacco, which you call "grey" tobacco.

'In the pockets of *B*, on the other hand, there was a little yellow tobacco dust, imitation Egyptian tobacco.

'But I now come to the most important point. The stains found on *Clothing B* were not grease-spots. They were old human bloodstains, probably arterial blood.

'The material has not been washed for some years. The man who was wearing the suit must have been literally drenched in blood. Finally, various tears suggest that there may have been a struggle, because in various parts, including the lapels, the weft has been ripped away as if by someone's finger-nails.

'*Clothing B* has a name-tab on it: Roger Morcel, tailor, rue Haute-Sauvenière, Liège.

'The revolver is a model which has not been manufactured for some years.

'If you would be good enough to leave me your address, I will send you a copy of the report which I have to draw up for my superiors.'

*

By eight o'clock that evening, Maigret was through with the formalities. The German police had handed over to him the dead man's clothing along with that in the suitcase, which the expert had called *Clothing B*. It had been decided that, until further orders, the body would be held at the disposal of the French authorities in the mortuary cold-storage unit.

Maigret had taken a copy of Joseph Van Damme's record: born in Liège of Flemish parents, business representative, then director of a broker's in his own name.

He was thirty-two and unmarried. He had only settled in Bremen three years before. After a difficult start, he seemed to be doing good business.

The Inspector went back to his room in the hotel, and sat for a long time on the edge of his bed, with the two fibre suitcases in front of him.

He had opened the communicating-door to the next room, where everything was still as it had been the previous day. He was struck by how little mess the incident had caused. On the wall, below a pink rose on the wallpaper, was a small brownish stain. The only bloodstain. On the table were the two sausage-rolls, still wrapped in paper. A fly had settled on them.

That morning, Maigret had sent to Paris photographs of the dead man, asking Police Headquarters to have them published in as many newspapers as possible.

Was that where the search should be made? At least the Inspector had an address in Paris: the one to which Jeunet sent himself thirty thousand-franc notes from Brussels.

Or should the search be made in Liège, where *Clothing B* had been bought some years earlier? Or in Rheims, where the dead man's shoes came from? Or in Brussels, where Jeunet had made his package of thirty thousand francs? Or in Bremen, where he had died, and where a certain Joseph Van Damme had gone and taken a quick look at his corpse, pretending he did not know him?

The hotel manager appeared and made a long speech in German, from which the Inspector gathered that he was being asked if the room where the incident had occurred could be tidied up and let again.

He grunted affirmatively, washed his hands, paid, and

went off with his two suitcases, their blatant shabbiness contrasting with his well-to-do appearance.

There was no reason why he should begin his inquiries one way rather than another. And if he settled for Paris, it was mainly because of the forcibly alien atmosphere of Germany, which constantly disrupted both his habits and way of thought, and finally had a depressing effect on him.

The tobacco, yellowish and very light, even took away his wish to smoke.

In the express, he slept, woke on the Belgian frontier at dawn, passed through Liège half an hour later and glanced half-heartedly out of the carriage window.

The train only stopped for thirty minutes, so Maigret did not have time to go to the rue Haute-Sauvenière.

At two in the afternoon, he got out at the Gare du Nord, and plunged into the Paris crowd. The first thing he did was to stop at a tobacco kiosk.

He had to hunt in his pockets a moment for some French money. Someone bumped into him. The two suitcases were at his feet. When he went to pick them up, only one was there. He looked round him in vain, realizing that it would be no good reporting it to the police.

Besides, one thing set his mind at rest. The suitcase which remained had a little string with two keys attached to the handle. It was the one which contained the clothing.

The thief had gone off with the suitcase of old newspapers.

Was it an ordinary thief, the kind that hangs round all stations? In which case, wasn't it odd that he had chosen such a shoddy-looking piece of luggage?

Maigret got into a taxi, enjoying both his pipe and the familiar hum of the street. He saw a photograph on the front page of a newspaper in a kiosk, and recognized, at a distance, the picture of Louis Jeunet, sent from Bremen.

He nearly dropped in at his house on the Boulevard Richard-Lenoir to change and to say hullo to his wife, but the incident at the station had upset him.

'If it really is *Clothing B* they're after, how can they have been told in Paris that I was bringing it or that I should be arriving at any special time?

It looked as if there were a number of mysterious circumstances attaching to the outline of that pallid face of the homeless man of Neuschanz and Bremen. Shadows were emerging, as though on a photographic plate immersed in developer.

They had to be defined, faces clarified, each one given a name; characters and entire lives reconstructed.

For the time being, there was nothing in the middle of the plate but an unclothed body, a head which the German doctors had patched up and restored to normal, and which stood out against the harsh light.

What were these shadows? First, that of a man who was running off with the suitcase that very moment, in Paris. Another who had tipped him off from Bremen or elsewhere. Perhaps it was the hearty Joseph Van Damme? Perhaps not. Then there was the person who, years earlier, had worn *Clothing B.* And the one who, in the struggle, had soaked it with his own blood. . . .

And then there was the one who had got the thirty thousand francs for the so-called Jeunet, or the one from whom the money had been stolen. . . .

The sun was shining, and people were sitting on the café terraces, which were heated by braziers. Drivers were yelling at each other. Swarms of human beings were crowding on to buses and trams.

Somewhere in that swirling crowd, and the crowds in Bremen, Brussels, Rheims, and elsewhere, two, three, four, or five persons would have to be arrested.

Perhaps more? Perhaps less. . . .

Maigret gazed affectionately at the grim façade of Police Headquarters, crossed the courtyard, holding his small suitcase, and greeted the office-boy by his Christian name.

'Did you get my telegram? Did you light the fire?'

'There's a lady here about the picture. She's been in the waiting-room two hours.'

151

Maigret did not bother to remove his coat and hat. He did not even put down the suitcase.

The waiting-room, at the end of the passage, with the Superintendent's offices each side of it, had frosted glass panels and was furnished with a few green velvet chairs. On the only brick wall, was a roll of police officers killed on official duty.

On one of the chairs sat a woman, still young, dressed with the typical correctness of the poor, suggesting long hours of sewing by lamplight with make-shift material.

Her black, woollen coat had a very narrow fur collar. Her hands, encased in grey cotton gloves, gripped a hand-bag which, like Maigret's suitcase, was of imitation leather.

Surely the Inspector must have been struck by a vague similarity between her and the dead man?

Not so much a similarity of features. But a similarity of expression, of *class* as it were.

She, too, had those same grey eyes, and the weary eyelids of one whose courage has deserted her. Her nostrils were pinched and her complexion dull.

She had been waiting for two hours and she had clearly not dared to change her seat or even move. She looked at Maigret through the glass door, not even hoping that here at last was the man she had come to see.

He opened the door.

'Would you come into my office, Madame?'

She seemed amazed when he showed her in ahead of him, and she stood for a moment, bewildered, in the middle of the room. Besides her bag, she was holding a crumpled newspaper on which could be seen half the photograph.

'I gather you know the man whose . . .'

Before he had finished speaking, she buried her face in her hands, bit her lip, and, stifling a sob, moaned:

'He's my husband, Monsieur.'

To hide his feelings, Maigret went and fetched a heavy arm-chair and pushed it towards her.

CHAPTER 3

The Herbalist's in the Rue Picpus

As soon as she could speak, she said:

'Did he suffer much?'

'No, Madame. I can assure you that death was instantaneous.'

She looked at the newspaper she was holding, and had to make an effort to speak:

'In the mouth?'

When the Inspector merely nodded, she said solemnly, and with sudden calm, staring at the floor, in the sort of tone she would have used to refer to a naughty child:

'He could never do anything the same as others!'

She did not look like anyone's mistress, or even anyone's wife. She was under thirty, yet she had the motherly tenderness, the calm gentleness of a nun.

The poor are used not to express their hopelessness, because life, work, and the hourly, daily calls of life lie for ever ahead of them. She wiped her eyes with her handkerchief. Her nose, which had become slightly red, prevented her from looking attractive.

Her lips, as she looked at the Inspector, were sometimes pursed in grief, sometimes wore a ghost of a smile.

'Do you mind if I ask you a few questions?' he said, sitting down at his desk. 'Was your husband's name really Louis Jeunet? When did he last leave you?'

She almost started crying again. Her eyes brimmed with tears. She had screwed her handkerchief into a very tight little ball between her fingers.

'Two years ago. But I saw him again once with his face pressed to the shop-window. If my mother hadn't been there . . .'

He realized that all he had to do was let her talk. She was doing it as much for her own sake as for his.

'You want to know all about our life, don't you? It's the only way to understand why Louis did this. My father was a male nurse in Beaujon. He had opened a small herbalist's in the rue Picpus, which my mother ran.

'Six years ago, my father died, and my mother and I continued to live off the business.

'I met Louis . . .'

'Did you say that was six years ago? Was he already called Jeunet?'

'Yes,' she replied in astonishment. 'He was a driller in a workshop in Belleville. He made a good living. I don't know why things happened so quickly. You can't imagine. He was impatient about everything. It was as if some fever were consuming him.

'I'd hardly been going out with him a month, when we married and he came to live with us.

'The living-quarters behind the shop are too small for three. We rented a room for my mother in the rue du Chemin-Vert. She left the business to me but, as she hadn't enough savings to live on, we used to give her two hundred francs a month.

'We were happy, I can promise you! Louis used to go off to work in the morning. My mother used to come and keep me company. He didn't go out in the evenings.

'I don't know how to explain it. But I always felt that something was wrong.

'You see, it was as if Louis wasn't our sort, as if the atmosphere got too much for him, sometimes.

'He was very loving . . .'

Her features softened. She looked almost beautiful as she confessed:

'I don't think there are many men like him. He'd take me in his arms all of a sudden. He'd gaze so hard into my eyes that it hurt. Then sometimes he'd unexpectedly push me away, in a way I've never seen anyone else do, and he'd

sigh to himself: "Still, I'm fond of you all right, Jeanne."
Then it'd all be over. He'd busy himself with one thing or
another, not even looking at me, spend hours fixing a bit
of furniture, making me a handy gadget or mending a clock.

'My mother didn't like him much, simply because she
realized he wasn't like everyone else.'

'Were there any objects among his possessions which he
kept specially carefully?'

'How did you know?'

She gave a little frightened start and said quickly:

'An old suit . . . Once, he came in when I'd taken it out
of a cardboard-box on top of the wardrobe and was brushing it. I was even going to mend the tears. The suit would
still have been good enough to wear in the house. Louis
snatched it from me, got angry and said some horrid things.
You'd have sworn he loathed me, that evening.

'It was a month after our marriage. Since when . . .'

She sighed, and looked at Maigret as if to say she was
sorry she had only such a feeble tale to tell him.

'Did he act more and more strangely?'

'It wasn't his fault, I'm sure! I think he was ill. He used
to brood. After we'd been happy for an hour in the kitchen
where we used to sit, I'd suddenly see him change. He'd
stop talking. He'd look at things and even me with an ugly
smile. Then he'd go and fling himself on his bed without
saying good night. . . .'

'Hadn't he any friends?'

'No. No one ever came to see him.'

'Didn't he travel or get any letters?'

'No. And he didn't like seeing people at home. Sometimes one of the neighbours who had no sewing-machine
used to come and have a go on mine. It was the surest way
of putting Louis in a temper.

'Not a normal sort of temper. Something deep down
inside. He was the one who seemed to be suffering.

'When I told him we were going to have a baby, he
stared at me like a madman.

'It was from then on, and especially after the baby was born, that he started to drink, in bouts, in spasms. . . .

'Yet I know he loved the baby! He used to look at him, from time to time, the way he used to look at me at first, adoringly. . . .

'The next day, he'd come back drunk, go to bed, lock the bedroom door, and spend whole hours, whole days there.

'The first few times, he cried and asked me to forgive him. Perhaps if mother hadn't interfered, I'd have managed to keep him. But my mother tried to preach to him. There were rows.

'Especially when Louis went two or three days without going to work.

'Towards the end, we were very unhappy. You know how it is, don't you? He became more and more beastly. My mother reminded him that it wasn't his house and turned him out twice.

'I'm sure it wasn't his fault. Something was driving him, driving him . . . Yet sometimes he'd look at me or his son the way I told you.

'Only it was much less often and it didn't last long. The last row was horrible. Mother was there. Louis had helped himself to some silver from the till and she called him a thief. He went quite pale, and his eyes all red, like on one of his bad days. He had a wild stare.

'I can still see him coming over to me as if he were going to strangle me. I was terrified and screamed out: "Louis!"

'He slammed the door so hard as he went out that the glass broke.

'That was two years ago. Some of the neighbours saw him pass by from time to time. I made inquiries at his factory in Belleville, but they told me he no longer worked there.

'But someone saw him in a small workshop in the rue de la Roquette which makes beer pumps.

'I saw him once after that, perhaps six months ago,

through the shop-window. Mother, who's living with me again, and the boy were in the shop. She wouldn't let me go to the door.

'Do you promise me that he didn't suffer, that he died straight away? He wasn't a happy man, you know. You must understand, now . . .'

She had lived her story through again with such intensity, and her husband moreover, had dominated her so completely that, as she talked, and she recalled his facial expressions, she unconsciously imitated them.

Maigret had been struck, from the start, by the disturbing likeness between this woman and the man in Bremen who had snapped his fingers and then fired a bullet into his mouth.

What was more, she seemed to have caught the consuming fever which she had just described. She had stopped talking, yet all her nerves were still on edge. Her breathing was shallow. She was waiting for something, she didn't know what.

'Didn't he ever talk to you about his past, his childhood?'

'No. He didn't talk much. All I know is that he was born in Aubervilliers. And I always thought he'd been educated above his station. He had lovely handwriting. He knew the Latin name for every plant. When the woman from the haberdasher's next door had a difficult letter to write, she used to come to him. . . .'

'And you never saw his family?'

'He told me, before we were married, that he was an orphan. There's something else I'd like to ask you, Inspector. Will he be brought back to France?'

When he hesitated, she turned away to hide her embarrassment and added:

'The herbalist's is my mother's now. So is the money. I know she wouldn't go to the expense of bringing back his body. Or even give me enough to go and see him. So, in that case . . .'

Her throat tightened and she hastily bent down to pick up her handkerchief, which had fallen on the floor.

'I will arrange for your husband to be brought back, Madame.'

She gave him a touching smile and dabbed at a tear on her cheek.

'You've understood, I can tell! You think like me, Inspector. It wasn't his fault. He was an unhappy man!'

'Did he ever have any large sums of money?'

'Only his pay. He used to give me it all at first. Then, when he started to drink . . .'

She gave another little smile, a very sad one, yet full of compassion.

She went away a little calmer, her narrow fur clutched tightly round her neck, still grasping her bag and the newspaper folded small in her left hand.

*

No. 18 rue de la Roquette turned out to be a really low-class hotel.

This part of the street is less than fifty yards from the Place de la Bastille. The Rue de Lappe, with its little dance-halls and its slums, leads into it.

Every ground floor is a bistro, and every house a hotel used by vagrants, permanent casual labourers, displaced persons, and prostitutes.

Yet a few workshops are squeezed into this disturbing refuge of penury, where, doors wide open, they hammer and handle oxyacetylene blow-lamps, and there is a constant flow of heavy lorries.

There is a sharp contrast between these active lives, these regular workers and busy employees with consignment notes, and the sordid, leering figures that hang about the area.

'Jeunet!' the Inspector growled, pushing open the door of the hotel office, on the mezzanine floor.

'Not here!'

'Has he still got his room?'

They had smelt the police and answered ill-humouredly.

'Yes, No. 19.'

'By the week? Or month?'

'By the month!'

'Have you any letters for him?'

They started to hedge. Finally, Maigret was handed the package Jeunet had sent himself from Brussels.

'Did he get many like this?'

'Now and then. . . .'

'Any other correspondence?'

'No. He may have got three packages altogether. A quiet fellow. I can't think why the police have got it in for him. . . .'

'Did he work?'

'At No. 65, up the road. . . .'

'Regularly?'

'It depended. Some weeks, yes. Others, no. . . .'

Maigret demanded the key of the room. But he found nothing there except a pair of unwearable shoes – the soles had come right away from the uppers – a tube which had contained aspirin and some mechanic's overalls, flung into a corner.

When he came down, he questioned the manager again, and learnt that Louis Jeunet never had any visitors, that he was never seen around with women and that, to all intents and purposes, he led a dull life, apart from occasional trips lasting three or four days.

But no one stays in a hotel in that area unless there is something funny going on. The manager knew that as well as Maigret. Eventually he grumbled:

'It's not what you think. Drink was his trouble. And how! Bouts of it. His weeklies, as my wife and I used to call them. He'd be all right for three weeks and go to work every day. Then, for a while, he'd drink away until he passed out cold on his bed. . . .'

'Wasn't there anything suspicious about him?'

But the man shrugged his shoulders as if to say that everyone who came to his establishment was suspicious.

At No. 65, they manufactured beer-pumps in a vast workshop open to the street.

Maigret was met by a foreman who had already seen Jeunet's picture in the paper.

'I was just about to write to the police,' he said. 'He was still working here last week. The fellow was earning eight francs fifty an hour!'

'When he was working.'

'You know about him? When he was working, yes! There's lots like him. But, as a rule, the others regularly have one too many or get really boozed on Saturdays. In his case, it came suddenly, without warning, a week on the trot. Once, when there was an urgent job on, I went and saw him in his room. Well, he was drinking there, all on his own, straight from a bottle on the floor by his bedside. It was no joke, I can tell you!'

*

Aubervilliers produced nothing. A Louis Jeunet, son of Gaston Jeunet, labourer, and of Berthe Marie Dufoin, domestic servant, was entered in the civil register. Gaston Jeunet had died ten years before. His wife had left the district.

Nothing was known about Louis Jeunet except that, six years before, he had written from Paris to get a copy of his birth certificate.

Yet the passport was a forgery, and therefore the man who killed himself in Bremen, and who had married the herbalist's daughter in the rue Picpus and had had a son by her, was not the real Jeunet!

The Prefecture records produced nothing either: no card in Jeunet's name, or with fingerprints corresponding to the dead man's, which had been taken in Germany.

So the wretched man had never had any account to settle with the law, either in France or abroad, because they kept up to date with the criminal records of most European countries.

It was only possible to delve back six years. This produced a Louis Jeunet, a driller, who worked, and lived the life of an honest workman.

He had married. He already owned *Clothing B* which was the cause of that first scene with his wife and which, years later, was to be the cause of his death.

He never went around with anyone and he received no letters. He seemed to know Latin, so he must have had an above-average education.

Back in his office, Maigret drew up a request for the body to the German police, dealt with a few current matters, and, with a sour, stubborn look, once again opened the yellow suitcase, the contents of which the expert in Bremen had so carefully labelled.

He added the package of thirty Belgian notes. Then he suddenly decided to break the string, copied down the numbers, and sent the list to the Brussels C.I.D., asking them to trace their origin.

He did all this laboriously, methodically, as though he were trying to convince himself that he was doing a useful job.

But from time to time he looked somewhat resentfully at the row of photographs, and his pen remained poised in the air as he gnawed at the stem of his pipe.

He was about to leave unwillingly, go home, and postpone his inquiries until the following day, when he was told that Rheims wanted him on the telephone.

It was about the picture published in the papers. The proprietor of the Café de Paris, in the rue Carnot, was convinced that he had seen the man in question in his establishment, six days before, and he remembered him because he had ultimately been forced to refuse to serve the customer, who was already drunk.

Maigret hesitated. For the second time, Rheims, where the dead man's shoes came from, was involved.

Now, these completely worn-out shoes had been bought several months earlier. Therefore, Louis Jeunet hadn't visited the town by accident.

An hour later, the Inspector took his seat in the Rheims express, and arrived there at ten o'clock in the evening. The Café de Paris, quite a smart establishment, was full of middle-class people. Three billiard-tables were in use. At several tables, cards were being played.

It was a typical French provincial café, where the customers shook hands with the cashier, and where the waiters were on familiar terms with those they served drinks. Local personalities and business representatives.

Here and there were silver-plated balls containing glass-cloths.

'I'm the Inspector you telephoned a short while ago . . .'

The proprietor was standing near the counter, keeping an eye on his staff, and at the same time handing out advice to the billiard-players.

'Ah, yes. Well, I've told you all I know. . . .'

He spoke quietly, as if he were slightly embarrassed.

'Anyway, he was sitting in that corner, near the third billiard-table, and he ordered a brandy, then a second and a third. It was about this time. The customers were giving him some funny looks because – how shall I put it? – he wasn't the sort who comes in here.'

'Had he any luggage?'

'An old suitcase, with a broken lock. I remember that, when he went out, the suitcase fell open and some old clothes dropped to the floor. He even asked for some string to tie it up.'

'Did he speak to anyone?'

The proprietor glanced at one of the billiard-players, a tall, thin, smartly-dressed fellow, who looked the sort of good player whose cannons the experts would follow with respect.

'Not exactly. Won't you have a drink? We could sit here, look!'

He chose a table to one side on which the trays were piled.

'About midnight, he was as white as this marble top. He had probably drunk eight or nine brandies. I didn't like the way he was staring. Drink does that to some people. They don't get excited, they don't wander about but, at a certain point, they fall flat on their faces. Everyone had noticed him. I went over and told him I couldn't serve him any more and he didn't object. . . .'

'Was there anyone still playing?'

'The ones you see at the third table. They're regulars who come here every evening, organize competitions, and make up a club. The man left. Then came the incident with the suitcase opening. I don't know how he was able to tie the string in the state he was in. These gentlemen shook my hand and left, and I remember one of them said: "We'll find him in the gutter somewhere!"'

The proprietor looked once more at the smartly-dressed player with the white, well-kept hands and impeccable tie, whose polished shoes creaked whenever he walked round the billiard-table.

'I don't see why I shouldn't tell you the whole story. In any case, I dare say it's just chance or a mistake. The next day, a commercial traveller, who comes here every month and who was here that evening, told me that, about one o'clock in the morning, the drunk and Monsieur Belloir were walking along side by side. He even saw the two of them go into Monsieur Belloir's house. . . .'

'He's the tall, fair man?'

'Yes. He lives five minutes away, in an attractive house in the rue de Vesle. He's the Vice-Chairman of the Banque de Crédit. . . .'

'Is the traveller here?'

'No. He's on his usual rounds, in the east. He won't be back till mid-November. I told him he must have made a mistake. But he stuck to his story. I almost mentioned it to Monsieur Belloir, as a joke. Then I didn't like to. He might have taken it badly, you see. I must ask you not to quote me on what I've just told you. Or at least, so that it doesn't seem to come from me. In my profession . . .'

The player, who had completed a break of forty-eight, looked round to take in the reactions, chalked the end of his cue with some green chalk, and, seeing Maigret with the proprietor, gave an imperceptible frown.

The latter, like most people who try to look relaxed, was wearing a worried, conspiratorial look.

'Your turn, Monsieur Émile!' Belloir called out from across the room.

CHAPTER 4

The Unexpected Visitor

THE house was a new one, and its design as well as the materials used revealed a studied elegance which created an impression of orderliness, comfort, comparative modernity, and ample means.

Red bricks, freshly repointed; stonework; a polished oak door, with brass fittings . . .

It was only half past eight in the morning when Maigret called, with the idea in the back of his mind of taking the Belloir family by surprise and seeing how they lived.

The front of the house, in any case, was worthy of the vice-chairman of a bank, and the impression was strengthened when the door was opened by a maid in a spotless apron. The entrance-hall was large and ended in a bevelled glass door. The walls were of imitation marble, and the floor of two-tone granite in geometric patterns.

To the left were double light-oak doors leading to the drawing-room and dining-room.

There was a coat-rack with some clothes on it, including an overcoat of a child of four or five, a big-bellied umbrella-stand with a gold-knobbed stick protruding from it.

The Inspector had only a second to take in the atmosphere of a solidly-organized way of living. He had hardly spoken Monsieur Belloir's name before the maid replied:

'If you would be good enough to follow me, *the gentlemen* are expecting you. . . .'

She walked towards the glass door. Through another half-opened door, the Inspector could see the dining-room, warm and clean, with a neatly laid table at which a young woman in a dressing-gown and a small boy of four were having breakfast.

Beyond the glass door was a light-coloured wooden

staircase, with a red-flowered stair carpet, secured at each step by a brass rod.

There was a large green plant on the landing. The maid was already turning the handle of another door, to a study, in which three men looked round simultaneously.

There was a sense of shock, of deep embarrassment, even of anxiety, which froze their looks. The only one who did not notice it was the maid who said in the most natural possible voice:

'Would you like to take off your coat?'

One of the three men was Belloir, neatly dressed, and his fair hair well brushed; the man next to him, less smart, was a stranger to Maigret; but the third was none other than Joseph Van Damme, the business-man from Bremen.

*

Two of them spoke at the same time. Belloir stepped forward with a frown, and said in a somewhat clipped, aloof voice which went with the *décor*:

'Monsieur?'

At the same time, Van Damme, trying to be his usual affable self, stretched out his hand to Maigret and exclaimed:

'Well, well! Fancy meeting you here. . . .'

The third man remained silent and watched the proceedings as if he had no idea what was going on.

'Excuse my disturbing you,' the Inspector began. 'I did not expect to break in on such an early meeting. . . .'

'Not at all! Not at all!' Van Damme retorted. 'Have a seat. Cigar?'

On the mahogany desk was a box. Van Damme hurried across, opened the box, and himself picked out a Havana, talking all the while.

'Wait while I find my lighter! I hope you won't summons me because it's not hall-marked! Why didn't you tell me in Bremen you knew Belloir? Just think, we could have travelled together! I left a few hours after you. I had a business telegram calling me to Paris, so I took the opportunity of coming to say hullo to Belloir. . . .'

The latter remained stiff and glanced from one to the other as if hoping for some explanation. Maigret turned to him and said:

'I will keep my visit as short as possible, in view of the fact that you are expecting someone. . . .'

'I am? How did you know?'

'Simple! Your maid told me that I was expected. Now, since you couldn't have been expecting me, then obviously . . .'

His eyes were twinkling, in spite of himself, but his face was expressionless.

'Inspector Maigret, Police Headquarters. You may have seen me yesterday evening in the Café de Paris, where I was trying to get some information about a case of mine.'

'Surely it's not the Bremen affair?' said Van Damme with feigned nonchalance.

'That's precisely what it is! Would you look at this photograph, Monsieur Belloir, and tell me if it is, in fact, that of a man you brought here one night last week?'

He held out a picture of the dead man. The vice-chairman of the bank bent down but did not look at it, or at any rate did not study it.

'I don't know the fellow,' he said, handing the photograph back to Maigret.

'Are you sure it's not the man who spoke to you when you were coming back from the Café de Paris?'

'What are you talking about?'

'You must forgive me if I persist. I am trying to obtain some information which is, in any case, of only minor importance. So I have taken the liberty of disturbing you, in the belief that you would not hesitate to come to the assistance of the Law. That evening, a drunk was sitting near the third billiard-table, where you were playing. He was noticed by all the customers. He went out shortly before you and, afterwards, when you left your friends, he came up to you . . .'

'I think I remember . . . He asked me for a light.'

'And you came back here with him, didn't you?'

Belloir gave a rather disagreeable smile.

'I don't know who told you this fairy story. I am not in the habit of picking up vagrants. . . .'

'You might have recognized him as a friend, or . . .'

'I choose my friends better than that!'

'Then you returned home alone?'

'I can assure you . . .'

'Was the man the same as the one whose picture I've just shown you?'

'I don't know. I didn't even look at him. . . .'

Van Damme had been listening with obvious impatience, and several times had been on the point of interrupting. The third man, who had a small brown beard and was dressed in black clothes of a kind still fashionable among certain artists, was gazing out of the window, now and then wiping off the glass the mist caused by his breath.

'In that case, I need only thank you and apologize once again, Monsieur Belloir . . .'

'Just a minute, Inspector!' Joseph Van Damme cut in. 'Surely you're not going to leave us like that? Please stay with us a moment, and Belloir will give us some of the old liqueur brandy which he always has in reserve. You know, I was hurt that you didn't come and dine with me in Bremen. I waited for you all evening. . . .'

'Did you travel by train?'

'By air. I nearly always travel by air, like most business-men, incidentally. In Paris, I felt like saying hullo to my old friend Belloir. We were students together. . . .'

'In Liège?'

'Yes. It's nearly ten years since we saw each other. I didn't even know he was married. It's odd to find him the father of a big boy. Haven't you finished with your suicide yet?'

Belloir had rung for the maid. He told her to bring the brandy and some glasses. Every movement he made was consciously slow and precise and betrayed how worried he was underneath.

'My inquiries have only just begun,' said Maigret casually. 'I can't tell if they will take a long time or if the case will be wound up in a day or two. . . .'

The front door bell rang. The three men exchanged furtive glances. Voices could be heard on the stairs. Someone said, in a fairly strong Belgian accent:

'Are they all up there? I know the way. It's all right. . . .'

And he called out from the door:

'Hello, all!'

Dead silence greeted his words. He looked round, saw Maigret, and glanced questioningly at his companions.

'Were . . . Were you expecting me?'

Belloir's features hardened. He went up to the Inspector:

'Jef Lombard, a friend,' he said between his teeth.

Then, emphasizing every syllable, he went on:

'Inspector Maigret of Police Headquarters. . . .'

The new arrival gave a start, and stammered in a flat and slightly absurd voice:

'Oh! . . . Good. . . . Fine. . . .'

In his confusion, he handed his overcoat to the maid and then hurried after her to fetch some cigarettes from his pocket.

*

'Another Belgian, Inspector. This is a real Belgian reunion. You must think it's some sort of conspiracy. . . . How about the brandy, Belloir? A cigar, Inspector? Jef Lombard is the only one who still lives in Liège. It so happens that business has brought us all to the same place at the same time, so we've decided to celebrate the occasion with a splendid blow-out. If I might . . .'

He looked at the others with a slight hesitation.

169

'You missed the dinner I wanted to give you in Bremen. Come and have lunch with us later on. . . .'

'Unfortunately, there are some things I have to do,' Maigret replied. 'Quite apart from which, it's time I left you to your business.'

Jef Lombard had gone over to the table. He was tall, thin, and lanky, with irregular features and a pale complexion.

'Ah! Here's the photograph I was looking for,' said the Inspector, as if to himself. 'I shan't ask you if you know this man, Monsieur Lombard, because that would be too miraculous a piece of luck. . . .'

Even so, he showed him the photograph, and he saw Lombard's Adam's apple protrude even more and perform a curious up-and-down movement.

'I don't know him. . . .' he managed to get out hoarsely.

Belloir was drumming on the desk with his manicured finger-tips. Joseph Van Damme was trying to think of something to say.

'So I shan't have the pleasure of seeing you again, Inspector? Are you returning to Paris?'

'I don't know yet. . . . My apologies, gentlemen.'

Van Damme shook hands with him, so the others had to follow suit. Belloir's hand was hard and dry. The bearded fellow offered his hesitantly. Jef Lombard was busy lighting a cigarette in a corner of the study, so he merely grunted and nodded his head.

Maigret brushed past the green plant that was sticking out of a huge china vase and once more felt the stair-carpet with the brass rods under his feet. From the hall, he could hear the shrill sound of a violin being played by a beginner and a woman's voice saying:

'Not so fast. . . . Elbow level with the chin. Easy, now!'

It was Madame Belloir and her son. He could see them from the street, through the drawing-room curtains.

*

It was two o'clock, and Maigret was finishing his lunch at the Café de Paris, when he saw Van Damme come in and glance round as if he were looking for someone. The business-man smiled when he saw the Inspector, and came over to him with his hand outstretched.

'So that's what you meant by things to do!' he said. 'Lunching all by yourself in a restaurant. I quite understand. You wanted to leave us to ourselves. . . .'

He evidently belonged to that category of men who cling on to one without being asked, and refuse to see that the way one greets them is not wholly encouraging.

Maigret took a malicious pleasure in remaining very aloof, yet Van Damme sat down at his table.

'Have you finished? In that case, let me give you a liqueur. Waiter! Let's see, what will you have, Inspector? An old Armagnac?'

He had the list of special liqueurs brought, called the proprietor, finally decided on some 1867 Armagnac, and asked for balloon glasses.

'By the way. . . . Are you going back to Paris? I'm returning this afternoon and, as I loathe the train, I'm proposing to hire a car. I could take you, if you like. What do you think of my friends?'

He sniffed his Armagnac critically and drew out a cigar-case from his pocket.

'Help yourself. They are very good. There's only one place in Bremen where you can get them and they import them direct from Havana.'

Maigret's face was at its most expressionless, and his eyes completely blank.

'It's funny, meeting again after several years,' Van Damme went on, apparently unable to endure the silence. 'When you begin, at twenty, you're all level with each other, so to speak. When you meet again, it's amazing to see what a gulf has sprung up between you. I don't wish to run them down. All the same, I wasn't really at home just now at Belloir's. . . .'

'That stifling provincial atmosphere. And Belloir himself, dressed up to the nines! Mind you, he hasn't done too badly. He married Morvandeau's daughter, Morvandeau the sprung-mattress man. All his brothers-in-law are in industry. And he's got quite a nice position in the bank and he'll be chairman one day or other. . . .'

'And the short man with the beard?' Maigret inquired.

'Oh, him. . . . He might do all right. I think he's a bit hard up, for the moment. He's a sculptor in Paris. Apparently, he has talent. But what can you expect? You saw him in that old-fashioned rig. Nothing modern about him. No business flair . . .'

'And Jef Lombard?'

'The grandest fellow in the world! When he was young, he was a real comedian. He'd have kept you in stitches for hours on end. . . .

'He wanted to be a painter. To earn a living, he drew for the newspapers. Then he worked as a photo-engraver, in Liège. He's married. I think his third's on the way. . . .

'What I mean is that I feel as if I'm suffocating when I'm with them. Petty lives and petty worries. It's not their fault, but I can't wait to get back to my business atmosphere. . . .'

He emptied his glass, and looked round the almost deserted room where a waiter was sitting at a table on the far side, reading the newspaper.

'That's agreed, then? You'll come back to Paris with me?'

'But aren't you taking the small man with the beard who came with you?'

'Janin? No! He'll have caught the train by now. . . .'

'Is he married?'

'Not exactly. But he always has some girl-friend or other living with him, sometimes for a week, sometimes even a year. Then he has a change! But he always introduces his female companion to you as Madame Janin. . . . Waiter! The same again!'

Maigret had to take care at times not to let his eye become too piercing. The proprietor himself came over and told him that he was wanted on the telephone. He had left the address of the Café de Paris at the Quai des Orfèvres.

It was some news from Brussels which had been wired to Police Headquarters. *The thirty thousand-franc notes had been issued by the Banque Générale de Belgique to a certain Louis Jeunet in payment of a cheque signed Maurice Belloir.*

When he opened the door of the telephone-box, Maigret noticed that Van Damme, not realizing he was being watched, had let his face relax. He immediately seemed less chubby, less pink, and, above all, less bursting with health and optimism.

He must have sensed that someone was looking at him, because he gave a start, and automatically became the hearty business-man again.

'That's agreed, then?' he said. 'You'll come with me? *Patron!* Will you arrange for us to be picked up by car and driven to Paris? A comfortable car, you understand? And while we're waiting, the same again. . . .'

He chewed the end of his cigar and, for a split second, as he was staring at the marble table-top, his eyes dulled and the corners of his mouth drooped as if the tobacco was too bitter for him.

'It's when you live abroad that you really appreciate French wines and liqueurs!'

The words rang hollow. There was clearly a deep gulf between them and the thoughts that were passing through his head.

Jef Lombard passed in the street. His figure was slightly blurred by the net curtains. He was alone. He was taking long, slow, gloomy strides and not bothering to look at what was going on in the town.

He was carrying a travelling-bag which reminded Maigret of the two yellow suitcases. But it was a better quality one, with two straps and a pocket for a visiting-card.

The heels of his shoes were beginning to wear down on

one side. His clothes were clearly not brushed every day. Jef Lombard was making for the station on foot.

Van Damme, a large platinum signet-ring on one finger, was wreathed in a cloud of fragrant smoke, spiced with the sharp tang of alcohol. The proprietor could be heard muttering over the telephone to the garage.

Belloir would be leaving his new house on his way to the marble entrance of the bank, while his wife took their son for a walk up and down the avenues.

Everyone would say good morning to him. His father-in-law was the biggest business-man in the area. His brothers-in-law were in industry. He had fine prospects.

Janin, with his black goatee and flowing cravat, would be on his way to Paris – third-class, Maigret would have betted.

Right at the bottom of the scale was the white-faced passenger from Neuschanz and Bremen, the husband of the herbalist in the rue Picpus, the driller from the rue de la Roquette, the solitary drinker, who used to stare at his wife through the shop-window, who sent himself banknotes wrapped like old newspapers, who bought sausage-rolls in a station buffet, and shot himself in the mouth because an old suit which was not his had been stolen from him.

'Are you ready, Inspector?'

Maigret gave a start and stared vaguely at his companion, so vaguely that the latter was embarrassed, tried to laugh – feebly! – and stammered:

'Were you dreaming? In any case, you seemed miles away. I bet you're still worrying about your suicide. . . .'

Not altogether. Because, just as he was asked this question, Maigret, without knowing why himself, was making up a strange list; the number of children involved in the story: one in the rue Picpus, with his mother and grandmother, in a shop smelling of mint and rubber; one in Rheims, learning to keep his elbow level with his chin, and drawing a bow across the strings of a violin; two in Liège, at Jef Lombard's, and a third on the way. . . .

'A last Armagnac. What do you say?'

'No thank you. That's enough. . . .'

'Come along! The stirrup-cup, one for the road. . . .'

Joseph Van Damme was the only one to laugh; he constantly felt the need, like a small boy who is afraid to go down into the cellar and who whistles to convince himself that he is brave.

CHAPTER 5

Breakdown at Luzancy

As they drove at high speed through the gathering dusk, there was rarely a moment's silence. Joseph Van Damme constantly found something to talk about and, with the help of the Armagnac, managed to keep up his high spirits.

The car was an old private saloon with worn cushions, flower-vases and marquetry pockets. The chauffeur was wearing a trench coat, and a knitted scarf round his neck.

After they had been driving for nearly two hours, they slowed down, and the car stopped by the side of the road about a mile from a village, the lights of which were just visible through the mist.

The chauffeur leant over the rear wheels, opened the door, and said that they had a puncture, and that it would take about a quarter of an hour to fix it.

The two men got out. The driver was already putting a jack under the axle, assuring them that he did not need any help.

Was it Maigret or Van Damme who suggested a stroll? In fact, neither did. It came about naturally. They took a few steps down the road, and noticed a narrow path at the end of which was a fast-flowing river.

'Look! The Marne,' said Van Damme. 'It's in flood.'

They followed the path slowly, smoking their cigars. They could hear an indistinct sound, and only found out where it came from when they reached the bank.

A hundred yards away, on the far side of the water, was a lock, Luzancy lock, its approaches deserted and its gates shut. Below the two men was the weir, with its creamy falls, its swirls and eddies, and its powerful current. The Marne was swollen.

In the darkness, they could make out the branches of

trees, even whole tree-trunks swept along by the current, crashing into the weir and finally shooting it.

There was only one light: the one on the lock in front of them.

At that very moment, Joseph Van Damme was in the middle of his speech, and saying:

'. . . Every year the Germans are making fantastic efforts to harness energy from rivers, and the Russians are copying them. They're building a dam in the Ukraine which will cost a hundred and twenty million dollars, and which will supply electric power to three provinces. . . .'

It was barely perceptible: his voice faltered on the words *electric power*. Then it went on as confidently as before. Then the man seemed to have to cough, and to take his handkerchief out of his pocket and wipe his nose.

They were less than eighteen inches from the water and suddenly Maigret, pushed from behind, lost his balance, swayed, and fell forwards. He clung with both hands to the grass on the bank; his feet were in the water, and his hat went floating over the weir.

Things happened quickly. The Inspector had been expecting that push. Some clods of earth gave way under his right hand.

But he had noticed a branch with some give, so he grasped it with his left.

It was barely a few seconds before he was on his knees on the towpath, then on his feet, and yelling at a figure vanishing into the distance:

'Stop!'

The odd thing was that Van Damme seemed afraid to run. He was making for the car, but hardly seemed to be hurrying. His knees were weak with fear and he kept looking round.

Head down and his neck buried in the collar of his overcoat, he let Maigret catch him up. He made only one gesture, a gesture of fury, as if he were thumping an imaginary table, and muttered between his teeth:

177

'Idiot!'

To be on the safe side, Maigret had pulled out his revolver. Without letting go of it, and without taking his eyes off his companion, he shook his trousers which were soaked to the knees. The water squelched from his shoes.

The chauffeur gave a few little hoots from the road to tell them that the car was ready to go again.

'Come on!' said the Inspector.

They went back to their seats in silence. Van Damme still had his cigar between his teeth. He avoided Maigret's eyes.

Ten miles. Twenty miles. A built-up area through which they slowed down; people wandering about the lighted streets. Then the main road again.

'Anyway, you can't arrest me. . . .'

The Inspector gave a start. The words, uttered slowly and stubbornly, were so unexpected. Yet they perfectly expressed what he was thinking.

They reached Meaux. The country gave place to the outer suburbs. A fine drizzle began to fall and, each time they passed a street-lamp, every drop became a star.

Then the Inspector, his mouth to the speaking-tube, said:

'Drive us to Police Headquarters, Quai des Orfèvres. . . .'

He filled his pipe. He could not light it because his matches were damp. He could not see his neighbour's face, which was turned towards the door, and which was now a mere profile, blurred by the shadows. But he could sense the anger in it.

There was now something hard, bitter, and intense in the atmosphere.

Even Maigret was sticking his lower jaw out grimly.

The tension was illustrated by an absurd incident, when the car stopped outside Police Headquarters. The Inspector got out first.

'Come on!' he said.

The chauffeur was waiting to be paid and Van Damme

did not appear to be doing anything about it. There was a moment of indecision. Then, Maigret, not unaware of the absurdity of the situation, said:

'Well? You hired the car. . . .'

'Excuse me. I travelled as a prisoner, so it's up to you to pay. . . .'

It was this detail which betrayed how far they had progressed since leaving Rheims, and the change that had come over the Belgian.

Maigret paid and, without a word, showed his companion the way. Closing the door of his office, the first thing he did was make up the stove.

He opened a cupboard, took out some clothes, and, ignoring his visitor, changed his trousers, socks, and shoes, and put his wet things to dry by the fire.

Van Damme had sat down without being asked. In the bright light, the change was even more striking.

He had left his false bonhomie, his out-spokenness and his somewhat forced smile behind in Luzancy, and he was waiting, his features drawn and a furtive look on his face.

Maigret kept busying himself about the room and pretending to ignore him, arranging his files and telephoning to his chief to ask him about something which had nothing to do with the case in hand.

Finally, planting himself in front of Van Damme, he said:

'Where, when, and how did you come to know the Bremen suicide who was travelling with a passport in the name of Louis Jeunet?'

The other gave an imperceptible start. But he glanced up with a determined look and said:

'In what capacity am I here?'

'Do you refuse to answer my question?'

Van Damme gave a laugh, a new kind of laugh, ironical and unpleasant.

'I know the law quite as well as you do, Inspector.

Either you are charging me and I shall wait until I see the warrant for my arrest, or else you are not charging me and I do not have to answer.

'In the first case, the law states that I may wait legal aid before speaking.'

Maigret did not get annoyed. He did not even seem put out by this attitude. Quite the contrary. He looked at his companion inquisitively, almost with satisfaction.

Thanks to the incident in Luzancy, Joseph Van Damme had been obliged to drop any pose. Not only the one he adopted with Maigret, but with everyone else, even himself.

Barely a trace remained of the hearty, superficial Bremen business-man, going from the big cafés to his modern office and from his office to the well-known restaurants. Nothing remained of the light-hearted, breezy commercial agent tackling his work and piling up money with the cheerful energy and zest of a man who enjoys life.

All that remained was a face, as though carved in wood, drained of colour, and it almost seemed as if, in the space of an hour, bags had formed under the eyes.

Yet, an hour earlier, Van Damme had still been a free man who, though he had something on his conscience, retained the self-assurance given him by his reputation, money, ability, and cunning.

He noticed the difference himself.

In Rheims, he used to pay for round after round of drinks. He would offer his companions the best cigars. He would give his orders and the proprietor would do his best to please him, telephone the garage and advise them to send their most comfortable car.

He was *someone*!

In Paris, he had refused to pay for the ride. He invoked the law. He seemed ready to argue, to defend himself inch by inch, dourly, like a man fighting for his life.

He was furious with himself. What he had said, after his gesture by the bank of the Marne, proved it.

He had planned nothing in advance. He did not know the

chauffeur. Even at the time of the breakdown, he had not immediately realized how he could make use of it.

It was only at the water's edge. Those swirls and eddies. The trees floating by as if they were dead leaves.

Stupidly, without thinking, he had given that push with his shoulder. . . .

He was furious. He guessed that his companion had been expecting that move.

He probably even realized that the game was up, and therefore he was all the more determined to fight back desperately.

He made as if to light another cigar. Maigret took it from his mouth, flung it into the coal-scuttle, and then went on and removed the hat which Van Damme had kept on his head.

*

'I must warn you that I have my work to do. If you do not propose to arrest me in accordance with official regulations, I must ask you to be good enough to release me. If you do not, I shall be forced to bring an action for arbitrary arrest.

'I may as well tell you that I shall strenuously deny any hand in the soaking you received. You stumbled on the slippery mud on the towpath. The chauffeur will confirm that I didn't try to run away, as I should have if I had really tried to drown you.

'As for the rest, I am still waiting to know what you have against me. I came to Paris on business. I can prove it. Then I went to Rheims to see an old friend, as highly-considered as myself.

'I was foolish enough, meeting you in Bremen where there are very few Frenchmen, to make a friend of you, take you out to eat and drink, and finally give you a lift back to Paris.

'You showed my friends and myself the photograph of a man we do not know. He killed himself. This has been materially proved. No one has brought an action so consequently there are no judicial steps to be taken.

'That is all I have to say to you. . . .'

Maigret pushed a spill into the stove, lit his pipe, and merely said:

'You are quite free. . . .'

He could not help smiling, because Van Damme was thrown right off balance by so easy a victory.

'What do you mean?'

'You're free! That's all. I may add that I am prepared to return your kindness and invite you to dinner. . . .'

He had seldom been in such high spirits. The other stared at him in astonishment verging on terror, as if each of his words was charged with hidden menace. He got up hesitantly.

'Am I free to return to Bremen?'

'Why not? You have just told me yourself that you are not guilty of any offence. . . .'

For a moment, it seemed that Van Damme was about to recover his self-assurance and cheerfulness, even accept the invitation to dinner, and explain away his action in Luzancy as clumsiness or a rush of blood to the head.

But Maigret's smile quenched this flicker of optimism. He seized his hat and clapped it on his head.

'What do I owe you for the car?'

'Nothing whatever. Only too glad to have been of service. . . .'

Were the man's lips trembling? He did not know how to take his leave. He tried to find something to say. Finally, he shrugged and made for the door, muttering, though it would have been hard to tell quite to whom or what the expression referred:

'Fool!'

Out on the staircase, where the Inspector was leaning over the banisters, watching him go, he repeated the same word.

Sergeant Lucas was passing with a handful of files, on his way to his boss's office.

'Quick! Get your hat . . . And coat. Follow that man to the end of the earth, if necessary. . . .'

Maigret took the files from his subordinate.

*

The Inspector had just completed a certain number of questionnaires, each headed by a name, to be sent out to the various divisions and returned to him with detailed information about the persons involved, namely: Maurice Belloir, vice-chairman of a bank, rue de Vesle, Rheims; Jef Lombard, photo-engraver, Liège; Gaston Janin, sculptor, rue Lepic, Paris; and Joseph Van Damme, import–export agent, Bremen.

He had reached the last card when the office-boy came and told him that a man wanted to see him in connexion with Louis Jeunet's suicide.

It was late. Police Headquarters was almost deserted. In the next office, though, an inspector was typing a report.

'Send him in!'

The person who was shown in stopped at the door, with an awkward, worried look. Maybe he was already regretting what he had done.

'Come in. Have a seat.'

Maigret took stock of him. He was tall and thin, with very fair hair, ill-shaven, and had on shabby clothes not unlike Louis Jeunet's. His overcoat had a button missing; its collar was greasy and its lapels unbrushed.

From other little details, his manner, and the way he sat down and looked about him, the Inspector summed him up as a casual worker, who, even if on the right side of the law, could not disguise his anxiety when confronted with the police.

'Have you come because of the picture that appeared in the newspapers? Why didn't you report straight away? The photograph has been out two days. . . .'

'I don't read the newspapers,' the man began. 'My wife

happened to bring back a piece of one wrapped round her shopping.'

Once before Maigret had been struck by these same mobile features, constantly twitching nostrils and, above all, this worried, morbidly worried look.

'Do you know Louis Jeunet?'

'I can't tell. It's a bad photograph. But I think . . . I think it's my brother. . . .'

Maigret let slip a sigh of relief. He felt that, this time, the mystery would be cleared up straight away. He went and planted himself with his back to the stove, the way he usually stood when he was in a good mood.

'In that case, your name must be Jeunet?'

'No. That's just it. That's why I hesitated to come. Yet it's definitely my brother. I'm sure of it, now I've seen a better photo on your desk. That scar, for instance! But I can't understand why he killed himself and, what's more, why he changed his name. . . .'

'What's yours?'

'Armand Lecocq d'Arneville. I've brought my papers.'

That movement, too, towards his pocket to take out his grimy passport, betrayed him as a casual worker, used to being under suspicion and having to show his identification papers.

'D'Arneville with a small d? In two words?'

'Yes.'

'You were born in Liège,' the Inspector continued, glancing at the passport. 'You are thirty-five. What is your profession?'

'At the moment, I'm a messenger in a factory in Issy-les-Moulineaux. My wife and I live in Grenelle.'

'You're down here as a mechanic.'

'I was once. I've done a bit of everything.'

'Including time. . . .' Maigret observed, turning over the pages of the passport. 'You're a deserter. . . .'

'There was an amnesty. I can explain. My father had money. He ran a tyre-business. I was only six when he left

184

my mother. She'd just had my brother Jean. That's how it all started. . . .

'We settled down in a small place in the rue de la Province, in Liège. In the early days, my father used to send us money for our upkeep fairly regularly.

'He led a gay life. He had mistresses. Once, when he brought us our monthly allowance, there was a woman in the car waiting down below. . . .

'There were rows. My father stopped paying, or at least only sent instalments. My mother used to go out cleaning and she gradually became half-mad.

'Not mad enough to be put away. But she used to accost people and tell them her troubles. She would wander round the streets, crying. . . .

'I hardly saw my brother. I used to go about with the local kids. We were carted off a dozen times to the police station. Then I was sent to work in an ironmonger's.

'I went home as little as possible. My mother was always crying, and she used to collect the old women in the neighbourhood and moan with them.

'When I was sixteen, I enlisted in the army, and applied to be sent to the Congo. I only stayed there a month. I hid in Matadi for a week. Then I stowed away on a passenger-ship bound for Europe,

'I was caught. I did time. I escaped and came to France and did all sorts of jobs.

'I've starved. I've slept in the Halles. I haven't always been perfect, but I swear that for the last four years I've been going steady.

'I've even got married. To a factory-girl who's keeping on with her job, because I don't earn much and I'm sometimes out of work.

'I've never tried to go back to Belgium. Someone told me that my mother died in a lunatic asylum and that my father was still alive.

'But he never wanted to know us. He's got another family. . . .'

The man gave a half-smile, as if to excuse himself.

'What about your brother?'

'That's different. Jean was the steady sort. He won a scholarship and went on to college. When I left Belgium for the Congo, he was only thirteen and I haven't seen him since.

'I sometimes had news when I ran into people from Liège. After college, some people helped him to study at the University.

'That was ten years ago. After that, all the Belgians I met told me they knew nothing about him, and that he must have gone abroad, because they never heard him mentioned.

'It was a shock to see the photograph, and especially to think that he'd died in Bremen, under a false name.

'You can't understand. I started off on the wrong foot. I've failed. I've been stupid.

'But when I think of Jean at thirteen... He was like me, but calmer, more serious. He used to read poetry, even then. He used to spend nights at his books, all alone, by the light of some stumps of candle a sacristan gave him.

'I was sure he'd make good. Look, as a small boy, he wouldn't have run round the streets for all the tea in China. In fact, the local bad boys used to jeer at him.

'I've always needed money, and I didn't hesitate to ask my mother. She went short so as to give it to me. She worshipped us. You don't understand when you're sixteen. But I remember I was horrible to her one day, because I'd promised to take a girl to the cinema.

'My mother was broke. I cried and threatened her. A charity organization had just given her some medicines so she went and sold them back.

'Do you understand? And now it's Jean who's dead, just like that, up there, under another name.

'I don't know what he's done. I can't believe he's gone the same way as me. You'd think the same if you'd known him as a boy.

'Do you know anything?'

Maigret handed him back his passport.

'Do you know any Belloirs, Van Dammes, Janins, and Lombards in Liège?'

'A Belloir, yes. His father was a local doctor. The son was a student. But they were "posh" people. I had nothing to do with them. . . .'

'What about the others?'

'I've heard the name Van Damme before. I think there used to be a big grocer's in the rue de la Cathédrale with that name. But it's so long ago.'

Then, after a moment's hesitation, Armand Lecocq d'Arneville added:

'Could I see Jean's body? Has it been brought back?'

'It will be in Paris tomorrow.'

'Are you quite sure he killed himself?'

Maigret looked away, embarrassed by the thought from which he could see no escape, that he had been involved in the incident and had been the unconscious cause of it.

His companion was screwing up his cap and shifting from one foot to another, waiting to be sent away. His deep-set eyes, and his pupils lost, like grey confetti, behind their pale eyelids, recalled so vividly the meek, worried eyes of the passenger from Neuschanz that Maigret felt a painful stab of remorse.

CHAPTER 6

The Hanged Men

IT was nine o'clock in the evening. Maigret was at home in the Boulevard Richard-Lenoir, without his collar or coat, and his wife was busy sewing, when Lucas came in drenched, brushing the rain, which had been coming down in bucketfuls, from his shoulders.

'The man's gone,' he said. 'So, as I didn't know if I ought to follow him abroad . . .'

'To Liège?'

'That's right! Did you already know? His luggage was at the Hôtel du Louvre. He had dinner there, changed and took the 6.19 p.m. for Liège. First-class single ticket. He bought a whole pile of magazines at the station bookstall. . . .'

'You'd think he gets under my feet on purpose!' the Inspector growled. 'In Bremen, when I didn't even know he exists, he introduces himself to me at the mortuary, asks me out to dinner and clings on to me. I arrive in Paris. He's here a few hours before or after me. Probably before, because he travelled by air. I go to Rheims and there he is ahead of me. I decide, an hour ago, to go to Liège tomorrow, and he's been there since this evening! To crown it all, he knows quite well that I'm going to turn up and that his merely being there practically constitutes a charge against him. . . .'

Lucas, who knew nothing about the case, suggested:

'Perhaps he wants to draw suspicion on himself so as to save someone else?'

'Is it to do with a crime?' Madame Maigret asked quietly, still sewing away.

Her husband got up with a sigh and gazed at the arm-chair where he had been so comfortably seated a moment earlier.

'What time is there still a train for Belgium?'

'There's only the night train now, at 9.30 p.m. It gets into Liège about six in the morning.'

'Will you pack my suitcase?' the Inspector said to his wife. 'How about a drink, Lucas? Help yourself. You know the cupboard. I've just got some of the plum brandy my sister-in-law makes herself, in Alsace. It's the long-necked bottle. . . .'

He dressed, removed *Clothing B* from the yellow fibre suitcase, wrapped it up well, and put it into his travelling-bag. Half an hour later, he left, accompanied by Lucas, who asked him while they were waiting for a taxi:

'What is this case? I haven't heard it mentioned back at H.Q.'

'I don't know much more about it myself,' the Inspector admitted. 'This odd sort of fellow died, right in front of me, idiotically, and there's a hell of a mix-up over what he did which I'm trying to sort out. I've been rushing at it like a wild boar, and I wouldn't be surprised if I didn't get my knuckles rapped for my pains. Here's a taxi! Shall I drop you in town?'

*

It was eight in the morning when he left the Hôtel du Chemin de Fer, facing the Guillemins station, in Liège. He had bathed and shaved; under his arm he was carrying a parcel containing not the whole of *Clothing B*, but only the coat. He found the rue Haute-Sauvenière, a steep, very busy street, and asked for Morcel's, the tailor. It was a poorly lit house, and a man in shirt-sleeves took the coat and turned it over and over in his hands, asking questions:

'It's a very old thing,' he declared, after considering it. 'It's torn. There's nothing to be done with it. . . .'

'It doesn't convey anything to you?'

'Nothing at all. The collar's badly cut. It's imitation English cloth, made in Verviers.'

The man began to chatter.

189

'Are you French? Does this coat belong to someone you know?'

Maigret sighed and took back the coat, while the other man kept talking, ending up where he should have started:

'You understand, I've only been here six months. If I'd made that suit, it wouldn't have had time to wear out. . . .'

'What about Monsieur Morcel?'

'He's at Robermont!'

'Is it far from here?'

The tailor laughed, delighted at his mistake, and explained:

'Robermont's the cemetery. Monsieur Morcel died at the beginning of the year and I took over the business. . . .'

Maigret found himself out in the street, with his parcel under his arm. He reached the rue Hors-Château, one of the oldest in the town where, at the far side of a courtyard, a zinc plaque bore the inscription: *Central Photo-engraving – Jef Lombard – Rapid work of all kinds.*

The Old Liège-style windows had small panes. In the middle of the small unevenly paved courtyard was a fountain carved with some former nobleman's arms.

The Inspector rang. He heard footsteps coming down from the first floor, and an old woman half-opened up and pointed to a glass door.

'All you have to do is push it. The workshop's at the end of the passage.'

It was a long room, lit by a glass roof. Two men in blue overalls were moving about among the zinc plates and trayfuls of acid. The floor was strewn with photographic proofs, and paper blotched with printer's ink.

The walls were covered with advertisements. Covers of magazines had been stuck on them, too.

'Monsieur Lombard?'

'He's in the office, with a gentleman. This way. Mind you don't get dirty. Turn to the left. It's the first door.'

The place must have been built bit by bit. You went up and down steps. Doors led into unused rooms.

It was both old-fashioned and oddly cheerful, like the old woman who'd been the first to see Maigret, and the workmen.

Arriving in an ill-lit passage, the Inspector heard voices, thought he recognized Joseph Van Damme's, and tried to listen. But they were too indistinct. He took a few more steps and the voices stopped. A head was poked through the half-open door. It was Jef Lombard's.

'Is it for me?' he called, not recognizing his visitor in the semi-darkness.

The office was a smaller room than the others, furnished with a table, two chairs, and shelves full of photographic plates. On the untidy table were bills, prospectuses, and headed notepaper from various business firms.

Van Damme was there, sitting on the corner of the desk. After a vague nod to Maigret, he made no move, and looked straight in front of him, scowling.

Jef Lombard was in working-clothes, his hands were dirty, and he had little black spots on his face.

'Can I help you?'

He cleared a chair covered with papers, pushed it over to the visitor, and hunted for the cigarette-end which he had put on a shelf. It was starting to burn the wood.

'Just a little information,' said the Inspector, without sitting down. 'I'm sorry to disturb you. I would like to know if, a few years ago, you knew a certain Jean Lecocq d'Arneville. . . .'

It was as if he'd pressed a trigger. Van Damme gave a start but took care not to turn towards Maigret. The photo-engraver bent down hastily to pick up a crumpled paper lying on the floor.

'I have . . . I think I have heard that name before,' he muttered. 'He's from Liège, isn't he?'

He had gone pale. He shifted a pile of photographic plates.

'I don't know what became of him . . . It . . . It's so long ago. . . .'

'Jef! Quick, Jef!'

It was a woman's voice from the maze of passages. A woman came running, out of breath, and stopped in front of the open door, so excited that her legs were trembling. She was mopping her brow with a corner of her apron. Maigret recognized the old woman who had let him in.

'Jef!'

Pale with emotion, eyes shining, he answered:

'What is it?'

'A girl! Quick!'

He looked round him, stammered something indistinct, and shot out of the door.

*

The two men were left alone. Van Damme took a cigar from his pocket, lit it slowly, and trod out the match. His face was hard, as at Police Headquarters. His mouth drooped and his jaws twitched as before.

But the Inspector pretended to take no notice of him and, hands in his pockets and pipe between his teeth, he began to wander round the office and examine the walls.

Only a few inches of wall were visible here and there because, wherever there were no shelves, drawings, water-colours, and paintings had been pinned up.

The paintings were not framed. They were simply canvases on stretchers, rather clumsy landscapes, with the grass and the leaves of the trees in the same thick green.

There were also a few caricatures, signed *Jef*, sometimes touched up with water-colour, sometimes cut out of a local paper.

But what struck Maigret was the large number of drawings of another kind, variations on the same theme. The paper had yellowed. A few dates helped to place the period when these sketches had been made as about a dozen years before.

They were differently composed, infinitely more romantic and, in ways, suggested a student imitating the style of Gustave Doré.

An early ink-sketch represented a hanged man swinging from a gibbet on which was perched an enormous crow. Hanging was the theme of at least thirty of these bits of work, either in pencil, ink, or water-colour.

There was the edge of a forest, with a man hanging from the branch of every tree. Somewhere else was a church steeple, and a human body hanging from both arms of a cross below the weather-cock.

There were hanged men of every kind. Some were dressed in sixteenth-century costume, forming a kind of Court of Miracles where everyone was swinging a few feet above the ground.

There was a hanged lunatic, in a top-hat and tail-coat, holding a stick, whose gibbet was a lamp-post.

Below another sketch was some writing: four lines from Villon's *Ballade des Pendus*.

There were dates, too, always the same period. All these macabre drawings, done ten years earlier, were now rubbing shoulders with captioned sketches for humorous news-papers, drawings for calendars, landscapes of the Ardennes, and advertising posters.

The steeple theme recurred, too. And the whole church. From the front, from the side, and from below. The main door, on its own. The gargoyles. The forecourt, with its six steps, which the perspective made seem vast.

Always the same church. As Maigret passed from wall to wall, he felt that Van Damme was growing agitated and ill at ease, perhaps even a prey to the same temptation as at Luzancy weir.

A quarter of an hour went by this way, and then Jef Lombard returned, his eyes moist. He wiped his forehead across which a lock of hair was straggling.

'You must forgive me,' he said. 'My wife has just given birth. To a girl. . . .'

There was a hint of pride in his voice but, as he spoke, he glanced anxiously from Maigret to Van Damme.

'It's my third child. Yet I'm just as overcome as the first

time. You saw my mother-in-law. She had eleven and yet she's sobbing for joy. She went and shouted the good news to the workmen and wanted to take them to see the baby. . . .'

His eyes followed Maigret's and came to rest on the steeple with the two hanged men. He became more nervous, and murmured with obvious embarrassment:

'Youthful indiscretions. They're very bad. But at the time I thought I'd be a great artist. . . .'

'It is a church in Liège?'

Jef did not answer immediately. Finally, he said, almost regretfully:

'It's been gone for seven years. It was demolished to build a new church. It wasn't beautiful. It hadn't even any style. But it was very old, with something mysterious about its design and the alleyways which surrounded it and which have since been cleared away. . . .'

'What was its name?'

'The church of Saint-Pholien. The new one, built on the same site, has the same name.'

Joseph Van Damme was fidgeting as if his nerves were raw. Underneath, he was ill at ease, though it showed only in scarcely perceptible movements, in his irregular breathing, his trembling fingers, and his leg which was pressed up against the desk, but which kept swinging.

'Were you married at the time?' Maigret inquired.

Lombard laughed.

'I was nineteen. I was studying at the Academy. Look!'

He pointed with a look of nostalgia, at a bad portrait, in dreary colours, where he was, however, still recognizable, thanks to the characteristic irregularity of his features. His hair was growing down his neck. He was wearing a black tunic, buttoned up to the neck, and a flowing cravat.

The picture was extravagantly romantic and there was even the traditional skull in the background.

'Just imagine if you'd told me then I was to be a photo-engraver!' said Jef Lombard ironically.

He seemed as embarrassed by Van Damme's presence as by Maigret's. But he obviously did not know how to get rid of them.

A workman came and asked him about a plate that was not ready.

'They can come back this afternoon!'

'Apparently that'll be too late!'

'Who cares? Tell them I've got a daughter. . . .'

His eyes, his gestures, and the pallor of his complexion, dotted with little spots of acid, betrayed a confused mixture of joy, nervousness, and anxiety.

'Will you have something? We'll go into the house.'

All three walked along the maze of passages and through the door. which the old woman had opened to Maigret earlier.

There were blue tiles in the passage. The place smelt clean, though there was a mawkish air about, possibly from the stuffiness of the sickroom.

'The two boys are at my brother's. This way.'

He opened the dining-room door. Only a glimmer of daylight filtered through the small window-panes. The furniture was gloomy, though the brass on show round the room reflected the light.

On the wall was a large portrait of a woman, signed *Jef*, clumsily painted, but clearly showing that he had tried to idealize his model.

Maigret took it to be his wife, looked around and, as he expected, found more hanged men. Better ones. Some that were thought worth framing.

'Will you have a glass of gin?'

The Inspector felt Joseph Van Damme's angry gaze on him. Every detail of the conversation seemed to infuriate him.

'You said just now that you knew Jean Lecocq d'Arneville. . . .'

Footsteps could be heard from the floor above, presumably the room in which the woman had had her baby.

'A casual acquaintance. . . .' Jef Lombard replied distractedly, straining to catch a low sound of wailing.

He raised his glass and said:

'To my daughter's health! And my wife's!'

He turned sharply, drained his glass at one gulp, and went and looked for some non-existent object in the sideboard to hide his confusion; but the Inspector still caught the dull sound of a stifled sob.

'I must go upstairs. Forgive me. . . . One of those days. . . .'

*

Van Damme and Maigret had not exchanged a word. While they were crossing the yard and skirting the well, the Inspector studied his companion ironically, wondering what he was going to do.

But once in the street, Van Damme merely touched the brim of his hat and went striding off to the right.

Taxis were rare in Liège. Maigret, unfamiliar with the trams, returned on foot to the Hôtel du Chemin de Fer, had lunch and made inquiries about the local newspapers.

At two o'clock, he went into the *Meuse* newspaper office just as Van Damme was leaving it. The two men passed within a yard of each other without a word of greeting, and the Inspector growled to himself:

'He keeps arriving ahead of me. . . .'

He went up to an official, asked if he could consult the newspaper files, and had to fill in a form and wait for an administrative permit.

Certain details had struck him: Armand Lecocq d'Arneville had learnt that his brother had left Liège at more or less the time that Jef Lombard was drawing hanged men with such morbid persistence.

And *Clothing B*, which the Neuschanz and Bremen vagrant was carrying about in his yellow suitcase, was very old – at least six years, according to the German expert – maybe ten!

'A light beer!'

Then there was silence, a heavy, unnatural silence. Van Damme stared out straight in front of him, his jaws clenched. Jef Lombard was still fidgeting, as if his clothes were too tight at the armholes. Belloir, stiff and aloof, was examining his nails and running a bit of match under the nail of his first finger to remove some dirt.

'Is Madame Lombard all right?'

Jef Lombard looked round, as if for support, then stared at the stove and stammered:

'Very well. Thank you. . . .'

There was a clock above the counter and Maigret counted a good five minutes before a word was spoken. Van Damme had let his cigar go out and was the only one to let his face wear a look of undisguised hatred.

Jef was the most interesting to watch. The events of the day had obviously conspired to set his nerves on edge. There wasn't a muscle in his face, however small, that wasn't twitching.

The four men's table was a complete oasis of silence in the café, where all the others were talking at the tops of their voices.

'*Belote* again!' someone called triumphantly from the right.

'*Tierce* high!' said another from the left rather doubtfully. 'Is it good?'

'Three beers! Three!' yelled the waiter.

Everything was alive and humming except the table where the four men were sitting, which seemed gradually to be surrounded by an invisible wall.

It was Jef who broke the spell. He bit his lower lip and got up, stammering:

'What the hell!'

He gave his companions a short, sharp, unhappy glance, took down his coat and hat, went to the door, and wrenched it open.

'I bet he's going to burst into tears,' mused Maigret.

He had sensed that sob of rage and desperation which had welled up in the photo-engraver's throat and made his Adam's apple quiver.

He turned towards Van Damme, who was examining the marble table-top, swallowed half his glass of beer, and wiped his lips with the back of his hand.

It was the same atmosphere, only ten times stronger, as in the house in Rheims, where Maigret had already forced himself on the same people. The Inspector's massive bulk helped to lend an air of menace to his imposed presence.

He was tall and broad, especially broad, thick and solid, and his rather ordinary clothes emphasized his rather plebeian build. He had a heavy face, and his eyes could remain bovine and motionless.

He was, in fact, like one of those figures in a child's nightmares with enormously large expressionless eyes who bear down on the sleeper as if to crush him.

It was something implacable, inhuman, like an elephant moving relentlessly towards its goal.

He was drinking, smoking his pipe, and gazing contentedly at the hand of the clock as it jerked forward, each minute, with a metallic click. An insipid clock.

He did not seem to be watching anyone in particular and yet he was on the look-out for the slightest sign of life left and right of him.

It was one of the most extraordinary hours in his career. In fact it lasted nearly an hour. Fifty-two minutes to be precise. A war of nerves.

Jef Lombard had been put out of action at the start. But the other two were hanging on.

There he was, between them, like a judge, but a judge who made no accusations and whose thoughts could not be read. What did he know? Why had he come? What was he doing? Was he waiting for the word or the gesture which would confirm his suspicions? Had he already found out the truth or was his self-assurance mere bluff?

What could any of them say? Talk again about a coincidence, a chance meeting?

Silence reigned. They were waiting, not even knowing what they were waiting for. They were waiting for something, yet nothing happened.

The hand of the clock shuddered forward every minute. There was a slight creak from the works. At first, they did not hear it. Now, it was deafening. There were three distinct parts to the movement: a first click, then the hand starting to move; then another click as if it were settling itself in its new place. And the face of the clock changed; the obtuse angle gradually became an acute angle. The two hands were about to coincide.

The waiter kept looking at their gloomy table in astonishment. Monsieur Belloir swallowed now and again. Maigret did not have to look at him to know what he was doing. He could hear him existing, breathing, going tense, and sometimes shifting his feet carefully, as if in church.

The customers were thinning out. The red cloths and cards disappeared from the tables and their pale marble-tops appeared. The waiter went out to pull down the shutters, while the manageress arranged the counters in small piles, according to their value.

'Are you staying on?' Belloir asked, his voice almost unrecognizable.

'How about you?'

'I . . . I don't know. . . .'

Then Van Damme rapped the table with a coin and asked the waiter:

'How much?'

'The round? Nine francs seventy-five. . . .'

All three were standing up, avoiding each other's eyes. The waiter helped them on with their coats.

'Good night, gentlemen.'

It was foggy outside and they could hardly see the lights of the street-lamps. All the shutters were closed. Somewhere in the distance, footsteps echoed along the pavement.

No one could decide which way to go. None of the three men wanted to take the responsibility for leading the way. Behind them, the door of the café was being locked and safety bars secured.

An alleyway, with a crooked row of old houses, led off to the left.

'Well, gentlemen,' said Maigret finally, 'all that remains is to wish you a good night. . . .'

Belloir's hand, which he shook first, was cold and nervous. Van Damme's, which he held out unwillingly, was moist and flabby.

The Inspector turned up his coat collar, gave a little cough, and began to walk alone, down the deserted street. All his senses were directed towards one object: he was listening for the merest sound, the least disturbance in the air which would warn him of danger.

His right hand was in his pocket, gripping the butt of his revolver. It seemed as if, in the network of alleyways which spread away to his left, isolated in Liège like a leper-colony, people were walking along hurriedly, trying not to make a noise.

He caught a low murmur of conversation, either very far away or very close to, he couldn't tell, because the fog was playing tricks with his senses.

Then, suddenly, he flung himself to one side, and flattened himself against a door. There was a muffled explosion and someone made off at full speed in the darkness.

Maigret walked forward a few steps, peered into the alleyway from which the shot had come, saw nothing but some dark patches which evidently led into blind alleys and, right at the end, two hundred yards away, a frosted-glass globe, a sign over a fish-and-chip shop.

A few moments later, he passed the shop. A girl walked out of it with a bagful of golden-brown chips. She made him a half-hearted proposition, and went off towards a better-lit street.

*

Maigret was writing away peacefully, pressing his pen on the paper with his huge index finger and, from time to time, ramming down the hot ash in his pipe.

He was in his room in the Hôtel du Chemin de Fer. The brightly-lit station-clock, which he could see through the window, said two in the morning.

Dear Lucas,

As one never knows how things will turn out, here are a few notes, which would enable you, should the need arise, to carry on with the inquiry I have begun.

(1) Last week, in Brussels, a shabbily-dressed man, looking like a tramp, made up a parcel of about thirty thousand-franc notes, and sent them to his own address in the rue de la Roquette, Paris. Inquiries will show that he often sent himself sums of this order, *but that he did not make use of them himself.* The proof is that the ashes of a large number of notes, deliberately burned, were found in his room.

He went by the name of Louis Jeunet and worked fairly regularly in a workshop in the same street.

He was married (see Madame Jeunet, herbalist, rue Picpus) and had one child. But he left his wife and child in unhappy circumstances, after some severe bouts of drunkenness.

In Brussels, after sending off the money, he bought a suitcase in which to put some things he was keeping in a hotel bedroom. I exchanged this suitcase for another, while he was on his way to Bremen.

Jeunet, *who did not seem to have considered suicide till then, and had bought something to eat for supper*, noticed that his things had been filched from him, and killed himself.

The object in question was an old suit which did not belong to him and which, some years earlier, had been torn during a struggle and soaked with blood. *The suit was made in Liège.*

In Bremen, a man came to see the corpse. His name was Joseph Van Damme, an import–export agent, *born in Liège.*

Back in Paris, I learnt that Louis Jeunet was, in fact, Jean Lecocq d'Arneville, *born in Liège,* who has not been heard of for a long time. He studied and even went to University. In Liège, from which he disappeared about ten years ago, there was nothing against him.

(2) In Rheims, Jean Lecocq d'Arneville was seen, one night before he left for Brussels, entering the house of Maurice Belloir, vice-chairman of a bank, *born in Liège*; the latter denied this meeting.

But the thirty thousand francs sent from Brussels have been traced to this same Belloir.

At Belloir's house I met: Van Damme, who had flown in from Bremen, Jef Lombard, a photo-engraver from Liège, and Gaston Janin, also *born in that town*.

As I was returning to Paris with Van Damme, he tried to push me into the Marne.

I found him again in Liège, at Jef Lombard's. The latter, ten years ago, spent his time painting, and the walls of his house are covered with drawings from that period representing hanged men.

In the newspaper offices I visited, the 15 February editions of the year of the hanged men had been torn out by Van Damme.

That evening, an unsigned letter promised me a complete explanation, and fixed a rendezvous in a café in the town. There I found not one man, but three: Belloir (who had come from Rheims), Van Damme, and Jef Lombard.

They greeted me with embarrassment. I am convinced that one of the three had decided to talk. The others seemed to be there merely to prevent him.

Jef Lombard, who was on edge, suddenly cleared off. I remained with the two others. I left them outside, after midnight, in the fog, and, a few seconds later, a shot was fired at me.

I concluded that one of the three had wanted to talk and also that one of the three had tried to get me out of the way.

It is obvious that, since this amounts to a confession of guilt, *the person concerned has only one course – to try again and not miss me.*

But which is it? Belloir, Van Damme, or Lombard?

I shall find out when he tries again. Since there may be an accident, I am taking the precaution of sending you these notes which will enable you to pick up the threads of the inquiry from the beginning.

As to the psychological aspect of the case, pay special attention to Madame Jeunet and Armand Lecocq, the dead man's brother.

I am now going to bed. My regards to everyone back there.

MAIGRET

*

The fog had cleared, leaving beads of white hoar-frost on the trees and every blade of grass in the Square d'Avroy, which Maigret was crossing.

A watery sun was shining in the pale blue sky, and the frost was gradually melting into little drops of clear water which were falling on to the gravel.

It was eight in the morning when the Inspector strode through the still-deserted Carré where the cinema billboards were leaning against closed shutters. Maigret stopped at a letter-box, dropped in his letter to Sergeant Lucas, and looked around him with a flicker of anxiety.

In this same town, in these same streets, bathed in pale sunshine, a man, at that same moment, was thinking about him, a man whose only hope of safety was to kill him. He had an advantage over the Inspector in that he knew the ground, as he had proved that night when he plunged into the tangle of alleyways.

He knew Maigret, too. Perhaps he was even watching him at that very moment, whereas the Inspector was unaware of his identity.

Was it Jef Lombard? Was the danger in that old house in the rue Hors-Château, where the woman and her baby were sleeping on the first floor, cared for by her good mother, while the unruffled workmen moved from one tray of acid to another, hustled by cyclist messengers from the newspapers?

Was it perhaps Joseph Van Damme, savage and morose, bold and scheming, who was spying on the Inspector from a place *to which he knew he would eventually come?*

Ever since Bremen, the latter had anticipated everything! Three lines in the German newspapers, and he had hurried along to the mortuary. He had lunched with Maigret and yet had arrived in Rheims before him.

He was the first in the rue Hors-Château. He had arrived at the newspaper offices before him.

Finally, he was at the Café de la Bourse.

It was true that there was nothing to prove that he

207

wasn't the one who wanted to talk. But nothing proved the contrary!

Perhaps it was Belloir, cold, formal, with all the arrogance of the upper-middle-class provincial. Perhaps he was the one whose only hope was to dispose of Maigret?

Or was it Gaston Janin, the little sculptor with the goatee? He had not been at the Café de la Bourse, but he could have been on the watch in the street.

How did it all link up with a hanged man swinging from the cross on a church? With those dozens of hanged men? With the forests of trees which bore no fruit but hanged men? With an old blood-stained suit, ripped at the lapels by frenzied nails?

The typists were going off to work. A municipal motor-sweeper was crawling along, with its two mechanical water jets, and its roller-shaped broom which swept the rubbish into the gutter.

At the street-corners, the town police, in their white enamel helmets, could be seen directing the traffic with their shiny white arms.

'Where's the main police-station?' Maigret inquired.

He was shown the way. He arrived while the charwomen were still busy cleaning, but a breezy clerk welcomed his fellow-policeman and, when the latter asked to see some police reports from ten years back, explaining that it was the month of February that interested him, he exclaimed:

'You're the second in twenty-four hours. You want to know if a certain Joséphine Bollant committed larceny about then, don't you?'

'Was there someone here?'

'Yesterday, about five in the afternoon. A fellow from Liège, who's done all right for himself abroad, even though he's still quite young. His father was a doctor. While he's got a nice business in Germany. . . .'

'Joseph Van Damme?'

'That's him! But he was wasting his time looking through the file, he couldn't find what he wanted. . . .'

'Will you show it me?'

It was a green file, where the daily reports were kept bound, in numerical order. There had been five reports on 15 February: two for drunkenness and rowdiness at night, one for shop-lifting, one for assault and battery, and the last for breaking and entering and stealing rabbits.

Maigret did not even read them. He looked at the numbers at the tops of the forms.

'Did Monsieur Van Damme examine the book himself?' he inquired.

'Yes. He sat in the office next door.'

'Thank you.'

The five reports were numbered: 237, 238, 239, 241, and 242.

In other words, one was missing and had been torn out, just as the newspapers had been torn from their files: it was No. 240.

A few minutes later, Maigret was out in the square behind the Hôtel de Ville, where cars were arriving for a wedding. In spite of himself, he had his ear cocked for the least sound; he was a shade nervous and was not enjoying it.

CHAPTER 8

Little Émile Klein

HE had timed it just right! It was nine o'clock. The staff were arriving at the Town Hall and crossing the main courtyard, pausing a moment to say good morning to each other on the handsome stone steps at the top of which a concierge with a braided cap and well-trimmed beard was smoking a pipe.

It was a meerschaum. Maigret noted the detail, for no special reason, possibly because the morning sun was reflected in it and because it was already seasoned. For a moment the Inspector envied the man, smoking away with greedy little puffs; he seemed like a symbol of peace and well-being.

The air was alive that morning, and became still more so as the sun rose in the sky. There was a glorious cacophony, shouts in Walloon dialect, the harsh clanging of the red and yellow trams, and the quadruple jets of an enormous fountain dominated by a Liège-style flight of steps, which was doing its best to drown the clamour of the nearby market.

Maigret saw Joseph Van Damme go up one side of the double staircase and disappear into the entrance-hall.

The Inspector hurried after him. Inside, the staircase went on up on two sides, meeting again on each floor. The two men came face to face on one of the landings, out of breath from running, and trying to appear natural to an official wearing a silver chain.

It was all very quick and poignant. A matter of precision, of a split second.

As he went up the staircase, Maigret had assumed that Van Damme had come there, as to the newspaper offices and the police station, simply to make something disappear.

One of the reports for 15 February had already been torn out.

But surely, as is the practice in most towns, the police would have sent the mayor a copy of the daily reports every morning?

'I should like to see the Town Clerk,' announced Maigret with van Damme only six feet away. 'It's urgent. . . .'

Their eyes met. They wondered whether to shake hands, decided not to and, when the official asked him what he wanted, the Bremen business-man simply murmured:

'It's nothing. I'll come back. . . .'

He went off. His footsteps grew fainter in the entrance-hall. Shortly afterwards, Maigret was shown into a luxurious office where the Town Clerk, buttoned up in his morning coat and high collar, set about finding the ten-year-old daily reports.

The air was warm and the carpets thick. A ray of sunshine lit up a bishop's crozier in a historical painting which occupied an entire panel on one of the walls.

After half an hour's search and an exchange of courtesies, Maigret discovered the reference to the stolen rabbits, and the reports for drunkenness and shoplifting. Then, between two miscellaneous items, came the following lines:

Police Constable Lacasse of No. 6 Division, was proceeding at six o'clock this morning to the Pont des Arches to take up point-duty and was passing the main door of the Church of Saint-Pholien, when he observed a body hanging from the door-knocker.

A doctor was urgently summoned but could only confirm the person's death, a man by the name of Émile Klein, a house-painter, twenty years old, born in Angleur and living in the rue du Pot-au-Noir.

Klein had apparently hanged himself, about the middle of the night, with a sash-cord. In his pockets were found only a few valueless objects and some small change.

Inquiries revealed that he had not been regularly employed for three months, and his action seems to have been the result of poverty.

His mother, Madame Klein, a widow, who lives on a modest pension in Angleur, has been notified.

*

Hours of feverish activity followed. Maigret plunged head-long down this new track. Yet, without altogether realizing it, he was less concerned with information about Klein than with meeting Van Damme.

Only if and when he came face to face with the business-man again, would he be anywhere near the truth. It had all begun in Bremen. And since then, every time the Inspector moved on a square, he had run into Van Damme.

The latter had seen him at the Town Hall, knew that he had read the report, and that he was on Klein's tracks.

Angleur produced nothing. The Inspector took a taxi into an industrial area of small, identical working-class houses, all the same sooty grey colour, in mean streets beneath the factory chimneys.

A woman was washing the doorstep of one of the houses, the one where Madame Klein had lived.

'She's been dead at least five years. . . .'

The shadow of Van Damme did not fall round there.

'Didn't her son live with her?'

'No. He came to a sticky end. He did away with himself on a church door. . . .'

That was all. Maigret merely learnt that Klein's father was a foreman in a coal mine and that, after his death, his wife lived on a small pension, sub-let the house, and only occupied an attic-room in it.

'To No. 6 Police Division,' he told the driver.

Constable Lagasse was still alive. But he barely remembered anything.

'It had been raining all night. He was soaked through and his red hair was plastered all over his face.'

'Was he tall? Or small?'

'On the small side.'

Then the Inspector went to the gendarmerie and spent

nearly an hour in their offices which smelt of leather and sweating horses.

'If he was twenty at the time, he must have gone before a military board. You did say Klein with a K?'

They found sheet No. 13 in the 'rejected' file. Maigret copied down the figures: *height* five foot two, *chest* thirty-two, and a note about '*weak lungs*'.

But there was still no clue leading to Van Damme. He was clearly to be found somewhere else. The only result of the morning's calls was to establish that *Suit B* had never belonged to the hanged man of Saint-Pholien, who was a little shrimp.

Klein had committed suicide. There had been no struggle and not a drop of blood had been spilt.

So where was the link with the Bremen tramp's suitcase and the death of Lecocq d'Arneville, alias Louis Jeunet?

*

'Drop me here. And tell me how to find the rue du Pot-au-Noir.'

'Behind the church. The one leading into the Quai Sainte-Barbe.'

When he arrived in front of Saint-Pholien, Maigret paid off the taxi. He was now looking at the new church which stood in the middle of a vast stretch of waste land.

To right and left of it were broad streets flanked by blocks of flats, about the same age as the church. But behind the latter, there was still an old district which had been partially demolished to make room for the church.

In a stationer's window Maigret found some picture-postcards of the old church, which was lower, squatter, and black all over. One wing was shored up with timbers. On three sides, low, sordid-looking houses backed on to its walls, giving the whole place a medieval appearance.

Nothing remained now of this courtyard of Miracles except a jumble of houses, separated by narrow streets and blind alleys, and pervaded by a nauseating stench of poverty.

The rue du Pot-au-Noir was barely two yards wide and down the middle of it flowed a stream of soapy water. Children were playing on the doorsteps. Inside, it was swarming with humanity.

It was dark in spite of the sun, which was bright but could not penetrate down the alleyway. A cooper had lit a brazier out in the street and was hooping barrels.

The numbers of the houses had completely faded. The Inspector had to inquire. When he asked for No. 7, he was shown a courtyard, from which came a noise of saws and planes.

On the far side was a workshop, with several carpenter's benches, at which three men were working. All the doors were open and glue was being melted on a stove.

One of the men looked up, put down his cigarette-end and waited for the visitor to speak.

'Did someone called Klein live here?'

The man looked round knowingly at his companions, pointed to a door and a dark staircase, and muttered:

'Up that way! There's someone already there.'

'A new tenant?'

He replied with an odd smile, which the Inspector only understood later on.

'Go and have a look. It's on the first floor. You can't miss it: it's the only door. . . .'

One of the workmen laughed softly as he worked his plane. Maigret started up the staircase in total darkness. A few steps up, the banisters were missing.

He struck a match and saw above him a door with no lock or handle; it seemed to be secured by a string tied to a rusty nail.

His hand in his revolver pocket, he pushed open the door with his knee, and was dazzled by the light which streamed through a stained-glass window with a third of its panes broken.

What Maigret saw was so unexpected that he looked around him for a moment before he could make out any details. Finally, in a corner, he saw a shape, a man leaning against the wall, fixing him with a savage glare: it was Joseph Van Damme.

'We were bound to end up here, weren't we?' declared the Inspector.

His voice echoed strangely in the stark, empty atmosphere.

Van Damme did not reply, but remained quite still, staring at him viciously.

*

It would have been impossible to understand the geography of the place unless you knew what type of building it had once been: part of a convent, a barracks, or a private house.

Nothing in it was square. Half the floor was boarded and the other half was made up of crooked flagstones, as in some old chapel.

The walls were white-washed, except for a rectangle of brown-coloured brick which presumably blocked up an old window. Through the stained-glass window could be seen a gable, a piece of guttering, and some crooked roofs in the background, in the direction of the Meuse.

But that was the least unexpected. The oddest thing was the complete illogicality of its contents, evocative of the mad-house or some huge practical joke.

Pell-mell on the floor were new, unfinished chairs, a door lying full length, with a mended panel, some pots of glue, broken saws, and boxes, from which straggled straw and shavings.

By contrast, in one corner, there was a kind of divan, or rather a spring mattress, partly covered with a piece of cretonne. Just above it dangled an odd-shaped lantern, with coloured glass, the sort sometimes to be seen in junk-shops.

Sections of an incomplete skeleton, the kind used by students, had been flung down on the divan. The ribs and the pelvis were still attached by hooks and were leaning forward like a rag doll.

Then there were the walls. The white walls had been covered with drawings, and painted frescoes.

This was the most incongruous aspect of the muddle: there were grimacing figures and inscriptions like *Long live Satan, grandfather of the world!*

On the floor was a Bible with a damaged cover. Elsewhere were crumpled sketches and yellowing papers, covered with a thick layer of dust.

There was another inscription over the door: *Welcome to the Damned!*

In the middle of all this rubbish, were the unfinished chairs, which smelt of the carpenter's shop, the glue-pots and rough deal planks, and an overturned stove, red with rust.

Finally, there was Joseph Van Damme, with his well-cut overcoat, carefully-shaved face, and impeccable shoes, Van Damme, who was still the man of the large Bremen brasseries, modern office-blocks, expensive dinners and glasses of old Armagnac. . . .

. . . Van Damme who drove his car and greeted important people, pointing out that the one in the fur coat was worth millions and that another had thirty cargo-boats on the high seas, and who, a little later, to the accompaniment of light music and the clinking of glasses and saucers, went and shook hands with all these magnates, feeling that he would soon be their equal. . . .

Van Damme suddenly looked like a hunted beast, motionless, his back still against the wall, the plaster whitening his shoulders, one hand in his overcoat pocket, glowering at Maigret.

'How much?'

Had he in fact spoken? Could the Inspector, in that fantastic atmosphere, have been the victim of a delusion?

He gave a start and upset a seatless chair, making a clatter.

Van Damme was scarlet in the face. Yet he had lost his healthy glow. There was panic, or desperation, as well as fury and the will to live, to triumph no matter what the cost, in his tensed-up features, in his expression, as he screwed up his last powers of resistance.

'What do you mean?'

Maigret went over to a pile of crumpled sketches which had been swept into a corner under the stained-glass window. Before getting an answer, he had time to spread out some nude sketches of a girl with coarse features and untidy hair, a vigorous well-formed body, swollen breasts, and broad hips.

'There's still time,' Van Damme went on. 'Fifty thousand? A hundred? . . .'

The Inspector glanced at him curiously. With barely concealed anxiety, the latter snapped:

'Two hundred thousand!'

There was fear in the air within the crooked walls of the wretched hovel. It was acrid, unhealthy, morbid.

Perhaps it was something more than fear: a repressed desire, a mad urge to kill. . . .

However, Maigret went on thumbing through the old papers, and found the same voluptuous girl, in different poses. As she posed, she seemed to have been gazing sullenly in front of her.

Once, the artist had tried draping her in the piece of cretonne which lay over the divan. On another occasion, he had drawn her in black stockings.

Behind her was a skull, which now lay at the foot of the spring mattress. Maigret remembered seeing this macabre head in one of Jef Lombard's portraits.

Links were forming, though still confusedly, between people and events, through time and space. With a somewhat nervous gesture, the Inspector spread out a new charcoal sketch which showed a young man with long hair, his shirt open across his chest, and on his chin the first signs of a beard.

He, too, was in a romantic pose. His head was three-quarters on, and seemed to be gazing into the future, as an eagle stares at the sun.

It was Jean Lecocq d'Arneville, who had committed suicide in that sordid Bremen hotel, the tramp who had not eaten his sausage-rolls.

'Two hundred thousand francs!'

Though it still betrayed the business-man, concerned with the slightest details and fluctuations of currency, the voice added:

'French francs!... Look, Inspector...'

Maigret sensed that pleading would soon give way to threats, and that the fear which throbbed in his voice would not take long to change into a growl of rage.

'There's still time. No official action has been taken. We're in Belgium....'

There was still a stump of candle in the lamp and the Inspector found an old paraffin-stove under the piles of papers on the floor.

'You are not on official business. And even... Give me a month....'

'In other words, it happened in December....'

Van Damme seemed to huddle closer to the wall. He stammered:

'What do you mean?'

'It is now November. In February, it will be ten years since Klein hanged himself. But you're only asking me for a month....'

'I don't understand....'

'Yes, you do!'

It was maddening to see Maigret still turning over the old papers with his left hand – the papers crackling as they brushed against each other – while his right hand remained thrust deep into his overcoat pocket.

'You understand quite well, Van Damme. If it were a question of Klein's death and if, for instance, he had been murdered, the time-limit would only come into force in

February, in other words, ten years afterwards. Yet you're only asking for a month. So it must have happened in December. . . .'

'You won't find anything. . . .'

His voice quavered, like a faulty gramophone.

'Then why are you frightened?'

He lifted up the springs of the bed. There was nothing underneath except dust and a barely identifiable crust of mouldy bread.

'Two hundred thousand francs. We could arrange it so that, later on . . .'

'Do you want your face slapped?'

It was so violent and unexpected, that for a moment Van Damme lost control, moved as if to protect himself, and, as he did so, unintentionally pulled out the automatic which he was gripping in his overcoat pocket.

He realized what he had done; for a second madness took hold of him but he couldn't bring himself to shoot.

'Drop that!'

His fingers opened. The automatic dropped to the floor near a pile of shavings.

Maigret turned his back on the enemy and continued to ferret about in the fantastic mass of heterogeneous objects. He picked up a sock which was also yellow and blotched with mildew.

'Tell me, Van Damme . . .'

He turned round, sensing something unusual in the air. He saw the man run his hand over his cheek and his fingers leave a damp streak.

'Are you crying?'

'Me?'

The *me* was aggressive, sardonic, desperate.

'Which branch of the army were you in?'

The other did not understand. He was ready to clutch at any straw of hope.

'I was in the E.S.L.R. The School for Reserve Second Lieutenants, at Beverloo. . . .'

'Infantry?'

'Cavalry.'

'In other words, you were then between five foot six and five foot eight. And you weighed under ten stone. So you must have filled out since. . . .'

Maigret pushed back a chair he had knocked into, picked up another scrap of paper, apparently part of a letter, with only one line on it:

My dear old friend . . .

But he kept watching Van Damme, who was trying to understand. Then, suddenly guessing, in hopeless confusion and his face contorted, he exclaimed:

'It wasn't me! I swear I've never worn that suit!'

Maigret gave his companion's revolver a kick and sent it skidding across to the other side of the room.

Why did he count up the children again just then? A small boy at Belloir's. Three kids in the rue Hors-Château, the last of whom had hardly opened its eyes. And the so-called Louis Jeunet's son.

On the floor lay an unsigned pastel sketch of the beautiful naked girl, arching her back.

There were hesitant footsteps on the stairs. A hand fumbled at the door, groping for the string which acted as a latch.

CHAPTER 9

The Companions of the Apocalypse

In the scene which followed, everything counted: words, silences, looks, even the involuntary twitch of a muscle. Everything was fraught with meaning, and behind the actors loomed the stark ghost of fear.

The door opened. Maurice Belloir appeared. He glanced first at Van Damme, huddled against the wall in one corner, and then at the automatic lying on the floor.

It was enough. He understood. Especially when he saw Maigret, his pipe between his teeth, still calmly thumbing through the old sketches.

'Lombard's coming!' Belloir blurted out, though it was not clear whether he was addressing the Inspector or his companion. 'I took a cab . . .'

These words alone were enough to show Maigret that the vice-chairman of the bank had thrown up the sponge. It was barely perceptible. His face was less strained, but there were tired and guilty inflexions in his voice.

All three looked at each other. Joseph Van Damme began:

'What's he . . .'

'He's like a madman. I tried to calm him down. But he got away. He went off, talking to himself and waving his arms. . . .'

'With a gun?' Maigret inquired.

'With a gun. . . .'

Maurice Belloir was listening with the unhappy look of a man who is shattered yet is trying in vain to control himself.

'Were both of you in the rue Hors-Château? Were you waiting for the result of my conversation with . . .'

He pointed to Van Damme. Belloir nodded assent.

'And did all three of you agree to offer me . . .'

He did not need to finish his sentence. They knew what he was referring to. They even understood what he meant when he was not speaking. It was as if they could hear what he was thinking.

Suddenly, there were hurried steps on the stairs. Someone stumbled, apparently fell on his face, and cursed angrily. A moment later, the door was kicked open and in the doorway stood Jef Lombard. He remained there for a moment, motionless, gazing at the three men with a terrifying stare.

He was shaking. He was in the grip of a fever, or perhaps some kind of madness.

Everything must have been dancing before his eyes, the figure of Belloir as he drew away from him, Van Damme's flushed face, and finally Maigret, with his broad shoulders, holding his breath and not stirring a finger.

To cap it all, there was all that fantastic junk, scattered drawings, and the naked girl, with only her chin and breasts showing, the lamp and the battered divan.

The scene could only have lasted a fraction of a second. At the end of Jef's long arm was a revolver.

Maigret watched him calmly. Even so, he heaved a sigh of relief when Jef Lombard threw the gun to the ground, clasped his head in his hands, broke into loud sobs, and groaned:

'I can't! I can't! Do you understand? I can't, damn it!'

He leant both arms against the wall, his shoulders were heaving, and he was sniffing audibly.

The Inspector went and shut the door because they could hear the noise of sawing and planing, as well as of kids squealing in the distance.

*

Jef Lombard wiped his face with his handkerchief, flicked back his hair, and looked round him with the vacant stare that people have after a nervous breakdown.

He had not yet entirely calmed down. His fingers were twitching. His nostrils were quivering. When he tried to speak, he had to bite his lip because another sob was welling up.

'To come to this!' he said in a voice made flat and cutting by sarcasm.

He tried to laugh, a desperate laugh.

'Nine years! Almost ten! I was left on my own, without a sou, and without a job. . . .'

He was talking to himself, no doubt unaware that he was staring hard at the picture of the nude – flesh in the raw.

'Ten years of daily grind, failure and difficulties of every sort! Yet I married. I wanted kids. I worked like a black to give them a decent life. A house, the workshop, everything. You saw it all. But what you didn't see were my efforts to build it all up. The discouragements. The bills at the beginning, which used to keep me awake at night. . . .'

He swallowed and ran his hand across his forehead. His Adam's apple rose and fell.

'So, anyway, I've just got a little daughter. I'm not sure if I've even looked at her! My wife, who's still in bed, doesn't understand, and stares at me, terrified, because she no longer recognizes me. The workmen keep asking me things and I don't know what to tell them. . . .

'Washed up! In a few days, suddenly! Undermined, destroyed, broken, smashed to bits! Everything! Ten years' work!

'And all because of . . .'

He clenched his fists, looked at the gun on the floor, and then at Maigret. He was at his wit's end.

'Let's get it over with!' he sighed, with a gesture of weariness. 'Who's going to do the talking? It's all so stupid!'

His words seemed to be addressed to the skull, to the piles of old sketches, and to the extravagant drawings on the walls.

'So stupid!' he repeated.

He looked as if he were going to cry again. But no. He was played out. The crisis was over. He went and sat on the edge of the divan, rested his elbows on his bony knees, cupped his chin in his hands, and stayed there, waiting.

He only moved to scratch a spot of mud off one of his trouser turn-ups with his nail.

*

'Am I disturbing you?'

It was a cheerful voice. The carpenter entered, covered in sawdust, glanced at the drawings decorating the walls, and then burst out laughing.

'So you came back to see all that?'

No one moved. Belloir was the only one who tried to appear natural.

'You remember you still owe me the twenty francs from last month? Oh, I haven't come to ask for them. I can't help laughing because, when you went away and left all this old rubbish, I remember you saying:

'"Maybe some day, a single one of these sketches will be worth more than this whole hovel put together. . . ."'

'I didn't believe it. Mind you, I held off painting the walls. One day, I brought along a frame-maker who sells pictures, and he took away two or three of the drawings. He gave me a hundred sous. Are you still painting?'

Eventually, he realized that there was something unusual going on. Joseph Van Damme was gazing stubbornly at the floor. Belloir was snapping his fingers impatiently.

'Wasn't it you who started a business in the Rue Hors-Château?' the carpenter went on to ask Jef. 'I've a nephew who worked for you. A tall, fair fellow. . . .'

'Possibly . . .' Jef sighed, looking away.

'I don't recognize you. Were you in the gang?'

The owner was addressing Maigret.

'No.'

'A weird crew! My wife didn't want me to let the place, then she advised me to sling them out, especially as they often didn't pay. But it amused me. First, it was which one could wear the biggest hat, then who could smoke the longest clay pipe! And they used to spend whole nights singing and drinking. There were some pretty girls here sometimes. By the way, Monsieur Lombard, do you know what became of the one on the ground there?'

'She married an inspector in the "Grand Bazar", and she now lives a hundred yards down the road. She's got a son who's at school with mine. . . .'

Lombard got up, walked over to the stained-glass window, and came back again, in such a state that the man decided to beat a retreat.

'Perhaps I'm disturbing you? I'll leave you to it. You know, if there's anything here that interests you . . . Naturally, I never meant to keep them because of the twenty francs. All I took was a landscape for my dining-room. . . .'

Out on the landing, he looked as if he were going to embark on a fresh speech. But he was called from below.

'Someone to see you, *patron.*'

'See you later, gentlemen. Very glad to have . . .'

His voice faded as the door closed again. Maigret had lit a pipe while he was talking. The carpenter's chatter had, after all, lowered the tension somewhat. So, when the Inspector began to speak and pointed to an inscription on the wall round one of the more extravagant drawings, Maurice Belloir replied almost naturally.

The inscription was: *The Companions of the Apocalypse.*

'Was that the name of your group?'

'Yes. I'll explain. It is too late, isn't it? That's just too bad for our wives and children. . . .'

But Jef Lombard cut in:

'I want to do the talking. Let me. . . .'

He started to pace up and down the room, glancing from time to time at some object or other, as though to illustrate his story.

'A little over ten years ago, I was studying painting at the Academy. I used to wear a broad-brimmed hat and a flowing cravat. There were two others with me. Gaston Janin, who was doing sculpture, and little Émile Klein. We used to adore parading up and down the Carré. . . . We were artists, you see. Each of us thought he'd be at least a Rembrandt. . . .

'It all began idiotically. We used to read a lot, especially writers of the Romantic period. We used to get carried away. We'd swear by one writer for a week. Then we'd drop him and take up another. . . .

'Little Émile Klein, whose mother lived in Angleur, rented this studio and we used to meet here. The medieval atmosphere, especially on winter evenings, made a great impression on us. We used to sing old songs and recite Villon. . . .

'I can't remember who discovered the *Apocalypse* and insisted on reading us whole chapters from it.

'One evening, we got to know a few students: Belloir, Armand Lecocq d'Arneville, Van Damme, and a fellow named Mortier, a Jew, whose father owned a sausage-skin and tripe shop not far from here.

'We were drinking. We brought them back here to the studio. The oldest of them wasn't even twenty-two.

'It was you, Van Damme, wasn't it?'

It was doing him good to talk. His steps became less jerky, his voice less hoarse, but after his fit of weeping, his face was still blotched with red and his lips swollen.

'I think it was my idea. To found a society, a group! I'd read stories about the secret societies which existed in German universities during the last century. A club which would link Art and Science!'

He could not help sneering when he looked at the walls.

'We were full of that kind of talk. It puffed us up with pride. On the one hand, there were the three daubers, Klein, Janin, and myself. That was Art. On the other, the students. We used to drink. We drank a lot. We drank in order to get ourselves even more worked up. We used to turn down the lights so as to produce a more mysterious atmosphere.

'We used to sleep here, too, you see. . . . Some on the divan, and the others on the floor. We used to smoke pipe after pipe. The air would grow thick.

'Then we used to sing choruses. There was nearly always someone who was sick and had to go and recover in the courtyard.

'This used to happen at two or three in the morning. We'd work ourselves up into a frenzy. The wine helped – cheap wine which turned our stomachs – as we plunged into the realms of metaphysics.

'I can still see little Émile Klein. He was the most nervous. His health was bad. His mother was poor; he lived on nothing and did without food so that he could drink.

'After we'd been drinking, we felt we were real geniuses!

'The student group was a bit more reasonable, because they weren't so poor, except for Lecocq d'Arneville. Belloir used to pinch a bottle of old Burgundy or liqueur from his parents. Van Damme used to bring some cold meat.

'We were convinced that people in the street used to look at us with a mixture of admiration and terror. We'd chosen a mysterious, high-sounding name: *The Companions of the Apocalypse*.

'I don't honestly think anyone had read the *Apocalypse* right through. It was just Klein who used to recite a few passages of it by heart when he was drunk.

'We'd arranged to split the rent, but Klein was allowed to live here.

'A few girls agreed to come and pose for nothing. Pose, and other things, of course! So we used to pretend we were Bohemians, and they were little street-girls! All that nonsense. . . .

'That's one of them on the floor. Dumb as a cow. But that didn't stop us painting her as a Madonna.

'Drink, that was the main thing. Never mind the expense, we had to whip up the atmosphere. I remember Klein trying to achieve the same result by upsetting a bottle of ether on the divan.

227

'And all of us working ourselves up until we were drunk and saw visions!

'God Almighty!'

Jef Lombard went and pressed his forehead against the steamy window. Then he came back with a new quaver in his voice.

'By working ourselves up into a frenzy, we ended up as packs of nerves. Especially those of us who didn't eat enough. Do you see what I mean? Little Émile Klein included. A kid who didn't eat, but kept himself going with loads of drink.

'Naturally, we re-discovered the world. We had our own ideas about all the great problems! We scoffed at the middle-class, society, and all established truths. . . .

'As soon as we'd gulped down a few drinks and the air was thick with smoke, we'd bandy the craziest ideas about! A mixture of Nietzsche, Karl Marx, Moses, Confucius, and Jesus Christ.

'For instance, let's see . . . I can't remember who it was who discovered that pain didn't exist and that it was only a figment of the imagination. I was so taken with the idea that, one night, in the middle of a breathless group, I stuck the end of a penknife into the fleshy part of my arm and tried to smile. . . .

'Then there were other things. We were an Élite, a little group of Geniuses brought together by chance. We soared above the conventional world of law and prejudice.

'A handful of gods, do you see? Gods who were sometimes starving to death, but who walked the streets proudly, dismissing the passers-by with contempt.

'We used to plan the future: Lecocq d'Arneville was to be a Tolstoy. Van Damme, who was doing a boring course at the School of Economics, was to revolutionize political economy and reverse all accepted ideas on the organization of the human race.

'Each of us had his place. There were poets, painters, and future heads of state.

'All on drink! And how! In the end, we were so used to getting carried away, that we'd hardly have got here, in the light of the lamp, with the skull from which we all drank, before each of us would manage to achieve the little frenzy he wanted, on his own. . . .

'Even the more modest of us could already see a marble plaque one day on the wall of the house: *Here met the famous Companions of the Apocalypse.* . . .

'It was a challenge to see who could bring the latest book, or come up with the most far-fetched ideas.

'It's pure chance that we didn't become anarchists. We used to discuss the question, solemnly. There had been an attempted assassination in Seville. We'd read the newspaper article out loud.

'I can't remember which of us cried out: "True genius is destructive!" . . .

'So this handful of young men used to discuss the subject for hours. We used to think up ways of manufacturing bombs. We used to wonder what it would be a good idea to blow up.

'Then Little Émile Klein, who was on his sixth or seventh glass, was sick. He rolled about on the floor, and all we could think about was what we'd do if something went wrong.

'That girl was with us. Her name was Henriette. She was crying.

'What nights they were! It was a point of honour not to leave until the lamplighter had passed and put out the lamps, and we'd go off, shivering, into the grey dawn.

'The ones who were well-off would climb in through a window, eat and sleep, and more or less repair the damage of the previous night.

'But the others, like Klein, Lecocq d'Arneville, and myself would wander the streets, nibble at a roll and gaze enviously at the shop-windows.

'I had no overcoat that year because I wanted to buy a broad-brimmed hat which cost a hundred and twenty francs.

'I used to make out that cold, like everything else, was

an illusion. So, fortified by our discussions, I told my father, a good, honest gunsmith's craftsman, who died since, that love of one's parents was the worst form of selfishness, and that a child's first duty was to deny his family. . . .

'He was a widower. He used to leave for work at six in the morning just as I was coming back. In the end, he used to leave earlier so as not to meet me, because my speeches frightened him. So he'd leave me notes on the table – *There's some cold meat in the cupboard. Father.*'

Jef's voice broke for a second or two. He looked at Belloir, who was sitting on the edge of a seatless chair staring at the floor, and then at Van Damme, who was tearing a cigar to shreds.

'There were seven of us,' Lombard said quietly. 'Seven Supermen! Seven Geniuses! Seven kids!

'Janin's still sculpting in Paris. Or at least he makes dummies for a big factory. From time to time, he works off his frustrations by doing a bust of his current girl-friend. . . .

'Belloir's in a bank. Van Damme's in business. I'm a photo-engraver.'

There was a silence charged with fear. Jef swallowed and went on, while the rings round his eyes seemed to grow darker:

'Klein hanged himself on the church-door. Lecocq shot himself in the mouth in Bremen. . . .'

Another silence. This time, Maurice Belloir, unable to sit still, got up, seemed to hesitate, and then went and stood in front of the stained-glass window. There was a peculiar sort of noise in his chest.

'And the last of you?' said Maigret. 'Mortier, wasn't it? The tripe-merchant's son.'

Lombard turned and stared at him with such frenzy that the Inspector anticipated another fit. Van Damme knocked over a chair.

'It was in December, wasn't it?'

Maigret was talking, but not missing the slightest twitch from any of his three companions.

'It'll be ten years ago in a month's time. The time-limit will expire in a month. . . .'

First he went and picked up Joseph Van Damme's automatic, and then the revolver which Jef had thrown on the floor shortly after his arrival.

He was not mistaken. Unable to hold out, Lombard clasped his head in his hands and moaned:

'My kids! My three kids!'

Then suddenly and unashamedly turning his cheeks wet with tears to the Inspector, he once again became hysterical and shouted:

'It was because of you, you, you alone, that I didn't even look at the girl, my last child. I couldn't even tell you what she's like. . . . Do you realize?'

CHAPTER 10

Christmas Eve in the Rue du Pot-au-Noir

THERE must have been a passing shower, a low, fast-moving cloud, because all the reflections of the sun suddenly vanished. And, as if someone had turned off a switch, the air became grey and dull, and everything seemed to wear a frown.

Maigret understood how those who used to meet there felt the need to soften the light with a multi-coloured lamp, make the most of the mysterious semi-darkness, and make the atmosphere heavy with a liberal supply of tobacco and drink.

He could imagine Klein waking up, the morning after those pathetic orgies, among the empty bottles, broken glasses, stale smell, and bluey-green light which filtered through the curtainless stained-glass window.

Jef Lombard was silent from exhaustion, and it was Maurice Belloir who spoke.

There was a sudden change, as if they had moved to a different wavelength. The photo-engraver had been shaken to the depths of his entire being; he was twitching, sobbing, hissing, pacing up and down; with alternating moments of agitation and calm, which could have been plotted on a graph, like a fever.

Belloir was in control, from head to foot, voice, expression, and movements; it was so obviously the result of an intense effort of will that it was painful to see.

He couldn't have cried. Or even twitched his lips. He was rigid all over.

'May I go on, Inspector? It will soon be dark and we've no light.'

It was not his fault that he brought up a material detail. Nor was it a lack of emotion. In fact, it was really his way of expressing himself.

'I think we were all sincere in our talks and discussions, and the dreams we voiced. But there were various degrees to our sincerity.

'Jef mentioned it. On the one hand, there were the rich ones, who went home afterwards and took root again in an atmosphere of security: Van Damme, Willy Mortier, and myself. Even Janin, who had everything he wanted.

'Willy Mortier was a special case, though. Here's just one instance. He was the only one who chose his mistresses from professional night-club entertainers and small-time dancers. He used to pay them. . . .

'A practical fellow. He was like his father, who arrived in Liège penniless, unashamedly chose the sausage-skin trade, and made a packet.

'Willy got five hundred francs a month pocket-money. Compared to what we all had, it was fabulous. He never set foot in the University, got his hard-up friends to take down the lectures, and passed his exams by means of "understandings" and bribes.

'He used to come here out of sheer curiosity. We had no ideas or tastes in common.

'I mean, his father used to buy pictures from artists, even though he had no time for them. He also bribed municipal councillors and even aldermen, to obtain certain favours. And he had no time for them, either. . . .

'Anyway, Willy despised us, too. He came here to measure the difference between himself, the rich boy and the rest.

'He didn't drink. He used to look disgusted at any of us who were drunk. Throughout our interminable discussions, he only came out with a few words, which were like a cold shower, words which hurt, because they dispelled all the false poetry we had managed to create.

'He loathed us and we loathed him! What's more, he was mean. Calculatedly mean. Klein didn't eat every day. One or other of us used to help him. But Mortier said:

'"I don't want there to be any money barriers between us. I don't want to be accepted just because I'm rich. . . ."

'So he gave his share and no more when we used to search in our pockets to go and fetch some drink.

'It was Lecocq d'Arneville who used to take down his lectures for him. I once heard Willy refuse to give him an advance on his work.

'He was the alien, hostile element, which you find in all groups of men.

'We tolerated him. But Klein, among others, when he was drunk, used to attack him violently and get things off his chest. Mortier, slightly pale, would listen to him contemptuously.

'I mentioned varying degrees of sincerity. The most sincere were undoubtedly Klein and Lecocq d'Arneville. They were so close, they could have been brothers. Both had had a tough childhood, and a hard-up mother. Both wanted to succeed, and were tormented by insuperable difficulties.

'So as to study in the evenings at the Academy, Klein had to work during the day as a house painter. He admitted to us that he felt giddy when he was sent up a ladder. Lecocq used to take down lectures, and give French lessons to foreign students. He often came and ate here. The stove must still be here somewhere. . . .'

It was on the floor, by the divan, and Jef kicked at it moodily.

*

Maurice Belloir, not a hair of whose well-groomed head was out of place, went on in his dull, expressionless voice:

'Since then, I've heard people in middle-class drawing-rooms in Rheims say jokingly:

'"Given certain circumstances, would you be able to kill a man?"

'Or the mandarin problem. You know. . . . *If all you had*

234

to do was press an electric button and kill a very rich mandarin in the heart of China to become his heir, would you do it? . . .

'Here, where the most outlandish subjects were an excuse for discussions which went on all night, the riddle of life and death had to come up, too. . . .

'It was shortly before Christmas. A news-item in the paper sparked it off. It had been snowing. Our ideas had to be different from the conventional ones, you see. So we got carried away by the theory that man is no more than a bit of mould on the earth's crust. What do his life or death matter? Pity is a mere disease. Big animals eat little ones. We eat the big animals. . . .

'Lombard told you the story of the penknife. How he stabbed himself to prove that pain didn't exist.

'Well, that night, there were three or four empty bottles lying about on the floor, and we were solemnly discussing the question of killing.

'After all, we were in the realms of pure theory, where anything is permissible. We cross-examined each other.

'"Would you dare?"

'Our eyes sparkled. Unhealthy shivers ran down our spines.

'"Why not? If life's nothing but chance, a skin disease on the earth's crust. . . ."

'"A stranger passing in the street?"

'Klein, who was most drunk, with dark rings round his eyes and his skin deathly pale, replied:

'"Yes!"

'We felt we were on the brink of the abyss. We were afraid to go any further. We were playing with danger, jesting with death, which we had conjured up and which now seemed to be prowling round us. . . .

'Someone – I think it was Van Damme – who had been a choirboy, sang the *Libera nos*, which priests chant over a coffin. We joined in the chorus. We wallowed in morbidity.

'But we didn't kill anyone, that night. At four in the morning, I jumped over the wall and went home. At eight o'clock, I was drinking coffee in the bosom of my family. It was simply a memory, do you understand? Like the memory of some stage-play that made you shudder.

'Klein stayed on here, in the rue du Pot-au-Noir. He nursed all these ideas too long in his big, sickly, head. They were eating at him. The next few days, he showed what he was thinking by asking sudden questions.

'"Do you really think it's difficult to kill someone?"

'We didn't want to hang back. But we weren't drunk any more. We said unconvincingly:

'"Of course not!"

'We may even have got a kick out of his childish hallucinations. But remember, we didn't want to start off any sort of drama. We were merely exploring the ground to the limit.

'When there's a fire, the onlookers, in spite of themselves, hope it'll go on, that it'll be a "splendid fire". When the water rises newspaper readers hope for "splendid floods" which they can talk about twenty years later.

'*Something of interest. It doesn't matter what!*

'It was Christmas Eve. Everyone brought some bottles. We drank and sang songs. Klein, half tight, kept taking one or other of us aside and saying:

'"Do you think I'm capable of killing?"

'No one was worried. At midnight, no one was sober. We were talking about fetching some more bottles.

'It was just then that Willy Mortier arrived, in a dinner-jacket, with a broad white shirt-front which seemed to absorb all the light. He was pink in the face and stank of scent. He told us that he had just come from a big smart reception.

'"Go and fetch some drink!" Klein yelled at him.

'"You're drunk, my friend. I simply came to say hullo. . . ."

'"Oh, no, it was to look at us!"

'No one could have guessed what was going to happen. Yet Klein's face was more terrifying than on any other

236

occasion when he had been drunk. He seemed quite small and thin next to the other fellow. His hair was ruffled, sweat was pouring from his forehead, and his tie was flapping.

'"You're a drunken pig, Klein!"

'"All right, so the pig says go and fetch some drink. . . ."

'I think Willy was scared at that point. He was vaguely aware that no one was laughing. Even so, he brazened it out.

'He had black curly hair that stank of scent.

'"I must say you're not exactly cheerful here," he remarked. "It was far more amusing with the stuffy crowd I came from. . . ."

'"Go and fetch some drink. . . ."

'Klein circled round him, his eyes blazing. A few of us were in one corner, discussing some theory of Kant's. Someone else was crying and swearing he wasn't fit to be alive. . . .

'No one was in control of himself. No one saw it all. Klein suddenly darted forward, a little bundle of taut nerves and struck him. . . .

'It looked as if he were ramming his head against the shirt-front. But then we saw blood spurting out. Willy had his mouth wide open. . . .'

*

'No!' Jef Lombard pleaded suddenly. He had got up and was looking at Belloir, dumbfounded.

Van Damme was once more flat up against the wall, his shoulders hunched.

But nothing could have stopped Belloir, not even if he had wanted to himself. It was growing dark. Their faces looked grey.

'Everyone was rushing about,' the voice went on. 'Klein was hunched up, a knife in his hand, and gazing in horror at Willy who was staggering about. These things never happen the way people imagine. I can't explain. . . .

'Mortier didn't fall. Yet the blood was pouring out of the hole in his shirt-front. I'm nearly sure he said:

'"Swine!"

'He just stood there, his legs slightly apart, as if to keep his balance. If it hadn't been for the blood, you'd have said he was the one who was drunk.

'He had big eyes. Just then, they seemed even bigger. He was gripping the button of his dinner-jacket with his left hand. With his right, he was feeling the seat of his trousers.

'Someone yelled in terror. I think it was Jef. We saw Willy's right hand slowly drawing a revolver from his pocket. A small, black, very hard, steel object.

'Klein was rolling on the floor, in the throes of a fit. A bottle fell down and was smashed.

'Willy wouldn't die. He was swaying imperceptibly. He looked at each of us in turn. He couldn't have been seeing straight. He raised his revolver. . . .

'Then someone went forward to grab the gun from him, slipped in the blood and they rolled together on the floor.

'They must have struggled a bit. Because Mortier wouldn't die, do you see? His eyes, those big eyes remained wide open!

'He was still trying to shoot. He kept on saying:

'"Swine!"

'The other fellow must have gripped his throat. In any case, he hadn't much longer to live.

'*I got in an awful mess, as the dinner-jacket lay there on the floor.*'

*

Van Damme and Jef Lombard were now staring in horror at their companion. Belloir continued:

'It was my hand that was round his neck! I was the one who slipped in the pool of blood!'

He was standing in the same place as he was then. But

238

now he was clean and neat, his shoes spotless and his suit well brushed.

He was wearing a large gold signet ring on his white, well-cared-for right hand, with its manicured nails.

'We stood there as if stunned. We put Klein to bed. He wanted to go and give himself up. No one spoke. I can't explain why. Yet I was perfectly clear in my mind. I can only repeat that people have the wrong ideas about such things. I dragged Van Damme out on to the landing and we whispered together. Klein never stopped struggling and yelling.

'The church-clock struck, but I don't know what time it was, as three of us went down the alleyway, carrying the body. The Meuse was in flood. There were eighteen inches of water on the Quai Sainte-Barbe and the current was very strong. The sluice-gates were open both up- and down-stream. In the light of the nearest street-lamp, we could just see the dark lump being swept away by the current.

'My suit was torn and blood-stained. I left it in the studio and Van Damme went and fetched me some clothes. Next day, I spun some yarn to my parents.'

'Did you all meet again?' Maigret inquired slowly.

'No. We left the rue du Pot-au-Noir in confusion. Lecocq d'Arneville stayed with Klein. Since then, we avoided each other, by mutual consent. When we met each other in town, we looked the other way.

'It so happened that Willy's body, thanks to the flood, was not recovered. He had always avoided talking about his connexions with us. He wasn't proud of being a friend of ours. People thought he'd run away. Then the inquiries shifted elsewhere, to low haunts where they thought he might have ended the night.

'I was the first to leave Liège, three weeks later. I broke off my studies abruptly and told my people that I wanted to go on with my career in France. I became a bank clerk in Paris.

'It was through the papers that I learnt that Klein had

hanged himself, the following February, on the door of Saint-Pholien.

'One day, I met Janin in Paris. We didn't mention the incident. But he told me that he, too, had settled in France.'

'I stayed on alone in Liège,' Jef Lombard muttered, looking down.

'You drew hanged men and church steeples,' Maigret retorted. 'Then you drew sketches for the newspapers. Then . . .'

He recalled the house in the rue Hors-Château, the windows with the small greenish panes, the fountain in the courtyard, his young wife's portrait, the photo-engraver's workshop, where posters and pages of newspapers were gradually encroaching on the walls covered with hanged men. . . .

And the kids. The third who had been born the previous day.

Ten years had slipped by, and gradually, everywhere, life had begun to carry on as before, with comparative ease.

Like the two others, Van Damme had wandered about Paris. Chance had taken him to Germany. His parents had left him some money. He had become an important business-man in Bremen.

Maurice Belloir had made a fine marriage. He had reached the top of the ladder.

Vice-chairman of a bank. A fine new house in the rue de Vesle. His boy learning the violin.

In the evenings, he played billiards with well-known figures like himself in the comfortable room in the Café de Paris.

Janin made do with chance female acquaintances, earned his living by making dummies, and, when his day was done, sculpted busts of his mistresses.

Lecocq d'Arneville had got married. Hadn't he a wife and child in the herbalist's in the rue Picpus?

Willy Mortier's father went on buying, cleaning and

selling lorry-loads and wagon-loads of intestines, subsidizing municipal counsellors and feathering his nest.

His daughter had married a cavalry officer and, when the latter did not wish to go into the business, Mortier had refused to hand over the agreed dowry.

The couple lived somewhere in a small garrison town.

The Stump of Candle

It was nearly dark. Their faces stood out against the murky background; their features looked sharper.

As if the semi-darkness had put him on edge, Lombard said nervously:

'Let's have some light!'

There was still a stump of candle in the lamp which had been hanging from the same nail there for years, along with the battered divan, the piece of cretonne, the broken skeleton and the sketches of the girl with the naked breasts, all kept there as security by the owner, who had never been paid.

Maigret lit it and coloured shapes danced on the walls, projected by the red, yellow, and blue glass, like a magic lantern.

'When did Lecocq d'Arneville come and see you for the first time?' the Inspector asked, looking at Maurice Belloir.

'It must have been about three years ago. I wasn't expecting it. The house you saw had just been finished. My boy had barely started to walk.

'I was struck by his resemblance to Klein. Not so much physically as morally. The same consuming fever. The same morbid nervousness.

'He came as an enemy. He was embittered. . . . Or desperate. I can't find the exact word.

'He sneered, talked sardonically, pretended to admire my house, my position, my life and character. Yet I felt he was ready to burst into tears, like Klein when he was drunk.

'He thought that I had forgotten. He was wrong. I simply wanted to live. Do you understand? That was why I had worked like a slave. Just so as to live.

'He hadn't been able to. It was true that he had lived with

242

Klein for two months after that Christmas night. We had left. They had stayed on, in this room, in ...

'I can't explain how I felt about Lecocq d'Arneville. After so many years, I found him just the same as he was before.

'It was as if life had carried on for some and stopped for others.

'He told me he had changed his name, because he didn't want to have anything around that reminded him of the horrible incident. He'd even changed his way of life. He hadn't opened a book since.

'He'd got it into his head to start a new life for himself, as a manual worker.

'I had to read this between the lines, because it was all flung at me with a mass of caustic comments, reproaches, and monstrous accusations.

'He'd failed, he'd made a mess of everything. But part of him was still bound up here.

'It was the same for all of us, I think. But not so intense. Not to that painful, unhealthy degree.

'I think Klein's face haunted him even more than Willy's.

'Married, with a child, he had some bad times. He went on the bottle. He was incapable, not only of being happy, but even of enjoying a moment of peace.

'He told me that he had adored his wife, and that he had left her because, when he was with her, he felt as if he were stealing.

'Stealing happiness. Happiness stolen from Klein. And the other man.

'I've thought about it a lot since, mind you. I think I've understood. We were playing with terrible ideas, with mysticism and morbidity.

'It was only a game. A kid's game. But at least two of us had got caught up in it. The two most fanatical.

'Klein and Lecocq d'Arneville. There'd been talk of killing. Klein wanted to do it. And then he killed himself.

Lecocq, horrified, his nerve gone, dragged this nightmare around with him for the rest of his life.

'The others and myself tried to escape and come to terms with normal life again.

'Lecocq d'Arneville, on the other hand, flung himself body and soul into his remorse, with the fury of despair. He had wrecked his life. He had wrecked his wife's and son's lives.

'Then he turned on us. That was why he came to see me. I didn't understand straight away.

'He looked at *my* house, *my* family, and *my* bank. I saw plainly that he thought it his duty to destroy it all.

'To avenge Klein. To avenge himself. . . .

'He threatened me. He had kept the suit with its stains and tears. It was the only material evidence of what happened that Christmas Eve.

'He asked me for money. A lot! Afterwards, he asked me for more.

'It was our Achilles' heel. All our positions, Van Damme's, Lombard's, mine, even Janin's, depended on money.

'A new nightmare had begun. Lecocq had not miscalculated. He went from one to the other, hawking that sinister suit of clothes round with him. With diabolical accuracy, he worked out just how much to ask for, so as to make things awkward for us.

'You saw my place, Inspector. Well, the house is mortgaged. My wife thinks her dowry is in the bank and untouched. There's not a sou left. And I did other things I shouldn't have.

'He went twice to Bremen to see Van Damme. He came to Liège.

'He was still embittered, still bent on destroying even anything that resembled happiness.

'There had been six of us round Willy's corpse. Klein was dead. Lecocq was living in a constant nightmare.

'So we all had to be equally miserable. He didn't even

244

spend the money. He lived as poorly as ever, like the time when he used to share a few sous' worth of sausage with Klein. He burnt the notes!

'Yet each of those burnt notes implied fantastic difficulties for us.

'For three years we've been struggling, each in his own town, Van Damme in Bremen, Jef in Liège, Janin in Paris, and myself in Rheims.

'For three years we hardly dared to write to each other, and then Lecocq plunged us back, against our will, into the atmosphere of the *Companions of the Apocalypse.*

'I've a wife. So has Lombard. We have kids. So we try and stick it out for their sake.

'The other day, Van Damme wired to us that Lecocq had killed himself and told us to meet here.

'We were all here. You arrived. After you left, we found out that it was you who had possession of the blood-stained suit, and that you were hot on the scent. . . .'

'Who stole one of my suitcases at the Gare du Nord?' Maigret inquired.

This time Van Damme replied:

'Janin did. I arrived before you. I was hiding there on one of the platforms.'

They all felt equally tired. The stump of candle would perhaps last another ten minutes, no more.

The Inspector moved carelessly and knocked into the skull which fell down and looked as if it were gnawing the floor.

'Who wrote to me at the Hôtel du Chemin de Fer?'

'I did,' Jef replied, without looking up. 'Because of my little girl. The little girl I haven't seen yet. Van Damme guessed. So did Belloir. Both of them were at the Café de la Bourse.'

'And was it you who fired?'

'Yes. I couldn't go on. I wanted to live. Live! With my wife and kids. So I was watching for you outside. I've fifty thousand francs worth of bills at the moment. Fifty

245

thousand francs that Lecocq d'Arneville burnt. But that's nothing. I'll pay them off. I'll do whatever's necessary. But feeling you there behind us. . . .'

Maigret turned to Van Damme.

'And you kept dashing ahead of me, trying to destroy the clues?'

They were silent. The candle flickered. The light filtering through the red glass of the lamp fell only on Jef Lombard.

Then, for the first time, Belloir's voice faltered.

'Ten years ago, immediately after the . . . the thing, I'd have accepted things,' he said. 'I'd bought a revolver, in case they came to arrest me. But ten years of life. Ten years of effort. Of struggle. And other things to consider: a wife, children . . . I think I could have pushed you into the Marne, too. Or fired at you that night outside the Café de la Bourse. . . .

'Because, in a month, less than that, in twenty-four days, the time-limit comes into force. . . .'

Right in the middle of the silence that followed, the candle suddenly gave a last flicker and went out. They were in complete and absolute darkness.

Maigret did not move. He knew that Lombard was standing to his left, Van Damme was leaning against the wall in front of him, and Belloir less than a pace behind him.

He waited, not even bothering to put his hand in his revolver pocket.

He distinctly felt that Belloir was shaking from head to foot, was gasping in fact. He struck a match and said:

'Shall we go?'

In the light of the flame, his eyes seemed even brighter. All four brushed against each other in the doorway, and then on the stairs. Van Damme stumbled because he had forgotten that there was no banister beyond the eighth step.

The carpenter's shop was closed. Through the curtains in a window, they could see an old woman knitting by the light of a small oil lamp.

'Was it along there?' said Maigret, pointing to the unevenly paved street which led to the embankment, a hundred yards off, where there was a gas lamp in a bracket on the corner of a wall.

'The Meuse came up to the third house,' Belloir replied. 'I had to go into the water up to my knees so as . . . so as to let him go with the current.'

They retraced their steps and skirted the new church in the middle of the waste ground which had still not been properly levelled.

Suddenly, they were in the town, with passers-by, red and yellow trams, cars and shop-windows.

To reach the town centre, they had to cross the Pont des Arches; the fast-flowing river was dashing itself noisily against the piles.

In the rue Hors-Château, they would be waiting for Jef Lombard: the workmen, downstairs, among the trays of acid and the plates that the cyclists from the newspapers would be asking for; the mother upstairs, with the dear old mother-in-law, and the little girl with her eyes still closed, lost in the white sheets of the bed. . . .

And the two older ones, who had to stay quiet in the dining-room decorated with pictures of hanged men.

And another mother, in Rheims, would be giving her son a violin lesson, while the maid was polishing all the brass stair-rods and dusting the china vase with the big green plant.

Work would be coming to an end in Bremen, in the office-building. The typist and the two clerks would be leaving the modern office, and as the electricity was switched off, the enamel letters: *Joseph Van Damme, Export and Import Agent* would be plunged in darkness.

Perhaps, in one of the brasseries, where they played Viennese music, some business-man with a shaven head would be remarking: 'Hullo! That Frenchman's not here. . . .'

In the rue Picpus, Madame Jeunet would be selling a

tooth-brush, or a couple of ounces of camomile, its pale leaves crackling in the packet.

The small boy would be doing his homework in the back of the shop.

The four men were walking in step. A breeze had sprung up, and it kept the clouds moving, so that from time to time there was bright moonlight.

Had they any idea where they were going?

They passed in front of a lighted café. A drunken man lurched out.

'I'm expected in Paris,' Maigret said, stopping suddenly.

As the three of them looked at him, not knowing whether to feel happy or desperate, and not daring to speak, he stuffed his hands into his pockets.

'There are five kids involved. . . .'

They were not even sure if they had heard him, because the Inspector had muttered the words to himself between his teeth. Now they could see only his broad back and his black overcoat with the velvet collar receding into the distance.

'One in the rue Picpus, three in the rue Hors-Château, one in Rheims. . . .'

*

After leaving the station, he went to the rue Picpus. There the concierge told him:

'It's not worth going up. Monsieur Janin isn't there. They thought it was bronchitis. But it turned out to be pneumonia, so they took him to hospital. . . .'

He then drove to the Quai des Orfèvres. Sergeant Lucas was there, busy telephoning to some bar-owner who had broken the law.

'Did you get my letter, *vieux*?'

'Is it all over? Did you fix things?'

'Did I hell!'

It was one of Maigret's favourite expressions.

'Did they run away? You know, I was darned worried

by that letter. I nearly made a dash to Liège. What were they? Anarchists? Forgers? A gang of international crooks?'

'Kids!' he murmured.

He threw the suitcase, containing what the German expert, in his long and detailed reports, had called *Clothing B*, into a cupboard.

'Come and have a beer, Lucas.'

'You don't seem too cheerful.'

'What ever gave you that idea, *vieux*? There's nothing funnier than life. . . . Are you coming?'

A few moments later, they were pushing the revolving doors of the Brasserie Dauphine.

Lucas had seldom been so worried. Instead of beer, his colleague swallowed down six Pernods, practically one on top of the other. In spite of this, his voice was not very steady, and there was an unusual misty look in his eyes as he said:

'Do you know something, *vieux*? Ten more cases like this and I'll pack it in. Because it would prove that there's a big fellow up there called God who's got it into his head to do our job for us. . . .'

It's true, though, that when he called the waiter, he did add:

'Don't worry. There won't be ten. . . . What's the news back at H.Q.? . . .'

MAIGRET
AND THE ENIGMATIC
LETT

TRANSLATED BY
DAPHNE WOODWARD

CHAPTER I

Age About 32, Height 5 ft 6 ins

Interpol to Sûreté, Paris:
   Xvzust Cracovie vimontra m ghks triv psot uv Pietr-le-Letton Breme vs tyz btolem.

Superintendent Maigret, of No. 1 Flying Squad, looked up from his desk; he had the impression that the iron stove which stood in the middle of his office, with its thick black pipe sloping up to the ceiling, was not roaring as loudly as it should. He pushed aside the paper he had been reading, rose ponderously to his feet, adjusted the damper and threw in three shovelfuls of coal.

Then, standing with his back to the stove, he filled a pipe, and tugged at his shirt collar; it was a low one, but it felt too tight.

He glanced at his watch; four o'clock. His jacket was hanging from a hook on the door.

Slowly he drifted back to his desk, where he read out the message in an undertone, decoding it as he went:

International Criminal Police Commission to Sûreté Générale, Paris:
   Police Cracow report Pietr the Lett passed through on way to Bremen.

Interpol, the International Criminal Police Commission, at that time had its headquarters in Vienna, from where, broadly speaking, it directed the campaign against gangsterism in Europe, its chief function being to maintain contact between the police forces in the different countries.

Maigret picked up a telegram, also written in *polcod* – the secret international language used by police headquarters all over the world. He read it aloud in 'clear':

Polizei – Praesidium, Bremen, to Sûreté, Paris:
   Pietr the Lett reported making for Amsterdam and Brussels.

A third telegram, from the Nederlandsche Centrale in Zake Internationale Misdadigers – the Netherlands police head-quarters – announced:

Pietr the Lett left for Paris 11 a.m. by North Star express coach 5 compartment G.263.

The final *polcod* telegram came from Brussels, and said:

Confirm Pietr the Lett passed through Brussels 2 p.m. in North Star compartment as reported by Amsterdam.

On the wall behind Maigret's desk was an enormous map, and he now planted himself in front of this, a tall, burly figure, hands in pockets and pipe clenched between his teeth.

His eyes travelled from the dot that stood for Cracow to the other dot that indicated the port of Bremen, and from there to Amsterdam and Brussels.

Again he looked at his watch. Twenty past four. The *North Star*, doing a steady 66 miles an hour, would now be some-where between Saint-Quentin and Compiègne.

No stop at the frontier. No slowing down. In coach 5, compartment G 263, Pietr the Lett was no doubt reading or looking out at the view.

Maigret went to a door and opened it, to reveal a cupboard with an enamel basin and tap. He washed his hands, ran a comb through his thick hair – which was dark brown, with only a few grey threads at the temples – and did his best to straighten a tie he could never persuade to look really neat.

It was November. Dusk was falling. From his office win-dow he could see a stretch of the Seine, the Place Saint Michel, and a floating wash-house, all shrouded in a blue haze through which the gas-lamps twinkled like stars as they lit up one by one.

He opened a drawer and glanced through a cable from the International Identification Bureau at Copenhagen:

Sûreté, Paris:

Pietr le Letton 32 169 01512 0224 0255 02732 03116 03233 03243 03325 03415 03522 04115 04144 04147 05221 . . . etc.

This time he took the trouble to translate aloud, and even

repeated the words several times, like a schoolboy going over a lesson:

'Apparent age 32 years. Height 5 ft 6½ ins. Nose: bridge straight, base horizontal, jutting out. Ears: large Original Border, crossed lobe, outward anti-tragus, lower fold straight; peculiarity – spaces between folds. Long face. Sparse light-blond eyebrows. Lower lip prominent, thick, drooping. Long neck. Eyes: halo around the pupil mid-yellow, periphery of the iris mid-green. Light blond hair.'

This was a verbal portrait of Pietr, or Piet, the Lett, and to the Superintendent it conveyed as much as a photograph. It described the man's general appearance: short, slight, youthful, with very fair hair, fair, thin eyebrows, greenish eyes, and a long neck.

It also gave a detailed description of Pietr's ears, so that Maigret could pick him out in a crowd even if his features were disguised.

Maigret took down his jacket, put it on, topped it with a heavy black overcoat, and placed a bowler hat on his head.

With a parting glance at the stove, which looked about to blow up, he left the office.

At the far end of a long corridor, on the landing that served as a waiting-room, he called out:

'Jean, don't forget my fire, will you?' And he began to descend the stairs. Here a rush of wind took him by surprise, and he had to step back into a recess to light his pipe.

The huge glass roof of the Gare du Nord gave no protection from the gusts of wind that swept the platforms. Several panes had been dislodged and lay in fragments on the lines. The lights were dim. People were muffled to the ears.

Beside one ticket-window, a group of travellers stood reading an ominous announcement:

'Channel gale . . .'

One woman, whose son was crossing to Folkestone, looked distraught and red-eyed. She was pouring out last-minute instructions to him, and making him promise, sheepishly, not to go on deck even for a moment.

Maigret stood at the entrance to platform 11, where a crowd had gathered to meet the *North Star*. All the big hotels, and Cook's, were represented.

Maigret did not move. Some of the others were growing irritable. One young woman, swathed in mink except for her legs in their sheer invisible stockings, was pacing to and fro, her stiletto heels clicking on the asphalt.

But he stood motionless, a bulky figure, his impressive shoulders casting a great shadow. People jostled him, but he swayed no more than a wall would have done.

The yellow dot of the train's light appeared in the distance. Hubbub broke out, the shouts of porters; the passengers began to plod towards the exit.

Two hundred of them had filed past before Maigret spotted among the throng a little man wearing an overcoat with a large green check pattern which was as unmistakably Nordic in cut as in colour.

The man was not hurrying. He was followed by three porters, and preceded by the representative of a luxury hotel in the Champs-Élysées, obsequiously clearing a path for him.

Age about 32. Height 5 ft 6½ ins. . . . Bridge of nose . . .

Maigret, showing no excitement, looked at the ears of the man in green. That settled it.

The man went close by him. One of the three porters bumped the Superintendent's leg with a suitcase.

At that moment one of the train staff came running up and spoke a few hurried words to the ticket-collector, who was standing by a chain that could be used to close the platform.

The chain was thereupon put up. Voices rose in protest.

The man in the green check overcoat had already reached the exit.

The Superintendent was smoking his pipe with short, rapid puffs. He went over to the official who had put up the chain.

'Police. What's the matter?'

'A body . . . They've just found . . .'

'Coach 5?'

'I believe so. . . .'

Life in the station was following its normal course. Only

256

platform 11 looked unusual. There were fifty people still there, prevented from leaving. They were growing impatient.

'Let them through,' said Maigret.

'But . . .'

'Let them through. . . .'

He watched this last batch file out. The loudspeaker was announcing the departure of a suburban train. Somewhere, people were running. Beside one of the *North Star* coaches, a little group stood waiting. Three men in railwaymen's uniforms.

The station-master arrived first, pompous but worried. Then a wheeled stretcher was pushed across the main hall of the station, past groups of people who stared after it uncomfortably, especially those about to board trains.

Maigret strode heavily along the platform, still smoking. Coach 1, Coach 2 . . . Coach 5.

This was where the group stood waiting at the door. The stretcher halted. The station-master was listening to the three men, who were all speaking at once.

'Police! . . . Where is he?'

They stared at him with obvious relief. His great bulk thrust into the excited group, making the rest look like nobodies.

'In the toilet. . . .'

Maigret hauled himself up the steps and found the open door of the toilet on his right. A body lay in a heap on the floor, bent double and strangely twisted.

The guard was giving orders from the platform:

'Shunt the coach into a siding. . . . Wait a minute! No. 62. . . . And inform the special Superintendent. . . .'

At first Maigret could only see the back of the man's neck. But he pushed aside the cap, which was perched askew, to reveal the left ear.

'H'm . . . "Crossed lobe, outward anti-tragus . . .",' he muttered.

There were a few drops of blood on the linoleum. He looked around him. The station employees were standing on the platform and the steps. The station-master was still talking.

Maigret tipped the man's head back; and his teeth tightened on the stem of his pipe.

If he had not seen the traveller in the green overcoat come out, if he had not seen him walking towards a car, accompanied by an interpreter from the Majestic, he might have doubted his own eyes.

The description fitted. The same small, fair, toothbrush moustache below a narrow-bridged nose. The same fair, thin eyebrows. The same greenish-grey eyes.

In other words, Pietr the Lett!

Maigret could not move in the cramped toilet. A tap no one had thought to turn off was still running and a jet of steam was escaping from a leaky joint in the pipe.

His shins were touching the corpse. He raised its head and shoulders and saw that the jacket and shirt bore scorch-marks across the chest, where a shot had been fired at point-blank range. It had made a big, blackish patch, partly covered by a purple-red bloodstain.

The Superintendent was struck by a small detail. He happened to notice one of the feet. It was lying sideways, twisted like the rest of the body, which had been pushed into a heap so that the door could be closed.

The foot was wearing a very ordinary cheap black shoe: it showed signs of having been re-soled, the heel was worn down on one side, and in the middle of the sole there was a round hole that had gradually worn right through.

The special station Superintendent had arrived, gold-braided and officious; standing on the platform, he fired his questions.

'What's the matter now? . . . Violence? . . . Suicide? . . . Mind you don't touch anything until the Public Prosecutor's men get here! . . . Careful! . . . It's my responsibility . . .'

Maigret had infinite difficulty in getting out of the toilet, entangled as he was in the corpse's legs. With a swift, professional gesture he felt the dead man's pockets, making sure they were empty, absolutely empty.

He stepped down from the train; his pipe had gone out, his

hat was askew, and there was a bloodstain on one of his cuffs.

'Hello, Maigret. You here? . . . What do you think?'

'Nothing! Go ahead. . . .'

'Suicide, surely?'

'If you like. . . . Have you rung the Public Prosecutor's office?'

'The moment I was informed. . . .'

A voice was bellowing through the loudspeaker. A few people had noticed that something unusual was going on; they stood a little way off, watching the empty train and the motionless group clustered outside coach 5.

Maigret left them all to it, walked out of the station and hailed a taxi.

'Majestic Hotel.'

The gale was blowing harder than ever. The streets were swept by whirlwinds that sent people reeling like drunkards. A tile crashed to the pavement. The buses rushed on their way.

The Champs-Élysées looked like a deserted race-track. It was just beginning to rain. The commissionaire outside the Majestic hurried over to the taxi with his huge red umbrella.

'Police! . . . Has someone just arrived off the *North Star*?'

The commissionaire promptly closed his umbrella.

'Yes, that is so.'

'Green overcoat, fair moustache? . . .'

'That's right. Ask reception.'

People were running to escape the downpour. Maigret walked into the hotel just in time to escape a flurry of rain-drops the size of walnuts and as cold as ice.

The impeccably dressed and imperturbable clerks and inter-preters behind the mahogany desk were unaffected by the weather.

'Police! . . . A new arrival – green overcoat, small fair moust —'

'Room 17. They're just taking his luggage up.'

The Friend of Millionaires

MAIGRET's presence at the Majestic inevitably carried a suggestion of hostility. He was a kind of foreign body its organism would not assimilate.

Not that he resembled the policeman dear to caricaturists. He had neither moustache nor heavy boots. His suit was of quite good material and cut; he shaved every morning and had well-kept hands.

But his frame was plebeian – huge and bony. Strong muscles swelled beneath his jacket and soon took the crease out of even a new pair of trousers.

He had a characteristic stance too, which even many of his own colleagues found annoying.

It expressed something more than self-confidence, and yet it was not conceit. He would arrive, massively, on the scene, and from that moment it seemed that everything must shatter against his rock-like form, no matter whether he was moving or standing still with feet planted slightly apart.

His pipe was clamped between his teeth. He was not going to remove it just because he was in the Majestic.

Perhaps, indeed, this vulgar, self-confident manner was assumed deliberately.

With his heavy, black, velvet-collared overcoat he made a conspicuous figure in the brightly-lit hall, where elegant women were coming and going amid whiffs of scent, shrill laughter, and whispers, greeted deferentially by the well-groomed staff.

Maigret paid no attention. He kept aloof from the bustle. The strains of a jazz orchestra drifted up to him from the underground ballroom, then died away, as though stopped by an impenetrable barrier.

As he began to go upstairs the liftman called to him, offering his services. But he did not even turn his head.

On the first floor, someone asked:

'Can I help you?'

The voice did not seem to reach his ears. He looked along the corridors with their endless, sickening expanse of red carpet, and went on and up.

On the second floor, hands in pockets, he began to read the room-numbers on their bronze plates. The door of No. 17 was open. Hotel servants in striped waistcoats were bringing in suitcases.

The new arrival had taken off his overcoat and stood, very slim and elegant in a worsted suit, smoking a cigarette with a cardboard mouthpiece and giving orders.

No. 17 was not a room but a suite – sitting-room, study, bedroom, and bathroom. The door was at a corner where two corridors met, and a big curved sofa stood outside, like a bench at a crossroads.

Maigret sat down on this, directly opposite the open door, stretched out his legs, and unbuttoned his overcoat.

Pietr the Lett noticed him, but went on giving orders, with no sign of surprise or annoyance. When the servants had finished arranging his trunks and suitcases on luggage stands, he came over and shut the door himself, holding it ajar for a second while he scrutinized the Superintendent.

Maigret had time to smoke three pipes and send away two floor-waiters and a chambermaid who came to ask what he was waiting for.

On the stroke of eight, Pietr the Lett emerged from his room, looking slimmer and more clean-cut than ever, in a dinner-jacket whose classic lines bore the mark of Savile Row.

He was bare-headed. His fair, close-cropped hair was beginning to retreat from a slightly receding forehead, and the pink skin showed faintly through it at the top of his head.

He had long, pale hands. On the fourth finger of his left hand he wore a heavy platinum signet ring with a yellow diamond on it.

He was again smoking a Russian cigarette with a cardboard

mouthpiece. He passed close by Maigret, halted as though tempted to speak to him, but then went on, looking thoughtful, towards the lift.

Ten minutes later he appeared in the dining-room and sat down at the table of Mr and Mrs Mortimer-Levingston, which was the centre of attention. Mrs Mortimer-Levingston had ten thousand pounds' worth of pearls round her neck. On the previous day her husband had put one of the biggest French motor-car firms on its feet again – keeping a majority of the shares for himself, of course.

The three of them were chatting gaily. Pietr the Lett talked volubly but quietly, leaning forward a little. He was entirely at ease, unaffected and nonchalant, although he could see Maigret's dark figure in the hall, through the glass partition.

The Superintendent was at the reception desk, asking to look at the visitors' book. He saw without surprise that the guest from Latvia had entered himself as 'Oswald Oppenheim, ship-owner, from Bremen'.

The man undoubtedly had a valid passport and a complete set of papers in that name, as in others.

And he had doubtless met the Mortimer-Levingstons before – in Berlin, Warsaw, London, or New York.

Had he come to Paris solely to meet them and bring off one of the colossal swindles in which he specialized?

His official description – Maigret had the card in his pocket – ran as follows:

'An extremely clever, dangerous man, of uncertain nationality, but Nordic origin. Thought to be Latvian or Estonian. Speaks Russian, French, English, and German fluently.

'Highly educated. Believed to be the leader of a powerful international gang, chiefly concerned in financial swindles.

'This gang has been traced at various times to Paris, Amsterdam (the Van Heuvel case), Berne (the United Shipbuilders case), Warsaw (the Lipmann case), and various other European cities, where its activities have been less positively identified.

'Most of Pietr the Lett's accomplices appear to be from the

English-speaking countries. One of those most frequently seen with him, and recognized as the presenter of the forged cheque at the Federal Bank in Berne, was killed while being arrested. He used to pass himself off as Major Howard, of the American Legion, but was discovered to be a former New York bootlegger, known in the United States as Fat Fred.

'Pietr the Lett has been arrested twice. Once at Wiesbaden, for fraudulently obtaining half a million marks from a Munich wholesaler, and once at Madrid for a similar transaction, the victim in that instance being a prominent member of Spanish court society.

'He used the same tactics on both occasions. He had a talk with his victim, and no doubt told him the stolen funds were in a safe place and that his arrest would not lead to their recovery.

'On each occasion the charge was withdrawn and the plaintiff presumably compensated.

'Has never been caught red-handed since.

'Probably has some connexion with the Maronnetti gang (which forges bank-notes and identity papers) and with the "wall-borers" gang in Cologne.'

There was also a persistent rumour in European police circles to the effect that as leader and 'treasurer' of several gangs, Pietr the Lett must have a handsome fortune put by under different names in banks, or even invested in the stock market.

He was now listening with a faint courteous smile to some story that Mrs Mortimer-Levingston was telling him, while his pale fingers plucked magnificent grapes from a large bunch.

'Excuse me, sir; may I have a word with you?'

Maigret was speaking to Mortimer-Levingston in the hall of the Majestic. Pietr the Lett had just gone up to his room, and so had the American's wife.

Mortimer-Levingston did not look at all the athletic Yankee; he was more like a Latin American.

He was tall and slim, with a very small head; his black hair was parted in the middle.

He looked permanently tired. His eyelids were dark and drooping. Indeed, he led an exhausting life, managing some-

263

how to put in regular appearances at Deauville, Miami, the Lido, Paris, Cannes, and Berlin, to join his yacht in some harbour, to complete a deal in a European city, or to be one of the judges at all the biggest boxing matches in New York and California.

He threw Maigret a supercilious glance and murmured without moving his lips:

'Who are you?'

'Superintendent Maigret, No. 1 Flying Squad.'

Mortimer-Levingston frowned almost imperceptibly, and paused with bent head, as though resolved to grant Maigret only a second of his time.

'Are you aware that you have been dining with Pietr the Lett?'

'Is that all you have to say to me?'

Maigret showed no surprise. He had expected some such retort. Putting his pipe between his teeth – for he had condescended to remove it before addressing the millionaire – he grunted:

'That's all!'

He looked rather smug. Mortimer-Levingston walked past him in icy silence, and went into the lift.

It was just after half past nine. The orchestra which had played during dinner now gave way to the jazz band. People were beginning to arrive from outside.

Maigret had not had dinner. He stood where he was, in the middle of the hall, with no sign of impatience. The manager kept glancing at him from a distance, looking worried and cross. Even the most junior employees scowled as they went past, and sometimes deliberately bumped into him.

The Majestic could not stomach him. He stood there obstinately, a great black, motionless patch, contrasting with the gilt, the bright lights, the fashionable crowd with its evening dress, fur coats, perfume, and vivacity.

Mrs Mortimer-Levingston was the first to emerge from the lift. She had changed her dress, and her shoulders were bare beneath a *lamé* cloak lined with ermine.

She seemed astonished that no one was waiting for her, and for a time she strolled about, her high, golden heels tapping rhythmically on the floor.

Suddenly she stopped at the mahogany desk where the clerks and interpreters were waiting, and spoke briefly to them. One of the clerks pressed a red button and picked up the telephone. . . .

Looking surprised, he summoned a page, who ran off to the lift.

Mrs Mortimer-Levingston was becoming visibly uneasy. Through the glass door a streamlined American limousine could be seen, parked just outside.

The page came back and spoke to the clerk, who in his turn said something to Mrs Mortimer-Levingston. She protested. She seemed to be saying:

'That's impossible!'

At this point Maigret walked upstairs, stopped at the door of room 17, and knocked. As he had expected after the scene he had just witnessed, there was no answer.

He opened the door; the sitting-room, he saw, was empty. In the bedroom, Pietr the Lett's dinner-jacket had been flung carelessly on the bed. A wardrobe trunk stood open. Pietr's patent-leather pumps lay on the carpet, far apart.

The manager arrived.

'You here already?' he grunted.

'So he's disappeared, has he?! Mortimer-Levingston as well! Is that it?'

'We mustn't get worked up. They're not in their rooms, but we're sure to find them somewhere about the hotel.'

'How many entrances are there?'

'Three. . . . One on the Champs-Élysées. One into the arcades. And the tradesmen's entrance in the rue de Ponthieu.'

'Is there a watchman there? Send for him.'

The manager took up the telephone. He was furious. He snapped at the switchboard operator who failed to understand him. All the time he glared at Maigret.

'What's the meaning of this?' he inquired, while they

waited for the watchman to arrive from his small glass-fronted box beside the tradesmen's entrance.

'Nothing. Or practically nothing, as they say. . . .'

'I hope there hasn't been a . . . a . . .'

The word that stuck in his throat was 'crime', that nightmare of every hotel-keeper in the world, from the humblest lodging-house keeper to the manager of the most luxurious 'palace'.

'We shall soon find out.'

Mrs Mortimer-Levingston appeared.

'Well?' she demanded.

The manager bowed and stammered something unintelligible. Approaching down the corridor was a little old man with an unkempt beard and slovenly clothes, quite out of keeping with the hotel. He was never supposed to come out from the wings, of course; otherwise he too would have worn a smart uniform and got shaved every morning.

'Did you see anyone go out?'

'When?'

'A few minutes ago.'

'One of the kitchen staff, I think. I didn't pay attention. . . . A man wearing a cap. . . .'

'Short and fair-haired?' Maigret put in.

'Yes. . . . I think so. . . . I didn't look. . . . He was walking fast. . . .'

'Nobody else?'

'I don't know. . . . I went to the corner of the street to buy an evening paper.'

Mrs Mortimer-Levingston was losing her self-control.

'Good Lord! Is this the way you search for someone?' she snapped, turning to Maigret. 'I'm told you're from the police. My husband may have been killed. . . . What are you waiting for?'

The heavy gaze that he turned on her was a hundred per cent Maigret. Utterly calm. Utterly indifferent. As though he had just heard a fly buzzing. As though he were looking at some completely commonplace object.

She was not used to being looked at like that. She bit her

lip, blushed scarlet under her make-up, and stamped her foot impatiently.

He went on gazing at her.

Then, driven past bearing, or perhaps not knowing what else to do, she broke into hysterics.

It was nearly midnight when Maigret got back to the Quai des Orfèvres. The storm was in full blast. The trees along the quay were tossing to and fro, and little waves were lapping the hull of the floating wash-house.

The offices of the Judicial Police were almost deserted. But Jean was still at his post, in the waiting-room that gave on to the corridors with their rows of empty offices.

Loud voices could be heard from the duty room. Here and there a thread of light showed under a door: a superintendent or inspector was still working on some inquiry. The engine of a police car suddenly snorted in the courtyard.

'Has Torrence got back?' asked Maigret.

'Just this minute.'

'How's my stove going?'

'I had to open the window a crack, it was so hot in your office. Water was running down the walls!'

'Order me some beer and sandwiches. Rolls, not sliced bread, remember!'

He opened a door and shouted:

'Torrence!'

Sergeant Torrence followed him to his office. Before leaving the Gare du Nord, Maigret had telephoned him to take up the investigation at this end.

The Superintendent was forty-five years old. Torrence was only thirty. But there was already something massive about him that suggested a not quite full-sized replica of Maigret.

They had handled many cases together, never uttering a superfluous word.

The Superintendent took off his overcoat and jacket and loosened his tie. Standing with his back to the stove, he paused to let the warmth get well into his bones before he asked:

'Well?'

'The Public Prosecutor called an emergency meeting. The Judicial Identification people took some photos, but they found no finger-prints. Except the dead man's, of course. There's no record of those in the files.'

'If I remember rightly, the Department has no file on Pietr?'

'Only his verbal portrait. No prints or measurements.'

'So there's nothing to prove that the corpse is not Pietr?'

'But there's nothing to prove that it is.'

Maigret had picked up his pipe and a tobacco pouch, which was empty except for a little brown dust. Automatically, Torrence held out an open packet of tobacco.

Silence. The pipe spluttered faintly. Then they heard footsteps and the clinking of glasses outside the door. Torrence opened it.

The waiter from the Brasserie Dauphine came in with a tray bearing six glasses of beer and four thick sandwiches, and put it down on the table.

'Will that be enough?' he inquired, noticing that Maigret was not alone.

'It'll do.'

Still smoking, the Superintendent settled down to eat and drink, after pushing a glass of beer towards his subordinate.

'So?'

'I questioned all the train crew. It turned out there was one man travelling without a ticket. Either the dead man or the murderer! They think he got in at Brussels on the wrong side of the train. It's easier to hide in a Pullman coach than in an ordinary one, because of the big luggage space in each coach. Pietr ordered tea between Brussels and the frontier; he was looking through a batch of English and French newspapers, including several financial ones. Between Maubeuge and Saint-Quentin he went out to the toilet. The steward remembers that, because as Pietr went past he said: "Bring me a whisky."'

'And he went back to his seat after a bit?'

'A quarter of an hour later he was sitting with his whisky in front of him. But the steward hadn't seen him come back.'

'Nobody tried to get into the toilet after that?'

'Oh yes. A woman passenger shook the door, but the handle wouldn't turn. After the train reached Paris, one of the crew managed to force the door open, and he found the mechanism had been put out of action with iron filings.'

'No one had seen the second Pietr until then?'

'No. He'd have been noticed, because he was wearing the kind of shabby clothes that aren't often seen on a Pullman train.'

'And the shot?'

'Fired point-blank from a 6-mm. automatic. It burnt the man so badly that the doctor says he could have died just from that.'

'No signs of a struggle?'

'None at all. His pockets were empty.'

'I know. . . .'

'Oh, sorry! . . . I did find this, in a small inside pocket in the waistcoat, which was fastened with a button.'

From his wallet Torrence brought out a transparent envelope; a lock of brown hair could be seen inside it.

'Give it here. . . .'

Maigret went on eating and drinking.

'A woman's hair, or a child's?'

'The official pathologist says it's a woman's. I left him a few hairs, and he promised to examine them thoroughly.'

'The post-mortem?'

'All over by ten o'clock. Age about thirty-two. Height 5 ft 6½ ins. No congenital defects, but one kidney was in a bad way, suggesting that the man was a heavy drinker. The stomach still contained tea and some almost completely digested food that couldn't be analysed then and there. They'll tackle that tomorrow. Once the tests are finished, the body will be taken to the Medico-Legal Institute and put on ice.'

Maigret wiped his mouth, returned to his favourite position in front of the stove, and held out a hand into which Torrence, as though by a conditioned reflex, again put his packet of tobacco.

'As for me,' said the Superintendent, 'I saw Pietr, or the man who's taken his place, settle into the Majestic and have dinner with the Mortimer-Levingstons, who seemed to be expecting him.'

'The multi-millionaires?'

'Yes. After dinner, Pietr went up to his suite. I warned the American, who went upstairs himself. The three of them must have intended to go out together, because a moment later Mrs Mortimer-Levingston came down, all dolled up for the evening. Ten minutes afterwards it was discovered that both men had disappeared.

'Pietr had changed from his dinner-jacket into something less conspicuous. He had put on a cap, too, and the porter took him for one of the kitchen staff. Mortimer-Levingston went off just as he was, in evening dress.'

Torrence said nothing. There was a long silence, during which they could hear the storm rattling the windows and the stove roaring.

'The luggage?' asked Torrence at last.

'Been through it. Nothing! Clothes. Linen. Suits. Shirts. Underwear. The complete outfit of a wealthy traveller. But not a single paper. The Mortimer-Levingston woman is convinced her husband has been murdered.'

A church bell rang somewhere. Maigret opened the desk drawer into which, that afternoon, he had thrust the telegrams about Pietr the Lett.

Then he looked at the map. He drew a line with his finger: Cracow, Bremen, Amsterdam, Brussels, Paris.

Near Saint-Quentin the finger paused for a moment: a man had died.

In Paris the line stopped abruptly. Two men had vanished, right in the Avenue des Champs-Élysées.

All that remained was some luggage in a hotel suite, and Mrs Mortimer-Levingston, as devoid of ideas as the wardrobe-trunk in the middle of the Latvian's bedroom.

Maigret's pipe was bubbling so exasperatingly that he took a bunch of feathers from another drawer and cleaned the stem; then he opened the stove and threw the dirty feathers into it.

Four of the beer-glasses were empty, their sides misted with thick froth. A man came out of one of the neighbouring offices, locked the door, and walked down the passage.

'One chap who's finished,' remarked Torrence. 'That's Lucas. He arrested two dope-peddlers this evening, after some mother's boy gave the show away.'

Maigret poked the stove and stood up again, red-faced. Absent-mindedly, he picked up the transparent envelope, took out the hair, and moved it about in the light from his lamp. Then he went back to the map. The invisible line marking the Latvian's journey described a definite curve, almost a semicircle.

Why go from Cracow up to Bremen, before coming down to Paris?

He was still holding the transparent envelope. 'This had a photograph in it,' he muttered to himself.

It was, in fact, the kind of envelope into which photographers put prints for their customers.

But it was of a size not seen nowadays except in villages and little country towns; what used to be called the 'album format'.

The photo it had once held must have been one of those pieces of cardboard half the size of a postcard, on which the actual picture was mounted, printed on a thin slip of glossy ivory-white paper.

'Is there anyone left in the laboratory?' the Superintendent asked suddenly.

'I imagine so. They must be working on the train business, developing their photos.'

There was only one full glass left on the table. Maigret emptied it at a gulp, and put on his jacket.

'Coming with me? That kind of photo usually has the photographer's name and address printed on it, incised or embossed.'

Torrence knew what he meant. They set out, following a maze of corridors and staircases, up to the attics of the Palais de Justice, and finally reached the Judicial Identification laboratory.

An expert took the envelope, felt it, almost seemed to sniff it. Then he sat down under a powerful lamp and pulled over a weird-looking machine mounted on wheels.

The principle is simple enough. If a piece of white paper is left for some time in contact with paper that is covered with print or written on in ink, whatever is thus printed or written on the second sheet will come off on to the first.

The result is invisible to the naked eye; but the transfer will show in a photograph.

Since there was a stove in the laboratory, Maigret inevitably drifted over to it. He stood there for nearly an hour, smoking pipe after pipe, while Torrence watched the photographer moving to and fro.

At last the door of a dark-room opened and a voice announced:

'Got it!'

'Well?'

'The photo was signed *Léon Moutel, art photographer, Quai des Belges, Fécamp.*'

It took an expert's instinct to read the faint marks on the plate, where Torrence, for instance, could see nothing but vague shadows.

'Want to see the photos of the body?' inquired the expert affably. 'They're magnificent! Although we were pretty short of space in that toilet in the train. Would you believe it, we had to sling the camera from the ceiling . . .'

'Is that an outside line?' Maigret interposed, pointing to the telephone.

'Yes. The switchboard operator leaves at nine o'clock. Then they connect me up with . . .'

The Superintendent rang up the Majestic. One of the interpreters took the call.

'Has Mr Mortimer-Levingston got back?'

'I will inquire, sir. Would you kindly tell me who . . .'

'The police.'

'He is not back.'

'And neither is Mr Oswald Oppenheim?'

'No.'

'What is Mrs Mortimer-Levingston doing?'

Silence.

'I asked you what Mrs Mortimer-Levingston was doing.'

'She . . . I believe she is in the bar.'

'In other words, she is drunk?'

'Well, she has had a few cocktails. She says she won't go up to her room again until her husband gets back. . . . Is it . . .'

'What?'

'Hello? This is the manager,' said a different voice. 'Are there any developments? Do you think the story will get into the papers?'

Cynically, Maigret rang off. To please the photographer, he glanced at the prints spread out on the driers; they were still damp and shiny.

Meanwhile he was saying to Torrence:

'You move into the Majestic, my lad. And take no notice whatsoever of the manager.'

'What about you, Chief?'

'I shall get back to my office. There's a train to Fécamp at half past five. Not worth going home and waking my wife. By the way – the Brasserie Dauphine will still be open. As you go past, order a glass of beer for me. . . .'

'Only one?' said Torrence, looking innocent.

'Yes, please, old chap. The waiter is bright enough to make it three or four. Tell him to bring a few sandwiches as well.'

One behind the other, they went down an interminable winding staircase.

The black-overalled photographer was left to the pleasure of contemplating the prints he had just made, which he now proceeded to number.

In an icy courtyard, the two policemen separated.

'If you go out of the Majestic for any reason, leave one of our fellows there!' enjoined the Superintendent. 'That's where I shall telephone if I need to.'

He went back to his office, and poked the stove as though he meant to break its bars.

CHAPTER 3

The Second Officer of the Seeteufel

LA BRÉAUTÉ station, where Superintendent Maigret left the main-line train from Paris to Le Havre at half past seven in the morning, gave him a foretaste of Fécamp.

An ill-lit refreshment room with grimy walls, and a buffet on which a few biscuits were mouldering and three bananas and five oranges were doing their best to form a pyramid.

The storm felt more violent here. The rain was coming down in buckets. To get from one platform to another meant wading up to one's knees in mud.

A repulsive little train, assembled from obsolete rolling-stock. Farms visible in faint outline in the pale daybreak, almost concealed by the streams of falling rain.

Fécamp! A dense reek of salt cod and herring. Stacks of barrels. Masts beyond the railway engines. A foghorn moaning somewhere.

'The Quai des Belges?'

Straight ahead. He only had to go on walking through the slimy puddles where fish scales glittered and fish offal lay rotting.

The art photographer was a shopkeeper and newsagent as well. He sold sou'westers, red sailcloth jerkins, seamen's jerseys, hempen rope, and New Year cards.

He was a puny, washed-out creature, who called his wife to the rescue as soon as the word 'police' was uttered. She was a handsome Norman type, who looked Maigret straight in the eye and almost seemed to be making advances to him.

'Could you tell me what photograph used to be in this envelope?'

It took a long time. Maigret had to prise the words out of the photographer one by one, doing his thinking for him.

To begin with, the photograph must be at least eight years

old, for he had given up making that format eight years ago, when he bought a new camera which took postcard-size photographs.

Who might have been photographed eight years ago? It took Monsieur Moutel a quarter of an hour to remember that he kept an album with a copy of every photograph produced in his studio.

His wife went to fetch it. Sailors went in and out. Children came to buy a pennyworth of sweets. Outside, the rigging creaked on the boats and the sea tumbled the pebbles against the breakwater.

Maigret, turning the pages of the album, gave a further detail:

'A young woman with very fine brown hair . . .'

That was enough.

'Madame Swaan!' exclaimed the photographer.

And he found the photo at once. It was the only time he had had a presentable sitter.

She was a pretty woman. She looked about twenty years old. The photo fitted the envelope perfectly.

'Who is she?'

'She still lives at Fécamp. But now she has a villa on the cliff, five minutes', walk from the Casino.'

'Married?'

'She wasn't in those days. She was the receptionist at the Railway Hotel.'

'Opposite the station, of course?'

'Yes, you must have seen it as you went by. She was an orphan, from a village near here. . . . Les Loges – do you know it? That's how she met a guest who was staying at the hotel – a foreigner. They got married. And now she lives in her villa, with her two children and a maid. . . .'

'Doesn't Monsieur Swaan live at Fécamp?'

There was a silence. The photographer and his wife exchanged glances. She spoke first.

'As you're from the police, we'd better tell you everything, hadn't we? In any case you'd find out. . . . It's nothing but rumours. . . . Monsieur Swaan is hardly ever at Fécamp. When he does come, he only stays a few days. ... Sometimes he doesn't even stay the night. ... The first time he arrived was soon after the war. The Newfoundland Fisheries were being restarted, after a five-year stoppage. ...

'The story was that he wanted to look into the question and invest money in the businesses that were being launched.

'He said he was a Norwegian. His first name is Olaf. The herring fishers, who sometimes go as far as Norway, say a lot of people there have that name. ...

'All the same, there was a rumour that he was really a German spy.

'So when he got married, people wouldn't have anything to do with his wife. ...

'Then it turned out he was a sailor, second officer of a German merchant vessel, and that was why he came so seldom. ...

'In the end the gossip died down, but people like us still don't trust him. ...'

'You say they have children?'

'Two. A little girl of three and a baby a few months old.'

Maigret detached the picture from the album and asked the way to the villa. It was still rather too early to call there.

For two hours he waited in a harbour café, listening to the fishermen discussing the herring season, which was in full swing. Five black trawlers were lying alongside the quay. Fish were being unloaded by the barrel and the air stank of them, in spite of the gale.

To get to the villa he went along the deserted promenade and round the closed casino, its walls still adorned with last summer's posters.

Finally he came to a steep path climbing up from the foot of the cliff. At intervals he passed the iron gate of a villa.

The one he was looking for turned out to be a comfortable-looking medium-sized red brick house. The garden, with its white gravel paths, was obviously well tended in the summer months, and there must be a fine view from the windows.

He rang the bell. A Great Dane came and sniffed at him through the gate – without barking, but looking all the fiercer for that. Maigret rang again, and a maid appeared. After shutting the dog into its kennel, she asked:

'What is it?'

She spoke with a local accent.

'I would like to see Monsieur Swaan, please.'

She seemed to hesitate.

'I don't know if Monsieur is at home. . . . I'll ask. . . .'

She had not opened the gate. It was still raining in torrents. Maigret was drenched.

He watched the servant go up the steps into the house. Then a curtain stirred at one of the windows. After a while the girl came back.

'Monsieur will not be home for several weeks. He's at Bremen. . . .'

'In that case I would like to speak to Madame Swaan.'

Again she hesitated, but finally opened the gate.

'Madame is not dressed yet. You will have to wait. . . .'

Dripping with water, he was shown into a trim living-room with white-curtained windows and a gleaming parquet floor.

The furniture was new, precisely the same as in any other middle-class home – good-quality stuff, in the style called 'modern' in 1900.

Light oak. Flowers in an 'artistic' stone jar in the middle of the table. Broderie anglaise table-mats.

But on a small side-table stood a magnificent embossed silver samovar, worth more than all the rest of the furniture put together.

There were sounds from somewhere on the first floor. Somewhere else, in one of the downstairs rooms, a baby was crying and another voice was speaking softly in a monotone, as though trying to comfort it.

At last, light footsteps came along the corridor. The door opened and Superintendent Maigret found himself confronted by a young woman who had dressed hurriedly in order to receive him.

She was of medium height, rather on the plump side, with a pretty, serious face that now wore an expression of vague uneasiness.

Nevertheless, she smiled as she said:

'Why didn't you sit down?'

Water was trickling from Maigret's overcoat, his trousers, and his shoes and forming little pools on the polished floor.

In such a state he could not possibly have sat down in one of the pale green velvet armchairs in that room.

'You are Madame Swaan, are you not?'

'Yes, Monsieur. . . .'

She looked inquiringly at him.

'Forgive me for disturbing you. It is just a formality. . . . I belong to the foreign supervisory department of the police force. We are making a census at the moment. . . .'

She said nothing. Her uneasiness seemed neither to increase nor to diminish.

'I believe Monsieur Swaan is of Swedish nationality?'

'No, Norwegian. . . . But to the French it is the same thing. . . . Even I, at first . . .'

'He is an officer in the merchant service?'

'Second officer of the *Seeteufel* of Bremen . . .'

'That's it. . . . So he works for a German company?'

Her colour deepened.

'The owners are German, yes. . . . At least on paper. . . .'

'Which means to say?'

'I don't see why I shouldn't tell you. . . . I expect you know that since the war there has been a lot of unemployment among merchant seamen. In this town alone you'll hear of several captains who could not get a boat and have had to sign on as second or third officers. Others have joined the Newfoundland or North Sea fishing fleets.'

She spoke rather hurriedly, but her voice was soft and steady.

'My husband didn't want to sign on for the Pacific, where there are more opportunities, because he would have been away from Europe for two years at a time. Soon after we were married, some Americans fitted out the *Seeteufel* in the name of a German ship-owner. And the reason Olaf came to Fécamp in the first place was to find out if there were any other schooners for sale here.

'Now you see what I mean. . . . They were to smuggle
drink to the United States. . . .

'Several big companies were floated, with American money.
Some are registered in France, others in Holland or Germany.

'It's for one of these that my husband is really working.
The *Seeteufel* is on what's called the "Rum Avenue run".

'So he has no connexion with Germany. . . .'

'Is he at sea just now?' asked Maigret, his eyes still on the
pretty face – which had a frank, even at times a touching
expression.

'I don't think so. You must realize that the ship doesn't sail
as regularly as a liner. But I always try to calculate the *Seeteufel*'s position as exactly as I can. At this moment she should
be at Bremen, or very nearly.'

'Have you ever been to Norway?'

'Never! I've hardly ever left Normandy. Just two or three
times, for short visits to Paris.'

'With your husband?'

'Yes. On our honeymoon, for one thing.'

'He's a fair-skinned man, isn't he?'

'Yes. . . . Why do you ask?'

'With a small, fair moustache, clipped short?'

'Yes . . . in fact I can show you a photograph of him.'

She opened a door and went out. Maigret heard her moving
about in the next room.

She was away longer than seemed reasonable. And from
other parts of the house came the sounds of doors opening and
shutting and of unaccountable footsteps coming and going.

At last she reappeared, looking rather disturbed and hesitant.

'I'm sorry,' she said. 'I can't put my hand on that photograph. With children about, the house is always in a
muddle. . . .'

'One more question. . . . To how many people have you
given a copy of this photo?'

He showed her the proof that the photographer had given
him. Madame Swaan blushed scarlet.

'I don't understand . . .' she faltered.

'Your husband has a copy of it, no doubt?'

'Yes. . . . We were engaged when . . .'

'No other man has a copy?'

She was on the verge of tears. Her lips trembled, betraying her bewilderment.

'No. . . .'

'Thank you, Madame. . . .'

As he was leaving, a little girl slipped out into the hall. Maigret had no need to inspect her features closely. She was the living image of Pietr the Lett!

'Olga!' her mother scolded, pushing the child towards a half-open door.

The Superintendent found himself outside again, in the rain and the blustering wind.

'Good-bye, Madame. . . .'

He caught a last glimpse of her as the door closed, and he felt he was leaving her in distress, after taking her by surprise in her cosy house.

And there were other subtle, indefinable signs of anxiety in the young mother's eyes as she closed the door behind him.

CHAPTER 4

The Drunken Russian

THERE are things that one doesn't boast about, which would sound comic if described in words, yet which call for a certain degree of heroism.

Maigret had had no sleep. From half past five to eight o'clock that morning he had been jolting along in draughty trains.

Ever since La Bréauté he had been drenched to the skin. Now, dirty water squelched out of his shoes at every step, his bowler hat was shapeless, his coat and jacket wringing wet.

The wind was hurling the rain against him so that it felt like repeated body-blows. The lane was deserted. It was no more than a steep path between garden walls, with a stream rushing down the middle.

He stood there for quite a time. Even his pipe, in his pocket, was wet. There was nowhere close to the house where he could hide. The best he could do was to flatten himself against a wall and wait.

Anyone who went by would see him and look round. He might have to wait there for hours and hours. He had no definite proof that there was a man in the house. And if there were, would he feel inclined to go out?

All the same, Maigret, glumly stuffing tobacco into his wet pipe, pressed back as far as possible into a slight bend in the wall.

This was no job for an officer of the Judicial Police. It was beginner's stuff. He had kept watch like this a hundred times, when he was between twenty-two and thirty years old.

He had a terrible job striking a match. The sandpaper was peeling off the box. If one of the wooden chips had not miraculously caught light at last, he would perhaps have gone away.

From where he stood, he could see nothing but a low wall and the green-painted gate of the villa. His feet were in a patch of brambles. There was a cold wind blowing down his neck.

Fécamp lay below, but he could not see it. He could only hear the crashing waves, with now and then the wail of a foghorn or the sound of a passing car.

He had been mounting guard for half an hour when a woman who looked like a cook came up the path, carrying a basket of provisions. She did not see Maigret till she was actually passing him. His huge form, standing motionless against a wall in that wind-swept lane, frightened her so badly that she began to run.

She probably worked in one of the houses higher up the hill. A few minutes later a man appeared at the bend in the lane; a woman joined him, then the pair of them went back indoors.

The situation was ridiculous. The Superintendent knew there was not one chance in ten that his vigil would lead to any result.

But he stuck to it, because of a vague impression; he could not even have called it a presentiment. It was more like a private theory, which he had never even worked out but which just stuck nebulously at the back of his mind; he called it the theory of the chink.

Every criminal, every gangster, is a human being. But he is first and foremost a gambler, an adversary; that is how the police are inclined to regard him, and as such they usually try to tackle him.

When a crime or felony is committed, it is dealt with on the strength of various more or less impersonal data. It is a problem with one – or more – unknown factors, to be solved, if possible, in the light of reason.

Maigret used the same procedure as anyone else. And like everyone else he employed the wonderful techniques devised by Bertillon, Reiss, Locard, and others, which have turned police work into a science.

But above all he sought for, waited for, and pounced on

the chink. In other words, the moment when the human being showed through the gambler.

At the Majestic he had been confronted by the gambler. Here, he sensed a difference. This quiet, neat villa was not one of the pawns in the game that Pietr the Lett was playing. That young woman, and the children Maigret had glimpsed and heard, belonged to an entirely different material and moral universe.

That was why he waited – though crossly, for he was much too fond of his big iron stove and his office, with the frothing beer-glasses on the table, to be anything but miserable in this clammy storm.

He had taken up his position shortly after ten o'clock. It was half past twelve by the time footsteps crunched on the gravel; the gate was opened by a quick, deft hand, and a figure appeared ten yards away.

The lie of the land allowed Maigret no retreat. So he stayed where he was, motionless, or rather, inert, planted firmly on legs to which his rain-soaked trousers clung in large, smooth patches.

The man who came out of the villa was wearing a shabby, belted trench-coat, its threadbare collar turned up. There was a grey cap on his head.

Thus clad, he looked very young. He set off down the hill, with his hands in his pockets and his hunched shoulders shivering because of the sudden change of temperature.

He had to pass within a yard of the Superintendent. That was the moment he chose to slacken his pace, take a packet of cigarettes from his pocket, and light one.

As though he were deliberately showing his face in the brightest possible light and letting the police officer have a good look at it!

Maigret allowed him to go a few steps farther, and then, frowning, set off in pursuit. His pipe had gone out. Every inch of his person expressed ill humour, coupled with an impatient determination to understand.

For the man in the trench-coat was and yet was not like the Lett. The same height – about five foot six. The same age, at a pinch, though in those clothes he looked more like twenty-six than thirty-two.

There was no reason why he should not be the subject of the 'verbal portrait' that Maigret knew by heart and of which he had a copy in his pocket.

And yet this was a different man! His eyes, for instance, had a softer, more pensive expression. They were a lighter grey, as though watered down by the rain.

He had no small, fair, toothbrush moustache. But that was not the only change in his appearance.

Other points occurred to Maigret. He was not dressed at all in the style of a merchant navy officer. Or even in a way befitting the villa, with its atmosphere of middle-class comfort.

His shoes were shabby, down at heel. He had turned up his trousers because of the mud, and the Superintendent saw that he was wearing grey cotton socks, faded and clumsily darned.

The trench-coat was all spotted and stained. The whole effect suggested a type well known to Maigret – the European vagrant, nearly always from Eastern Europe, who haunts the lowest type of Paris lodging-house, sometimes sleeps in railway stations, seldom ventures into the provinces, and then travels third-class or ticketless on the steps of trains or in goods trucks.

A few minutes later he had proof of this. Fécamp had no real brothels; but behind the harbour there were two or three sordid dives more popular with stokers than with fishermen.

Ten yards away from these establishments stood a respectable, clean, well-lit café.

But the man in the trench-coat went straight past this, stepped unhesitatingly into the most squalid of the dives, and propped his elbows on the bar with a gesture that spoke for itself.

It was a familiar gesture, casual, vulgar. Even had he wanted to, Maigret could not have imitated it.

He went in, too. The man had ordered an absinthe substitute, and stood without a word, vacant-eyed, showing no interest in Maigret, who stood beside him.

Beneath the man's unbuttoned coat collar, the Superintendent saw a grubby shirt: another thing that cannot be faked! That shirt, and that collar, reduced to a mere string, had been worn for days and nights, more likely for weeks on end. The wearer had slept in them, heaven knows where. He had sweated in them, been rained on in them.

The suit had a certain style about it, but it bore the same marks, spoke of the same filthy, vagabond life.

'Same again.'

The man's glass was empty. The café-keeper refilled it and poured out a dram of spirits for Maigret.

'So here you are again, eh?'

The man made no reply; he drank his second apéritif at one gulp, like the first, and pushed his glass back across the counter, indicating that he wanted another refill.

'Will you have something to eat? I've got some soused herring. . . .'

Maigret had manoeuvred himself across to a little stove and now stood with his back to it, as shiny as a wet umbrella. The patron was not to be discouraged. With a wink at the Superintendent, he spoke to the customer in the trench-coat again.

'By the way, there was a fellow-countryman of yours in here last week. A Russian from Archangel. He came off a Swedish three-master that had to put in here because of the storm. He hadn't much time to get tight, I can tell you! They had a hell of a lot of work. . . . Sails torn, two masts gone – the devil's own mess.'

The other man, now at his fourth absinthe, was drinking with concentration. The *patron* filled his glass the moment it was empty, each time with a conspiratorial wink at Maigret.

'As for Captain Swaan, he's not been back since the last time I saw you. . . .'

Maigret started. The man in the trench-coat, who had just emptied his fifth glass of neat spirits, lurched across to the stove, knocking into the Superintendent, and held out his hands to warm them.

'I'll have a herring after all,' he said.

He spoke with a fairly strong accent – Russian, so far as Maigret could judge.

There they were, side by side, practically rubbing shoulders. Several times the man passed his hand over his face, and his eyes were becoming dimmer and dimmer.

'Where's my glass?' he demanded impatiently.

It had to be put into his hand. As he drank, he stared hard at Maigret and screwed up his face in disgust.

There was no mistaking his expression! And as though to make his sentiments even clearer, he flung his glass on the floor, clutched the back of a chair to steady himself, and muttered something in a foreign language.

The *patron*, slightly perturbed, invented some reason for passing close to Maigret and said in what was meant to be a whisper, but loud enough for not a word to escape the Russian:

'Take no notice! He's always like that. . . .'

The man laughed, a smothered, drunken laugh. He subsided on to the chair, dropped his head into his hands, and sat motionless until a plate of soused herring was thrust on to the table between his elbows.

The café-keeper shook him by the shoulder.

'Eat! It'll do you good. . . .'

The man laughed again, with a bitter coughing sound. He turned his head, looking for Maigret, stared impudently at him and pushed the plate of herring off the table.

'Wan'a drink!'

The *patron* raised his hands to heaven and growled apologetically:

'Oh, these Russians!'

And he swivelled a finger round on his forehead.

Maigret had pushed back his bowler hat. Grey steam was rising from his clothes. He had only reached his second dram.

'I'll have a herring,' he said.

He was eating it with a piece of bread when the Russian rose shakily to his feet, looked round as though not knowing what to do next, and laughed jeeringly, for the third time, as his eyes fell on Maigret.

Then he reeled over to the bar, took a glass off the shelf, and lifted a bottle out of the pewter basin where it was standing in cold water.

He helped himself without looking to see what it was, clicking his tongue as he drank.

Finally he produced a hundred-franc note from his pocket.

'That enough, clot?' he demanded, and tossed the note into the air. The publican had to fish it out of the sink.

The Russian tugged at the door handle, but the door would not open. There was nearly a row, because the café-keeper tried to help the man, who kept pushing him away with his elbow.

At last the trench-coat vanished into the mist and rain, going along the quay towards the station.

'Queer fellow!' sighed the publican to Maigret, who was paying his bill.

'Does he come here often?'

'Every now and then. . . . He once spent the night on the bench where you were sitting. . . . He's Russian. So I was told by some Russian sailors that came in one day when he was here. It seems he's an educated man. Did you notice his hands?'

'Don't you think he's very like Captain Swaan?'

'Oh, you know him? Yes, indeed! Not so much that one could take one for the other, but all the same . . . For a long time I thought they were brothers. . . .'

The putty-coloured figure disappeared round a corner. Maigret began to hurry.

He caught up with the Russian just as he was entering the third-class waiting-room at the station, where he slumped on to a bench and put his head between his hands again.

An hour later they were seated in the same compartment, together with a cattle-dealer from Yvetot, who proceeded to tell Maigret funny stories in the Normandy patois, nudging him with his elbow now and then to call his attention to their neighbour.

The Russian slid down imperceptibly until he was huddled on the seat with his pallid face sunk on his chest and his mouth open; his breath reeked of alcohol.

CHAPTER 5

At the Roi de Sicile

THE Russian woke at La Bréauté and did not go to sleep again. Indeed, the Havre–Paris express was so full that Maigret and his companion had to stand in the corridor, outside the doors of two neighbouring compartments, looking out at the blurred scenery which rushed past the windows and was gradually swallowed up by the falling night.

The man in the trench-coat took not the slightest notice of the police officer. Nor did he try to escape from him in the crowd at Saint-Lazare station.

On the contrary, he went slowly down the wide staircase, noticed that his packet of cigarettes was soaking wet, bought another at the tobacconist's shop in the station, almost stopped at the refreshment bar. Changing his mind, he set out along the pavement, dragging his feet – a depressing figure, for he seemed utterly indifferent to his surroundings, so listless as to be incapable of any response.

It is a long walk from Saint-Lazare to the Hôtel de Ville, right through the centre of the city, and between six and seven in the evening crowds are pouring out on to the pavements and cars rush along the streets in a steady flow, like blood circulating through the human body.

The narrow-shouldered Russian, in his tightly-belted raincoat with its mud stains and grease spots, and his down-at-heel shoes, stumbled through the bustle, under the lights, getting jostled and pushed, never pausing or looking behind him.

He took the shortest route, down the rue du 4 Septembre and through Les Halles; he obviously knew the way well.

Reaching the Jewish quarter, centred on its nucleus, the rue des Rosiers, he walked past shops with Yiddish inscriptions, kosher butchers, and bakeries that displayed unleavened bread.

At the corner of an alley as long and dark as a tunnel, a woman tried to take his arm; but she released him, looking scared, without his having uttered a word.

At last he came to the rue du Roi de Sicile, a crooked street fringed with blind alleys, narrow passages, and crowded courtyards – still half Jewish, but already half a Polish colony – and here, after two hundred yards, he turned into the lobby of a hotel.

The name of the place, displayed in ceramic letters, was Au Roi de Sicile.

Below it were inscriptions in Hebrew, Polish, and other incomprehensible languages, probably including Russian.

Next door was a yawning gap with the remains of a house that had been shored up by beams.

It was still raining, but this backwater was sheltered from the wind.

Maigret heard the sound of a window being slammed on the third floor of the hotel. Showing no more hesitation than the Russian, he went in.

No door to the lobby: the stairs went straight up. On the first floor was a kind of glass-fronted box, where a Jewish family sat eating.

The Superintendent knocked. Instead of opening the door, someone pushed up a little window. A sour smell came out. The Jew wore a black skull-cap. His fat wife went on eating.

'What do you want?'

'Police! What is the name of the resident who has just come in?'

The man muttered something in his own language, produced a dog-eared ledger from a drawer, and pushed it through the window without a word.

At the same moment Maigret sensed that he was being watched from the dark staircase. Turning his head sharply, he saw an eye glittering about ten steps above him.

'Which room?'

'Thirty-two.'

He turned the pages of the register, and read:

'Fédor Yurovich, aged 28, born at Vilna, labourer, and Anna Gorskin, aged 25, born at Odessa, no occupation.'

The Jew had returned to his seat and his meal, like a man with a clear conscience. Maigret drummed on the pane, and he got up again, slowly and reluctantly.

'How long has he been living here?'

'About three years.'

'And Anna Gorskin?'

'She was here before him. . . . Four and a half years, maybe.'

'What do they live on?'

'You saw him. He's a working man.'

'Come off it!' Maigret exclaimed, in a tone that effectively changed the other man's attitude.

'The rest is no business of mine, is it?' he remarked, his manner more ingratiating. 'He pays regularly. He comes and goes; it's not my job to trail him. . . .'

'Does he have visitors?'

'Now and then. . . . I've got more than sixty residents, and I can't keep an eye on all of them. So long as they don't get up to any mischief! . . . Anyhow, if you're from the police, you must know the house. My books have always been in order. Sergeant Vermouillet will tell you so. He's the one who calls here every week. . . .'

Maigret suddenly wheeled round and called out:

'Come down, Anna Gorskin!'

There was a faint sound on the stairs, and then came footsteps. Finally, a woman emerged into the ray of light.

She looked older than her registered age of 25. A question of race, no doubt. Like many Jewish women of her age, she had put on weight, but without losing all trace of beauty. She had wonderful eyes, the whites very clear and brilliant and the pupils velvety black.

But in other respects she displayed a slovenliness which

spoilt the impression. Her black hair was greasy and unkempt, hanging down to her shoulders in thick strands. She wore a shabby dressing-gown, which hung open, showing her underwear. Her stockings were rolled down below podgy knees.

'What were you doing on the stairs?'

'I live here. . . .'

Maigret realized at once what kind of woman he had to deal with. Passionate and shameless, she was spoiling for a fight. At the slightest excuse she would start a scene, rouse the whole house with her screams, and probably make the wildest accusations.

Perhaps she knew her position was unassailable. At any rate she was staring defiantly at the enemy.

'You'd do better to keep an eye on your boy-friend.'

'That's my business.'

The hotel-keeper stood at his little window, turning his head from left to right and back again with a grieved reproachful expression; but there was amusement in his eyes.

'When did Fédor leave you?'

'Last night. . . . At eleven o'clock.'

She was lying, obviously. But a head-on clash with her would do no good. Unless he went the whole hog and took her off to the station.

'Where does he work?'

'Where he pleases.'

Her breasts were quivering under the half-open dressing-gown. Her lip curled disdainfully.

'What do the police want with Fédor?'

Maigret thought it better to lower his voice as he said:

'Get along upstairs. . . .'

'When I choose! I don't take orders from you.'

To retort would merely provoke some ridiculous incident which might prejudice his investigation.

Maigret closed the ledger and handed it back to the hotel-keeper.

'It's in order, isn't it?' said the latter, who had signed to the young woman to keep quiet.

But she stayed where she was, hands on hips, half of her

body visible in the light from the lodge, the other half in darkness.

The Superintendent looked at her again. She met his eye and could not resist muttering:

'Oh, I'm not afraid of you!'

He shrugged his shoulders and went away downstairs, brushing against the whitewashed wall on either side.

In the passage he ran into two collarless Poles, who looked away when they saw him coming.

The street was wet, the cobbles gleaming.

In every corner, in every little patch of darkness, up the blind alleys and the corridors, one could sense the presence of a swarming mass of humanity, a sly, shameful life. Shadows slunk along the walls. The shops were selling goods unknown to French people even by name.

Less than a hundred yards away were the rue de Rivoli and the rue Saint-Antoine – wide and well-lit, with their buses, their shops, and their police.

Maigret stopped a flap-eared urchin who was running past, by grabbing his shoulder, and said:

'Go and fetch me a policeman from the Place Saint-Paul.'

But the child stared at him, completely baffled, and stammered something unintelligible. He did not know a word of French!

The Superintendent's eye fell on a ragged figure.

'Here's five francs,' he said. 'Take this note to the cop in the Place Saint-Paul.'

The tramp understood. Ten minutes later a uniformed policeman appeared.

'Ring up the Judicial Police and tell them to send me an inspector at once. Dufour, if possible.'

He paced up and down for a good half-hour after that. People went into the hotel. Others came out. But the second window from the left on the third floor was still lit up.

Anna Gorskin appeared in the doorway. She had put on a greenish coat over her dressing-gown. Her head was bare, and in spite of the rain her feet were shod in red satin mules.

She splashed across the street. Maigret drew back into the shadows. She went into a shop, came out again after a few minutes with her arms full of little white parcels, topped by two bottles, and disappeared back into the hotel.

Inspector Dufour arrived at last. He was a man of 35 who spoke three languages fairly fluently; this made him useful, despite his passion for complicating even the simplest matters.

He would work up an ordinary burglary or a smash-and-grab case into a mysterious drama and then lose his head in the middle of it.

But being uncommonly tenacious, he was the very man for a specific assignment, such as watching a house or trailing somebody.

Maigret gave him a description of Fédor Yurovich and his mistress.

'I'll send you one of the other chaps. If either of those two comes out, you follow him or her; but someone must stay here on guard. Understand?'

'This is still the *North Star* business? The Mafia was responsible for that, wasn't it?'

The Superintendent thought it best to go away. A quarter of an hour later he was back at the Quai des Orfèvres, had sent another detective to join Dufour, and was bending over his stove and cursing Jean, who had not managed to get it red hot.

His wet overcoat, on its hanger, was quite stiff and still kept the shape of his shoulders.

'Did my wife ring up?'

'Yes, this morning. We told her you were off on a job.'

She was accustomed to that. He knew that when he got home she would just kiss him, move her saucepans about on the stove, and fill a plate with savoury stew. At most she might venture – once he had sat down to table and she was watching him with her chin propped on her hands – to inquire:

'Everything all right?'

Whether at midday or at five in the afternoon, he would find a meal ready just the same.

'Torrence?' he asked Jean.

'He telephoned at seven o'clock this morning.'

'From the Majestic?'

'I don't know. He asked if you had left.'

'And then?'

'He rang up again in the afternoon, at ten past five. He asked me to tell you he was waiting for you.'

Maigret had had nothing to eat all day except a herring. He stood for a few minutes in front of his stove, which was beginning to roar, for he had an inimitable gift for coaxing the most sullen coals into flame.

At last he strode heavily to the cupboard, which concealed a wash-basin, a towel, a mirror, and a suitcase. He carried the suitcase into the middle of the room, undressed, put on dry clothes and a clean shirt, and ran hesitant fingers across his unshaven chin.

'Oh, never mind. . . .'

He threw a longing glance at the stove which was now burning so well, placed two chairs close to it, and draped his wet garments carefully over them. The last of the previous night's sandwiches was still lying on his desk and he wolfed it down, standing ready to leave. But there was no beer, and his throat felt rather dry.

'If anything turns up for me, I'm at the Majestic,' he said to Jean. 'Tell them to telephone me there.'

And at last he settled back into a taxi.

CHAPTER 6

Third Interval

MAIGRET found that his colleague Torrence was not in the hall, but in a room on the first floor, where an excellent dinner was being served. The Sergeant gave the ghost of a wink.

'It's the manager!' he explained. 'He'd rather have me up here than downstairs. He almost implored me to accept this room and the delicious meals he's been sending up to me.'

Speaking softly, he pointed to a door.

'The Mortimer-Levingstons are through there. . . .'

'So Mortimer-Levingston got back?'

'About six o'clock this morning – wet, muddy, and furious, with his clothes all covered in chalk, or whitewash.'

'What did he say?'

'Nothing. He tried to get up to his room without being seen. But they told him his wife was waiting for him in the bar. And she was! She had finally invited a Brazilian couple to drink with her. The bar stayed open just for them. She was dreadfully tight.'

'So then?'

'He turned pale. His lips curled. He nodded curtly to the Brazilians and then took hold of his wife by the waist and dragged her away without a word. I think she must have slept until four in the afternoon. There wasn't a sound from their suite before that. Then I heard whispers. Mortimer-Levingston rang downstairs for the newspapers.'

'They said nothing about the business, I hope?'

'Nothing. They obeyed instructions. Just a short paragraph to say a body's been found in the *North Star* and the police think it's suicide.'

'What happened next?'

'The waiter brought them up some *citron pressé*. At six o'clock Mortimer-Levingston came down to the hall, looking worried; he passed close by me two or three times. He sent off cables in cipher to his New York bank and to his secretary, who's been in London for the last few days.'

'Is that all?'

'At the moment they're just finishing dinner. Oysters, roast chicken, and salad. I get told about everything that goes on. The manager is so delighted to have shut me up here that he can't do too much for me. For instance, he came up just now to tell me that the Mortimer-Levingstons have seats for the play at the Gymnase – a four-act thing called *L'Épopée*. I forget who it's by....'

'What about Pietr's rooms?'

'Nothing doing. Nobody has been in there. I locked the door and stuffed a little ball of wax into the lock, so no one can get in without my finding out....'

Maigret had picked up a leg of chicken and was gnawing it unashamedly, while looking round in vain for a stove. In the end he sat down on the radiator and inquired:

'Anything to drink?'

Torrence poured him out a glass of excellent white Mâcon, and he swallowed it with relish. At that moment there was a light knock on the door and a servant came in, looking furtive.

'The manager sent me to tell you that Mr and Mrs Mortimer-Levingston have ordered their car.'

Maigret looked at the table, still loaded with food; his face wore the same mournful expression with which he had gazed at his office stove.

'I'll go,' he said regretfully. 'You stay here.'

He tidied himself up a little in front of the mirror, wiped his mouth and chin. A moment later he was waiting in a taxi for the Mortimer-Levingstons to come out to their car.

They soon appeared, he in a black overcoat which hid his evening dress, she swathed in furs as on the previous night.

She must be tired, for her husband was supporting her discreetly with one hand. The car started without a sound.

Maigret did not know that the Gymnase was having a first night, and he almost failed to get in. Municipal Guards were lined up on the pavement, and an awning stretched from the entrance to the kerb, where a small crowd had gathered, in spite of the rain, to watch the invited audience emerge from their cars.

The Superintendent had to ask to see the manager, and was kept hanging about in passages, looking conspicuous, the only man in a lounge suit.

'It's not that I object!' exclaimed the frenzied manager, waving his hands. 'But you are the twentieth person that's asked me for "a seat in a corner"! There isn't a seat left! And you're not even wearing a dinner-jacket!'

He was being summoned from all sides.

'You see! Put yourself in my shoes!'

In the end Maigret stood with his back to a door, among the usherettes and programme-sellers.

The Mortimer-Levingstons had a box. There were six people in it, including a princess and a cabinet minister. People went in and out. Hands were kissed and smiles exchanged.

The curtain rose to reveal a sunny garden. There were cries of 'Hush!' Whispers. Stumbling feet. Then the first actor's voice was heard, still hesitant but growing firmer, building up atmosphere.

But late-comers were still pushing in, and the cries of 'Hush!' began again. Somewhere, a woman tittered.

Mortimer-Levingston looked more aristocratic than ever. Evening dress suited him wonderfully, the white shirt-front setting off his sallow complexion.

Had he seen Maigret, or had he not? An usherette brought the Superintendent a stool, which he was obliged to share with a stout lady in black silk, the mother of one of the actresses.

First interval. Second interval. Comings and goings between the boxes. Spurious exhilaration. Greetings exchanged between the stalls and the dress circle.

The corridors, the foyer, and even the stairs were buzzing

like a hive of bees. Names were whispered, the names of maharajahs, financiers, statesmen, artists.

Mortimer-Levingston left his seat three times, appearing first in a stage box and then in the stalls, chatting with a former Prime Minister, whose booming laugh could be heard twenty rows away.

End of the third act. Flowers on the stage. An ovation for one skinny actress. The banging of tipped-up seats, the clatter of feet surging across the parquet.

When Maigret looked round at the Americans' box, Mortimer-Levingston had vanished.

Fourth and last act. This was the time for anyone who had any pretext for doing so to make for the wings and the actors' and actresses' dressing-rooms. Other people were besieging the cloakrooms or worrying about cars and taxis.

Maigret wasted a good ten minutes hunting round the theatre. Then he had to go outside, hatless and coatless, to question the police, the commissionaire, and the Municipal Guards.

At last he was told that Mortimer's olive-green limousine had just left. Someone showed him where it had been parked, outside a dive frequented by programme-sellers.

The car had driven off towards the Porte Saint-Martin. The American had not collected his coat and hat.

There were groups of spectators outside, enjoying the fresh air in any spot where they could find shelter from the rain.

The Superintendent smoked his pipe, with his hands in his pockets and a stubborn, withdrawn, angry face. The bell began to ring. People streamed back into the theatre. Even the Municipal Guards disappeared, to watch the last act.

The Boulevards looked dishevelled, as they do at eleven o'clock at night. The streaks of rain falling past the street lamps were thinning. A cinema was spewing out its audience, while the staff turned out the lights and carried the notices inside before closing for the night.

People were gathered under a street lamp, waiting for a bus. When it came there were squabbles, because the queue-ticket dispenser had run out. A policeman intervened, and long after the bus had gone was still in heated argument with a fat indignant man.

At last a limousine glided alongside the kerb. Almost before it stopped, Mortimer-Levingston, bare-headed, still in his evening clothes, opened the door, bounded up the steps of the theatre, and disappeared into the warmly lighted corridor.

Maigret looked at the chauffeur, one-hundred-per-cent American, hard-featured, with a jutting jaw, motionless in his seat as though his uniform held him rigid.

The commissionaire opened one of the quilted doors just a crack. Mortimer-Levingston was standing up at the back of his box. An actor was speaking disjointed, sardonic phrases. The curtain fell. Flowers. A burst of applause.

A rush for the doors. Cries of 'Hush!' The actor announced the author's name, and then fetched him from the stage box to take a call.

Mortimer-Levingston was kissing some hands, shaking others, giving a hundred-franc tip to the woman who brought his coat and hat.

His wife was pale, with mauve circles under her eyes. After they got into the car there was a moment of indecision.

The couple were arguing. Mrs Mortimer-Levingston was protesting irritably. Her husband lit a cigarette and closed his lighter with an angry snap.

Finally he said something into the speaking-trumpet, and the car drove off, followed by Maigret's taxi.

It was half past twelve. Rue La Fayette. The whitish pillars of the Trinité church, surrounded by scaffolding. Rue de Clichy.

The limousine stopped in the rue Fontaine outside Pickwick's Bar. Commissionaire in blue and gold. Cloakroom. Red curtain held back; the sound of a tango.

Maigret followed and sat down near the door, at a table

which must always have been empty, for it stood right in the draught.

The Mortimer-Levingstons had sat down close to the jazz band. He was looking at the menu, giving his order. A professional dancer stopped in front of Mrs Mortimer-Levingston, with a low bow.

She rose and danced. Levingston's eyes followed her with a curious persistence. She exchanged a few words with her partner, but did not once glance towards the corner where Maigret was sitting.

Here, among the evening dresses and dinner-jackets, there were a few foreigners in informal dress.

The Superintendent waved away a dance hostess who made as if to sit down at his table. The compulsory bottle of champagne was placed before him.

Paper festoons dangled everywhere. Balls of cotton wool were flying through the air. One hit Maigret on the nose, and he scowled at the old lady who had thrown it at him.

Mrs Mortimer-Levingston had returned to her seat. Her partner roamed round the floor and then made for the exit, lighting a cigarette.

Suddenly he lifted a corner of the red velvet curtain, and disappeared. About three minutes elapsed before it occurred to Maigret to put his head outside.

The dancer was not there.

The rest of the evening was long and dreary. The Mortimer-Levingstons ate a copious supper – caviar, *truffes au champagne, homard à l'américaine*, cheese.

Mrs Mortimer-Levingston did not dance again.

Maigret hated champagne, but he sipped it because he was thirsty. There were some salted almonds on his table; unfortunately he ate them, and they parched his tongue.

He looked at his watch: two o'clock.

The nightclub was emptying now. A girl dancer did her number, which was received with complete indifference. A drunken foreigner with three women at his table was making more noise than all the rest of the customers put together.

The dance partner, who had returned after a quarter of an

hour, had partnered several other ladies. But now it was over. The place had an air of weariness.

Mrs Mortimer-Levingston was grey-faced, with drooping eyelids.

Her husband beckoned to the attendant, who brought her fur wrap and his overcoat and opera hat.

Maigret had the impression that the dancer, standing beside the saxophonist, was watching him anxiously, while making conversation.

He summoned the *maître d'hôtel*, who kept him waiting, so that several moments were lost.

When the Superintendent finally got outside, the Americans' car was turning the corner of the rue Notre-Dame-de-Lorette. Half a dozen empty taxis were waiting at the kerb.

He went towards one of them.

A shot rang out, and Maigret put his hand to his chest, looked round, saw nothing, but heard footsteps hurrying away down the rue Pigalle.

He went on for several yards, as though propelled by his own momentum. The doorman ran up to support him. People were coming out of Pickwick's to see what had happened. Among them, Maigret noticed the tense face of the male dancer.

CHAPTER 7

Maigret Gives Up the Game

TAXI drivers who work the night shift in Montmartre understand at the slightest hint – often, indeed with no explanation at all.

When the shot was fired, one of those waiting outside Pickwick's Bar had been about to open the door of his cab for Maigret. He did not know the Superintendent, but may have guessed from his bearing that he was a police officer.

People were running from a small café across the street. In a few seconds there would be quite a crowd surrounding the wounded man. At this point the driver sprang to the aid of the doorman, who was holding Maigret up but did not know what to do with him. And in less than half a minute the taxi was driving away, with Maigret inside.

The taxi drove straight on for about ten minutes, and then stopped in an empty street. The driver got out, opened the door, and saw his passenger sitting in an almost natural position, with one hand inside his jacket.

'I see it's nothing serious; I thought not. Where shall I take you?'

Maigret looked rather upset, nevertheless – precisely because the wound was only superficial. The bullet had torn the flesh on his chest, grazed past a rib, and come out again near the shoulder-blade.

'Police Headquarters.'

The driver grunted something inaudible. On the way, the Superintendent changed his mind.

'Take me to the Majestic – the tradesmen's entrance, in the rue de Ponthieu.'

He had rolled his handkerchief into a ball and pressed it against the wound, and now he found the bleeding had stopped.

As they drove on towards the heart of Paris, his face began to show less pain and more anxiety.

The driver offered to help him out of the taxi, but he waved the man away and crossed the pavement with a firm step. He found the night porter dozing behind the window of his cubby-hole in the narrow passage.

'Has anything happened?'

'What do you mean?'

It was cold. Maigret went back to pay the taxi driver, who grumbled again at receiving only a hundred francs after his remarkable feat.

Even now Maigret made an impressive figure. The hand clutching the handkerchief was still pressed against his chest, under his coat. He held one shoulder higher than the other, and he was careful to husband his strength. He felt a bit light-headed. Sometimes he felt that he was wavering, and had to make an effort to pull himself together, to recover his usual exactness of perception and movement.

He went up an iron staircase, opened a door, found himself in a passage, lost his way in a labyrinth of corridors, and ended up on another staircase, identical with the first but bearing a different number.

He had lost his way in the back corridors of the hotel. Fortunately he ran into a white-capped assistant cook, who watched his approach with great alarm.

'Show me the way to the first floor – the room next to Mr Mortimer-Levingston's suite.'

But the young cook did not know the guests by name, and he was upset at the sight of the five streaks of blood Maigret had left on his face when he had rubbed his hand over it.

This giant roaming about in the narrow service corridors, with a black overcoat slung from his shoulders, the empty sleeves dangling, and one hand resting motionless on his chest, making a bulge under his jacket and waistcoat, quite terrified the young man.

'Police!' said Maigret impatiently.

He could feel dizziness coming over him. His wound was burning, as though long needles were stabbing through it.

In the end the cook set off, without a backward glance. A little later, Maigret felt a carpet under his feet. He realized that he was now out of the servants' quarters and in the hotel proper. He looked at the numbers of the rooms. He was on the odd-number side.

At last he met a scared chambermaid.

'Where is Mr Mortimer-Levingston's room?'

'On the floor below. . . . But . . . you . . .'

He went down one flight. Meanwhile a rumour was circulating among the staff that a strange, wounded, ghostly man was wandering about the hotel.

He leant against the wall for a moment and left a blood-stain on it, while three small drops, very dark red, fell on the carpet.

Eventually he found the Mortimer-Levingstons' suite, and next to it the door of the room Torrence was using. He went up to it, walking slightly askew, and pushed it open.

'Torrence!'

The lights were on. The table was still cluttered with plates of food and bottles.

Maigret's thick brows came together. He could not see his colleague. But there was a kind of hospital smell about the place.

He advanced a few paces, still feeling confused. And halted abruptly beside a sofa.

A foot in a black shoe was sticking out from under it.

He had to make three attempts. As soon as he took his hand away from his wound it began to bleed alarmingly.

Finally he seized the napkin which lay on the table, and pushed it inside his waistcoat, which he then buckled very tightly. The smell that hung about the room made him feel sick.

With fumbling hands he lifted a corner of the sofa and swivelled it on two legs.

As he had expected, it was Torrence that lay there, curled

up, with one arm twisted, as though they had broken his bones in order to cram him into a narrow space.

There was a bandage covering the lower part of his face, but it was not tied. Maigret knelt down.

All his movements were steady, in fact very slow, no doubt because of his own condition. His hand seemed reluctant to feel the other man's chest. And when it reached the heart, the Superintendent froze and remained motionless, kneeling on the carpet, his eyes fixed on his companion.

Torrence was dead. Maigret's lips twitched imperceptibly. His fists clenched; his eyes clouded, and he uttered a terrible oath in the silent closed room.

It could have been ridiculous. But in fact it was terrible. Tragic. Terrifying.

Maigret's face had hardened. He was not weeping. He was probably incapable of that. But his features expressed such fury and grief, and such amazement, that he looked almost stupefied.

Torrence was 30 years old. For the last five years he had virtually been working solely with the Superintendent.

His mouth was open, as though in a desperate effort to get a breath of air.

On the floor above, just over the dead man's body, a hotel guest pulled off his shoes. Maigret glared round, looking for an enemy. He was breathing heavily.

Several minutes went by, and when Maigret rose to his feet it was because he could feel that something sinister was creeping through his own body.

He made his way to the window, opened it, and saw the Avenue des Champs-Élysées lying empty below. He let the breeze cool his forehead for a moment, and then went back to pick up the bandage he had taken off Torrence's face.

It was a damask table napkin, embroidered with the monogram of the Majestic. It still smelt faintly of chloroform. Maigret stood there, his mind a blank except for a few inchoate thoughts, which kept colliding in the vacuum and setting up grievous echoes.

Once again he leant his shoulder against the wall, as he had done in the corridor; and the lines of his face suddenly sagged. He looked old, disheartened. At that moment, perhaps, he came near to bursting into tears. But he was too tall, too massive, cast in too tough a mould.

The sofa was pulled sideways, touching the untidy table, where some cigarette-ends lay on a plate among chicken bones.

The Superintendent put out his hand towards the telephone. But he did not pick it up. With an angry snap of his fingers, he went back to the body and stood staring at it.

With a bitter, ironical grimace he reflected on the regulations, the Public Prosecutor's Department, the formalities, the precautions to be taken.

What did all that matter? This was Torrence! Almost a part of himself!

Torrence, a member of the firm, who . . .

He undid the man's waistcoat – so feverish beneath his apparent calm that he pulled off two buttons. And then he noticed something, and turned pale.

On the shirt front, level with the centre of the heart, there was a little brown speck.

Not even as big as a dried pea. Just one drop of blood had escaped, and had dried into a clot the size of a pinhead.

Maigret stared, misty-eyed, his face contorted with an indignation for which he could find no words.

It was horrible; but it revealed the true master-criminal. No need to search further. He knew the method, having read about it a few months previously in a German criminological magazine.

First the chloroform-soaked napkin, rendering the victim helpless in twenty or thirty seconds. Then the long needle, which the murderer unhurriedly drives in between two ribs, seeking the heart, plucking out its life silently and with no mess.

Precisely the same crime had been committed at Hamburg six months ago.

A bullet may go wide of the mark, or merely wound. Maigret was a proof of that. It makes both noise and mess.

A needle driven into the heart of a man lying inert kills him scientifically, with no possibility of error.

The Superintendent remembered something. That evening, when the manager sent a message that the Mortimer-Levingstons were leaving for the theatre, he had been sitting on the radiator, gnawing the leg of a chicken and feeling suddenly so comfortable that he had almost decided to keep watch in the hotel himself and send Torrence to the theatre.

The thought upset him. He looked at his subordinate with embarrassment, feeling thoroughly uncomfortable, unable to decide whether it was because of his wound, his emotion, or the whiffs of chloroform.

The idea of opening a proper, official investigation did not even occur to him.

It was Torrence that lay there! Torrence, with whom he had been through every campaign in the last few years. Torrence, who understood him at the least word or sign.

Torrence; with his mouth open as though still trying to swallow a little oxygen, still trying to keep alive. And Maigret, unable to weep, felt ill, uneasy, sick at heart, with a weight on his shoulders.

He returned to the telephone and spoke into it, so softly that the operator had to ask him to repeat his number twice over.

'*Préfecture*. . . . Yes. Hello? *Préfecture?* . . . Who is that? Who? Tarraud? . . . Listen, my boy. Get over to the Chief's place. . . . Yes, to his home. . . . And tell him – tell him to come to me at the Majestic. Right away. Room . . . I don't know the number, but they'll show him. What? No, nothing else. . . .

'Hello. . . . What did you say? . . . No, I'm all right.'

He rang off, for the other man was asking questions, thinking his voice sounded strange and his instructions even stranger.

For a moment he stood there, arms hanging at his sides. He kept his eyes averted from the corner where Torrence lay. Catching sight of himself in a mirror, he noticed that the blood had soaked through the napkin. Then, with great difficulty, he took off his jacket.

An hour later the Director of the Criminal Investigation Department knocked at the door, to which he had been led by a member of the hotel staff; it opened a crack, and he saw Maigret peering out.

'You can go,' said the Superintendent to the hotel employee, in an expressionless voice.

And not until the man was out of sight did he open the door wider. Only then did the Director see that Maigret was naked to the waist. The door into the bathroom stood wide open. There were pools of reddish water on the floor.

'Shut the door quickly,' ordered the Superintendent, regardless of the other man's rank.

Maigret had a long purple gash on the right side of his chest. His braces were hanging down over his thighs.

He jerked his head towards Torrence's corner, laid a finger on his lips and said: 'Sssh!'

A shudder ran down the Director's spine:

'Dead?' he queried in sudden alarm.

Maigret's head sank forward.

'Will you lend me a hand, Chief?' he murmured sadly.

'But ... you. ... It's very serious. ...'

'Ssh! ... The bullet came out again, that's the main thing. ... Help me to wrap all this up in the towel.'

He had put the dinner dishes on the floor and cut the table-cloth in two.

'Pietr the Lett's gang,' he explained. 'They didn't get me. But they got my lad Torrence. ...'

'Have you cleaned the wound?'

'Yes. First with soap and then with iodine.'

'You really think? ...'

'It'll do for the moment. ... It was a needle, Chief. They killed him with a needle, after putting him to sleep. ...'

He was a different man. It was like seeing and hearing him through a gauze curtain that blurred all sights and sounds.

'Pass me my shirt. . . .'

A toneless voice. Measured, unsteady movements. A blank face.

'It was essential that you should come. Seeing that it was one of us. Besides, I didn't want any fuss. Let them come and fetch him presently. Not a word in the papers. You trust me, don't you, Chief?'

Yet there was a slight quiver in his voice. It touched the other man, who took him by the hand.

'Now then, Maigret! What's come over you?'

'Nothing. . . . I'm perfectly calm, I assure you. I don't think I have ever felt calmer. But now it's between them and me. You understand?'

The Director helped him on with his waistcoat and jacket. Maigret looked deformed because of the bandage, which thickened his waist and made his figure bulge in places as though he had rolls of fat.

He glanced at his reflection in the mirror, and pulled an ironical face. He was well aware of his sloppy appearance. This was not the formidable, flawless block of granite with which he liked to confront his adversaries.

His pale, blood-streaked face looked puffy, with a suggestion of bags under the eyes.

'Thanks, Chief. . . . You think it can be arranged, about Torrence?'

'To avoid publicity? Yes. . . . I'll tell the Public Prosecutor. . . . I'll see him myself.'

'Good! Now I'll get to work.'

He said this as he tried to tidy his dishevelled hair. Then he walked across to Torrence's body, hesitated, and asked his companion:

'I can close his eyes, can't I? . . . I think he'd rather it was me. . . .'

His fingers were trembling. He kept them on the dead man's eyelids for a long moment, like a caress. The Director, feeling the strain, called imploringly:

'Maigret!'

The Superintendent stood up and threw a last glance round

him. 'Good-bye, Chief. ... Don't let them tell my wife I've
been hurt. ...'

For a second he stood in the doorway, entirely filling it.
The Director nearly called him back, feeling anxious about
him.

During the war, some of his fellow-soldiers had said good-
bye to him like that, with the same tranquillity, the same unnatural gentleness, before going into action.

And those were the ones that never came back.

CHAPTER 8

The Killer

THE international gangs that specialize in large-scale swindles seldom go in for killing.

One can even take it as axiomatic that they do not kill people, at any rate not those they have decided to relieve of a large sum of money. Their thefts are committed by more scientific methods, and most of their associates are gentlemen who never handle a weapon.

But they do kill occasionally, to settle their own accounts. One or two insoluble murders are committed somewhere or other every year. In most cases the victim cannot be identified, and is buried under a name known to be false.

It means he is either a traitor to the gang, a man who becomes talkative when he is drunk and has lapsed from discretion now and then, or a subordinate whose ambition is a threat to his bosses.

In America, the land of the specialist, executions of this kind are never carried out by a member of the gang. Experts known as 'killers' are called in; like State executioners, they have their own assistants and their scale of fees.

It has sometimes been the same in Europe. Among others there was the notorious Polish gang whose leaders all ended on the scaffold; their services were enlisted several times by criminals of higher standing who did not wish to soil their hands with blood.

Maigret was aware of this when he went downstairs and across to the reception desk of the Majestic.

'When a visitor telephones for food, who takes the call?' he inquired.

'A special head waiter in charge of room service.'

'At night as well?'

'No. After nine o'clock it is a member of the night staff.'

'Who is to be found? . . .'

'In the basement.'

'Tell someone to take me there.'

Again he went behind the scenes of the luxury bee-hive designed for a thousand guests. He found an employee sitting at a switchboard in a room next to the kitchens. A ledger lay open in front of him. This was the slack time.

'Did Sergeant Torrence ring for you between nine o'clock yesterday evening and two o'clock this morning?'

'Torrence?'

'The police officer in the blue room, next to No. 3,' the clerk explained in professional terms.

'No, he didn't.'

'And no one went up there?'

The reasoning was elementary. Torrence had been attacked in that room, and therefore by someone who had gone in there. To gag his victim, the murderer must have been standing behind him. And Torrence had had no suspicion.

Nobody but a hotel waiter satisfied those conditions; he might have been sent for by Torrence, or he might have come of his own accord, to clear the table.

Showing no excitement, Maigret put his question in a different way.

'Which member of the staff went off duty early?'

The switchboard operator looked astonished.

'How did you know? What a coincidence! . . . Pepito had a phone call to say his brother was ill. . . .'

'What time was that?'

'About ten o'clock.'

'Where was he then?'

'Upstairs.'

'Which telephone did he take the call on?'

They rang through to the main switchboard. The operator on duty said he had passed no call to Pepito.

Things were moving quickly! But Maigret remained impassive and glum.

'Where is his card? You must have a card. . . .'

'Not exactly a card. . . . At least, not for what we call the dining-room staff. They change so often.'

They had to go to the secretary's office, which was empty at that hour. But Maigret had the books brought out, and found what he was looking for:

Pepito Moretto, Hôtel Beauséjour, 3 rue des Batignolles. Took up service on . . .

'Get me the Hôtel Beauséjour on the telephone.'

Meanwhile, questioning another employee, he learnt that Pepito Moretto, recommended by an Italian head waiter, had come to the Majestic three days before the Mortimer-Levingstons. His work had been perfectly satisfactory. He had begun in the dining-room and afterwards been transferred, at his own request, to room service.

The Hôtel Beauséjour came on the line.

'Hello. . . . Will you get me Pepito Moretto? Hello. . . . What's that? . . . With his luggage? . . . Three o'clock in the morning? . . . Thank you. . . . Hello! . . . One more thing. Were his letters delivered at your hotel? . . . None at all? . . . Thank you. That is all.'

And Maigret rang off, still maintaining his unnatural calm.

'What time is it?' he asked.

'Ten past five.'

'Call me a taxi.'

He told the driver to take him to Pickwick's Bar.

'It closes at four o'clock, you know?'

'Never mind.'

The taxi stopped outside the nightclub. The shutters were closed, but there was light showing under the door. Maigret knew that in most night spots the staff, who may number forty or more, usually have supper before going home.

They sit down to eat in the room the clients have just left, while the paper streamers are being swept up and the charwomen are beginning their work.

However, Maigret did not ring the bell at Pickwick's. Turning his back on the place, he noticed a *café-tabac* at the corner of the rue Fontaine, of the kind where nightclub staff are apt to congregate during the evening, between two jazz numbers or after closing-time.

This *bistro* was still open. When Maigret went in, three men were leaning on the bar, drinking coffee laced with brandy and talking shop.

'Isn't Pepito here?'

'He left a long time ago,' replied the *patron*.

The Superintendent noticed that one of the customers, who had perhaps recognized him, was signalling to the proprietor to keep quiet.

'I had an appointment with him for two o'clock,' he resumed.

'He was here then. . . .'

'I know. I sent him a message by one of the dancers across the road.'

'José?'

'That's it. He must have told Pepito I couldn't get away.'

'José did come, that's true. . . . I think they were talking together. . . .'

The customer who had made signs to the *patron* was now drumming with his fingers on the bar. He was pale with anger, for the few words that had slipped out were enough to explain what had happened.

At ten o'clock that night, or shortly before, Pepito had murdered Torrence at the Majestic.

He must have had very precise instructions, for he had immediately left his work, on the pretext that his brother had telephoned, and gone to the café at the corner of the rue Fontaine, where he had waited.

At a certain moment the dancer just referred to as José had crossed the street and given him a message, which was childishly obvious – he was to shoot Maigret the moment he came out of Pickwick's.

In other words, two crimes within a few hours. And the only two men who were dangerous to Pietr the Lett would be disposed of!

Pepito had fired his shot and run away, having played his

part. He had not been seen, so he could go and fetch his belongings from the Hôtel Beauséjour.

Maigret paid for his drink and left; glancing back he saw the three customers bombarding the *patron* with reproaches.

He knocked on the door of Pickwick's Bar, and it was opened by a charwoman.

As he had expected, the staff were at supper, seated round the tables, which had been lined up in a row. There were remains of chicken, partridge, dessert, whatever the clients had not finished off. Thirty heads turned towards the Superintendent.

'Is it long since José left?'

'Oh yes – directly after . . .'

But the head waiter recognized Maigret, whom he had waited upon himself, and he nudged the speaker with his elbow.

Maigret did not beat about the bush.

'Give me his address! The right one, or you'll be sorry.'

'I don't know. . . . Only the proprietor. . . .'

'Where is he?'

'Gone to his country place at La Varenne.'

'Give me the register.'

'But . . .'

'Quiet!'

They pretended to hunt through the drawers in a small office behind the orchestra platform. Maigret pushed them aside and at once found the ledger, where he read:

José Latourie, 71 rue Lepic.

He went out as he had come in, with a heavy step, while the waiters, still alarmed, resumed their meal.

He was only a few yards from the rue Lepic. But No. 71 is fairly high up the steep hill. He had to stop twice, out of breath. At last he came to the door of a hotel, similar to the Beauséjour but more squalid, and rang the bell. The door opened automatically. He knocked on a small round window in the corridor, and a sleepy night porter eventually emerged.

'José Latourie?'

The man looked at the row of keys hanging at the head of his bed.

'Not in yet. His key is here. . . .'

'Give it to me. Police.'

'But . . .'

'Quick!'

The fact was that no one opposed him that night. Yet he was not as stern and unbending as usual. But perhaps they sensed vaguely that this was worse.

'Which floor?'

'Fourth.'

The room was long, narrow and stuffy. The bed was un-made. José, like most of his kind, must have stayed in bed till four o'clock in the afternoon, after which hour hotel-keepers refuse to have rooms done.

An old pyjama jacket, threadbare at the neck and elbows, was lying on the sheet. On the floor was a pair of dancing pumps, trodden down at the back and with holes in the soles, now used as bedroom slippers.

A travelling bag in imitation leather contained only some old newspapers and a pair of patched black trousers.

Above the wash-basin lay a cake of soap, a pot of ointment, a few aspirins, and a tube of veronal.

On the ground was a screw of paper which Maigret picked up and carefully unfolded. One sniff was enough to inform him that it had contained heroin.

Fifteen minutes later, after hunting everywhere, he noticed a hole in the rep cover of the only arm-chair, pushed his finger into it, and pulled out, one by one, eleven packets of the same drug, each containing one gramme.

He put them in his wallet and went downstairs. In the Place Blanche he approached a policeman, to whom he gave certain instructions. The constable went up the rue Lepic and stationed himself near No. 71.

Maigret remembered the black-haired young man, a sickly shifty-eyed gigolo who had bumped into his table in his agitation, after going out to speak to Moretto.

He had been afraid to go home when the thing was over, preferring to sacrifice his three miserable suits and the eleven small packets – though at the retail price these would be worth at least a thousand francs.

He would be caught one day, for his nerve was poor and he must be haunted by fear.

Pepito was infinitely more self-possessed. He might be waiting on some station platform to catch the first train. He might have gone to ground in the suburbs, or simply have moved to a hotel in another district.

Maigret hailed a taxi and almost gave the address of the Majestic. But he calculated that they would not yet have finished there. In other words, Torrence would still be in that room.

'Quai des Orfèvres,' he said.

Walking past Jean, he realized that the man already knew what had happened, and he turned his head aside almost guiltily.

He paid no attention to his stove. He did not take off his jacket or his shirt collar.

For two hours he sat motionless, with his elbows on the desk, and it was daylight by the time it occurred to him to look at a paper which must have been put there during the night.

'To Superintendent Maigret. Urgent.

'A man in evening dress came to the Hôtel du Roi de Sicile about eleven-thirty and remained for ten minutes. He left again in a private car. The Russian has not been out.'

Maigret's expression did not change. And now, news came pouring in. First there was a telephone call from the police station in the Courcelles district.

'A certain José Latourie, a professional dancing-partner, has been found dead outside the gate of the Parc Monceau. He had three knife wounds. His wallet had not been stolen. The time and circumstances of the crime are unknown.'

Not to Maigret. He could imagine them at once. Pepito Moretto coming up behind the young man as he left Pickwick's, thinking he was too upset and liable to give the show away, killing him without even bothering to take his wallet and identity papers – perhaps out of bravado.

'You think you can trace us through him? Well, here he is!' Pepito seemed to be saying.

Half past eight. The voice of the manager of the Majestic came over the telephone.

'Hello? . . . Superintendent Maigret? . . . It's incredible, preposterous! . . . A few minutes ago there was a ring from No. 17. No. 17! . . . You remember? The room that . . .'

'That Oswald Oppenheim was in. Yes. Well?'

'I sent a waiter along. . . . Oppenheim was lying in bed as though nothing had happened, and he asked for his breakfast. . . .'

CHAPTER 9

Oswald Oppenheim's Return

MAIGRET had been sitting still for two hours. When he tried to stand up he could scarcely move his arms, and he had to ring for Jean to help him on with his coat.

'Get a taxi for me.'

A few minutes later he walked into Dr Lecourbe's house in the rue Monsieur-le-Prince. There were six people in the waiting-room, but he was taken round, through the flat, and as soon as the consulting room was free he went in.

It was an hour before he came out again. He was carrying himself more stiffly than before, and the rings round his eyes had darkened so much that his whole expression had altered, as though he had made up his face.

'Rue du Roi-de-Sicile. I'll tell you when to stop.'

From a distance he saw his two inspectors patrolling outside the hotel. He got out of the taxi and joined them.

'He's not come out?'

'No. One or the other of us has been here all the time.'

'Who has left the hotel?'

'A little bent-up old man, and then two young chaps, and then a woman of about thirty. . . .'

Maigret asked, with a shrug and a sigh:

'Had the old man got a beard?'

'Yes. . . .'

He left them without a word, and went up the narrow staircase and past the lodge. A moment later he was rattling the door of Room 32. A woman's voice replied in an unknown language. The door gave way, and he saw Anna Gorskin getting out of bed, half naked.

'Where's your boy-friend?' he demanded.

He spoke curtly, like a man in a hurry, not bothering to look round the place.

'Get out! . . . You have no right! . . .' shouted the woman.

But he, impassive, bent to pick up the familiar trench-coat from the floor. He seemed to be looking for something else. He saw Fédor Yurovich's greyish trousers at the foot of the bed.

There were no man's shoes in the room, however.

Anna, who was struggling into her dressing-gown, stared at him ferociously.

'You think because we're foreigners . . .'

He did not wait for her burst of rage. He went out calmly, closing the door, which she reopened before he had gone down one flight of stairs. She stood on the landing, breathing heavily, without a word. She leant over the banisters to watch him, and suddenly, unable to restrain her irresistible urge to do something, anything, she spat.

The spittle fell with a soft splash, missing him by a couple of inches.

'Well? . . .' asked Inspector Dufour.

'Watch the woman. *She* won't be able to disguise herself as an old man. . . .'

'You mean to say that? . . .'

Oh no – he didn't mean to say anything! He was in no mood for argument. He got back into his taxi.

'The Majestic.'

Uneasy and humiliated, the inspector watched him go.

'Do what you can!' called Maigret.

He didn't want to hurt the man's feelings, either. It wasn't his fault that he had been tricked. Hadn't Maigret himself allowed Torrence to be killed?

The manager was waiting for him at the entrance, which indicated an entirely new attitude.

'Well. . . . You understand. . . . I don't know what to do next. . . . They came and fetched your . . . your friend. . . . They assured me that nothing would appear in the papers. . . . But the *other man* is here. *Here!*'

'No one saw him come in?'

'No one. That's just what ... Listen. I told you on the telephone, he rang his bell. ... When the waiter went in, he ordered coffee. He was in bed. ...'

'And Mortimer-Levingston?'

'You think there is a connexion? Impossible! He's a celebrity. ... Cabinet ministers and bankers have called on him at this very hotel! ...'

'What is Oppenheim doing now?'

'He has just had a bath. I think he is getting dressed.'

'And Mortimer-Levingston?'

'The Mortimer-Levingstons haven't rung yet. They are still asleep.'

'Give me a description of Pepito Moretto.'

'Oh yes. ... I was told ... Personally, I never saw him. Not to notice him, I mean. We have such a large staff! But I have made inquiries. A small, swarthy, black-haired, stocky man, who never said a word from one day to the next. ...'

Maigret wrote this down on a sheet of paper and put it into an envelope which he addressed to his chief. With the finger-prints that must certainly have been found in the rooms where Torrence was killed, that ought to be enough.

'Have this taken to the Préfecture.'

'Yes, Superintendent.'

The manager had become positively suave, for he felt that the affair might take on disastrous proportions.

'What are you going to do?'

But the Superintendent was already walking away, with an awkward chunky gait. He stopped in the middle of the hall, looking like a visitor to some historic church who is trying to guess, without the verger's help, what interesting features it possesses.

A ray of sunshine appeared, and the hall of the Majestic glittered like gold.

At nine o'clock in the morning it was practically deserted. A few people were having breakfast at widely scattered tables, reading their newspapers.

After a time Maigret sank into a cane chair beside the little fountain, which for some reason was not working that day. The goldfish in the ceramic pool remained obstinately motionless, merely opening and shutting their mouths vacantly.

This reminded the Superintendent of Torrence's open mouth. The recollection must have distressed him considerably, because he shifted about for a long time before finding a position that suited him.

A few servants were coming and going. Maigret followed them with his eyes, aware that a shot might be fired at any moment.

The issue had become as crucial as that.

The fact that Maigret had identified Oppenheim as Pietr the Lett was of no great consequence, and he was not in much danger from that.

Pietr was at no pains to hide himself, he was defying the police, convinced that they could bring no charge against him.

To prove him right, there was that series of telegrams following him step by step from Cracow to Bremen, Bremen to Amsterdam, Amsterdam to Brussels, and Brussels to Paris.

But then there had been the dead man on the *North Star*. And above all there had been Maigret's discovery that there was an unexpected connexion between Pietr the Lett and Mortimer-Levingston.

That discovery had brought matters to a head.

Pietr was a self-confessed bandit, who simply said to the international police:

'Catch me at it if you can!'

Whereas Mortimer-Levingston was universally regarded as a pillar of respectability.

There were two people who might have guessed the relationship between Pietr and Mortimer-Levingston.

And that very evening, Torrence had been killed and Maigret shot at in the rue Fontaine.

A third person, hapless and probably knowing little or nothing, but a possible starting-point for a new investigation, had also been liquidated – José Latourie, the gigolo.

Now Mortimer-Levingston and the Lett, their confidence

presumably restored by the triple murder, had gone back to their places. There they were, upstairs in their luxurious suites, giving orders by telephone to the staff of a great hotel, taking baths, having breakfast, getting dressed.

Maigret was waiting for them all by himself, seated uncomfortably in a cane arm-chair, one side of his chest stiff and throbbing, his right arm almost paralysed by a dull ache.

He had the power to arrest them. But he knew it would be no use. It might conceivably be possible to collect evidence against Pietr the Lett, alias Fédor Yurovich, alias Oswald Oppenheim – who had doubtless been known by plenty of other names as well, perhaps including that of Olaf Swaan.

But against Mortimer-Levingston, the American multimillionaire? Within an hour of his arrest there would be a protest from the United States Ambassador. The French banks and the many companies of which he was a director would make a stir in political circles.

What proof? What clue? The fact that he had walked off for a few hours in the wake of Pietr the Lett?

That he had gone to Pickwick's for supper, and his wife had danced with José Latourie?

That a police inspector had seen him go into a squalid hotel called the Roi de Sicile?

All that would be torn to shreds! Apologies would have to be offered, and even steps taken, such as dismissing Maigret – ostensibly, at any rate – as a sop to the United States.

Torrence was dead!

He must have passed through this hall, on a stretcher, as dawn began to break. Unless the manager, anxious not to confront any early-rising client with a painful sight, had persuaded the stretcher-bearers to go out through the servants' quarters.

Probably he had. The narrow passages, the winding stairs, where the stretcher must have banged into the hand-rail.

The telephone rang, behind the mahogany counter.

People bustling to and fro. Flurried orders.

The manager came over.

'Mrs Mortimer-Levingston is leaving. . . . They have just

rung down for her trunk to be fetched. . . . The car has arrived.'

Maigret smiled frostily.

'What train?' he asked.

'She is catching the Berlin plane from Le Bourget.'

Before he had finished speaking she appeared, wearing a greyish travelling coat and carrying a crocodile handbag. She was walking quickly. But on reaching the revolving door she could not resist a backward glance.

To make certain that she saw him, Maigret rose, with an effort. He was positive that she bit her lip and went out still more hurriedly, gesticulating as she gave her orders to the chauffeur.

The manager was called away. The Superintendent was left alone, standing beside the fountain, which suddenly began to work. There must be a fixed time for turning the water on.

It was ten o'clock.

He smiled again, to himself, and sat down heavily but cautiously, for his wound was becoming more and more painful, and hurt him at the slightest movement.

'They're getting rid of the weaklings. . . .'

For that was it, right enough! After José Latourie, who had been regarded as unstable and dismissed from the scene with three knife-stabs in the chest, they were getting rid of Mrs Mortimer-Levingston, who might also be intimidated. She was being sent to Berlin. That was privileged treatment!

The tough nuts remained: Pietr the Lett, who was taking an interminable time to get dressed; Mortimer-Levingston, who had doubtless lost nothing of his aristocratic bearing; and Pepito Moretto, the gang's 'killer'.

All of them, linked by invisible threads, were getting ready.

The enemy was there, in their midst, in the middle of the hall, where signs of life were now beginning to appear. He was sitting motionless in a wicker arm-chair, with his legs stretched out, while the fountain tinkled close by and its fine spray blew into his face like dust.

One of the lifts came down and stopped.

Pietr the Lett was the first to emerge, wearing a superb cinnamon-coloured suit and with a Henry Clay between his lips.

He was at home here. He was paying for it. Casual, self-assured, he strolled round the hall, pausing here and there in front of the showcases which the big shops maintain in luxury hotels. He asked one of the page-boys for a light, he inspected a board on which the latest foreign exchange rates were posted up; he came to a halt within three yards of Maigret, beside the fountain, staring fixedly at the artificial-looking goldfish. Finally he flicked the ash from his cigar into the pool, and walked off towards the reading-room.

CHAPTER 10

A Restless Way

PIETR THE LETT glanced through several newspapers, paying particular attention to the *Revaler Bote*, an Estonian periodical of which the Majestic had only one old copy, presumably left by some departing guest.

Shortly before eleven o'clock he lit another cigar, walked across the hall, and sent a page-boy to fetch his hat.

Thanks to the sunshine flooding on to one side of the Champs-Élysées, it was fairly warm outside.

Pietr went out wearing a grey felt hat and no overcoat, and strolled slowly up to the Étoile, like a man just taking a breath of air.

Maigret followed at a short distance, making no attempt to conceal himself. He did not find the walk enjoyable, for his movements were hampered by the dressing on his chest.

At the corner of the rue de Berry he heard a faint whistle a few steps away, but paid no attention. The whistle was repeated. At this he looked round, and saw Inspector Dufour, making mysterious signs to indicate that he had something to tell his chief.

The Inspector was standing in the rue de Berry, pretending to be engrossed in the contemplation of a chemist's window, so that his gestures seemed to be addressed to the wax head of a woman, one cheek of which was carefully covered with eczema.

'Come here! Come along! Quick. . . .' said Maigret.

Dufour was hurt and offended. For the last hour he had been prowling in the vicinity of the Majestic, employing the most cunning ruses, and now the Superintendent was ordering him to show himself in broad daylight!

'What's going on?'

'It's that Gorskin woman. . . .'

'Gone out?'

'She's here. . . . And now you've made me come forward, she can see us both at this moment. . . .'

Maigret looked round him.

'Where is she?'

'The Select. . . . She's sitting inside. . . . Look, though: the curtain's moving. . . .'

'Keep watching.'

'Without hiding myself?'

'Go and drink an *apéritif* at the table next to hers, if you like.'

As matters now stood in this contest, it would be pointless to play hide-and-seek. Maigret walked on. After two hundred yards he again saw Pietr the Lett, who had not tried to exploit the conversation by dodging away.

Why should he? The game was being played on new ground. The opponents could see one another. The cards were practically on the table.

Pietr went twice up and down from the Étoile to the Rond-Point des Champs-Élysées, and in the end Maigret knew every smallest detail of his appearance, had summed up his physical characteristics in full.

Physically Pietr was elegant, fine-drawn, in fact with more distinction than Mortimer-Levingston, for instance; but his was a Nordic type of distinction.

The Superintendent had studied several men of that kind, all intellectuals. And his Latin mind had been thoroughly perplexed by those he had known in the Latin quarter, during a period of medical studies which he had not completed.

He remembered one of them, a thin, blond Pole; at the age of 22 he had already shown signs of incipient baldness; back in his own country his mother was a charwoman; and for seven solid years he had attended lectures at the Sorbonne, with no socks on his feet, and with literally nothing to eat but a piece of bread and one egg, day after day.

As he could not afford to buy the set books, he had been forced to study in the public libraries.

He knew nothing about Paris, about women, or about the French character. But almost before his studies were completed, he was offered an important professorship at Warsaw university. Five years later, Maigret saw him again in Paris, as aloof, short-spoken, and cold as ever; he was a member of a delegation of foreign scientists, and he dined with the President.

The Superintendent had known others of his kind. Not all of them were of equal quality. But nearly all were astonishing, because of the number and variety of things they wanted to learn and did learn.

Study for the sake of study! Like that Belgian university professor who knew all the Far Eastern dialects (some forty of them), but had never set foot in Asia and was not in the least interested in the nations whose languages he analysed in his dilettante way.

The grey-green eyes of Pietr the Lett expressed that kind of determination. And yet, no sooner had one decided to classify him with the race of intellectuals than one noticed other points which reopened the whole question.

It was as though the shadow of Fédor Yurovich, the Russian vagabond in the trench-coat, were cast over the clear-cut figure at the Majestic.

That they were one and the same man was already a moral certainty and fast becoming a material one.

On the evening he arrived in Paris, Pietr had vanished. Next morning Maigret had found him at Fécamp, in the guise of Fédor Yurovich.

He had gone to the Hôtel du Roi de Sicile. A few hours later, Mortimer-Levingston had visited the hotel. Several people had come out after that, including an old, bearded man.

And in the morning, Pietr the Lett had been back again at the Majestic.

The astounding thing was that apart from a rather striking physical resemblance the two personalities had absolutely nothing in common.

Fédor Yurovich was unmistakably a vagabond Slav, a melancholy, rock-bottom down-and-out. Not one false note.

Not one slip, for instance, while he was leaning on the bar in that low dive at Fécamp.

On the other hand there was not a flaw in the personality of Pietr the Lett – a well-bred intellectual from head to foot, in his manner of asking a page-boy for a light, in the angle at which he wore his grey felt hat – which was of the best English make – in his nonchalant manner of savouring the sunlit air of the Champs-Élysées or looking at a shop window.

And this perfection was not just superficial. Maigret knew what it was to play a part: the police do not disguise themselves and make up their faces as often as people think, but it has to be done at times.

But Maigret in disguise was still Maigret in certain ways, certain facial expressions or mannerisms.

Maigret as a big cattle-dealer, for instance (he had done that, and brought it off) would be *acting* the cattle-dealer. But he would not *be* one. He would never get into the skin of the part.

Whereas Pietr–Fédor was Pietr or Fédor through and through.

In short, the Superintendent's impression was that the man was both characters at one and the same time, not only in get-up but in essence.

He had been alternating between these two utterly different lives, no doubt for a long time, perhaps from the very first.

These were only disconnected ideas, flowing in on Maigret while he walked slowly along, relishing the mild atmosphere.

But all of a sudden the Lett's personality splintered.

The circumstances that led to this were significant. He had come to a halt opposite Fouquet's, and even begun to cross the Champs-Élysées, with the obvious intention of taking an *apéritif* at the bar of that fashionable establishment.

But he changed his mind, went on along the same side of the avenue, and suddenly, quickening his pace, darted into the rue Washington.

In that street there is a *bistro* of the type to be found in the heart of all the wealthiest districts, serving taxi-drivers and domestic servants.

Pietr went in. The Superintendent followed close behind, just as he was ordering an absinthe substitute.

He was standing by the horseshoe-shaped bar, which a blue-aproned waiter wiped from time to time with a dirty cloth. To his left was a group of dusty bricklayers. To his right, a man in the uniform of the gas company.

Pietr looked thoroughly out of place, with his air of refinement and the quiet, flawless elegance of his clothes.

His little toothbrush moustache and his thin eyebrows looked too blond and glistening. He was staring at Maigret, not face to face, but in a mirror.

And the Superintendent noted that his lips were quivering, his nostrils imperceptibly narrowed.

Pietr must be watching his step. At first he drank slowly, but soon he gulped down what remained in his glass and jerked his finger in a way that meant:

'Fill it up!'

Maigret had ordered a vermouth. In this little bar he looked even taller and bulkier than usual. He never took his eyes off Pietr.

In a way, he was in two places at once. Two pictures were overlaid, as they had been a few minutes earlier. The squalid café at Fécamp formed a backcloth to the present scene. Pietr was a double figure. Maigret saw him simultaneously in his light-brown suit and in a shabby raincoat.

'I tell yer I ain't puttin' up with it no longer!' said one of the bricklayers, banging his glass on the counter.

Pietr was drinking his third opal-coloured *apéritif*; the smell of aniseed drifted into Maigret's nostrils.

The gas man had shifted his position in such a way that Maigret and Pietr were now side by side, their elbows touching.

Maigret was two heads taller than the other man. They were both facing a mirror, and staring at each other in its grey, limpid surface.

The Lett's eyes were the first of his features to become blurred. He snapped his thin white fingers, pointed to his glass, and passed a hand across his forehead.

And then, little by little, a kind of battle began in his face. At one moment it was the features of the Majestic's client that Maigret saw in the mirror; then it was the harassed face of Anna Gorskin's lover.

But this second face never came right to the surface. It was thrust back by a desperate muscular effort. Only the eyes were always Fédor's eyes.

The man's left hand was clinging to the edge of the counter. His body swayed to and fro.

Maigret tried an experiment. In his pocket was the picture of Madame Swaan that he had taken from the Fécamp photographer's album.

'What do I owe you?' he asked the waiter.

'Two francs twenty.'

He pretended to be hunting in his wallet, and dropped the photo, which fell into a puddle between the up-curved edges of the counter.

He ignored it, and held out a five-franc note. But he was staring hard into the mirror.

The waiter had picked up the photograph and, with profuse apologies, was wiping it on his apron.

Pietr the Lett stood there stony-eyed, clutching his glass. Not a muscle moved in his face.

Then, suddenly, there was a faint, unexpected sound, so sharp that the *patron*, busy at the cash desk, swung round on his heel.

Pietr's hand opened, and the fragments of his glass fell on the counter.

He had crushed it to pieces, slowly. Blood was trickling from a narrow cut on his forefinger.

He threw down a hundred-franc note in front of him and walked out, not glancing at Maigret.

Now he was making straight for the Majestic. No trace of intoxication. His appearance was the same as when he set out, his step as firm.

Stubbornly, Maigret followed at his heels. Coming in sight

of the hotel, he saw a car drive away, and recognized it. It was the car of the Judicial Identification Service, removing the police cameras and the apparatus which had been used to detect finger-prints.

This encounter took the wind out of his sails. For a second he lost confidence, as though he were drifting, with nothing to hold on to.

He went past the Select. Through the window, Inspector Dufour made a signal which was supposed to be confidential, but in fact drew all eyes unerringly to Anna Gorskin's table.

'Mortimer-Levingston?' queried the Superintendent, pausing at the reception desk of the hotel.

'He has just left by car for the American Embassy, where he is lunching.'

Pietr the Lett went to his own table in the dining-room, which was empty.

'Will you be lunching too?' the manager asked Maigret.

'Yes – put me at his table.'

The manager nearly choked.

'At his . . . That's not possible! The room is completely empty, and . . .'

'I said at his table.'

Unwilling to admit defeat, the manager ran after Maigret.

'Listen! He's sure to make a scene. . . . I can put you somewhere where you'll be able to see him just as well.'

'I said at his table.'

It was then, as he strolled about in the hall, that he noticed he was tired. A subtle fatigue that was affecting his whole body, in fact his whole being, flesh and spirit alike.

He dropped into the wicker arm-chair where he had sat earlier in the morning. A couple consisting of a lady of very ripe years and an over-elegant young man rose at once, and the woman, fidgeting irritably with her lorgnette, said in a voice loud enough to be overheard:

'These big hotels are becoming impossible. Just look at that. . . .'

'That' was Maigret, who couldn't even raise a smile.

CHAPTER 11

The Woman with the Revolver

'HELLO? . . . Hm . . . It *is* you, isn't it?'

'Maigret speaking, yes,' sighed the Superintendent, who had recognized the voice of Inspector Dufour.

'Shh . . . I'll be brief, Chief. . . . She went to the ladies. . . . Left handbag on table. . . . I went over . . . . Revolver in it.'

'Is she still there?'

'Yes, eating. . . .'

Dufour, in the telephone box, must be looking conspiratorial, making cryptic gestures of alarm. Maigret rang off without comment. He hadn't the heart to reply. These little eccentricities, which usually amused him, now gave him a kind of nausea.

The manager had resignedly ordered a place to be laid opposite Pietr, who was already at the table and had asked the head waiter:

'Who is that place for?'

'I don't know, Monsieur. Those are my orders. . . .'

And he had not pursued the point. An English family of five now came noisily into the dining-room and took some of the chill out of the atmosphere.

Leaving his hat and heavy overcoat with an attendant, Maigret walked across the room and paused before sitting down, even giving the ghost of a bow.

But Pietr did not appear to notice him. The four or five *apéritifs* he had swallowed were forgotten. He was cold, punctilious, his movements were precise.

Not for a second did he show the least sign of nerves; his abstracted gaze looked more like that of an engineer with a technical problem on his mind.

He drank little, but he had chosen one of the best burgundies of the last twenty years.

He ate sparingly: omelet *aux fines herbes*, escalope, and *crème fraîche*.

Between courses he sat with his hands folded on the table, waiting with no sign of impatience, heedless of what went on around him.

The dining-room was filling up.

'Your moustache is coming unstuck,' said Maigret suddenly.

Pietr showed no sign of having heard; only, after a moment, he brushed his upper lip casually with two fingers. It was true, though hardly perceptible.

The Superintendent's calm was a byword at the Préfecture, but now even he had some difficulty in keeping his composure.

And during the remainder of the afternoon it was to be sorely tried.

Not that he had expected Pietr to make any compromising move before his very eyes.

But in the morning he had seemed to show the first signs of a breakdown. Might there not be some hope of driving him beyond his limit, by the perpetual presence of Maigret's bulk, looming like an immovable barrier between him and the light?

The Lett took coffee in the hall, sent upstairs for a light overcoat, strolled down the Champs-Élysées, and, a little after two o'clock, went into a neighbouring cinema.

He stayed there until six o'clock, without exchanging a word with anyone, writing anything, or making the slightest ambiguous move.

Leaning back in his seat, he attentively followed the plot of a trivial film. When, after this, he was walking to the Place de l'Opéra, where he took an *apéritif*, had he glanced round he would have noticed that Maigret was showing signs of wilting. He might even have sensed that the Superintendent was beginning to lose his self-confidence.

So much so, that during the hours spent in the dark, staring at the screen with its fleeting images, which he made no attempt to follow, Maigret had all the time been contemplating the possibility of making an immediate arrest.

But he knew so well what would happen if he did! There was no conclusive material evidence. And a whole barrage of influences would instantly be brought to bear on the examining magistrate, the Public Prosecutor, even the Foreign Minister and the Minister of Justice!

He was walking with his shoulders slightly bent, his wound was smarting, and his right arm growing stiffer and stiffer. And the doctor had told him very seriously:

'If the pain spreads, come here as quickly as you can. It means that the wound is becoming infected. . . .'

And if it did? As though he had time to think about that!

'Just look at that!' a woman at the Majestic had exclaimed before lunch.

Well, yes. 'That' was a police officer, trying to prevent a group of big criminals from continuing their exploits, and determined to avenge a colleague who had been murdered in that very hotel!

'That' was a man who did not get his clothes from a London tailor, who had no time to have his hands manicured every morning, and whose wife had been cooking wasted meals for him for the last three days, resigned to knowing nothing of his whereabouts.

'That' was a senior police Superintendent, with a salary of two thousand two hundred francs a month, who, once he had finished a case and the murderers were behind bars, had to sit down with a sheet of paper in front of him, make out a list of his expenses, attach all the receipts and vouchers, and then argue it out with the cashier!

Maigret had no car, no fortune, no staff of assistants. And if he did venture to use the services of one or two police officers, he had to explain, afterwards, why he had needed them.

Pietr the Lett, sitting three yards away, paid for his *apéritif* with a fifty-franc note and left the change. It was a mania with him, or a form of bluff. Then he went into a men's shop and, no doubt for the fun of it, spent half an hour selecting twelve ties and three dressing-gowns, laid his card on the counter, and left, escorted to the door by a faultlessly-attired salesman.

The wound must definitely be getting inflamed. Sometimes great stabs shot through Maigret's shoulder, and he had a sick feeling in his chest, as though his stomach were involved in the business.

Rue de la Paix. Place Vendôme. Faubourg Saint-Honoré. Pietr the Lett strolled on. . . .

At last the Majestic, where the page-boys rushed forward to spin the revolving door for him.

'Chief . . .'

'You again?'

Inspector Dufour stepped hesitantly out of the shadows, looking careworn.

'Listen. . . . She's disappeared. . . .'

'What on earth do you mean?'

'I did my best, I swear I did! She walked out of the Select. A moment later she went into No. 52, a dress shop. I waited an hour before asking the doorman. She had not been seen in the first-floor showroom. She'd simply walked through the building, which has another entrance in the rue de Berry. . . .'

'Very well.'

'What shall I do?'

'Take a rest.'

Dufour caught the Superintendent's eye and hastily averted his own.

'I do assure you . . .'

To his stupefaction, Maigret patted him on the shoulder.

'You're a good chap, Dufour. Just stop worrying old man.'

And he went into the Majestic, intercepted the manager's grimace and answered it with a smile.

'Pietr the Lett?'

'He has just gone up to his room.'

Maigret turned to one of the lifts.

'Second floor.'

He filled his pipe, and suddenly realized – smiling again, rather more sourly than before – that he had forgotten to smoke for several hours.

At the door of No. 17 he knocked without hesitation. A voice called to him to come in. He did so, closing the door behind him.

In spite of the central heating, there was a log fire in the sitting-room, by way of decoration. Pietr, leaning on the mantelpiece, was pushing a burning paper with his toe to hasten its destruction.

Maigret realized at a glance that the man was not so calm as before; but he had sufficient hold over himself to conceal his delight.

With one of his huge hands he grasped the back of a tiny gilded chair, which he carried to within a yard of the fire. There he set it down again on its spindle-legs and seated himself astride it.

Was it because he had his pipe between his teeth again? Or because his whole being had got its second wind after the recent hours of dejection, or rather indecision?

In any case, at that moment he looked larger than ever. He was double-strength Maigret, so to speak. A block hewn out of weathered oak, or solid rock.

He propped both elbows on the chair-back. He looked as though he would be capable, if driven beyond endurance, of seizing the other man's neck in one enormous hand and banging his head against the wall.

'Is Mortimer-Levingston back?' he rapped out.

Pietr, who was watching the paper burn, raised his head slowly. 'I don't know. . . .'

His fists were clenched, a point that did not escape Maigret. Nor did it escape him that a suitcase, which had not been in the suite before, was standing near the bedroom door.

It was a cheap travelling-case, worth about a hundred francs at most, and looked quite out of place in these surroundings.

'What's in that?'

No reply. But Pietr's face twitched nervously. After a moment he asked:

'Are you arresting me?'

And it almost seemed that beneath its anxiety his voice held a note of relief.

'Not yet.'

Maigret rose, went over to the suitcase, and pushed it with his toe to the fireplace, where he opened it.

Inside was a brand-new ready-made grey suit; someone had forgotten to unpick the label, on which a serial number was marked.

The Inspector picked up the telephone.

'Hello? . . . Has Mortimer-Levingston come in? . . . No? . . . And no one has asked for room 17? . . . Hello? . . . Yes. . . . A parcel from a man's shop on the Grands Boulevards? No need to send that up.'

He rang off and asked in a surly voice:

'Where is Anna Gorskin?'

He felt he was getting somewhere at last.

'Look for yourself. . . .'

'In other words she isn't here. . . . But she has been here. . . . She brought this suitcase, and a letter. . . .'

With a rapid movement, Pietr pushed down the fragments of burnt paper, so that nothing remained except ashes.

The Superintendent realized that this was not the moment to take chances; he was on the right lines, but the least slip would rob him of his advantage.

From force of habit he stood up and moved closer to the fire – so abruptly that Pietr jumped and made as though to defend himself. He broke off the gesture, flushing as he realized his mistake.

For Maigret only planted himself with his back to the fire. He was smoking his pipe in short, thick puffs.

Silence now reigned, so long and so full of implications that it jarred on the nerves.

Pietr was on tenterhooks, but determined to keep his countenance. As a retort to Maigret's pipe, he lit a cigar.

The Superintendent began to pace up and down. He leant on the little table that held the telephone, almost shattering it with his weight.

The other man did not notice that he had pressed the bell without lifting the receiver. The result was instantaneous. The telephone rang. A voice from the office inquired:

'Hello? . . . Did you call?'

'Hello? . . . Yes. . . . What did you say?'

'Hello? . . . This is the manager's office. . . .'

Maigret went on imperturbably:

'Hello? . . . Yes. . . . Mortimer-Levingston? Thank you. . . . I'll see him presently. . . .'

'Hello? Hello?'

He had scarcely rung off when the ring came again. The manager's voice asked urgently:

'What is going on? I don't understand!'

'Blast!' thundered Maigret.

He looked searchingly at Pietr, whose pallor had increased and who, at least for a second, was obviously tempted to bolt for the door.

'That was nothing,' Maigret told him. 'Only Mortimer-Levingston coming back. I had asked them to let me know.'

He saw beads of sweat on the other man's brow.

'We were speaking of the suitcase and the letter that came with it. . . . Anna Gorskin. . . .'

'Anna does not come into this.'

'Excuse me. . . . I thought. . . . Wasn't the letter from her?'

'Listen. . . .'

Pietr was trembling. It was obvious. And he was unusually tense. His face, his whole body, jerked and twitched.

'Listen!'

'I'm listening,' said Maigret shortly, still with his back to the fire.

He had slipped his hand into his hip-pocket.

He needed only a second to take aim. He was smiling, but behind his smile could be sensed a concentration strained to the utmost limit.

'Well? I tell you I'm listening. . . .'

But Pietr seized a bottle of whisky, muttering through his teeth:

'All right, then!'

And he poured himself a full glass, swallowed it at one draught, and stood looking at the Superintendent with Fédor Yurovich's glassy stare, a drop of spirit gleaming on his chin.

CHAPTER 12

The Two Pietrs

MAIGRET had never witnessed such lightning intoxication. True, he had never before seen a man swallow a whole tumblerful of whisky at one gulp, refill it, empty it again, fill it for the third time, shake the bottle, and drink the neat spirits to the last drop.

The effect was alarming. Pietr the Lett flushed crimson; a moment later the blood drained from his face, but scarlet blotches were left on his cheeks. His lips turned pale. He clutched at the table, tottered a few steps, then articulated with drunken insouciance:

'You asked for it, didn't you?'

And he broke into a strange laugh that expressed an infinity of emotions – fear, irony, bitterness, perhaps desperation. Trying to prop himself on a chair, he knocked it over. Wiping his damp forehead, he resumed:

'You know, you wouldn't have brought it off all on your own. . . . It's just luck. . . .'

Maigret did not stir. He felt so embarrassed that he almost put an end to the scene by making the other man swallow or inhale an antidote.

He was witnessing the same transformation as in the morning, but ten times, a hundred times more drastic.

Just now he had been dealing with a man in complete control of himself, a man whose keen intelligence was backed by exceptional will-power. A man of the world, possessing wide culture and the most polished manners.

And all at once there was nothing left but a bundle of nerves, a puppet whose strings had gone haywire, a livid grimacing countenance that centred in a pair of glaucous eyes.

The man was laughing! But amidst his laughter and his aimless gesticulations he was straining his ears, bending forward as though listening for some sound beneath his feet.

And underneath was the Mortimer-Levingstons' suite.

'It was well planned,' he said in an unnaturally hoarse voice. 'And you wouldn't have been able to see through it! Sheer luck, I tell you, or rather, a run of lucky chances.'

He bumped into the wall and stayed there, leaning in a twisted position. His features contorted – for this self-induced drunkenness, which was almost a form of poisoning, must have given him a headache.

'Come on. . . . Try to tell me, while there's still time, which Pietr I am. . . . You think Pietr's just a clown, don't you?'

It was repulsive yet pathetic, comic and yet horrible. And the man's galloping intoxication was growing worse with every second.

'It's funny that they haven't come! . . . But they will. . . . And then. . . . Hurry up! . . . Guess! Which Pietr am I?'

His attitude suddenly changed, he clutched his head in his hands and an expression of physical suffering came over his face.

'You'll never understand. . . . The story of the two Pietrs. . . . It's a bit like the story of Cain and Abel. . . . You're a Catholic, I suppose. . . . In my country we're Protestants, and we live with the Bible. But it's no use. . . . I'm certain Cain was an innocent, trusting kind of chap, whereas that fellow Abel . . .'

Footsteps sounded in the corridor. The door opened.

Even Maigret was so startled that he had to bite harder on the stem of his pipe.

For it was Mortimer-Levingston that came in, fur-coated, with the jovial face of a man who has just dined well in good company.

A slight aroma of liqueurs and cigar-smoke hovered round him.

The moment he stepped into the sitting-room his face changed. The colour left it. Maigret noticed an irregularity of feature which was hard to define but which gave something disturbing to his appearance.

343

One could feel that he had arrived from out of doors; a little fresh air was still caught in the folds of his clothes.

The scene was being played from two directions at once. Maigret could not see it all.

He chose to watch Pietr, who, having recovered from his first shock, was now trying to rally his wits. But it was too late. The dose had been too strong. Realizing this himself, he was desperately straining his will-power to the limit.

His features twisted. He must be peering at people and objects through a distorting fog. When he let go of the table he stumbled, but miraculously recovered his balance, after heeling over at a perilous angle.

'My dear Mor —' he began.

But he met the Superintendent's eye, and continued with a change of tone:

'Oh, all right! All . . .'

The door banged. Footsteps were heard, hurrying away. It was Mortimer-Levingston beating a retreat. At the same moment, Pietr dropped into a chair.

Maigret reached the door with one bound. Before rushing out, he paused and listened.

But it was no longer possible to distinguish the American's footsteps among all the varied sounds in the hotel.

'I tell you, you asked for it!' stammered Pietr, and went on muttering thickly, in an unknown language.

Maigret locked the door, hurried along the passage, and ran down a staircase.

He reached the first floor just in time to intercept a woman who was running away. He noticed a smell of gunpowder.

With his left hand he clutched the woman by her clothes. His right came down heavily on her wrist, and a revolver fell to the floor. In falling it went off, and the bullet shattered a pane of glass in the lift.

The woman struggled. She was unusually strong. The Superintendent, unable to subdue her by any other means, twisted her wrist, and she fell on her knees, screeching:

'Coward!'

The hotel was beginning to stir. Unusual noises were

echoing through all the corridors, emerging from every nook and cranny.

The first person to appear was a chambermaid in a black and white uniform. She raised her hands to heaven and fled in terror.

'Keep still!' ordered Maigret, addressing his captive, not the maid.

Both women stopped moving.

'Mercy! I haven't done anything!' cried the chambermaid.

After that, the chaos got worse and worse. People appeared from all sides. In one group the manager was waving his arms. In another there were women in evening dress; and an appalling din was rising from the whole scene.

Maigret decided to bend down and slip handcuffs on his prisoner, who was none other than Anna Gorskin. She resisted. In the struggle her dress tore, and she was reduced to her usual state of half-nakedness, but looking magnificent, with her flashing eyes and curling lips.

'Mortimer-Levingston's room?' Maigret called to the manager.

But the manager was completely out of his depth. And Maigret was all alone among the jostling, panic-stricken crowd, where to make matters worse the women were all screaming, weeping, or stampeding.

The American's suite was only a few yards away. The Superintendent had no need to open the door; it was wide open already. On the floor lay a bleeding body, still moving.

Maigret now ran back to the floor above, banged on the door he had locked with his own hand, heard not a sound, turned the key.

Pietr the Lett's rooms were empty!

The suitcase was still on the floor, near the fireplace, with the cheap suit thrown across it.

Cold air was blowing in through the open window, which gave on to a yard scarcely bigger than a chimney.

Below were the dark rectangular shapes of three doorways.

Maigret walked heavily downstairs again, and saw that the crowd had grown calmer. A doctor had been found among the hotel guests. But the women – and the men, for that matter – were taking little notice of Mortimer-Levingston, or of the doctor bending over him.

All eyes were turned on Anna Gorskin, who had collapsed in the corridor, her wrists shackled by the handcuffs, her face furious, and was hurling insults and threats at the spectators.

Her hat had slipped off, and greasy black locks of hair were dangling over her face.

One of the hotel interpreters came out of the lift with the broken pane; with him was a uniformed policeman.

'Clear the place,' Maigret ordered.

He heard vague sounds of protest behind his back. He loomed so large that he seemed to fill the corridor.

Ponderous and implacable, he walked across to Mortimer-Levingston's body.

'Well?'

The doctor was a German who spoke very little French; he launched into a lengthy explanation in a mixture of the two languages.

The lower part of Mortimer-Levingston's face had literally vanished, leaving nothing but a great red and blackish wound.

But the mouth opened, a mouth which was not quite a mouth any more, and a babbling sound emerged, with a gush of blood.

No one understood, neither Maigret, nor the doctor – who was later discovered to be a professor of Bonn University – nor the two or three people who were standing close by.

Mortimer-Levingston's fur coat was spattered with cigar ash. One of his hands lay open, with the fingers spread wide.

'Dead?' asked the Superintendent.

The doctor shook his head, and both of them fell silent.

The uproar in the passage was dying away. The policeman was pushing back the excited crowd, a step at a time, despite all resistance.

Mortimer-Levingston's lips closed, then parted again. The doctor knelt motionless for a few seconds.

Then he stood up and said, as though relieved of a heavy burden:

'Dead, *ja*. It was difficult . . .'

Someone had trodden on the edge of the fur coat, which bore the clear print of a boot.

The police officer, in his silver-braided uniform, had been standing silently for a moment in the open doorway.

'What shall I? . . .'

'Get rid of everyone. The lot,' commanded Maigret.

'The woman is screaming . . . .'

'Let her scream.'

And he went and planted himself in front of the fireplace, which had no fire in it.

CHAPTER 13

The Ugala Corporation

EVERY race has its own smell, loathed by other races. Superintendent Maigret had opened the window and was smoking steadily, but faint odours were still making him feel queasy.

Was the Hôtel du Roi de Sicile impregnated with them? Or the street? The smell had first met his nostrils when the black-capped hotel-keeper opened his little window a crack. And it had thickened as he climbed the stairs.

In Anna Gorskin's room you could cut it with a knife. There was food lying all over the place, for one thing. Flaccid sausages of a repulsive shade of pink, thickly speckled with garlic. A plate with some fried fish floating in a sour liquid.

Butts of Russian cigarettes. Dregs of tea in half a dozen cups.

And sheets and underwear that seemed to be still damp, the sourness of a bedroom that was never aired.

It was in the mattress, which he had unstitched, that Maigret found the little grey linen bag.

Photographs and a certificate tumbled out of it.

One of the photos showed a steep, cobbled street, lined with old houses, step-gabled in the Dutch manner, but white-washed. The black lines of windows, doors, and ledges stood out sharply against the harsh whiteness of the walls.

The house in the foreground bore an inscription in letters that had something of both Gothic and Russian script about them:

6 RÜTSEP

MAX JOHANNSON

TAILOR

It was a big house. A beam jutting from the gable carried a

pulley, used in the old days to hoist sacks of corn up to the loft. A flight of six steps, with an iron handrail, led from the street to the front door.

On these steps was a family group, clustered round a short, greying, colourless man of about forty – the tailor, no doubt – with a solemn, aloof expression.

His wife, in a satin dress strained to bursting-point, was seated in a carved wooden chair. She was smiling genially at the camera, though her lips were slightly compressed, so as to look 'genteel'.

In front of them were two children, holding hands. Two boys, six or eight years old, dressed in knickerbockers that came below their knees, black stockings, and white sailor shirts with embroidered collars and cuffs.

The same age! The same height! The same striking resemblance to the tailor.

But there was no mistaking the difference of character between them.

One wore a determined expression, and stared at the camera aggressively, with a kind of defiance.

The other was looking stealthily at his brother. Looking at him trustfully, admiringly.

The photographer's name was stamped at the bottom: *K. Akel, Pskov.*

The second photograph was larger and even more enlightening. It had been taken at a public dinner. Three long tables, loaded with plates and bottles, stood at right-angles to the camera. In the background, on a grey wall, hung a banner showing six flags, a coat of arms bearing a device of which the details were indistinguishable, two crossed swords, and a hunting-horn.

The diners were students, eighteen to twenty years old. They wore caps with narrow peaks edged in silver and velvet crowns, doubtless of the livid green shade so popular with the Germans and their Northern neighbours.

The young men had close-cropped hair and, in most cases, strongly marked features.

Some of them were grinning broadly at the camera. Others

were holding up curiously shaped carved wooden beer-mugs. A few had shut their eyes, dazzled by the flashlight.

Prominently displayed on the middle table was a slate on which was written:

UGALA CORPORATION
TARTU

It was one of those students' associations which exist in every university in the world.

Erect in front of the banner was a young man who stood out from all the others.

For one thing he was bare-headed, with a shaven crown that threw his features into strong emphasis.

And while most of his companions were in ordinary clothes, he wore a dinner-jacket – in which he looked slightly gawky, for his shoulders were not yet broad enough for it. Across his white waistcoat hung a broad ribbon, like that of the highest class of the Legion of Honour.

These were the presidential insignia.

Strangely enough, although most of the guests were looking towards the camera, the shyer ones, by some instinct, kept their eyes on their young leader.

And the one who was gazing at him the most intently was his double, seated at his side and craning his neck so as not to lose sight of him.

The student with the beribboned chest and the student who was devouring him with his eyes were, beyond question, the same as the two little boys outside the house at Pskov, the sons of Johannson the tailor.

The certificate was inscribed in Latin on vellum, in imitation of an ancient document. With a lavish use of archaic terms, it proclaimed a certain Hans Johannson, student of philosophy, to be a Companion of the Ugala Corporation.

And the document was signed: *Pietr Johannson, Grand Master of the Corporation.*

The linen bag also contained a packet tied with string in which there were more photographs and some letters written in Russian.

The photographs bore the name of a firm at Vilna. One of them showed a Jewish woman about fifty years of age, stout, sour-faced, and festooned with pearls like a statue in a church.

Her resemblance to Anna Gorskin was evident at a glance. And one of the other photographs showed Anna herself, at the age of sixteen or so, wearing an ermine-trimmed hat.

The heading on all the letters was the same, in three languages:

EPHRAIM GORSKIN
WHOLESALE FURRIER
FINE SIBERIAN SKINS A SPECIALITY
VILNA — WARSAW

Maigret was unable to read the writing below. But he noticed that one phrase, which recurred in several of the letters, was heavily underlined.

He put these papers into his pocket and to satisfy his conscience made a final tour of the room.

It had been occupied by the same person for so long that it had lost its impersonal, hotel-bedroom atmosphere.

The story of Anna Gorskin could be read in every trifling object, in the stains on the wallpaper, and even on the linen.

Hairs were scattered all over the place — coarse, greasy, black hairs.

Hundreds of cigarette ends. Biscuits in tins and broken biscuits on the floor. A jar of preserved ginger. A big tin containing the remains of a preserved goose, a Polish brand. A pot of caviar, vodka, whisky. A little pot which proved, when Maigret sniffed it, to contain a remnant of unprocessed opium, in compressed wafers.

Half an hour later, back at the Préfecture, he was having the letters translated to him. Certain passages caught his attention:

... Your mother's legs are getting more and more swollen. ...
... Your mother asks whether your ankles still swell when you do

351

*a lot of walking; she thinks you may have the same trouble as she
has....*

*... We are not too much worried, although the question of Vilna is
not settled. We are caught between the Lithuanians and the Poles....
But they both hate the Jews....*

*... Will you inquire about Monsieur Levassor, 65 rue d'Haute-
ville: he has ordered some skins from me, but gives no banker's
reference....*

*... When you have finished your studies you must get married and
come into the business with your husband. Your mother is no help to
me at all nowadays....*

*... Your mother sits all day in her chair.... Her temper is
becoming impossible.... You ought to come home....*

*Goldstein's son, who got here a fortnight ago, says your name is
not down at the Sorbonne. I told him that was a lie, and ...*

Your mother has had to be tapped for dropsy....

*... You have been seen in Paris in the wrong sort of company. I
wish to have an explanation....*

*... I have had some more unsatisfactory information about you.
As soon as business permits, I shall come to see for myself....*

*... If it were not that your mother refuses to be left alone, and the
doctor says there is no hope for her, I would come and fetch you at
once....*

I order you to return.

... I am sending you five hundred zloty for your train-fare....

... If you are not back in a month's time, I shall curse you....

Then more about the mother's legs. Then an account of the
girl's life in Paris, as told by a Jewish student on his return to
Vilna.

Unless you come home immediately, all is over between us.

And a final letter.

*How have you been managing for the last year, now I have
stopped sending you money? Your mother is very unhappy. And she
blames me for all that has happened.*

Superintendent Maigret did not laugh once. He put the papers in his drawer, locked it, wrote several telegrams, and then made his way to the detention cells.

Anna Gorskin had spent the night in the common lock-up. But Maigret had afterwards given orders for her to be put in a separate cell.

He began by opening the spy-hole. Anna Gorskin was sitting on a stool. She did not start, but turned her head slowly towards the door and glared disdainfully at her visitor.

He went in, and watched her for some time without a word. He knew it would be no use fencing with her, putting the kind of indirect questions that sometimes extract an involuntary confession.

She was too cool-headed to be caught in that kind of trap, and he would only lose face by attempting it.

So he merely growled:

'Will you confess?'

'Nothing!'

'You still deny you killed Mortimer-Levingston?'

'I deny it.'

'You deny that you bought that grey suit for your accomplice?'

'I deny it.'

'You deny sending it up to his room at the Majestic, with a letter in which you informed him you were going to kill Mortimer-Levingston and told him where to meet you outside?'

'I deny it.'

'What were you doing at the Majestic?'

'I was looking for Mrs Goldstein's room.'

'There is nobody of that name staying at the hotel.'

'I did not know that.'

'And why did I find you running away with a gun in your hand?'

'In the first-floor passage I saw a man shoot another and then drop his gun. I picked it up for fear he would shoot me too. I was running to warn the staff.'

'You had never seen Mortimer-Levingston before?'

'No.'

'But he went to the Roi de Sicile.'

'There are sixty people living in the hotel.'

'You don't know Pietr the Lett, or Oppenheim, either?'

'No.'

'That doesn't make sense.'

'I should worry.'

'We shall find the shopkeeper who sold you the grey suit.'

'Bring him along.'

'I have informed your father, at Vilna.'

At this she started, for the first time. But in a flash she jeered:

'If you want him to come here, send him the train-fare. Otherwise . . .'

Maigret kept his temper, watching her with a curiosity not entirely devoid of sympathy. For she had guts.

At first sight her evidence did not hold water. The facts seemed to speak for themselves.

But it is precisely in such circumstances that the police, more often than not, find themselves unable to refute the defendant's denials with conclusive evidence.

And in this case there was none! The revolver was not known to the Paris gunsmiths. So there was nothing to prove that it belonged to Anna Gorskin.

What about her presence at the Majestic when the crime was committed? But people can wander about in a large hotel as freely as they can in the street. She claimed to have been looking for someone? That was not necessarily impossible.

Nobody had seen her fire the shot. Nothing remained of the letter that Pietr the Lett had burnt.

Circumstantial evidence? There was any amount of that. But juries will not convict on circumstantial evidence, they mistrust even the most conclusive proof, in their dread of committing a miscarriage of justice – the bogy always conjured up by the defence.

Maigret played his last card:

'I have a report that Pietr is at Fécamp.'

This time he got a reaction. Anna Gorskin jumped. But telling herself that he was lying, she recovered her calm, and retorted nonchalantly:

'So what?'

'An anonymous letter, which is now being checked, says he is hiding in a house belonging to a man called Swaan.'

Her dark eyes, as she looked up at him, were grave, almost tragic.

Maigret, glancing absent-mindedly at Anna's ankles, saw that as her mother had feared she was dropsical.

Her scanty hair was dishevelled and her scalp showed through it. Her black dress was dirty.

And her upper lip showed distinct signs of a moustache.

All the same, she was beautiful, in a vulgar, animal way. Her eyes still fixed on the Superintendent, her lips curled in scorn, her body slightly drawn back, or rather crouched down, instinctively sensing danger, she snarled:

'If you know all that, why ask me questions?'

Then her eyes flashed and she went on, with an insulting laugh:

'Unless you are afraid of compromising *her*! That's it, isn't it? . . . Ha! It doesn't matter about me. A foreigner. A tart, going down the drain in the ghetto. . . . But as for her, well . . .'

Carried away by passion, she was about to break her silence. Maigret, feeling she might be put off by his concentrated attention, assumed an air of indifference and turned his head aside.

'Well – nothing! You hear me!' she screamed. 'Get out! Let me alone! Nothing, I tell you! Not a thing!'

And she flung herself on the ground, with a movement that could not have been anticipated, even by someone with experience of such women.

A fit of hysterics! Her features were distorted. She lay writhing, great shudders convulsing her body.

Only a moment ago she had been beautiful; now she was hideous. She was pulling out her hair in handfuls, regardless of the pain.

Maigret was not disconcerted. He had seen this kind of thing a hundred times before. He picked up the water-jug from the floor. It was empty.

He called a warder.

'Fill this quickly.'

Soon afterwards he was splashing cold water straight into Anna's face. She gasped, her lips parted eagerly, she looked at him without recognition, and at last fell into a stupor.

Even then, a superficial tremor passed over her from time to time.

Maigret lowered the bed, which, in accordance with regulations, was tilted against the wall, straightened the wafer-thin mattress, and with an effort lifted Anna on to it.

He did all this without a shade of resentment, with a gentleness of which he might have been thought incapable. He pulled down the unfortunate woman's skirt over her knees, felt her pulse, and stood at the bedside for a long time, looking at her.

Seen thus, she had the worn features of a woman of thirty-five. Her forehead in particular was lined with slight wrinkles that were not usually visible.

But her hands were pretty and graceful – plump, the nails smeared with cheap varnish.

Maigret filled himself a pipe, prodding it slowly and lightly with his forefinger, like a man uncertain what to do next. For a few moments he strode about the cell, the door of which was still ajar.

Suddenly he wheeled round in astonishment, doubting his own ears.

The blanket had just been pulled up over Anna Gorskin's head. All that could now be seen of her was a shapeless lump beneath the ugly grey covering.

And the lump was moving, shaken by spasms. Listening hard, he became aware of stifled sobs.

Maigret went out quietly, shut the door behind him and walked past the warder. After ten paces, however, he came back, and rapped out in a surly tone:

'Have her meals brought in from the Restaurant Dauphine.'

CHAPTER 14

Two Telegrams

MAIGRET read them aloud to Coméliau, the examining magistrate, who seemed worried.

The first was Mrs Mortimer-Levingston's reply to the telegram informing her that her husband had been murdered.

Berlin. Hôtel Modern. Sick, high fever, unable travel Stop Stones will do necessary.

Maigret smiled sourly.

'You understand? On the other hand, here is a telegram from the Wilhelmstrasse. It's in *polcod*, so I'll translate it.'

Mrs Mortimer-Levingston arrived by air staying Hôtel Modern Berlin where she received telegram Paris on returning from theatre Stop Went to bed and sent for American doctor Pelgrad Stop Doctor claims right to professional secrecy Stop Should we insist on visit from police doctor Stop Hotel servant noticed no symptoms.

'As you see, Monsieur Coméliau, the lady has no desire to be questioned by the French police. Not that I am suggesting she was hand-in-glove with her husband. On the contrary, I feel sure he kept her in the dark about ninety-nine per cent of his activities. Mortimer-Levingston was not the man to confide in a woman, and particularly not in his own wife. But the other evening at Pickwick's Bar she certainly gave a message to a professional dancing-partner, who is now being kept on ice at the Medico-Legal Institute. Maybe that was the one time necessity compelled Mortimer-Levingston to make use of her.'

'And who is Stones?' inquired the magistrate.

'Mortimer-Levingston's private secretary. He served as a link between his chief and his different business ventures. When the crime took place he had been in London for a week. Staying at the Victoria Hotel. I took care not to inform him. But I rang up Scotland Yard and asked them to get hold of him. You realize that at the time when the London police got to the Victoria, Mortimer-Levingston's death had not been announced in England, though the Press may have had wind of it. All the same, the bird had flown. Stones left a few minutes before the arrival of the police.'

The magistrate looked gloomily at the pile of letters and telegrams cluttering up his desk.

The death of a multi-millionaire affects the lives of thousands of people. And all Mortimer-Levingston's business associates were alarmed by the fact that he had met a violent end.

'You think we ought to spread the rumour that it was a crime of passion?' Monsieur Coméliau queried dubiously.

'I think it would be wise. If not, you'll start a panic on the Stock Exchange right away, and ruin some perfectly respectable businesses, including several French firms that Mortimer-Levingston had recently pumped money into.'

'Of course. But . . .'

'Wait a minute! The American Ambassador will ask you for evidence. . . . And you haven't got any! Neither have I. . . .'

The magistrate wiped his glasses.

'So? . . .'

'Nothing! . . . I'm expecting news from Dufour, who has been at Fécamp since yesterday. . . . Let Mortimer-Levingston have a handsome funeral. What does it matter anyhow? There'll be speeches, official deputations. . . .'

For the last few minutes the magistrate had been watching Maigret curiously.

'There's something funny about you,' he remarked suddenly.

The Superintendent smiled and said in a confidential tone: 'Morphine.'

'What!'

'Don't worry, I'm not an addict yet. Only an injection in my chest. . . . The doctors want to remove two of my ribs, they say it's absolutely essential. But it'll be an endless business! I shall have to go into a nursing-home and stay there for I don't know how many weeks. . . . I asked them for two or three days' respite. At worst it seems I shall only lose a third rib. Two more than Adam. But now you're making a tragedy of it, like everyone else. . . . That shows you haven't argued it out with Professor Cochet, the man who's rummaged about inside practically all the high and mighty in the world. . . . He'd tell you, as he told me, that thousands of people get along with all kinds of bits and pieces missing.

'The Prime Minister of Czechoslovakia, for instance. . . . Cochet removed one of his kidneys. . . . I saw it. . . . He showed me lungs, stomachs, all sorts of things. . . . And their owners are going about their business all over the world.'

He looked at his watch and growled below his breath:

'That chap Dufour . . .'

His face resumed its gravity. The magistrate's office was hazy with the smoke from his pipe. Maigret seemed quite at home there, sitting on a corner of the desk.

'I think I'd do better to get down to Fécamp myself,' he remarked at last with a sigh. 'There's a train in an hour.'

'Nasty business,' Monsieur Coméliau concluded, pushing aside the file.

The Superintendent was lost in contemplation of the clouds of pipe-smoke enveloping him. The spluttering of his pipe was the only sound that disturbed, or rather punctuated the silence.

'Look at this photo!' he said suddenly.

He was holding out the one taken at Pskov, with the tailor's white-gabled house, the pulley under the eaves, the six steps up to the door, the mother seated, the father self-consciously posing, and the two little boys with their embroidered sailor collars.

'That's in Russia! I had to look it up in the atlas. Near the Baltic. There are several little countries there – Estonia, Latvia, Lithuania. . . . Encircled by Poland and Russia. The frontiers haven't managed to coincide with the races. The language changes from one village to the next, in some districts. And there are the Jews as well, scattered everywhere, but a people set apart, all the same. Not to mention the communists. There's fighting along the frontiers. There are ultra-nationalist armies. . . . The people live off the fir-trees in the forests. The poor are poorer than elsewhere. Some of them die of cold and hunger. . . .

'Some of the intelligentsia are in favour of German culture, others prefer Slav culture, and others want local traditions and the old dialects. . . .

'Some of the peasants look like Lapps or Kalmuks, some are hulking, fair-haired chaps, and then there's a whole mass of Jews and part-Jews, who eat garlic and slaughter their livestock differently from the rest. . . .'

Maigret took back the photograph from the magistrate, who had glanced at it without much interest.

'Quaint kids,' was his only comment.

Handing him the photo again, the Superintendent asked:

'Could you say which of them I'm looking for?'

There was still three quarters of an hour before the train left. Monsieur Coméliau looked at each boy in turn – the one who seemed to be defying the camera, and his brother, looking away from it as though seeking his advice.

'Photographs like that are terribly revealing,' Maigret went on. 'One wonders how those chaps' parents and teachers can have failed to guess at a glance what lay ahead of them.

'Take a good look at the father. . . . He was killed in a riot, one evening when street fighting broke out between the nationalists and the communists. . . . He didn't belong to either side. . . . He had just gone out to buy bread. . . . I got that piece of information by sheer accident from the proprietor of the Roi de Sicile, who comes from Pskov. . . .

'The mother is still alive, and living in that house. On Sundays she wears national costume, with a tall cap with ear-flaps. . . .

'The children . . .'

He broke off.

'Mortimer-Levingston,' he began again, with a change of tone, 'was born on a farm in Ohio and began his career selling bootlaces in San Francisco. Anna Gorskin was born at Odessa and brought up at Vilna. Mrs Mortimer-Levingston's parents were Scots, who emigrated to Florida when she was still a child.

'And they all assemble here in Paris, a stone's throw from Notre-Dame. . . . As for my own father, he was a gamekeeper on one of the oldest estates in the Loire valley.'

He glanced again at the time, and then pointed to the boy in the photograph who was gazing with admiration at his brother.

'And now I must go and lay my hands on that lad.'

He knocked out his pipe into the coal-scuttle and just stopped himself from automatically refilling the stove.

A few moments later Monsieur Coméliau, polishing his gold-rimmed spectacles, observed to his clerk:

'Don't you find Maigret rather changed? He seemed to me . . . how can I put it . . . a little on edge . . . a little . . .'

After searching in vain for the right word, he broke off with:

'What the devil are all these foreigners doing in France?'

Then, seizing the Mortimer file, he began to dictate:

'*The year one thousand nine hundred . . .*'

Inspector Dufour was standing at the same corner where Maigret had waited, on a recent stormy morning, for the man in the trench-coat to come out. This was for the good reason that there was no other bend in the entire length of the steep lane which, after serving as a path to the few villas on the cliff-side, dwindled to a mere track and finally petered out in the close-cropped grass.

Dufour was dressed in black leggings, a short, half-belted overcoat, and a sailor's cap, such as everyone wears at Fécamp; he must have bought them as soon as he arrived.

'Well?' asked Maigret, coming up to him in the dark.

'Everything's going fine, Chief.'

The Superintendent found this somewhat alarming.

'What's going fine?'

'The man hasn't gone in, or come out. . . . If he got to Fécamp before I did, and went into that house, he must be there still.'

'Tell me exactly what has happened.'

'Yesterday morning, nothing. The maid went to do the shopping. In the evening I arranged for Inspector Bornier to relieve me. No one went in or came out during the night. At ten o'clock the lights went off. . . .'

'And then?'

'This morning I took over again, while Bornier went to get some sleep. . . . He'll be coming along to replace me. . . . The maid went out shopping about nine o'clock, the same as yesterday. . . . The lady of the house went out half an hour ago. . . . She'll soon be coming home. . . . I suppose she's gone to pay a call.'

Maigret said nothing. He was well aware of the inadequacy of this supervision. But how many men would it take to keep a really strict watch?

Merely to guard the villa, three would be none too many. And there ought to be one inspector tailing the servant and another following 'the lady of the house', as Dufour called her.

'It's half an hour since she went out?'

'Yes. . . . Hello, here comes Bornier. . . . I'm due for a meal. I've had nothing all day except a sandwich, and my feet are frozen.'

'Off you go.'

Bornier was a very young man, just starting in the Flying Squad.

'I met Madame Swaan,' he said.

'Where? When?'

'On the quay. Just a minute ago. . . . She was going towards the lower jetty.'

'All alone?'

'All alone. . . . I almost followed her. Then I said to myself that Dufour would be waiting for me. . . . The jetty is a dead end, so she can't go far.'

'How was she dressed?'

'In a dark coat. . . . I didn't specially notice.'

'Shall I go now?' asked Dufour.

'I told you to already.'

'If anything turns up you'll let me know, won't you? All you have to do is ring the hotel doorbell three times running.'

This was too silly! Maigret scarcely heard him. Saying to Bornier: 'Stay there!' he suddenly walked up to the gate of the villa Swaan and tugged so hard at the bell that he nearly pulled it out. He could see a light on the ground floor, in what he knew to be the dining-room.

He waited five minutes, but nobody appeared, so he climbed the wall – a low one – strode up to the door, and banged on it with his fist.

'Who is there?' a frightened voice quavered from inside; and the children began screaming.

'Police! Open the door!'

Hesitation. Scuffling footsteps.

'Hurry up!'

The corridor was in darkness. As he went in, Maigret could just make out the white patch of the maid's apron.

'Madame Swaan?'

At that moment a door opened and he saw the little girl he had noticed on his previous visit.

The servant did not move. She had her back to the wall and one could feel she was rigid with fright.

'Who did you meet this morning?'

'I promise you, Inspector ...'

She burst into tears.

'I swear I ...'

'Monsieur Swaan?'

'No. ... I. ... It was ... Madame's ... brother-in-law. ... He gave me a letter for her. ...'

'Where was he?'

'Outside the butcher's. ... He was waiting for me. ...'

'Had he asked you to do anything like that before?'

'No. ... Never. ... I never saw him outside this house.'

'Do you know where he asked Madame Swaan to meet him?'

'I don't know anything. ... Madame was upset all day. She

asked me questions, too. . . . She wanted to know how he looked. I told her the truth – that he looked like a man who's going to do something dreadful. When he came up to me I felt frightened, truly I did.'

Maigret suddenly walked out, leaving the front door open.

CHAPTER 15

The Man on the Rock

INSPECTOR BORNIER, new to his job, was considerably startled when his superior went past him at a run, brushing by without a word while the door of the villa still stood open.

Twice he called out:

'Superintendent! . . . Superintendent!'

But Maigret never looked round. He did not slow down until a few minutes later he came out into the Étretat road, where there were a few people about. Here he turned to the right, splashing through the mud on the quay, and began running again as he made for the lower jetty.

He had not gone a hundred yards when he saw the outline of a woman. He changed direction in order to pass closer to her. A trawler was unloading, and a lantern hung in the shrouds.

He stopped to give the woman time to reach the circle of light, and saw that it was Madame Swaan. Her face was convulsed, wild-eyed, and she was hurrying along with an unsteady gait, as though picking her way through muddy pools and avoiding them only by a miracle.

The Superintendent was just about to go up to her, and even took a few steps in her direction. But ahead of him he glimpsed the deserted jetty, a long black line stretching into the night with waves splashing up on either side.

It was in that direction that he hurried on. Once past the trawler there was not a soul to be seen. The red and green lights of the channel shone through the darkness. The lighthouse perched on the rocks flashed its beacon at fifteen-second intervals over a wide patch of sea and lit up the nearer cliff-face, lending it, for that brief instant, a kind of ghostly life.

Maigret bumped into some bollards and found himself on

the jetty, which was built on piles, surrounded by crashing waves.

His eyes searched the darkness. He could hear a boat hooting to be let out of the lock.

In front of him was the dark tumult of the sea. Behind him, the town, with its shops and its slippery cobbles.

He walked on quickly, pausing now and then to gaze round with growing apprehension.

Not knowing the lie of the land, he went out of his way in trying to take a short cut. The jetty led him to the foot of a semaphore showing three black balls, which he counted without being aware of it.

Farther on, he leant over the railing, looking down at the great patches of white foam that swirled between the rocks.

His hat blew away. He chased it, but was too late to prevent it from falling into the sea.

Seagulls were uttering piercing cries above his head, and occasionally a white wing flashed against the sky.

Had Madame Swaan found nobody at the meeting-place? Had her companion had time to get away? Was he dead?

Maigret was consumed with impatience, convinced that he would have his answer in a matter of seconds.

He reached the green light and circled round the iron girders that supported it.

Nobody there! And the waves rolled in, one by one, to attack the breakwater – rearing up, tottering, retreating in a great whitish trough, only to return with fresh impetus.

An occasional sound of pebbles grinding against one another. The dim outline of the empty casino.

Maigret was looking for a man!

Turning back, he scrambled down to the beach, among stones that looked, in the darkness, like monstrous potatoes.

He was on a level with the waves now, and their spray blew into his face.

It was then he noticed that the tide was out and the jetty surrounded by a ring of black rocks, with water dashing up and bubbling round them.

It was a miracle that he noticed the man at all. At the first glance he took him for some inanimate object, a vague shadow among shadows.

He looked harder. It was on the farthest rock, where the waves reared their crests most proudly before crashing over in a cloud of spray.

There was something living there. . . .

To reach it, Maigret had to thread his way between the piles supporting the jetty along which he had been walking a few minutes earlier.

The stones were covered with seaweed. His feet slipped. He could hear a surging murmur made up of many sounds – like the scampering of hundreds of crabs, the bursting of bubbles or of sea-grown berries, and the imperceptible quivering of the mussels that coated the lower halves of the baulks on which the jetty rested.

Once, Maigret lost his footing, and one leg sank up to the knee in a pool of water.

He could not see the man any longer, but he was going in the right direction.

The man must have come out here when the tide was lower, for the Superintendent was suddenly halted by a pool two yards across. He groped for the bottom of it with his right foot and nearly fell forward. In the end he had to swing himself over by the crossbeams.

It was one of those occasions when a man prefers to have nobody watching him. He made uncoordinated movements. He constantly missed his mark, like a clumsy acrobat. But he went on, just by sheer momentum. He fell; he picked himself up again. He floundered, undignified and ungraceful.

He cut his cheek, and could never say afterwards whether he had done it in falling flat on the rocks, or scraped it on a nail projecting from one of the beams.

He had another glimpse of the man – hardly believing his eyes because the figure was so still and looked so like one of those stones which, from a distance, resemble human shapes.

After a certain point, the water was lapping round his

shins. He was no seaman. Without realizing it, he began to quicken his pace. At last he reached the group of rocks where the man was perched. Maigret was three feet above him and ten or fifteen paces away.

It did not occur to him to take out his revolver. He went forward, walking on tiptoe where the ground permitted it, loosening pebbles with a rattle that was drowned by the noise of the tide.

Then, suddenly, without a pause, he leapt on the motionless figure, caught the man's neck in the crook of his elbow, and pushed him over backwards.

The two nearly slipped down, to be swept away by the extra-powerful wave which broke at that instant. It was pure chance that that did not happen. Made deliberately ten times, the same move might have gone wrong every time.

The man, who had not seen his aggressor, was squirming like an eel. His head was wedged, but his body wriggled with an agility which in these surroundings was almost super-human.

Maigret did not want to choke him. He was only trying to keep him still. He had one foot hooked round the farthest pile of the jetty, and that was holding up the pair of them.

His opponent's resistance was brief. It had been merely a spontaneous, animal reaction.

As soon as he had had time to think – or at any rate as soon as he caught sight of Maigret, whose face was almost touching his own – he stopped moving.

He blinked his eyes to indicate surrender, and as soon as his neck was released he pointed vaguely to the heaving mass of water and faltered in a voice that had not yet recovered its strength:

'Take care . . .'

'Shall we have a talk, Hans Johannson?' said Maigret, digging his fingers into the slippery seaweed.

Later he was to admit that at that precise moment his companion could have sent him flying into the water with one kick.

The opportunity lasted for only a second, but Johannson,

crouching beside the first baulk of timber, made no attempt to take advantage of it.

Later, too, Maigret frankly admitted that for a moment he had had to clutch his prisoner's foot, to help himself up the rock.

Then, without a word, the two of them set out on the return journey. The tide was already higher. Not far from the shore they were cut off by the same pool that had delayed the Superintendent on his way out, and which was now deeper.

Pietr stepped into it first, was out of his depth after three yards, splashed, spat, and finally emerged, up to his waist in water.

Maigret threw himself forward. At one moment he shut his eyes, feeling that his body was too heavy to be kept afloat.

The two men came together again, drenched and dripping, on the pebbly beach.

'Did she talk?' asked Pietr in a lifeless voice – a voice which at all events held no echo of what makes a man cling to life.

Maigret could have lied to him. But he preferred to answer:
'She didn't say a word. . . . But I know.'

They could not possibly stay where they were. In that wind their wet clothes were turning into icy bandages. Pietr's teeth began chattering first. In the faint moonlight Maigret saw that his lips were blue.

He had no moustache. This was the anxious face of Fédor Yurovich, the face of the little boy at Pskov, devouring his brother with his eyes. But although those eyes were of the same misty grey, there was now a painful intensity in their expression.

Making a three-quarter turn to the right, the two men could see the cliff, with two or three specks of light shining from it – the villas, including Madame Swaan's.

And when the pencil of light from the lighthouse swept past, they could dimly make out the roof that sheltered her, with her two children and the frightened servant.

'Come,' said Maigret.
'To the police station?'

The voice was resigned, or rather, indifferent.
'No.'

He knew one of the hotels beside the harbour – Chez Léon –
and had noticed one entrance that was only used in the
summer, by the few people who came to Fécamp for seaside
holidays. This door led to a room which in the season was
used to serve fairly expensive meals.

In winter-time the fishermen were quite satisfied to drink
and eat oysters and herrings in the main café.

This was the door that Maigret opened. He walked with his
companion across the dark room and ended up in the kitchen,
where a little maid uttered a cry of astonishment.

'Fetch the boss.'

Without moving from the spot, she shouted:

'Monsieur Léon! ... Monsieur Léon ...'

'A room,' said the Superintendent, when Monsieur Léon
arrived.

'Monsieur Maigret! ... But you're wet ... Have you? ...'

'A room. Quickly!'

'There's no fire in the bedrooms! ... And a hot-water
bottle will never be enough to ...'

'You must have a couple of dressing-gowns?'

'Yes, of course. ... My own ... but ...'

He was three heads shorter than the Superintendent.

'Bring them along!'

They went up a steep staircase with sharp, unexpected
bends in it. The room was clean. Monsieur Léon closed the
shutters and suggested:

'A hot toddy, eh? ... A stiff one!'

'That's it. ... But the dressing-gowns first of all.'

Maigret was beginning to feel ill again, from the cold. The
injured side of his chest felt frozen.

For the next few minutes he and his companion behaved
with the easy informality of soldiers in barracks. They undressed in front of each other. Monsieur Léon opened the
door a crack and slipped his arm inside, with two dressing-
gowns draped over it.

'Give me the biggest one,' said the Superintendent.

The Lett compared the two.

Holding one of them out to his companion, he caught sight of the sopping bandage, and his face twitched.

'Is it serious?'

'Two or three ribs to be removed one of these days.'

This was followed by a silence. Monsieur Léon broke it by inquiring from outside:

'Getting on all right?'

'Come in.'

Maigret's dressing-gown scarcely reached his knees, leaving a pair of bulging, hairy calves uncovered.

The Lett, slight and pale, with his fair hair and slender ankles, in this garb had the elegance of an acrobat.

'The toddy will be along at once. I'd better put your things to dry, hadn't I?' said Monsieur Léon. He gathered up the two soggy heaps of clothing, went to the head of the stairs and shouted:

'Well, Henriette? Where's that toddy?'

Then he came back with a caution:

'Don't talk too loud. There's a commercial traveller from Le Havre in the next room, and he has to catch a train at five o'clock tomorrow morning.'

CHAPTER 16

The Bottles of Rum

It would perhaps be an exaggeration to suggest that in the course of an inquiry cordial relations often develop between the police and the individual from whom they are trying to obtain a confession.

But unless the criminal is a mere soulless brute, a kind of intimacy nearly always grows up. No doubt owing to the fact that for weeks, sometimes for months, the detective and the offender are concentrating entirely on one another.

The detective is doing his level best to get some idea of the criminal's past life, to reconstruct his ideas and anticipate his slightest reactions.

For both, it is a matter of life and death. And when they come face to face, the situation is sufficiently dramatic to break down the barrier of polite indifference that in ordinary circumstances divides one man from another.

Detectives have been known, after catching a criminal, at the cost of strenuous efforts, to grow attached to him, visit him in jail, and give him moral support till the very moment when he mounts the scaffold.

This partly accounts for the behaviour of the two men once they were alone in the room. The hotel-keeper had brought in a charcoal stove, and a kettle stood singing on it. Close at hand, flanked by two glasses and a sugar basin, stood a tall bottle of rum.

They were both cold. Huddled in their borrowed dressing-gowns, they bent over the inadequate stove, which was not enough to warm them.

Their attitude had the casual ease of the guardroom or the barracks, an informality seldom found except among men for whom social conventions have temporarily ceased to count.

Perhaps it was simply because they were cold. Or more

likely because both were suddenly overwhelmed by fatigue.

It was over! No words were needed to convince them of that!

So they dropped into their respective chairs and stretched out their hands towards the kettle, staring vaguely at the blue enamel stove, which formed a kind of bond between them.

It was the Lett who picked up the bottle of rum and, with deft movements, prepared the two glasses of toddy.

After taking a few sips, Maigret asked:

'Did you mean to kill her?'

The reply came at once, with equal simplicity:

'I couldn't do it.'

But the man's whole face was working, contorted by a tic that seemed to give him no respite.

Sometimes he blinked rapidly, several times in succession; sometimes his lips twisted this way or that; sometimes his nostrils quivered.

Pietr's firm, intelligent features were becoming blurred.

The Russian was gaining the upper hand – the tramp with the overstrained nerves, whose movements Maigret did not bother to watch.

Thus he failed to notice that his companion had seized the bottle of rum, filled his glass and emptied it at one gulp, and that his eyes were beginning to glisten.

'Pietr was her husband? . . . He and Olaf Swaan were one and the same person, isn't that so?'

The Lett could not keep still. He got up and looked round for cigarettes; but there were none to be found, which seemed to distress him. As he went past the table where the stove stood, he helped himself to some more rum.

'That's not the place to begin,' he said.

Looking his companion straight in the face, he added:

'You know everything, or practically everything, don't you?'

'The two brothers at Pskov . . . twins, I suppose? You're Hans, the one who looked so admiringly and submissively at the other.'

'When we were still quite small, he began to treat me like a servant. . . . Not only when we were by ourselves, but in front of our schoolfriends. . . . He didn't say "servant", he said "slave". . . . He had noticed that I liked it. . . . I *did* like it. I still don't know why. . . . I saw everything through his eyes. . . . I would have died for him. . . . Later on, when . . .'

'Later on, when . . .?'

Twitching features. Blinking. A mouthful of rum.

Then a shrug, as much as to say:

'Oh well. . . .'

And he resumed in a steady voice:

'Later on, when I fell in love with a woman, I don't think my devotion to her was greater. . . . Probably less. I used to fight the other boys if they questioned his leadership. I wasn't as strong as they were, but I felt a kind of exhilaration when they knocked me about.'

'You often get that sort of bossiness with twins,' observed Maigret as he mixed himself another toddy. 'Excuse me a moment.'

Going to the door, he called to the proprietor to ask for his pipe, which had been carried off with his clothes, and for a packet of tobacco.

'And could I have some cigarettes?' his companion put in.

'And some cigarettes, *patron*. . . . *Gauloises bleues!*'

He sat down again. Both men waited in silence till the maid had brought what they wanted and gone away again.

'You were at Tartu University together . . .' Maigret began again.

The Lett could not sit still. As he smoked he bit into his cigarette, spat out flakes of tobacco, strode jerkily to and fro, picked up a vase that stood on the mantelpiece, put it down in a different place. His words came with feverish haste.

'That's where it began, yes. My brother was the best student of his year. All the professors were interested in him. The other students accepted him as a leader. So much so that although he was one of the youngest, they elected him President of *Ugala*.

'We used to drink a lot of beer in the local taverns. I drank

374

most of all. I don't know why I started drinking at that early age. I had no reason for it. Anyhow, I've been drinking all my life.

'I think it was chiefly because after a few glasses I could begin to imagine a world made to my own measure, where I should play a brilliant part. . . .

'Pietr was very hard on me. He used to call me a "dirty Russian". You don't know what that means! Our mother's mother was Russian. And in our country, especially after the war, the Russians were regarded as lazy, drunken idlers. . . .

'At that time the communists were provoking riots. My brother collected the members of *Ugala*, they went to a barracks and armed themselves, and then they started fighting, right in the middle of the town.

'I was afraid. . . . It wasn't my fault. . . . I was frightened. . . . I couldn't walk. . . . I stayed in a tavern behind closed shutters, and sat there drinking till it was all over. . . .

'I wanted to be a great dramatist, like Chekhov. I knew all his plays by heart. But Pietr laughed and said:

'"You'll never be anything but a wash-out!"

'There was a whole year of disturbances and riots, with life completely disrupted. The army wasn't strong enough to keep order, so the civilians formed themselves into armed bands, to defend the town.

'As leader of the *Ugala* boys, my brother became a person of importance, taken seriously even by the most respectable citizens. Before his moustache began to grow he was being tipped as a future statesman in an independent Estonia.

'But order was restored, and then a scandal came to light and had to be hushed up. When the accounts were drawn up it turned out that Pietr had used *Ugala* chiefly for his own ends.

'He was a member of several committees, and he'd been cooking the books of all of them.

'He had to leave the country. . . . He went to Berlin, and wrote to me to join him there.

'That's where we both started our careers.'

Maigret was watching the other man's over-excited face.

'Who did the forgeries?'

'Pietr taught me to imitate every kind of writing, and sent me to study chemistry. I lived in one small room and he gave me 200 marks a month. . . . A few weeks later he bought himself a car to take his mistresses for drives. . . .

'Mostly, we used to touch up cheques. . . . Pietr would give me a ten-mark cheque, I would alter it to ten thousand marks, and he would get cash for it – in Switzerland or Holland; once even in Spain. . . .

'I used to drink a great deal. He despised me and ill-treated me. Once I nearly got him caught, unintentionally, because of a forgery that wasn't quite as good as the others.

'He thrashed me with a walking-stick. . . .

'And I didn't say a word! I still admired him. . . . I don't know why. . . . But everybody was impressed by him. . . . There was a time when, if he'd wanted to, he might have married the daughter of a German cabinet minister. . . .

'Because of that bungled cheque we had to move to France; at first I lived in the rue de l'École-de-Médecine. . . .

'Pietr wasn't working alone any more. He had joined up with several international gangs. . . . He was travelling abroad a lot, and making less and less use of me. . . . Only now and again, for forgeries, because I had got very handy at that job. . . .

'He used to give me a little money.

'"Drinking is all you'll ever be fit for, you dirty Russian!" he kept saying.

'One day he told me he was going to America on some terrific job that would make him the equivalent of a multi-millionaire. He ordered me to move to the country, because the Paris police had already questioned me several times.

'"All I want is for you to keep quiet! That's not too much to ask, is it?"

'At the same time he ordered me to find him a whole batch of false passports, and I did.

'Then I went to Le Havre. . . .'

'And there you met the future Madame Swaan. . . . Her name was Berthe.'

A silence. The other man's Adam's apple swelled in his throat.

At last he broke out:

'How I longed to become *something*, then! She was the receptionist at the hotel where I was staying. . . . She used to see me coming back drunk every night. . . . And she scolded me. . . .

'She was very young, but serious. She made me think of a home, and children. . . .

'One evening when she was telling me off and I wasn't too hopelessly tight, I wept in her arms, and I believe I promised to mend my ways.

'And I think I'd have kept my word. I was fed up with everything! Sick of dragging around. . . .

'It lasted nearly a month. . . . Silly, when you come to think of it. . . . On Sundays we used to go and listen to the band in the public gardens. . . . It was autumn. . . . We'd walk back by the harbour and look at the boats. . . .

'We didn't talk about love. . . . She said she was my friend. . . . But I knew that one day. . . .

'Oh yes! . . . One day, my brother came back. . . . He needed me in a hurry. . . . He had a whole suitcase full of cheques to be doctored. . . . Heaven knows how he'd collected so many! They were drawn on every big bank in the world. . . .

'On this occasion he'd turned himself into an officer of the merchant navy, by the name of Olaf Swaan. . . .

'He took a room at my hotel. . . . For weeks on end, while I was doctoring the cheques – for that's a delicate job! – he went round all the ports along that coast, looking for boats to buy. . . .

'His new scheme was going well. He told me he had concluded an arrangement with one of the biggest American tycoons – who wasn't to appear openly in the business, of course.

'They were trying to bring all the most important international gangs under one leadership.

'The bootleggers had already reached agreement. . . . Now they needed small boats to smuggle the drink. . . .

'Do I need to tell you the rest? Pietr had cut off my supply of alcohol, so as to force me to work. . . . I was shut up in my room all day, surrounded by watchmaker's eyeglasses, bottles of acid, pens, inks of all kinds, and even a portable printing-press. . . .

'One day I went into my brother's room without warning.

'Berthe was in his arms. . . .'

He grabbed the bottle, which was down to its dregs by now, and emptied it at one draught.

'I left,' he concluded, in a voice that sounded strange. 'It was all I could do. I left. . . . I caught a train. I trailed round all the *bistros* in Paris for days and days. . . . I ended up in the rue du Roi de Sicile, dead drunk and as sick as a dog!'

CHAPTER 17

Hans and His Mistress

'IT seems to be my fate to be pitied by women. When I came round, Anna was fussing over me. . . .

'And she took it into her head to stop me drinking, too! . . . She treated me like a child, the same as Berthe used to do! . . .'

He laughed. His eyes were misty. It was exhausting to watch his restless movements and the play of his features.

'But she stuck to it. As for Pietr . . . Well, I suppose it's not for nothing that we're twins; we must have *some* things in common.

'I told you he could have married a German girl from one of the best families. . . . But no! He married Berthe, a little later, when she had left her job and gone to work at Fécamp. . . . He didn't tell her the truth.

'I can understand it all. . . . The need to have a decent, quiet corner somewhere, you know. . . .

'He has children! . . .'

This seemed to be too much! The man's voice broke. Real tears came into his eyes; but they dried at once, as though his eyelids had scorched them up.

'Until this very morning she still believed she'd married a real captain in the merchant navy. . . .

'He came now and then to stay with her and the kids – it might be for a couple of days, or for a month. . . .

'Meantime, I couldn't get rid of the other one. . . . Anna. . . .

'Heaven alone knows why she loved me. . . . But she did, that's certain. . . .

'And I treated her the way I'd been treated all my life by my brother. . . . I used to insult her. . . . I was always humiliating her. . . .

'When I got tight she used to cry. . . . And I used to drink on purpose! . . .

379

'I even took opium and all kinds of filth. . . . On purpose! . . .

'Then I fell ill, and she nursed me for weeks. . . . Because this broke down in the end. . . .' He pointed at his body with an air of disgust. Then he said imploringly:

'Won't you ask for some drink?'

After only a second's hesitation, Maigret went to the head of the stairs and called:

'Send up some more rum!'

The Lett did not thank him.

'From time to time I would run away to Fécamp, to hang about the villa where Berthe had gone to live. . . . I can see her now, pushing her first baby in its pram. . . .

'Pietr had been forced to tell her I was his brother, because of the resemblance. . . .

'One day I had another idea. . . . Way back, when we were kids, I used to imitate Pietr's manner, out of admiration for him. . . .

'Now I was tormented by so many strange ideas that one day I dressed up like him and went to Fécamp. . . .

'The servant had no suspicion. . . . But as I was about to go in, the little girl appeared, and called:

'"Papa! . . ."

'I'm a fool! I ran away! But the idea was fixed in my mind. . . .

'At rare intervals Pietr used to send word for me to meet him. . . . He needed something forged. . . .

'And I'd do it! Why?

'I hated him, and yet I was still under his thumb. . . .

'He was dealing in millions, staying in big hotels, appearing in society. . . .

'Twice he was caught, and both times he got away with it. . . .

'I never concerned myself with his organization, but you'll have guessed the kind of set-up, as I did. So long as he was on his own, or with only a handful of accomplices, he'd kept to moderate-sized affairs. . . .

'But he caught the attention of Mortimer-Levingston,

whom I never met till the other day. . . . My brother had brains, daring, one might even say genius. Mortimer-Levingston had the veneer of respectability and a well-established international reputation. . . .

'Pietr's job was to rope in the big sharks, under his leadership, and organize the deals.

'Mortimer-Levingston acted as their banker. . . .

'All that meant nothing to me. . . . As my brother had predicted, when I was only a student at Tartu, I was a washout. . . . And like all washouts, I was drinking, alternating between bouts of depression and excitement. . . .

'I had just one lifeline. I still wonder why I clung to it through all that buffeting. I suppose because it was associated with my only glimpse of possible happiness: Berthe. . . .

'As ill-luck would have it, I went down there last month. . . . Berthe gave me advice. . . . And she added:

'"Why don't you follow your brother's example?"

'Then I was suddenly struck by an idea. I couldn't understand why I hadn't thought of it sooner. . . .

'I could actually become Pietr, whenever I chose!

'A few days later he wrote to say he was coming to France and would be needing me.

'I went to Brussels to wait for him. I got into the train on the wrong side and hid behind a pile of suitcases until I saw him get up to go to the toilet. I was there first. . . .

'I killed him! I'd just swallowed a whole bottle of Belgian gin. The hardest part of it was getting him undressed and into my own clothes. . . .'

He drank greedily, with an eagerness Maigret would not have thought possible.

'When you first spoke to Mortimer-Levingston, at the Majestic, did he notice anything?'

'I rather think so. But only as a vague suspicion. At that time I had only one idea – to see Berthe again. . . .

'I wanted to tell her the truth. . . . I felt no real remorse, and yet I couldn't take advantage of my crime. . . . In Pietr's trunk there were all sorts of clothes. . . . I dressed up like a tramp, in my usual style. I left the hotel by the back way. . . . I felt Mortimer-Levingston was following me, and it took me two hours to shake him off. . . .

'Then I hired a car and had myself driven to Fécamp. . . .

'Berthe couldn't understand why I'd come. . . . And once I was in front of her, and she was asking me questions, I no longer had the courage to confess!

'You arrived on the scene. . . . I saw you from the window. . . . I told Berthe the police were after me for theft, and asked her to save me.

'After you left, she said:

'"And now, go! You are dishonouring your brother's house. . . ."

'Yes, she really said that! And I left! And we went back to Paris, you and I. . . .

'There I found Anna. . . . A scene, of course! Tears! . . . At midnight, Mortimer-Levingston arrived. By this time he'd understood everything, and threatened to have me killed unless I took Pietr's place once and for all. . . .

'It was a very serious matter for him. . . . Pietr was his only contact with the gangs. . . . Without him, he had no hold over them. . . .

'Back to the Majestic. . . . And you after me! . . . I heard some talk about a detective being killed. . . . I saw you, all stiff inside your jacket. . . .

'You'll never know how sick I was of life. . . .

'At the idea that I was doomed to act the part of my brother for the rest of my days. . . .

'You remember the little bar? . . . And the photo you dropped? . . .

'When Mortimer-Levingston came to the Roi de Sicile, Anna had objected. . . . She felt the arrangement was to her disadvantage. . . . She realized that my new role would take me away from her. . . .

'That evening, in my room at the Majestic, I found a parcel and a letter. . . .'

'An off-the-peg grey suit and a note from Anna to say she

was going to kill Mortimer-Levingston, and appointing a place for you to meet her. . . .'

The atmosphere was now thick with smoke, and warmer. The outlines of things were becoming hazy. . . .

'You came here to kill Berthe,' said Maigret deliberately.

His companion was drinking. He emptied his glass before he replied, clutching the mantelpiece to keep himself upright.

'To put an end to everything! Including myself! . . . I was sick of it all! . . . I had one idea left, of the kind my brother used to call typically Russian. . . . That Berthe and I should die together, in each other's arms. . . .'

He broke off, to say in a changed voice:

'Idiotic! It takes a quart of spirits to give one an idea like that. . . . There was a policeman outside the gate. . . . I was sober by then. . . . I wandered about. . . . This morning I gave the maid a note asking my sister-in-law to meet me on the lower jetty, and telling her that unless she brought me a little money herself, I should be caught. . . .

'Revolting, wasn't it? . . .

'She came. . . .'

Then, propping his elbows on the marble chimney-piece, he suddenly burst into tears – not like a man, but like a child. In a voice half choked by sobs, he continued his story.

'I hadn't the courage. . . . It was almost dark. . . . The sea was roaring. . . . And her face – with the first signs of anxiety. . . . I told her everything. . . . Everything! Including the murder! . . . Yes, with the change of clothes in the cramped space in the toilet. . . . Then, because she looked as though she were out of her mind, I swore it wasn't true. . . . Wait! Not about the crime. . . . But about Pietr being a scoundrel. . . . I shouted at her that I'd made that up, to revenge myself. . . . I expect she believed me. . . . *One always believes things like that.* . . . She dropped her bag on the ground, with the money she had brought. And she said . . . No. She couldn't speak.'

Raising his head, he turned his tortured face towards Maigret and tried to take a step forward – but staggered and had to clutch at the mantelpiece.

'Pass me the bottle, you. . . .'

And in the 'you' there was a note of gruff affection.

'Here. Give me that photo a minute. . . . You know . . .'

Maigret produced Berthe's photograph from his pocket. This was his only mistake throughout the whole business – the mistake of imagining that at that moment it was she who was foremost in Hans's thoughts.

'No. . . . The other. . . .'

The one of the two little boys with sailor collars.

The Lett gazed at it as though in a trance. The Superintendent was looking at it upside down, but he could see the admiration with which the fairer boy was watching his brother.

'They took away my gun with my clothes,' Hans suddenly said in a flat, colourless voice, as he looked round him.

Maigret's face was scarlet. He pointed awkwardly to the bed, where his own revolver lay.

At that the Lett relaxed his grip on the chimney-piece. He was not staggering now. He had mustered all his strength.

He walked past, within a yard of the Superintendent. They were both in dressing-gowns. They had shared the bottles of rum.

Their two chairs were still facing each other on either side of the charcoal stove.

Their eyes met. Maigret had not the heart to turn his head away. He was expecting a pause.

But Hans went by, very erect, and sat down on the edge of the bed; the springs creaked.

The second bottle had a little rum left in it. The Superintendent picked it up. It clinked against his glass as he poured.

He drank slowly. Or rather he pretended to drink. He was holding his breath.

At last came a report. He drained his glass at one gulp.

In official language, the story ran:

On – November 19 – , at 10 p.m., Hans Johansson, born at Pskov, Russia, of Estonian nationality, no occupation, resident in the rue du Roi de Sicile, Paris, having confessed to the murder of his

384

brother, Pietr Johannson, killed in the North Star express on –
November of the same year, took his own life by shooting himself in
the mouth, shortly after being arrested, at Fécamp, by Superintendent
Maigret of No. 1 Flying Squad.

The projectile, of 6 mm. calibre, passed through the roof of the
mouth and lodged in the brain. Death was instantaneous.

The body was transported, for the necessary formalities, to the
Medico-Legal Institute, which delivered a receipt for it.

CHAPTER 18

The Wounded Man

THE ambulance men left, though not until they had enjoyed a glass of Madame Maigret's own plum brandy – she prepared it every year in her native village in Alsace, where she always returned for the summer holidays.

When the door had closed behind them and the sound of their footsteps was dying away down the stairs, she went into the bedroom, where the wallpaper was patterned with bunches of roses.

Maigret, looking a little tired, with narrow dark rings round his eyes, lay in the big bed whose most prominent feature was a red silk eiderdown.

'Did they hurt you?' asked his wife, as she tidied the room.

'Not too badly. . . .'

'Are you allowed to eat?'

'A little. . . .'

'Fancy you being operated on by the surgeon who's done all those kings, and people like Clemenceau and Courteline. . . .'

She opened the window to shake out a rug on which one of the ambulance men had left footmarks. Then she went into the kitchen, shifted a saucepan on the stove, took off the lid, and put it on again slightly to one side.

'Tell me, dear . . .' she began when she came back.

'What?'

'Do *you* believe that business about a crime of passion?'

'Who are you talking about?'

'About that Anna Gorskin, whose trial opens today, the woman who lived in the rue du Roi de Sicile and says she was in love with Mortimer-Levingston and killed him out of jealousy.'

'Oh, so it's today?'

'It doesn't make sense.'

'Well, you know, life is so complicated. . . . You might pull my pillow up.'

'You think she'll be acquitted?'

'A lot of those women are!'

'That's just what I'm saying. . . . Wasn't she mixed up in your case?'

'Vaguely. . . .' he sighed.

Madame Maigret shrugged her shoulders. 'It's a lot of use being married to a member of the Judicial Police!'

But she said this with a smile.

'When anything happens,' she added, 'I hear about it from the concierge. . . . She has a nephew who's a journalist. . . .'

This time Maigret laughed too.

Before his operation he had gone twice to see Anna in the women's prison.

The first time she had scratched his face.

The second time she had given him information which had led to the arrest, on the following day, at a lodging-house in the Bagnolet district, of Pepito Moretto, the murderer of Torrence and of José Latourie.

Days and days without news! From time to time a telephone call from the ends of the earth, which did little to reassure her. And then, one fine morning, Maigret had come home, looking completely done up, collapsed into his chair, and gasped:

'Go and fetch the doctor. . . .'

Now she was bustling happily about the flat, pretending to grumble, just for the principle of the thing; stirring the stew that bubbled in her saucepan, carrying buckets of water here and there, opening windows and shutting them again, and from time to time inquiring:

'A pipe?'

On the last occasion there was no reply.

Maigret was asleep, the lower half of his body buried under the red eiderdown, his head sunk into the big, soft pillow, his features in repose, while all these homely sounds fluttered round him.

In the Palais de Justice, Anna Gorskin was fighting for her life.

Pepito Moretto, in the Santé prison, knew that his was doomed. In the cell where he was kept under permanent observation, he prowled ceaselessly round and round beneath the gloomy eye of a gaoler, whose face was divided into squares by the grating in the door.

At Pskov, an old woman in national costume, the flaps of her bonnet pulled down over her cheeks, would now be on the way to church, her sledge gliding over the snow while a drunken coachman lashed at a pony which trotted jerkily, like a clockwork toy.

MORE ABOUT PENGUINS
AND PELICANS

For further information about books available from Penguins please write to Dept EP, Penguin Books Ltd, Harmondsworth, Middlesex UB7 0DA.

In the U.S.A.: For a complete list of books available from Penguins in the United States write to Dept DG, Penguin Books, 299 Murray Hill Parkway, East Rutherford, New Jersey 07073.

In Canada: For a complete list of books available from Penguins in Canada write to Penguin Books Canada Ltd, 2801 John Street, Markham, Ontario L3R 1B4.

In Australia: For a complete list of books available from Penguins in Australia write to the Marketing Department, Penguin Books Australia Ltd, P.O. Box 257, Ringwood, Victoria 3134.

In New Zealand: For a complete list of books available from Penguins in New Zealand write to the Marketing Department, Penguin Books (N.Z.) Ltd, P.O. Box 4019, Auckland 10.

Georges Simenon

A selection

MAIGRET'S CHRISTMAS

A soft cough in the dark . . . the rasp of a match . . . the sigh of a smoke cloud – Maigret at work.

Here are nine entrancing stories featuring that laconic pipe-puffing detective, Chief Superintendent Maigret. Some are set in Paris, some deep in the provinces – there are memorable scenes in Maigret's office at the Quai des Orfèvres, a remote country inn and the bustling streets and cafés of Paris.

Maigret's patience, ingenuity and compassion are put to the test and, as we follow him through the various stages of his career, and even into a not uneventful retirement, we catch a rare glimpse of Maigret at home as well as at work.

MAIGRET AND THE GHOST

Three stories by the writer who blends, *par excellence*, the light and the shadow, cynicism and compassion . . .

Maigret and the Hotel Majestic finds Superintendent Maigret investigating the murder of a woman whose strangled body was found in a hotel basement. There are several suspects . . .

Three Beds in Manhattan is the poignant story of two lonely people who meet in a bar in Greenwich Village. Unable to part, they drift from one sordid bar to another as they talk over their past lives and muse on the future.

In *Maigret and the Ghost* a plain-clothes detective is shot and the young woman with whom he had been spending the night vanishes. Maigret's investigations lead him into the world of art-collecting as the story draws to a dramatic close.

G. K. Chesterton

THE PENGUIN
COMPLETE FATHER BROWN

All forty-nine sensational cases investigated by the high-priest of detective fiction, Father Brown.

Immortalized in these famous stories, G. K. Chesterton's little Norfolk priest has entertained and endeared himself to countless generations of readers. For, as his admirers know, Father Brown's cherubic face and unworldly simplicity, his glasses and his huge umbrella, disguise a quite uncanny understanding of the criminal mind at work . . .

This Penguin Omnibus edition contains:

THE INNOCENCE OF FATHER BROWN
THE WISDOM OF FATHER BROWN
THE INCREDULITY OF FATHER BROWN
THE SECRET OF FATHER BROWN
THE SCANDAL OF FATHER BROWN

THE MAN WHO WAS THURSDAY

A secret society of revolutionaries has sworn to destroy the world.

There are seven members of the Central Anarchist Council who, for reasons of security, call themselves by the names of the days of the week – Sunday, Monday, and so on. But events soon cast a doubt on their real identities. Thursday, for example, is not the passionate young poet he appears to be, but a Scotland Yard Detective. Who and what are the others?

As this brilliantly funny detective story develops into a rich, paradoxical nightmare, Chesterton probes some of the mysteries of human behaviour and belief.

and

THE NAPOLEON OF NOTTING HILL

Wilkie Collins

THE MOONSTONE
Edited by J. I. M. Stewart

'The first, the longest, and the best of modern English detective novels,' wrote T. S. Eliot of *The Moonstone*. In the infancy of a craft Wilkie Collins grasped the essential ingredients with the confident intuition of a master. Few of his successors have attempted anything on so magnificent a scale: few have equalled his ability at creating mystery, suspense and atmosphere, and hardly any could have maintained the reader's interest so unfalteringly over so many pages.

THE WOMAN IN WHITE
Edited by Julian Symons

The Woman in White was a tremendous success when it first appeared in 1860 – Gladstone put off a theatre party in order to read it. Thackeray sat up all night to finish it – and it has not lost its power to enthral, as much for the force and flexibility of Wilkie Collins' characterization as for its masterful plotting and maintenance of suspense. From the moment when 'the Woman' first appears to Walter Hartright on the moonlit road in North London, the reader is caught up in the spell of the book and held by it to the end. Among the many memorable characters the finest is generally agreed to be Count Fosco, the Napoleonic villain whose corpulent figure and eccentric habits add actuality to his melodramatic role. If *The Moonstone* was the first great detective novel, *The Woman in White* is probably still the greatest mystery thriller in the language.

Sir Arthur Conan Doyle

A STUDY IN SCARLET

'There's the scarlet thread of murder running through the colourless skein of life, and our duty is to unravel it, and isolate it, and expose every inch of it.'

In this, their first adventure, Sherlock Holmes and Dr Watson uncover a thrilling story of murder, love and revenge, which began years before in Salt Lake City . . .

THE HOUND OF THE BASKERVILLES

The ancient legend of the hound of the Baskervilles had persisted in family history for generations. And it was Sir Charles's mysterious death in the grounds of Baskerville Hall that brought Sherlock Holmes to the scene of one of his most famous and intriguing cases.

'He was running, Watson – running desperately, running for his life, running until he burst his heart and fell dead upon his face . . .' What had it been, then, looming through the darkness, that could have inspired such terror? A spectral hound loosed from hell; or a creature of infinite patience and cunning, with a smiling face and a murderous heart . . .

and

THE SIGN OF FOUR
THE VALLEY OF FEAR
THE ADVENTURES OF SHERLOCK HOLMES
THE CASE-BOOK OF SHERLOCK HOLMES
THE MEMOIRS OF SHERLOCK HOLMES
THE RETURN OF SHERLOCK HOLMES
HIS LAST BOW
THE PENGUIN COMPLETE SHERLOCK HOLMES

Also published in Penguins

THE RIVALS OF SHERLOCK HOLMES
Early Detective Stories
Edited by Hugh Greene

In these thirteen stories, Hugh Greene gives enchanting proof that Sherlock Holmes stood by no means alone as a master-sleuth in late-Victorian and Edwardian London. Some, like Martin Hewitt and Dr Thorndyke, are sharp and sea-green incorruptible. But such men as Romney Pringle and the sinister Dorrington, while just as acute, have no purity of motive . . .

Among the undeservedly forgotten authors are Max Pemberton, Arthur Morrison, Guy Boothby, William Le Queux, R. Austin Freeman and Ernest Bramah.

MORE RIVALS OF
SHERLOCK HOLMES
Edited by Hugh Greene

'She drew off her left glove, a delicate, crinkled suede affair, and offered her bare hand to the surgeon . . .

' "The forefinger," she explained calmly, "I should like to have it amputated at the first joint please." '

– from Jacques Futrell's 'The Superfluous Finger', one of the stories in this elegant collection of Edwardian tales of cosmopolitan crime.

Dashiell Hammett

THE BIG KNOCKOVER
AND OTHER STORIES

'Dashiell Hammett gave murder back to the kind of people that commit it for reasons, not just to provide a corpse; and with the means at hand, not with handwrought duelling pistols, curare, and tropical fish' – Raymond Chandler

Here are ten classic suspense stories from the twenties and thirties – selected and introduced by Lillian Hellman. Hammett's Continental Op – tough, tired, intelligent, a snap-brimmed Sir Galahad with a Browning – was the prototype for a whole new tradition of Private Eye thrillers.

THE THIN MAN

Retirement suited Nick just fine. He had a pretty wife called Nora, a Schnauzer called Asta, and a taste for good Scotch.

All it took was a little persuasion. Like four .32 bullets, a blonde, the newspapers, the cops, and a junked-up hoodlum in his bedroom. Nick Charles, former Trans-American Detective Agency Ace, was back in business!

Julian Symons

THE BLACKHEATH POISONINGS

'A superb detective novel of an original kind, which, while offering the reader as much information as anyone, ends with a surprising and totally unexpected conclusion. At the same time his evocation of this late Victorian epoch – a kind of black *Diary of a Nobody* – seems to ring true in every respect' – *The Times Literary Supplement*

THE TELL-TALE HEART
The Life and Works of Edgar Allan Poe

'Mr Symons' analysis of Poe's divided self is uncondescending, and does not simplify his subject. On the contrary, he rescues Poe from Freudians, symbolists, moralists and other simplifiers. By indicating the ramifications of the two selves, he restores to Poe his depth and mystery. He manages to be both incisive and finely circumspect . . . And he even makes you like Poe most of the time' – John Carey in the *Sunday Times*

BLOODY MURDER

'An urbane and scholarly account of the crime novel . . . from its beginnings with Poe and Vidocq down to the immediate present' – Michael Gilbert in the *Sunday Telegraph*

'Can be heartily recommended to anyone who has ever enjoyed a detective story or a crime novel' – Kingsley Amis in the *Spectator*

P. G. Wodehouse

A selection

LIFE AT BLANDINGS

'For Wodehouse there has been no fall of Man . . . the gardens of Blandings Castle are the original gardens from which we are all exiled' – Evelyn Waugh

In his inimitable style, P. G. Wodehouse entices us into the demesne of Blandings Castle – an apparent paradise where it is eternal high summer, with jolly house-parties, tea on the lawn and love trysts in the rose garden. But for Clarence, ninth Earl of Emsworth, there is always something to disturb this tranquil scene, from avoiding his forceful sister, Lady Constance Keeble, to foiling unscrupulous attempts to nobble his beloved pig, the Empress of Blandings, and bailing out the vacuous Hon. Freddie Threepwood from his numerous scrapes. Without at least one imposter on the premises, Blandings Castle is never quite itself.

Dornford Yates

BERRY AND CO.

Rich, sophisticated, devoted – five unforgettable characters!

Once again Berry and Co. become mixed up in a series of madcap adventures – an anxious pursuit across the Hampshire countryside for a prized Rolls Royce, preventing Vandy (a detested cousin) reaching the buried Pleydell treasure first, and saving Nobby from the clutches of Blue Bandala's owner.

ADÈLE AND CO.

When Jill, Duchess of Padua, has her priceless pearls stolen, along with Adèle and Daphne's jewels (and Berry's cufflinks), Berry and Co. face an impossible task in their attempts to recover them – particularly when they discover that Auntie Emma, a ruthless professional criminal, hopes to beat them to it.

Throwing caution to the wind, Berry, Jonah and Boy embark on a thrilling chase which takes them from Paris to the Pyrenees, and, at the end of the day, it is the irrepressible Berry who is the hero of the hour.

JONAH AND CO.

Vintage Yates – thrilling, witty and exhilarating!

In this inimitable collection of stories we learn, among other things, why Eulalie is cut dead, how Nobby discovers that the biggest receiver in France has not yet retired – and find out about an affair of the heart . . .